Other Titles by Virginia Brown from Bell Bridge Books

Divas are Forever

by

Virginia Brown

Bell Bridge Books

This is a work of fiction. Names, characters, places and incidents are either the products of the author's imagination or are used fictitiously. Any resemblance to actual persons (living or dead), events or locations is entirely coincidental.

Bell Bridge Books
PO BOX 300921
Memphis, TN 38130
Print ISBN: 978-1-61194-461-7

Bell Bridge Books is an Imprint of BelleBooks, Inc.

Copyright © 2018 by Virginia Brown

Published in the United States of America.

We at BelleBooks enjoy hearing from readers.
Visit our websites
BelleBooks.com
BellBridgeBooks.com
ImaJinnBooks.com

10 9 8 7 6 5 4 3 2 1

Cover design: Debra Dixon
Interior design: Hank Smith
Photo/Art credits:
Shoes © Dahliamm | Dreamstime.com
Pug (manipulated) © Roman Chernyshev | Dreamstime.com

:Lfde:01:

To My Readers

Many of the details about activities offered during the annual April pilgrimage in Holly Springs are accurate. However, I have taken great license with details involving the planning and execution of certain activities, for which I hope the Holly Springs Garden Club—and the ladies of the historical railroad depot—will forgive me. Although the true crime statistics for Holly Springs average only one murder a year, it's a lot more fun to keep the police department and the madcap Divas busy chasing after fictional criminals. I hope you agree!

Dedication

This is dedicated to one of our original Depot Divas, Ginger Kemp, who left us suddenly last August. Ginger was one of the guiding spirits of the Dixie Divas, funny, sarcastic, and prone to hilarious episodes she loved to retell. One of her favorite sayings was, "Well, sunny beaches," in moments of frustration. So when it's repeated by one of the Dixie Divas, you'll know I'm channeling Ginger again.

Ginger—I hope you're happily reclining on a sunny beach and enjoying eternity while regaling others with your wonderful sense of humor and stories. We miss you terribly.

Chapter 1

"I CAN'T BELIEVE Miranda Watson has the nerve to leave the house wearing that," said my first cousin and best friend Bitty Hollandale. "Some women just shouldn't wear a sundress. Bless her heart."

Since we were sitting in Budgie's café, where we had gone after a trip to the optometrist to check Bitty's eyes, and since Miranda looked just fine, I put some of Bitty's ire down to the fact she'd just had her eyes dilated. To her horror, she'd also been prescribed eyeglasses. Bitty likes to think she's still in her thirties. She's not. We're in our early fifties, and I'm two months older than her, which she likes to repeat often to annoy me. It only bothers me when she pretends I'm years older in front of people who don't know us.

It's hard to find someone in Holly Springs, Mississippi, who doesn't know us.

My name is Eureka May Truevine, but everyone who knows me calls me Trinket. Bitty's name is really Elisabeth, but Bitty suits her much better. We tend to prefer nicknames in the South. I was just glad to be called Trinket instead of Booger. Or worse.

We were born here and grew up here, and even though I'd gone off following my then husband to random jobs around the country for most of my adult life, residents had been reacquainted with me since my return a little over a year ago. In fact, Bitty and I both had become notorious for a recently acquired talent for solving murders. It's a gift—one I haven't been able to return.

Unfortunately for me, Bitty rather likes the gift. She's easily bored. I'm not. I can find a ton of things to occupy my time and mind that don't involve shock, terror, and firearms.

"Yes," I said to soothe Bitty's judgment of Miranda Watson's dress, "bless her heart."

Bless her heart is a frequent Southern phrase that is multi-purpose. It can be added in a kind tone to lessen the sting of comments like, "She's so buck-toothed, she can eat an apple through a picket fence," or "He's three sandwiches short of a picnic." My father prefers to say,

"He's half a bubble off-plumb," which is some kind of carpentry term. And as noted, the phrase can also be used to critique a person's attire, manners, character, or actions.

"Be nice," I hissed at Bitty as the subject of our conversation spied us in the corner and sailed toward us, waving and smiling.

"She's only in a good mood because she finally found a man who can stand her," Bitty grumbled, but her tone had softened. I knew she wouldn't be rude in public unless provoked. It's just not good manners. Besides, Miranda had apologized several times for the tacky things she'd printed about us in her weekly gossip column in the *South Reporter* the year before. While her comments hadn't been directed at any one person, they had been unjust—but not unfounded—about our social club, the Dixie Divas. We do tend to be rather exuberant at our monthly meetings.

"Trinket Truevine," Miranda said to me, "you're just the person I'm looking for."

I cringed inside. Any time someone says that to me, I'm rarely glad they found me.

"Really?" I said politely. "Here I am. How's Chitling?"

Chitling is her pet pig, purchased under the misnomer of miniature pig, now not so mini. Miranda only bought her to mimic Bitty, who has been known to wag her pet pug any and every place allowed. While Bitty buys her pug, Chen Ling—whom I'd dubbed Chitling long before Miranda adopted her pet pig, just to annoy my cousin—all kinds of clothes studded with real diamonds that should never be wasted on a dog, Miranda doesn't have Bitty's budget, so she has to substitute with rhinestones. It just doesn't look the same.

Miranda shook her head and sighed. Her bleached blond hair formed a helmet atop her head, remarkably like Bitty's hairdo. Not a strand moved. An F-3 tornado couldn't muss hair on either of their heads.

"Chitling is growing like a weed," she said. "I've put her on a diet, but Dr. Coltrane said she's going to get a lot bigger anyway."

"Well," observed Bitty, "pigs do grow, you know."

The pig had, as I'd predicted, grown quite a bit and was no longer able to be tucked under her arm and carted around like Bitty hauls her pug. It's amazing what a proper diet and a growth spurt can accomplish. Local grocery stores and public venues must have given a collective sigh of relief at the news the pig would no longer shop at their establishments.

"They certainly do grow fast," Miranda replied as she pulled out a chair to sit down. "Trinket, I hear that you're going to greet tourists at Six Chimneys for the pilgrimage this year. Is that right?"

Despite my resistance, I'd been drafted by my dear cousin to stand on her front sidewalk to greet people during our annual pilgrimage when antebellum homes are open to the public, and people can soak up a way of life long past. And of course, there will be Confederate soldiers in uniform roaming around, a tour of Hillcrest Cemetery, often referred to as "Little Arlington," a visit to the railroad depot, and a host of other activities regarding The War. That's the Civil War, for the uninitiated. We tend to refer to it with capital letters as if it's the only war America has endured. For the South, it was a dreadful time with great losses suffered in lives, land, and livelihoods. For the country, it was a devastating experience.

Being Southern, we like to commemorate such things. I'm not sure why, unless it's to be a reminder of how far we've come since then, or a matter of pride that we were beaten but not conquered. Then again, that's true of all Americans. We can be bloodied but not bowed.

But I digress. I replied to Miranda's question with an affirmative, "Yes, Bitty has me conscripted into her service. I'm going to stand on her sidewalk and hand out leaflets about her house, while I try not to melt in the heat or suffer a sinus attack. Why do you ask?"

"It is hot for April," Miranda agreed. "We've had unseasonable weather this year. I'm compiling a list of houses and people who'll be participating in the pilgrimage."

Bitty said, "But the Garden Club has already done that. We have programs with houses listed and a map to give tourists. You were there and voted on the arrangements."

"I know. I'm just giving an overview for my column. Since it's going to be in the *Memphis Commercial Appeal* as well as the *South Reporter*"—she paused to preen about having a byline in the widely-read Memphis newspaper instead of just the local paper—"I thought it'd be nice if this year we have a sort of *Grande Belle* to organize one of the attractions. You know there's going to be a reenactment of General Van Dorn's raid and burning of supplies at the railroad depot—without the actual fire, of course—so we need an organizer to coordinate everything. I did have Maisie Truett, but she's come down with the flu. So, I think Trinket would be a perfect replacement."

I brightened at the thought. Would there be a way to avoid

standing on a sidewalk and greeting tourists while wearing hoop skirts and a hat? If so, it sounded like a good plan to me.

"I can help," I said, before Bitty could object. "I'm sure there are a lot of other ladies who would just *love* to take my place at Six Chimneys."

Bitty narrowed her eyes. She looked like a Siamese cat, just blue slits glaring at me. I ignored her. Sometimes that was the best thing.

"Great," Miranda said enthusiastically. She didn't seem to notice Bitty glowering like a lump of radioactive waste; she took a notebook out of a purse as big as an overnight case and scribbled in it. "I'll put you down as supply organizer for the Friday and Saturday raid on the depot. Sammy Simpson is going to take care of the historical details. You just have to make sure there are enough Confederate and Yankee uniforms. Oh, and convince some of the men to be Yankees instead of Confederates. There are always a few who want to be stubborn."

Suddenly, it didn't sound so stress-free. I'm familiar with the strong sentiment a lot of the re-enactors have for playing the enemy. One year, the Union's General Grant defected to the Confederate side during a particularly rousing battle. I suppose he just couldn't help himself.

"Do you have a list of the participants?" I asked.

"I'll make you a copy and bring it to you at Carolann's shop. Are you working tomorrow?"

I nodded. "Yes, I'll be there from one to six."

Miranda beamed. "Thank you, Trinket. You have no idea how helpful you're going to be. Bye, Bitty. Y'all take care."

After she sailed back out of the café, her voluminous flowered sundress blossoming like an entire garden, I went back to my banana pudding and coffee. I tried to avoid Bitty's gaze. I could feel her eyes burning into me until finally I put down my spoon and looked at her.

"Go ahead and say it now. Get it out of your system," I said.

"I don't know what you mean, Trinket."

"Yes, you do."

Bitty stuck her chin in the air and stared at a black and white photo of the Eiffel Tower on the brick wall. Budgie's is supposed to be the French Market Café now, but since we all knew it when it was still owned by Budgie instead of just managed by her, the locals still call it Budgie's.

Bitty drummed her long fingernails against the table top. "Really, you're free to make your own decisions. I had hoped you would be there for me so we could work together, but apparently that's too much to ask. If you prefer to be a traitor, there's nothing I can do about it."

I rolled my eyes. I couldn't help it. But I said quite calmly, "Your boys will be here on spring break from Ole Miss. Between Brandon and Clayton, I'm sure you'll have plenty of help. Besides—you know I'm not that excited about wearing hoop skirts and a corset. I'd faint in the heat. Then who would you have to help?"

"Brandon and Clayton are in the reenactment, as you very well know, and if you fainted, I'd be the first one there with a cold rag and smelling salts."

I lifted my brows at her. "Do you even know what smelling salts are?"

"Ammonia powder. Mama used to keep them around when Aunt Imogene visited. She was always fainting over something."

"Probably an excess of snuff," I suggested, and we both laughed.

With the contentious moment behind us, Bitty finally accepted my decision to allow my post at her front door to be given to someone else. It was a relief, since she likes to be in control and had it in her head that I was the best person to greet tourists visiting Six Chimneys, her lovely antebellum home. I envisioned melting in the heat, clad in a corset and pantaloons under hoop skirts and stifling satin. Bitty probably envisioned a willing accomplice should she take it in her head to do something silly. Being separated would save us both.

"Maybe Heather," she said, mentioning her son Brandon's girlfriend. "If they're still together."

"Is there a chance they might not be?"

"Well, you know young men and women. They've been together nearly a year. Unless it's serious, I figure the romance may have run its course."

Since I wasn't about to comment either way on the possibility of a serious romance or a break-up, I said, "Heather would be perfect. She probably knows as much about your house as I do. It has a wonderful history."

"It does have a rich history, doesn't it? I've become a guardian of those who lived there before. A keeper of their stories, their spirits that live on . . ." She gestured toward an imaginary spirit. "I have been given a great responsibility."

I barely kept myself from rolling my eyes. Sometimes Bitty likes to be dramatic. Sometimes she watches too much TV.

"So," I said to drag her back from her place in history or the spirit world, "if you know someone who needs a corset and hoop skirt for the pilgrimage, mine will be available. I'm sure it can be altered in time if they get right on it."

Bitty eyed me. "Dream on. You're the only six-foot woman in Holly Springs."

"Five-nine, and I'm willing to be generous and donate the dress."

"I'll alert the media. Wait—Miranda is the media. Tell her about your donation."

Bitty sounded peevish, so I decided we needed another topic of conversation. "How is Maria handling all the cleaning for the pilgrimage this year? Last year, she quit three times."

"Oh, she's doing much better this year. She's only quit twice. I pay her extra since her son Ricardo is going to college next year. She's really the best maid I've ever had."

"If not for the fact your house is always clean, and I know you don't clean, I'd think you made up Maria. I've never seen her."

"She comes very early. It's like magic. I wake up, and my house is clean."

"So when does she do your bedroom? I mean, it's always clean too."

"I'm not a light sleeper."

"That's an understatement. A shotgun going off over your head wouldn't wake you."

Bitty smiled. "I suppose Aunt Anna has Cherryhill ready for the tour?"

Aunt Anna is my seventy-ish mother, and Cherryhill is our hundred and sixty-eight-year-old ancestral house. During The War it had the distinction of being burned by the Yankees, as did several houses in the Holly Springs area, but fortunately, the blaze didn't completely destroy it. Around the turn of the twentieth century, however, another fire did a lot of damage. We tend to ignore that fact during the pilgrimage. Tourists are much more impressed by Yankee depredations than faulty wiring.

Daddy grew up in the house, as did Bitty's father, who died some years ago. While Bitty's father married old money, my daddy kept the house and land, and he and my mother reared four children. Just my twin sister Emerald and I are left. My older brothers were killed during the Vietnam War when we were still pretty young. Cherryhill has seen great sorrow as well as great joy over the years.

"Mama has been cleaning for almost a week," I answered Bitty. "She's had Daddy in the basement and the attic bringing out all our antique furniture, dishes, and vintage curtains."

"I hope she gets the mothball smell out of them before the tour." Bitty finished her last bite of chess pie and followed it with coffee while I scraped the final bit of banana pudding out of my bowl.

And then, just because we both love to annoy one another and I felt reckless, I said, "I hope you still fit into your dress. It was pretty tight last year, if I remember correctly. Luckily, I don't have to worry about my dress fitting since I won't be needing it."

It was my turn to needle her about weight, since she'd been badgering me relentlessly about getting too fat to fit into my hoop skirt. I was deliriously happy I wasn't going to have to wear it after all, so I felt a bit cocky about the whole thing.

Sometimes I shoot myself in the foot with my big mouth.

Bitty looked at me and smiled her Grinch smile. If she'd turned green, she could have easily posed for the Dr. Seuss book.

"You do know that everyone who participates in the pilgrimage wears a costume, don't you, dear?"

"Not true," I said. "Miranda didn't say one word about me wearing a hoop skirt."

"You'll see," was all she said, and a feeling of dread came over me. "Say it ain't so . . ."

"Oh, it's so."

Alas, the next day I discovered Bitty was right when Miranda showed up at Silk Promises, the lingerie shop where I worked. She had brought the list of those participating in the battle at the railroad depot.

"Your dress is ready for Friday, isn't it?" she asked.

I felt lightheaded. Gloom enveloped me. I'd hoped, up until the last minute, that I would be spared the ignominy of appearing in public in hoop skirts and a hat.

"Yes," I said with a sigh. "It's ready. Are you sure I have to wear it?"

Miranda blinked. She reminded me of the Mimi character on the old *Drew Carey Show*, who'd had her blond hair all teased up and wore too much bright blue or green eye shadow. It looked like Miranda had multiple sets of eyes, so I just picked out a pair to gaze into hopefully, but to no avail. The bottom set of eyes blinked at me again.

"Why yes, of course you have to wear it. How else will tourists know you're one of the pilgrimage guides?"

"Uh, I can wear a name tag?" When I get the same kind of look from someone not blood kin to me that I get from Bitty or my mother, I know I've crossed over the line. So I added, "But of course, I can wear the tag on my dress, I suppose."

Miranda nodded. "If you don't want to ruin the material with a pin, I can get you a name tag on a cord around your neck."

Since I didn't give two figs about pinholes in a dress I didn't want to wear, I just said, "Oh, I don't want to be a bother. Whatever you give me will be fine."

I didn't mean a word of that, but Mama had always stressed courtesy in situations that I deemed uncomfortable. Good manners are one of the Top Three Things Southern Girls Learn. I think the list used to have a Top Twenty, but times being what they are, getting a more modern Southern Girl to learn the Top Three can be difficult enough.

1. A lady must have good manners, on all occasions.
2. A lady must never curse, chew gum, smoke, or be intoxicated in public.
3. A lady must always dress appropriately and modestly.

Needless to say, those rules have been broken countless times over the years. I was a rebellious child. I joined sit-ins, grew my hair down to my butt, and smoked those slim cigarettes popular in the '70s. I wore bell-bottom pants and halter tops in public. I cursed when I felt it necessary, and I drank beer with my friends in public. Yet I always said "ma'am" and "sir" to my elders and wrote thank-you notes for Christmas and birthday gifts. Once I had a child of my own, however, the responsibility to rear her as I had been reared overwhelmed me, and I had reverted to the teachings of my childhood. My Michelle has excellent manners.

I count myself fortunate not to have grown up with the same rules that Bitty had to learn in her youth. Her mama came from money. Money creates its own set of rules. There are a ton of social graces that go along with being a debutante that I never had to think about. Bitty thought about them. I can't say she paid much attention to them unless absolutely required, though. And I'm sure she hasn't paid attention to them since then. But she likes to remind me that she never got arrested at a sit-in.

So knowing all the rules and adhering to all the rules are two different prospects. I was polite to Miranda the entire time I was fighting the desire to make a public scene.

When she left the shop, I turned to look at Carolann, the owner of Silk Promises and my employer. "Damn," I said, thereby breaking Rule Number 2.

Carolann Barnett, a New Age adherent with hair the color of a brush fire, tie-dyed clothes, and peace signs on several chains around her neck, just laughed. "It's not so bad, Trinket. The pilgrimage will be over before you know it. Then you'll get to put up your feet and be happy it's behind you."

"Promises, promises." I sighed. "It's not that I don't like the pilgrimage. I do. I love the tours through gorgeous homes, the history of Holly Springs, and the craft fairs at the railroad depot and on the courthouse lawn. I like the reenactments and seeing all the young women and girls in beautiful dresses. I like seeing handsome young men in uniforms, whether they're gray or blue. But I'm quite sure that something will go wrong, and I'll be smack in the middle of it."

"What's the worst thing that can happen?" Carolann asked in a reasonable tone. "If it rains, people will still be able to tour the homes and watch a reenactment from the depot. There's the concert Saturday night and the Sunday brunch at Montrose. Our museum has great exhibits and more period clothes than the Pink Palace Museum up in Memphis. So, what could possibly go wrong?"

"I don't know. Something always does. There'll be a train wreck. The depot will catch fire. Bitty will put another bullet hole in her back door."

"The police haven't given her back her gun yet," Carolann reminded me.

"She has more. Jackson Lee makes her keep them in a gun safe, but she has a key. You'd think she'd listen to him since he's her boyfriend as well as her attorney, but you know Bitty. And I know I sound ridiculous, but when Bitty and I are involved in anything, something *always* goes wrong. It's inevitable."

"I think you're worrying for nothing. The pilgrimage has always been a success."

I shook my head. "That's because Bitty and I have never been involved in the planning together. We're like lightning rods. Mark my words—there will be trouble."

Have I mentioned that sometimes I can be psychic?

THE HOLLY SPRINGS Railroad Depot is a beautiful building. Sections of it date back to the 1850s, the most modern being updated in the 1940s. In recent years, the family who owns the elegant structure has gotten it on the historic register and made repairs, keeping it within historic guidelines. The ground floor with baggage room and waiting rooms have opened to the public a few times during tours and events, and renovation is complete in the dining room where William Faulkner used to sit in the restaurant and watch passengers and workmen. Back then, regular customers would often complain about the thinness of the ham. "Turn off the fan so my ham won't fly away," they would say. Faulkner even referred to the ham in his novel, *The Reivers*.

On the second floor are rooms where passengers used to stay while waiting for the next train to take them to their destination, still outfitted with antique furniture and linens and enough unique pieces to make Bitty salivate at just the mention of them. After a visit, I thought I was going to have to revive her with antique smelling salts when she stumbled home with her eyes still glazed in rapture. She's a true antiques devotée.

I just like nice furniture that's comfortable. Bitty considers me a barbarian.

It was sheer pandemonium in the hours leading up to the first reenactment. While I had been given the responsibility of assigning gray or blue uniforms, there were a few protests. It's not easy to watch grown men bicker like children over a prized toy. Seven of the participants had their own uniforms—all gray—so there wasn't an issue with them. Bitty's sons, Brandon and Clayton, wore their own gray uniforms. Unfortunately, those soldiers without uniforms preferred to wear the eight gray ones. None wanted to wear the eight Union blues.

"Some of you have to wear the blue," I said in what I thought was a reasonable tone. "But if you want to, you can die quickly in the fighting."

That seemed to be acceptable. I soon had eight more Rebels and eight doomed Yankees; history be damned. Three of the Confederates had horses. None of the horses required uniforms, thank heavens. I'm not sure I could have coped.

It was a lovely Friday, I had completed my mission of organizing the uniforms, and I made sure everyone had an appropriate weapon— that was nearly as difficult as assigning the uniforms—and the reenactment went off without a hitch. Sammy Simpson was wonderful at his task. He had stationed Rebels around the depot and directed

Yankees to cots near the stacked "supplies" of food, clothing, weapons, and munitions. Since the original raid had been at dawn, we had to improvise. Yankees "slept" at their posts and were routed by the Rebels. It went just splendidly. Once the smoke cleared, all the players got a rousing round of applause, especially Confederate General Van Dorn, who was played by a quite convincing Riley Powers.

After the reenactment was over for the day, I collected all the borrowed uniforms and counted the weapons, checking them off the list before I put them all in a locked chest. Then I caught a ride back up the hill with Sammy. He was the only one with a van big enough to hold a woman in hoop skirts and a wide-brimmed hat. It was a fairly pleasant ride. Sammy was a tall, lanky man with a weather-beaten face and good manners. He was pleased that his attention to detail had gone off so well and entertained me with a few horror stories from the past.

"One year this fool—and I won't divulge his name—showed up on his mare that was in heat. Instead of a reenactment of Grant's occupation, we had a sex education simulation. All the other horses were geldings, but that didn't mean they'd forgotten what nature intended them to do. Riley Powers nearly fell out of the saddle when his horse tried to climb on top of the mare."

"I missed a lot in my years away," I said, and Sammy nodded.

"Some things are best heard and not experienced," he observed, and I had to agree.

All in all, it wasn't a bad first day out of two, and I actually looked forward to the final reenactment. I can be so foolish. Saturday's feature was an excellent example of optimism gone awry.

As we gathered at the depot for the final performance, my positivity wavered. Right off the bat, Walter Simpson declared that he wasn't about to wear a Yankee uniform no matter what I said. Tall, thin, wrinkled as a peach pit, he glared at me and shook a bony finger in my face.

"I've always been a Confederate, and I ain't about to change that now."

"But this isn't the actual war," I said in a vain attempt at reason. "We're just replaying an historic event. Since you were a Rebel yesterday, and Royal Stewart got in a bar fight last night and can't get out of jail in time, we need another Yankee. Besides him, you're the only tall man who fits into this uniform."

I didn't want to be rude and point out the obvious, that all the men who didn't already have their own uniforms ran to fat and fatter. Since Walter's authentic uniform had succumbed to moths years ago, I hoped he'd cooperate. But I saw how upset he was and decided it wasn't worth hurt feelings to continue.

Before I could say anything, Sammy came up and said, "Grand-dad, wear the blue so it won't look like the Rebels are fighting each other instead of Yankees. We need to have a fair amount of enemy to shoot at, and I don't want it to look like a massacre."

Walter threw his arms up in the air. "Fine. I'll wear the damn thing. Just don't expect me to do it again next year. Gimme the hat too. I'll cover my face so no one knows it's me."

With that vital matter settled, I gave Walter the blue uniform, and he went inside the depot to change into it, muttering to himself but more cooperative. I looked up at Sammy.

"Thanks. I was beginning to think *I'd* have to wear it. It's probably more comfortable than a corset, but I'm not sure I could stuff myself into it."

Sammy grinned. "He's a hardheaded old coot. And I bet you'd look fine in Yankee blue."

"Maybe. I'm already wearing Confederate gray. If I could do a Rebel yell, I'd probably join the battle."

"I'm sure you'd do a very nice Rebel yell."

"Only if stuck with a hatpin. Did your grandfather bring his own weapon?"

"I brought one from his gun collection. Period appropriate, of course."

"Thank heavens. I'm not eager for an argument where firearms are involved."

Sammy laughed, and I focused on checking off the names of those who borrowed a rifle, sword, or pistol from the supply kept just for the reenactments. Many had their own swords or rifles, but some always had to borrow. No soldier was properly dressed without a weapon.

The temperature was perfect April weather for Holly Springs. The sun was shining, it was warm enough to wear sundresses, but not so warm I overheated in that god-awful corset, hoop, petticoats, pantaloons, gray satin dress, and a wide-brimmed hat with fresh flowers on the red band around the crown. I was pretty sure I looked like a gray mule in a straw hat.

While Sammy Simpson coordinated the placement of soldiers, I guided tourists to the area cordoned off for them and handed out pamphlets explaining the importance of General Van Dorn's raid on the railroad depot. It may have seemed counter-productive to the tourists, but in December 1862, it had made perfect sense. A lot of Yankee supplies and bales of cotton had been stored along the tracks at the depot. Back then the supplies were meant to be sent south to Vicksburg, and the cotton was to be sent to northern markets. Rebel soldiers had caught the entire Yankee camp by surprise, routed them from their positions, and confiscated the depot supplies. What they couldn't use or carry had been set on fire. Because of Van Dorn's preemptive strike, the Yankee occupation of Vicksburg had been delayed for six months, and local history was then made.

We did our best to channel the historic raid. Shots rang out as the Yankees returned Rebel rifle-fire. Horsemen raced back and forth as tourists watched from under the front awning of the historic railroad depot. Smoke bombs went off, giving an appearance of fire, and layers billowed around the one-story brick building that was the freight depot; supplies were stacked in front of it for the reenactment. There was shouting and hollering and lots of unmistakable Rebel yells. Yankee soldiers were captured and held as prisoners, wagons of precious "supplies" were trundled away, and tourists cheered and clapped as Confederates won the day. Van Dorn had pulled off the perfect coup with little loss of life. It was a Confederate victory that still resonates in Holly Springs. It was quite impressive.

Only a couple of "bodies" littered the ground around the railroad tracks. Conflicting tales from eyewitnesses to the original raid had been passed down as to how many or even if there had been any casualties. Some accounts say six soldiers died, some say there'd been one death, and others say none were killed. For the reenactment, four soldiers lay "dead" near the freight office for dramatic effect.

Brandon and Clayton had participated in the raid quite enthusiastically. I saw their blond heads bobbing about among the Confederate and Union uniforms. Brandon carried an old rifle handed down on Bitty's mother's side of the family. It had seen action in Shiloh and at Brice's Crossroads, but age had taken its toll on the weapon, and it was inoperable. Clayton carried an old sword, brandishing it about his head as he forced Yankee "prisoners" to swear an oath of allegiance to the South and be paroled by signing an agreement to resign from future fighting, just as had been done in 1862.

Tourists applauded as the reenactment came to an end, and I breathed a sigh of relief that my part in the pilgrimage was done for the year. There had been no mishaps. I congratulated myself on avoiding complete disaster.

All re-enactors took their final bows, and the dead rose from the ground to join them.

All but one.

A Yankee soldier lay sprawled near the freight office, unheeding to calls that he could rise. One of the Confederate soldiers walked over to nudge him, laughing and saying the war was over. The soldier didn't respond.

A trickle of alarm rippled down my spine. Something wasn't right. That quickly became apparent to the soldier who tried to rouse him, and he knelt down to peer at the still form. After a swift check, he swiveled around in obvious distress, holding up a bloodied hand.

"He's been hurt. I think he's dead!"

Chaos immediately ensued. Other re-enactors rushed forward, someone yelled for a doctor, tourists milled about in confusion, and one of the horsemen dismounted and forgot about his horse. It ran off, hooves clattering against pavement as it headed for parts unknown. I stood stock-still, staring at the scene in horror.

Once again, I had been too quick to congratulate myself.

Chapter 2

HOLLY SPRINGS' police are very efficient and thorough. Although constrained by pesky things like laws, they still manage to solve a remarkable number of crimes, including murder. I had little doubt they'd find out what happened fairly quickly.

Brandon and Clayton stood next to me as we silently watched the coroner and police do their jobs. A white van stood ready to take away the erstwhile Yankee soldier. His name had not yet been officially divulged, although we all knew it was Walter Simpson, Sammy Simpson's grandfather. Sammy stood by, white-faced and weeping, saying over and over to anyone who'd listen that he couldn't believe this was happening.

He wasn't alone.

While most of the tourists had been herded to another area until police could question them as to what they'd seen, those of us involved in the re-creation of the raid had been grouped in a different area. Stunned to silence, we stood beneath the overhang of the railroad depot right outside the former baggage room, close enough to see what was going on, yet far enough away to remain ignorant of what was being said. Yellow crime tape had been strung from a former hitching post to a sawhorse provided to cordon off the area and back to another post, forming a large triangle of sorts along the tracks.

Police kept spectators at bay while plainclothes officers questioned all the participants. There were so many witnesses, uniformed officers conducted interviews as well. Those being questioned were taken into the dining room. Cardboard cutouts of Rebel and Yankee soldiers watched over the scene like silent witnesses.

"Miz Truevine," officer Rodney Farrell said politely as he took me aside, "what can you tell me about the events?"

"Very little. Like all the others, I was watching the battle. It was confusing with soldiers firing everywhere and the smoke from those bombs burning my eyes. I didn't even know anyone was hurt until afterward."

"Yes, ma'am. So you didn't see who was firing what weapon?"

"Is that what killed him? He was *shot*? Who would put real bullets into their gun?"

I hadn't really expected the deputy to reply to my question and he didn't. It'd been more of an observation than a question anyway. It was inconceivable to me that someone wouldn't know better than to load a real bullet.

"Who was responsible for assigning the weapons?" Farrell asked next.

I gulped. "That would be me. I have my list right here."

When I handed my clipboard to him he scanned it and nodded, then said he was taking it as evidence. "What else do you know about these weapons, Miz Truevine?"

"Not much." When Deputy Farrell looked up at me with a frown I shrugged. "Sorry. These are the props used for reenactments. That's all I know."

"Where are they kept when not being used?"

"In that locked chest." I indicated a battered old Army chest against the depot wall. "I put them in it last night and locked it. I got the key and unlocked it this morning."

"And who holds the key?"

"Sammy Simpson. He's in charge of this particular reenactment."

"Is he the only one with a key?"

I shook my head. "I don't know. I would imagine not, since he's not the only one who conducts reenactments. There are probably several keys, but you'd have to check with Sammy or maybe members of the Garden Club."

"Are you sure there's nothing else you can tell me about these firearms, Miz Truevine?"

"Yes, pretty sure. I'm not well-acquainted with guns."

What I know about firearms can be condensed to one word: dangerous. While I realize the weapon itself isn't dangerous, but the person holding it, in my experience, the two were not always conducive to safety when inadvisably coupled. Like Bitty.

Since Bitty wasn't anywhere near the scene of this shooting, I was relieved that our future involvement in the investigation was limited to concern instead of active participation. It's very wearing on my nerves to find myself in the middle of criminal enterprise.

"Did you happen to see the victim fall?" asked the deputy, still pursuing any leads he might glean from me, and again, I shook my head.

"No, I was watching General Van Dorn. Riley Powers did very well. I could almost believe he was a real general, shouting orders."

As I talked to the deputy I saw one of the officers collecting all rifles, pistols, swords, and bayonets used in the reenactment. Each weapon was tagged, identified by the owner's name and contact information. I heard Brandon protest that his rifle belonged to his mama's family and she'd be fit to be tied if anything happened to it. He was right. Bitty is a firm believer in holding on to family heirlooms, even those that are for show more than purpose.

The officer assured him that the rifle would be returned as soon as it'd been through a ballistic test to rule it out as the weapon that killed Walter Simpson. That left me to wonder why they'd also seized the swords and bayonets, but as I didn't want to participate in the questioning any longer than necessary, I said nothing. We watched as an officer tagged the rifle so that Brandon was satisfied it'd been properly marked.

Farrell asked me a few more questions; where I'd been standing in relation to the victim, if I heard him say anything or anyone say anything to him, then he moved on to the next witness, my nephew. Clayton is younger by five minutes than Brandon. The identical twins had been born to Bitty and her first husband, Frank Caldwell, who was now serving a fifteen- to twenty-five-year sentence in a Federal prison.

Apparently, the government has little tolerance for Ponzi schemes that tend to rob the poor to give to the rich. Who knew?

Clayton told basically the same story as I had, except he repeated that Walter complained that he'd had to play a Yankee, and next year he wanted to be on the right side. "He said it wasn't fair that he had to play a Yankee, and he was pretty mad about it," added Clayton.

"Did he say he was angry with anyone in particular?" Farrell looked up from writing notes in his little book.

Clayton hesitated, then said, "Not really, sir. He just mostly said he didn't want to be a Yankee 'cause they stole his family's home, and he wasn't about to forget that."

I remembered the story. The Simpson family had been in the Holly Springs area since 1835 and had their house first occupied, looted, then burned down by Yankees. After The War, the carpet-baggers stole their land. It took over a decade for them to get it all back, and they'd had no intention of parting with it again. It'd stayed in the Simpson family since 1878. Apparently, Walter Simpson had inherited their resentment along with the house and land.

"What do you mean, 'not really'?" Farrell asked Clayton. "Who was Walter Simpson angry with?"

Clayton glanced over at me, and I nodded encouragement. Then he said, "Just my aunt. He said she made him wear the blue, and he should have just gone on home right then."

I blinked. Well, it was true, but it did sound bad. Rodney Farrell looked over at me. "Did you know he was angry with you, Miz Truevine?"

"Walter didn't make it a secret, Deputy," I said dryly. "He stomped around muttering for a good half hour before the reenactment began."

"Why did you make him wear the blue uniform?"

"He was the only one who'd fit into it, and we needed one more Yankee to even out the participating sides."

Farrell nodded. "I see. And where were you standing when he was shot?"

"Unarmed, in full view of about fifty tourists, as well as everyone else. Just ask anyone."

"I will."

Officer Farrell moved on to question Brandon, who stood on my other side. He asked basically the same questions, and Brandon answered much the same as we had, with one minor exception. "Our rifle hasn't worked right for years. I just use it for show."

Farrell scribbled in his notebook. "You gave that rifle to one of our officers?"

"Yessir. It's about as useless as Clayton's sword, though."

"When was the last time you fired the weapon?"

Brandon repeated, "It hasn't worked right for years. I'd say it hasn't fired properly since General Forrest whipped the Yankees at Brice's Crossroads."

Farrell smiled. "Most of these old weapons are like that. So it's genuine and not one of those reproductions?"

"Yessir. Still has the paper cartridges. It's an Enfield and fires the .58 caliber bullets. Or it would, if it worked. You're not going to keep it, are you? Mama will be pretty upset."

"Once ballistics is done, it'll be returned to you. Be sure to tell your mama that so she doesn't come down to the station all het up and ready for war."

Brandon grinned. "I will. Mama can get riled up, that's for sure."

That was an understatement. I was surprised she wasn't already down at the depot raising Cain about her boys being in harm's way. Officer Farrell moved on, and those of us still clustered by the depot discussed our various theories.

Most of us came to the conclusion that someone had accidentally left real bullets in their rifle or pistol instead of the blanks always used in reenactments. It happened, although not once in the seventy-five years of pilgrimage history had anyone been killed at a reenactment.

It was a good thing the reenactment had been early in the day, because it took the whole day for them to talk to all the witnesses. Tourists were allowed to leave at last, and finally only the locals were left to wander off toward home.

With the questioning over for the moment, those of us involved in the reenactment were all dismissed, with the caveat that we go down to the police station within twenty-four hours to be fingerprinted. As the Holly Springs police already had my prints due to an unfortunate event the previous year, I was exempt. So I headed straight for Bitty's house with Brandon and Clayton right behind me.

She was pacing her entrance hall and looking anxiously out the front door. When she saw us pull up in our cars, the door flew open, and she met us on the porch, her long pale skirts whirling around her ankles as she came to a stop.

"It's about time y'all got here. That awful Lieutenant Stone made me stay away," she fumed. "I was on my way as soon as I heard about it, but he met me at the stop sign and told me to go on back home until they got things sorted out. He said he figured I'd be down there in everybody's way so wanted to head me off, and unless I felt like spending the night in jail, I'd just better keep myself home. Can you believe that?"

I could, but I wasn't about to say that to Bitty. It'd been a trying enough day. Instead of saying anything that could be misunderstood, I said, "I hope you have some sweet tea left. I'm parched."

Bitty always has sweet tea, as do most Southern households. The methods for brewing it may be different, the amount of sweetness may vary, additives may differ, but there's a cold pitcher of tea in pretty much every Southerner's home. In my family, we like our tea sweet and strong. Sugar has to be added while the brewed tea is still hot or it doesn't dissolve properly. It never tastes right if added to cold tea. Of course, iced tea without sugar is almost sacrilege.

The boys took their tea upstairs, but I drank mine standing close to the refrigerator in case I wanted more. The horror of a sudden death hovered too close, and I craved normalcy, or what passed for normalcy around Bitty. She fussed around the kitchen, mostly complaining about being left out of the excitement, and after my second glass of tea, I felt more human. I still wore the hoop skirt, corset, and bloomers and was dying to get out of them before they melded into my skin. I don't know how our ancestors managed. The corset alone is torture. Add long cotton bloomers and a hoop petticoat under the yards of skirt material, and it should be banned by Geneva Convention standards.

Bitty was still wearing her dress, too. It was a lovely cream color with delicate rosebuds sewn into the scoop neckline, off the shoulder, a rose-colored sash cinching her small waist. She has a Barbie doll figure—incredibly large bosom, impossibly small waist, and hips like a twelve-year-old boy. She's also five-two in her stocking feet, five-six in the stilettos she likes to wear.

My dress had been chosen by my cousin and was gray satin. It did have a red sash that gave it some color, but I looked like a rocky volcanic island in the blasted thing. Bitty claimed the dark material hid my extra twenty pounds. I'm only fifteen pounds overweight and told her she just didn't want my outfit to compete with her dress. She can be very competitive.

"I'm going home to change clothes," I said after my third glass of sweet tea. "I feel fat as a tick in this thing."

Bitty looked surprised. "You can't go home yet. The pilgrimage has to continue despite everything. We're supposed to hand out programs at the music concert being held at Montrose tonight."

I flapped my arms in the air. "Why do you always obligate me to things without asking me first? I want to go home. I don't want to go hand out programs."

"My, my, you're a bit overwrought. It's been a terrible day. Here. I have just the thing to calm you."

I wasn't a bit surprised when she got out the Jack Daniel's. I shook my head. "No way. If I drink that, I may be testy to tourists. If I'm going to be drafted into service, the least I can do is be sober."

"That's one way to look at it. However, I consider it a public service if we're in a good mood."

I thought about it a moment. She had a point. A little bit of mood elevator could be a good thing. By our third tipple, I was very relaxed and even jovial.

"Maybe handing out programs will be fun," I said with a giggle. "Where's our limo?"

Bitty looked a bit alarmed. "Have you eaten today?" she asked me, and when I shook my head, she said I should eat a sandwich. "I think you're a bit too happy. Pimento cheese okay?"

"That'll be just fine. Is our limo on the way?"

"Brandon or Clayton will be our limo."

I pictured us all three in the boys' small sports car and started laughing. "I can sit on the trunk," I offered. "The two of you in the front . . . good thing I lost my hat. I don't think it'd make it to Montrose. Anyway, I look like Sally Field in *The Flying Nun* in that stupid thing. If a good wind came up, off I'd go into the wild blue yonder . . ."

Bitty added extra pimento cheese to white bread and put it on a plate. "Eat all of it," she commanded. "I'm going to freshen up. You'll eat it, right?"

"Aye, aye, Captain." I saluted her rather smartly, I thought, but somehow poked a finger into my right eye. It made me wince. Bitty insisted I sit at the table to eat, but since it was too hard to squeeze my hoop skirt between chair and table, I ended up just hovering. The sandwich was delicious. I've always loved Aunt Sarah's pimento cheese. The recipe has been a guarded secret, known only by a few. My mother has a copy of it that she's never shared with me or anyone that I know of; she insists Aunt Sarah left out an ingredient when she gave it to her since it doesn't taste quite like hers. Sharita Stone, who cooks all Bitty's meals once a week and freezes them, uses the original recipe. I think Bitty asked her to sign a confidentiality clause before giving her the recipe card. She needn't have bothered. Sharita's very trustworthy.

Her brother is Lieutenant Marcus Stone of the Holly Springs police. He's not as nice to us as he used to be, probably because we only see him in moments of extreme stress. Murder is always stressful.

I ate most of my sandwich before I noticed Chen Ling watching me. Bitty got her from a rescue on a temporary basis, but since it was a match made in doggy heaven, she's never returned her. They have a symbiotic relationship: Bitty waits on Chen Ling hand and foot, and Chen Ling likes it. While the pug may not care about the cute clothes and diamond collars, I would like for someone to be so generous to me.

"Here," I said to the grumpy geriatric gremlin at my feet. "Have some sandwich."

Chitling loves people food, in particular Aunt Sarah's pimento cheese. Since Dr. Kit Coltrane is her vet, he's warned Bitty about the pitfalls of feeding her unhealthy food. Bitty tries her best to avoid it and has put the pug on a diet. Said pug does her best to wheedle, charm, or steal food, and pimento cheese is her weakness. Because I felt generous, I gave her a small bite. She reciprocated by trying to grab the rest of it from my hand. She only has three front fangs, but she's really good at using them to her advantage. I barely got my hand back in one piece.

"Are you feeding her people food?" a voice demanded, and I looked around to see Bitty right behind me.

"No," I lied. "She stole it."

"Honestly, Trinket, you're going to be useless tonight, I can just tell. If we didn't have to be there in fifteen minutes, I'd make you a pot of coffee. They'll have some there. Don't talk to *anyone* until I can get you a large cup of black coffee, you hear?"

I smiled. Then I hiccupped. Bitty rolled her eyes.

Brandon ended up driving us to Montrose in Bitty's Franklin Benz. It was back from the repair shop where it'd undergone major cosmetic surgery for a fender bender a couple months before. We call it the Franklin Benz because her second ex-husband Franklin's alimony payment and big settlement had bought it. It's really just a regular Mercedes sedan.

Montrose was lit up for the night like a gorgeous lady at a grand ball. The antebellum red brick house is Classic Greek Revival with four white columns and a graceful curved staircase to the second floor. The parlor was set up for a concert, with elegant Queen Anne chairs for the guests. I heard the unmistakable sound of strings tuning up. Bitty grabbed me by the arm.

"Stay right here," she said. "I'm fixing to get you some coffee."

"Will do," I replied with another salute. This time my finger stayed out of my eye.

I felt much better, actually. The sandwich had done its work and soaked up some of the Jack Daniel's. But it obviously made Bitty happy to tend to me, so I just nodded and smiled as she disappeared in the direction of the kitchen. A tufted velvet bench sat to one side, and I went to sit on it to wait for my little caretaker's return.

Just as I reached the bench the front door opened again, and a throng of people entered the hall. It was getting crowded, so I sat down.

I forgot I had on a petticoat with stiff, unyielding hoops.

I didn't adjust for the hoops as I'd been taught, and my skirt and petticoat snapped up to obscure my face and vision. It happened so quickly, I didn't have time to react. All of a sudden, I went from sitting gracefully to exposing myself to a room full of strangers. Oh, I had on the long bloomers and stockings, and though I hadn't fit into the high-button shoes, I wore sensible, flat ballet-style slippers. I also wore a corset tied tightly enough to cut off the circulation to the entire lower half of my body. At that instant, I would have preferred it to be around my neck so that I was spared the immediate shrieks of dismay and bursts of laughter from startled spectators.

For a paralyzing moment, I did nothing. Time seemed suspended in some kind of warp. It probably wasn't nearly as long as it felt, but I somehow managed to push my skirt and petticoat back down and pretend nothing had happened. That's a lot harder than one might think. I had to hold down the rebellious hoops with one hand and adjust my posture to accommodate the curve of the hoop I had sat on. It finally slid free, and my skirts stayed in place. The hoop quivered with a threat of repeating the action, so I balled up my fists and cudgeled it into submission.

People were still laughing, and I gazed toward the other room, ignoring them as if I had no idea I'd just shown complete strangers my underwear. My face felt hot, and beads of sweat trickled down the back of my neck. I patted a curl of my hair back into place, then smoothed the ugly gray skirt. If I'd had a lace fan, I'd have been fanning myself furiously. Then a voice cut into my attempt at invisibility, and I cringed inside.

"Why, Trinket Truevine, is that you? I declare, you haven't changed a bit!"

I couldn't very well ignore the owner of the voice because she was standing right in front of me, so I looked up.

To my chagrin, it was a classmate from my brief sojourn at Ole Miss. I'd dropped out to go off to protests with my future husband, a man with six-pack abs and the work ethic of a grasshopper. She'd gone on to graduate and marry a football jock who made a fortune on Wall Street. I heard she'd divorced and remarried a couple times. I hadn't seen her in nearly twenty years, and I couldn't imagine why she was in Holly Springs.

I put a smile on my face and lied, "Darlene Landers, it's good to see you."

She smiled back at me, her eyes turning up at the corners like a sly cat. "I'd say it's good to see you too, but I'm not sure if we were meant to see so much of you."

I forced a laugh. "Sometimes the hoops get away from me. Have you moved back to this area?"

Darlene tossed back her dark hair and glanced behind her. I saw a tall man hovering by the door. He smiled when she waggled her fingers at him. She turned back to me. "We've been looking at real estate near here. Derek and I thought that with all the kids grown, it'd be nice to live closer to my mother. She's getting up in years. So we thought we'd find a small place to buy in the area. Derek is from Illinois, so I brought him to see some of the historical aspects of life in the South, like this pilgrimage."

If I remembered correctly, Darlene was from Oxford. She'd married Early James right after graduation and six months before their first child was born. On one of my visits back home, I'd attended a baby shower for her. It'd been so long ago it felt like forever.

I managed a smile and feigned interest. "Well, I hope he's enjoying the pilgrimage."

"He seems to be. We've signed up for the brunch here tomorrow, too. Are you still married to Perry?"

"We were divorced last year," I said. "I came home to help my parents now that they're in their seventies."

I've noticed that when you meet up with someone from school and it's been a couple decades, there's really not that much to talk about after you run through the list of spouses and kids. Darlene expressed a few more niceties about the pilgrimage events, then right before she turned to leave she said, "Wasn't someone murdered during the reenactment today?"

"I think it was an accident. We don't know yet."

Darlene nodded. "It was murder."

A bit startled by her obvious certainty, I asked, "Why do you say that?"

"Honey, when a rich man drops dead from a bullet wound, you can trust that it's not an accident."

"But Walter Simpson wasn't rich. I mean, he had some property, but I never heard he was wealthy enough to be murdered. How do you know for sure that he was shot?"

"Please. It's all over North Mississippi. It was even on the evening news. Well, I hear the orchestra tuning up, so we'd better go in. Good to see you again, Trinket."

As she walked over to her husband standing by the door I pondered her comments. I was sure the police hadn't ruled cause of death yet. It'd only been a few hours. Maybe I should have been watching the evening news instead of drinking Jack Daniel's with Bitty.

"Here's your coffee," my cousin said at my elbow, and I turned to look at her.

"Was Walter Simpson very wealthy?"

She blinked a few times before answering. "He was quite comfortable, but I'm not sure you'd call him wealthy. Why?"

"Because someone just mentioned he was probably murdered for his money."

Bitty shoved the coffee into my hand. "Drink all of this right now. I think you're having some kind of hallucination."

I took the coffee. "No, seriously. Do you remember Darlene Landers?"

"Dated Early James and graduated magna cum pregnant?" She nodded. "I do. Why?"

"She's here with her new husband and—"

"Tall, gray hair, and big nose?" Bitty interrupted me, and when I nodded she said, "Derek Pratt. He's a Yankee."

"He's from Illinois, yes. To get to my point, Darlene said when a rich man dies from a bullet wound, you can bet it's murder."

"That sounds about right. Drink your coffee. You look all flushed."

Since I was probably still flushed from the humiliation of having my skirts fly up over my head in the middle of a crowd, and I had no intention of sharing that with Bitty, I drank my coffee. I handed her the empty cup, and she passed me a stack of programs.

"Give these out at the door while I make sure there are some available for those already seated."

I stood at the door with programs for those attending the concert, and Bitty flitted about through the crowd, meeting and greeting. She's a social butterfly. I'm more of a shy brown moth. It's not that I don't enjoy going to concerts, speaking to people I've just met, or just making small talk. I do. I'm just not the expert at it that Bitty is. She's a Belle. That's with a capital *B*. She can carry on a conversation with complete strangers and charm them, flattering and teasing at the same time.

The few times I tried my hand at being a Belle, I came off as a Bitch. That's with a capital *B*, too. So I stuck with what I know best. I smiled and handed out programs.

By the time the concert was over, I was exhausted. It'd been a long weekend. I just wanted to go home and crawl into bed with the covers over my head. I thought Bitty would never stop mingling with garden club members and guests. I sagged against a doorframe and waited for Madame Butterfly to stop flitting. Sometimes it took a while.

Finally, she glided toward me, her face glowing like a Halloween lantern. "Well, Trinket, we're done for this year. Tomorrow is the Sunday brunch, and we aren't participating in that, so you're free to pack away your dress until next time."

I just looked at her. She was having such a good night, I knew I shouldn't ruin it by telling her there was no way I'd be joining the festivities next year. Even if I did, it certainly wouldn't be in a dress that made me look like a shiny gray boulder. So I smiled and nodded.

We went outside on the beautifully lit sidewalk to wait for Brandon or Clayton to arrive. It was a lovely night: a bit chilly with a slight breeze blowing, but winter was definitely over. I hoped for a summer that wouldn't make me feel like a boiling crawfish every time I went outside, but I realized that living in Mississippi, hot weather is pretty much a certainty. So I just enjoyed the excellent weather while I could.

Bitty shivered. "I should have worn a shawl," she said.

"You really are a hothouse flower, aren't you," I observed.

"I have delicate skin. I'm not like some people who bake in the sun and look like a dried apple doll by the age of forty. I preserve my magnolia skin as much as possible."

"Magnolia skin? Delicate? Who sold you your magic mirror—Walt Disney?"

Actually, Bitty does have lovely skin and very few blemishes, but she also sees a plastic surgeon on a regular basis and gets Botox injections. I've informed her that Botox is a poison, but so far she hasn't paid me the least bit of attention. She hears what she wants to hear. I'm a lot like that myself. Still, I recalled a tanning bed in her not-so-distant past.

"Jealousy is an ugly thing, Trinket." Bitty patted an imaginary stray strand of blond hair back into place. "Of course, you're entitled to it, I suppose. It must be difficult for you, being so close to me and all."

There's little I like better than swapping insults with Bitty. I've heard that keeping brain cells active prevents senile dementia.

"Not really," I said. "But since I don't live in Oz with you and the rest of the Munchkins, I'm more closely acquainted with reality."

Bitty patted me on the arm. "Oh honey, you've been so bitter since that tornado dropped a house on your sister. Try to get past it."

I had just opened my mouth to mention flying monkeys when Bitty's Mercedes pulled up in front of Montrose, and we went out to the curb. Brandon leaned across the front seat to open the door for his mother while I got into the back. I manhandled the hoops into submission and stretched out my legs with a sigh of relief. It was over. Thank God. I wasn't sure I could have endured too much more. I'm not as hardy as Bitty when it comes to social excess.

Once back at her house, I went upstairs to retrieve my clothes I'd left there earlier. I'd discovered that putting on a corset properly required two people: one to pull the laces tight and one to shriek in agony. I'd done my part admirably. Just the sight of my Lee jeans and long-sleeved tee shirt formed my decision that I couldn't go another minute or three wearing all the accouterments of a nineteenth century victim. I got out of the blamed things as quickly as I could. It wasn't easy undoing the corset laces, but I managed it. Desperation helped.

I threw the dress, corset, stockings, and petticoats over my arm and went downstairs. "Here," I said to Bitty, who was still clad in her lovely dress, "you can burn these now."

She looked shocked. "Are you insane?"

"Probably. If not, I'm sure I wouldn't have let myself be talked into wearing this dress, much less the corset. Guantanamo prisoners don't suffer this much."

"I'll have these cleaned and stored for you until next time," she replied, taking the vile things from me.

"Dream on, Endora. Not even a twitch of your nose and generous sprinkling of fairy dust could accomplish my return to corset duty."

"It was Samantha who twitched her nose. Endora just snapped her fingers."

"Whatever. Reruns of *Bewitched* aside, I have done my part. My involvement with the next pilgrimage will be as a contented tourist."

When Bitty didn't respond, I knew she intended to talk me into it again next year. I was determined to resist. There were some things too horrible to contemplate.

"Darlene Landers was right, you know," Bitty said as she took my pilgrimage garments to her laundry room. I followed behind her, not too closely just in case she made an unexpected stop or detour.

"About what?" I asked.

Bitty set my clothes down on a granite counter and got a hanger and dry cleaner bag off a rack. "Walter Simpson was shot through the heart."

"Who told you that?"

"Rayna."

Rayna Blue is a founding member of the Dixie Divas. The Divas are a local club of women-only members who meet once a month to eat good food, sip exotic drinks or sweet tea, according to personal preferences, and generally misbehave. It's a great way to relax. No men are allowed at these meetings except as entertainment or to tend bar; we're inclined to get raucous on occasion, but we're usually harmless. There are no requirements to be a Diva, except being female and having a sense of humor. All ages and professions are welcome. Membership stays at about a dozen, for reasons of space and notoriety.

At any rate, Rayna's husband Rob Rainey is a bail bondsman and insurance claims investigator, so she usually knows such details long before they're made public. It comes in very handy on occasion.

I watched Bitty slide the gray satin dress onto a padded hanger and put it on the rack; she put the coiled-up petticoat on a separate hanger, put corset, pantalets, and stockings into a small mesh bag and attached it to the hanger, then covered it all with a dry cleaner's bag, all ready to be cleaned and stored.

"Do the police think it was an accident?" I asked after I digested the information that a man I had been speaking with just hours earlier had been shot through the heart. I'd hoped for an accident. Deliberate murder was too horrible to contemplate.

"I'm not sure what the police think. Darlene thinks it was murder, and she might be on to something. Whether it was accident or murder, Walter Simpson is just as dead."

"Now that I think about it, Rodney Farrell questioned me as if it could be a murder. I suppose they have to do that just in case. But still . . ."

"Rodney Farrell isn't sure that gravity is a law," said Bitty. She and Deputy Farrell didn't always get along, so it wasn't surprising she felt that way. "I wouldn't worry so much about what he said. He just follows orders."

"True. There's going to be a thorough investigation, I'm sure. Poor Walter. I just wish I hadn't made him wear a Yankee uniform," I said. "Now he won't get to wear the gray next year."

Bitty turned to look at me. "That's not your fault, Trinket. It wouldn't matter what uniform he wore if it was his time. What's going to happen just happens, whether we want it to or not."

I nodded. "True. Still, I wish he'd gotten to wear what he wanted. He was so unhappy at having to wear the Yankee uniform, but he was the only one who could still fit in it."

Bitty patted me on the arm. "It's all right, sugar. After all, someone had to be the enemy. It was just his turn, that's all."

That struck me as pretty philosophical. Especially for Bitty. Sometimes we just have to take our turns being the bad guy, so to speak. I've had to do it several times in my life, and it's one of those things that is not very pleasant. But someone has to do it.

It was a good thing I felt that way, because it wasn't long before I had to take my turn as the bad guy again. It was just as unpleasant as I remembered.

I ended up staying the night in Bitty's guest room; I hadn't been asleep but an hour or two when I was awakened by a rude shaking. It jerked me from a sound sleep, and I sat up, swinging one arm outward.

"Hey!" Bitty protested, ducking just in time. "Be careful, Trinket. You nearly decapitated me."

"What are you doing?" I peered at her; light from the hallway behind put her in silhouette, but I could still see pink everything, including whatever was smeared on her face.

"Brandon just called. His car broke down, and we have to go get him. I want company."

"Haven't you ever heard of Triple A?" I grumbled. "Where is he?"

"JB's. He called a tow truck, but the guy couldn't give him a lift home. And everyone else has already left."

"That's what, half a mile? Oh, never mind. Fine. Let me find my slippers, and I'll come with you."

That's how I found myself in my jammies and bunny slippers, sitting in the front seat of Bitty's car with a pug on my lap at three in the morning. My eyes were scratchy from lack of sleep, and I was rather irritable.

"He could have walked home by now," I muttered as Bitty steered the Benz down the street toward Van Buren. JB's is the local late-night spot for music and drinks, right on the court square. It's close to Budgie's, so we often end up there during the day if we want a drink that isn't tea or coffee.

At three in the morning, Holly Springs' court square was pretty much deserted. Traffic signals and security lights were about the only lights still on. The sidewalk in front of JB's was empty, no sign of Brandon.

"Maybe he walked home," I said rather grumpily. "He's probably there wondering where we are, if he noticed your car gone."

"He specifically said he needed a ride, but he didn't say why," Bitty murmured, peering out the windshield at the dark, shadowed sidewalks. She slowed the car to a crawl. "It's only been about ten minutes since he called. I know he said JB's. Where could he be?"

"In your kitchen having a late snack, is my guess."

"I don't know. He sounded a bit upset. He should have stayed home and not gone out, but he said he was going crazy, thinking about poor Walter Simpson. He ran to help, you know, and saw him lying there, lifeless—it's a lot for a young man to face."

I agreed. But all I said aloud was, "Why isn't Clayton with him? I thought they did most things together."

"Clayton is asleep."

I turned in the seat to stare at her. "What? Why didn't you send him instead of getting me out of bed? I knew I should have gone home tonight, but *No,* you said, *You'll sleep better here,* and *You can go home after a good night's rest.* So here I am, at three in the morning, on a rescue mission for someone who isn't even—"

A sudden thud on the passenger-side door interrupted my waspish whine, accompanied by a shrill bark from Chen Ling, still sitting in my lap like a furry Buddha. It scared me, and I let out a high-pitched, *"Eek!"*

Bitty braked sharply, and I lurched forward, squashing the pug as the seatbelt cut into my stomach and shoulder. I threw my hands up to brace myself against the dash. If we'd been going at a normal speed, the dog and I both would be tasting airbag. My heart raced as I looked out the window. I caught a glimpse of blond hair and relaxed slightly. It had to be Brandon.

Bitty hit the electric locks, and Brandon jerked open the back door. He flung himself inside, breathing heavily. "Go!" he shouted to Bitty, and she hit the gas.

There was a powerful engine under the hood of that Benz. We hurtled down Van Dorn toward Craft at a speed far too fast for my tastes. Bitty didn't slow up until we passed the dollar store. I had no idea if she ran the light at Memphis Street.

"What's going on?" I asked Brandon as Bitty braked at the stop sign. If it hadn't been a dead end, I'm not sure she would have slowed down at all. We turned left on two wheels.

"Didn't you see him?" Brandon asked, still breathing heavily. "Some idiot chased me all the way to the library and back."

"Who was it? And why?"

Brandon leaned forward, gripping the back of the front seat with both hands. "I have no idea. I was minding my own business, although I was still pretty pissed about whoever sabotaged my car, and—"

"Wait a minute," Bitty interrupted. "Someone did something to your car?"

"Yeah. It wouldn't start. It looked like they took the coil wire. I would have left it there, but the top was down, and I didn't want whoever messed with it to come back to finish the job. So I had it towed."

"Is that why you wanted a ride home?" I asked, half-turning to look at him. Chitling took exception to being disturbed and growled, but I ignored her. "You didn't want to risk walking?"

"Kinda. Whoever did it spray-painted a few rude suggestions, and I figured they'd stick around to watch my reaction."

"You should have called the police," said Bitty, and a glance at her showed her lips set in a taut line. "This town has gone nuts. First Walter, now this. Do you think they were trying to do something bad to you?"

"Truthfully, I thought it was one of the guys messing with me at first. It looked like just whipped cream all over the car. Clayton had already gone, and the other guys offered me a ride home, but I wanted to stay for the tow truck. I thought the driver would give me a lift, but he had two guys with him and no room."

Brandon paused. "I think he thought it was funny. Turned out it was paint and not whipped cream, too. Anyway, he hadn't been gone but a minute when someone came up behind me and smacked me in the back. I turned around, but it was some guy in a mask, one of those Halloween rubber ones. When he went to hit me again, I grabbed the bat out of his hands, and he took off so I chased him. Then he took out a big knife and chased me until I got back up here and saw your car."

"No idea who it was?" I asked, and Brandon shook his head.

"No. He wasn't a big guy, though. At first, I thought it might be someone I'd had a fight with a while back, but he's a lot bigger."

"It could have been a friend of his, or a brother," I suggested, and Brandon nodded.

"Could have been. Hey, hold on—I think that's him!"

Bitty had turned down a side street to come around and back up to Van Dorn, and a man dressed in dark clothes and a hoodie walked down the street toward the cemetery. When she sped up, he took off running through some yards. Brandon opened the back door, and Bitty shrieked at him not to get out. He fussed a little but closed the door, opening the window to lean out and search the dark, empty yards and streets.

We circled the block twice, but whoever it was had gone into the night. Or into one of the houses.

"I guess we lost him," said Bitty, and I had to admit, I was pretty relieved.

"He could be in the cemetery," said Brandon, and I shook my head.

"No way. I'm not riding through the cemetery at three in the morning, I don't care who chased you."

"Trinket's right," said Bitty after a moment, and I was pleased until she added, "The gates are locked at night."

We ended up going home, and of course Chitling had piddled in my lap, so I took a shower and put on a dry muumuu. When I went downstairs, Bitty and Brandon were talking.

"We think it was just a practical joke," said Bitty and took a sip of her wine. Some of the pink stuff she wears on her face at night had worn off, so she looked like a deranged harlequin.

I took the glass of wine she offered me. "Some joke. Chasing a person with a knife can be dangerous."

Brandon nodded. "Maybe they were just trying to scare me. Otherwise, why hit me with the bat first? I'm going to find out who's behind it and teach them a lesson."

"Let it go," said Bitty, and I looked at her over the rim of my wine glass. She was serious. "It will only end up worse, I'm afraid. Promise me you'll just put this behind you. No harm was done to anything but your car, and I'll pay for that. I don't want to risk someone getting really mad and doing something worse."

She had a point. Brandon finally agreed, and we all went to bed. I lay in the guest room gazing up at the canopy over my bed, thinking it'd been a pretty long day. And after all that had happened, it was disconcerting for someone to think it amusing to threaten anyone with a knife. It could be just a college-boy prank, but I didn't like it. It seemed to me that Brandon had made an enemy of someone.

Chapter 3

"WELL, IN THE FIRST place," I said to my mama at our kitchen table a couple days later, "anytime someone you haven't seen in decades comes up to you and knows who you are immediately, it's a bit of an insult. Especially when they say you haven't changed a bit."

Mama nodded understanding. "It implies that either you looked twenty years older when you were in school, or that they're lying their socks off."

"I always lean toward the latter explanation." I was a bit grumpy. "Of course, in Bitty's case, she still looks like she did in school because cosmetic surgery is a wonderful thing, and she has too much money and time on her hands."

After a moment Mama said, "Bless her heart."

"Bitty said I'm too sensitive. She said I've been away too long and have forgotten what people really mean when they say things like that."

"It's possible, sugar."

I sighed. "I know. But I've been back home for over a year. You'd think I would have relearned the translations from Belle to English by now."

"That's okay, hon." Mama patted the back of my hand. "It'll all come back to you soon."

"I'm not so sure. I never get the implications of what's said until later, when it's far too late to say something snarky back to them."

"If it's any consolation," Mama said after a moment, "Darlene Landers' great-great- grandmother was a Yankee carpetbagger from Ohio. A very nice lady, according to what I've heard, but that whole side of the family came down here from up north after The War."

"Thank you, Mama," I said, knowing that she had done her best to console me. It just doesn't mean as much to me as it does to my parents or to the generations before them. A lot of us have moved on from old resentments.

Walter Simpson was not one of them, however. His bitter resentment of the family's ill fortunes during the nineteenth century was legendary in Holly Springs. I could imagine how difficult it must have been for him to play the part of a Yankee, even in a reenactment.

"I tried to be fair," I said aloud. "But Royal Stewart got into a bar fight and was taken off to jail, so there wasn't anyone who fit into his uniform. What else was I to do?"

Mama blinked at me in confusion, and I realized she'd not followed my internal switch of conversational topic.

"Sorry," I said. "I was thinking about Mr. Simpson."

Mama sighed. "Honestly, Trinket, your thought processes are too quick for me to follow. Don't you worry about Walter Simpson being angry with you at the reenactment. He was more than capable of leaving if he didn't want to stay. He had his own reasons for agreeing. What happened to him is terrible, but you aren't responsible in any way. Now, I need to go check on your father. He's out riding that blamed tractor around the fields. He's probably scaring the neighbors."

"We don't have any neighbors," I argued needlessly. Cherryhill sits on ten acres, all that's left of the once expansive farm. Over the years, chunks of land had been sold to housing developers and a few individuals, so ten acres was all that's left of the original tract of land my Truevine ancestors had farmed for decades. There's no one to leave it to but me. Emerald, my twin sister, lives out in the Northwest and doesn't plan to ever come home to live. Getting her to come home to visit is a major coup. My only child, Michelle, lives down in Georgia and may one day want to come back to live, but I rather doubted it. I'm sure that eventually it will be sold, and I can only hope it will be to someone who appreciates a dying cherry orchard, creaky old house, and a barn full of stray cats. I've heard there are crazy people who can be bamboozled into taking a chance on someone else's heritage. Maybe they'd come in and make their own heritage after I'm gone. That'd be a nice thing to have happen.

So while my mother went outside to check on Daddy, who had recently taken to riding the John Deere over rutted fields that had once been home to cows, I got up from the table and got myself a glass of sweet tea. Mama and Daddy lived in the downstairs, having turned the parlor into their main bedroom so they don't have to climb the stairs, and I have the entire upstairs to myself. It's rather nice.

I didn't have to work at my part-time job for a few days since Carolann's niece was in town and wanted to work with her aunt, so I had some unexpected free time. I had anticipated a lovely interlude of lazy days catching up on my reading, drinking sweet tea, and swinging in the new hammock Daddy had strung between two of the old cherry trees. Now that the pilgrimage was behind us, Bitty had plans with Jackson Lee Brunetti, her significant other. They planned to go on a trip to Europe. I was sure Bitty would come back with new clothes from all the Paris designers she could find. Lord knows, she has enough money.

Jackson Lee is an expert lawyer with an almost mythical reputation; he's been known to get his clients unbelievable deals in lawsuits, get the guilty acquitted or the best possible sentences, and just his name had been known to prompt opposing lawyers to advise their clients to take a deal instead of going to trial.

He'd been in love with Bitty for quite a while. She finally took notice of him the year before, and since then, they've been a couple with a proclivity to nauseatingly sweet pet names. I didn't even want to think about what they called each other in private.

My relationship with our local vet, Dr. Kit Coltrane, was much less sugary. Neither of us was prone to syrupy sweet murmurings. Thank heavens. We had a friendship as well as a closer relationship. No, I'm not going into any details. I'm sure there's a rule against that in the Top Twenty Things Southern Girls Learn.

After I went upstairs and picked out a book I hadn't had time to read, I went back into the kitchen for my sweet tea. Daddy had come in while I was upstairs deciding on which book to read first. He had snippets of cut grass on his cheek as well as his flannel shirt. I brushed off a rather large piece of nutgrass and asked if he'd had any trouble with the tractor.

"Nope, she runs like new," he said. "Spike did a bang-up job on her, I have to say that."

Since it was my clueless cousin's fault the John Deere had stopped running, I said, "Bitty will be thrilled to hear it." I drank some of my tea, refilled it from the pitcher, and held up my book. "I'm going out to swing in the hammock and read. I intend to be a lady of leisure for the next few days."

"But I'm mowing the grass," Daddy protested.

"It can't be that high. It's only April."

"We've had warm weather, and weeds get started early."

I put my hands on my hips. "You just want to play on your tractor, don't you?"

"Well, I needed to find out if it's in good working order before the grass gets too high. It took quite a beating, you know."

He was right, but I didn't want a replay of how Bitty had abused his tractor in one of her manic schemes, so I just said, "It's fine now. Can't you mow later?"

"I'll just mow the orchard first. I can trim the grass later, I suppose."

I kissed him on the cheek. "Thank you, Daddy."

My father and I are a lot alike in some ways. I got my height from him, since he's still over six feet despite age robbing him of an inch or so; my mother is very petite, and her silver hair was once blond. My sister Emerald got Mama's height, small bone structure, and lovely blond hair. I got Daddy's height and the Truevine tendency to collect annoying fat cells in random parts of my anatomy. I also got the darker hair, although it's always had streaks of red that's called dark auburn on the boxes of color I buy at Walmart. I had to start coloring my hair after Mama's crazy dog decided all the gray on my head was his enemy, the squirrel. He'd look at me and bark ferociously. It was rather unpleasant.

Since Daddy and I had struck a truce, I didn't want to be too greedy. I took my sweet tea and book up to my room to wait for him to finish mowing the orchard. There's a long enclosed porch across the entire back of the room. At one time before air conditioning, it'd been used as a sleeping porch. Now it has windows that lift and screens to keep out mosquitos or other parasites. I raised the windows to let in a cooling breeze and chose a big, overstuffed chair to curl up in with my book and tea. I'd gotten behind on my reading. I've always loved to read, especially as a child.

When I had graduated from Dick and Jane and Spot, I gravitated toward stories with horses, like *Black Beauty*, *My Friend Flicka*, and an old book titled *Ticktock and Jim*. Jim is the boy in the story, and he and his pony had some grand adventures. I'd always begged for a pony. Daddy always replied that we had cows, but he wouldn't let me ride them. Bitty had a pony, and at the tender age of six, she'd ridden over to my house, and we'd gone off on some grand adventures of our own. It was an activity we enthusiastically pursued for the rest of our childhood. Very few of our adventures had parental approval. We also spent a great deal of our youth grounded to our homes, where we did numerous chores to atone for our sins. The upside of being grounded was that we watched a lot of TV and became acquainted with characters like Samantha and Darrin, Lucy and Ethel, Rob and Laura, Andy and Barney, and Scooby-Doo and Shaggy. I still remember *77*

Sunset Strip reruns with great fondness. My oldest brother emulated the character Kookie by combing his hair all the time. We just loved to tease him about it.

To this day, Bitty and I enjoy reliving our childhoods. My mother often remarks that we never left our childhoods. She may be right.

The smell of freshly cut grass drifted through the window screens and into the room as I curled up to read, the drone of the mower familiar and soothing. Before I knew it, I was waking up and it was afternoon. I'm not a person who naps often or well. One of the reasons for that is my state of confusion upon waking, as if I've just arrived in a time machine and can't figure out where I am or why I'm there. My tongue is usually thick and I've drooled on myself, and any attempt at conversation is marred by the fact I can't properly form words.

I had a crick in my neck from having fallen asleep with my head bent over, my book had fallen to the floor, and all the ice in my sweet tea had melted. Watered down tea is not on the list of my favorite things. So I stumbled downstairs with my head bent in what I feared would be a permanent and unattractive position. I had my tea glass in one hand and a Kleenex to wipe the drool off my chin in my other. I'm sure I walked like Quasimodo, from *The Hunchback of Notre Dame* fame.

Of course, the very first person I saw upon staggering into the kitchen was Kit Coltrane. Just his voice can make my heart go pitty-pat, as if I were sixteen again. The actual sight of him can skyrocket my blood pressure. Not just because he's quite handsome, which he is, but because he has a warm, wonderful smile and he really likes me. I'm always a little awed by the last. I'm also puzzled by it, but I figure *What the heck?* If he's attracted to tall, eccentric women with an extra fifteen pounds cleverly hidden in sweatpants or Lee jeans, who am I to argue?

"Hey, gorgeous," he said with a grin, and I said something back in a jumble of syllables that passed for the English language.

"Whd dun hm do how her."

Kit is very polite. His mama raised him right, and he didn't say anything at all tacky. He just nodded as if he understood. "I came out to check on one of your mama's sick cats."

My parents had decided to be caretakers of a vast legion of stray cats that congregate in the barn quite punctually twice a day. They don't have to be summoned, but my father likes to yodel for them, just in case one has missed its internal dietary clock. It's rather like hog calling but without the *suu-eee*. When one of the furry stomachs on feet comes down with an ailment, the vet is immediately contacted. Kit makes house calls.

Since I wasn't at my best and hoped he hadn't noticed, I smiled and headed for the tea. By the time I reached the refrigerator, I was coherent enough to ask if he'd like a glass. He gave me another one of his devastating smiles.

"I have to give a round of injections, but as soon as I get back in, I would love a glass of sweet tea. No lemon."

"No problem," I said brightly.

As soon as he was out the door, I raced upstairs for my bathroom. I scrubbed drool off my chin, brushed my teeth, checked my underarm deodorant, brushed snarls out of my hair, and then spritzed a light perfume over my clothes. Really, one of the perks of being over fifty is that I don't have to worry as much about my appearance as long as I'm clean and neat-looking. But put an eligible man into that equation, and it changes the dynamics. While I haven't gone as far as Bitty in spraying lacquer on my hair until it would survive a nuclear explosion, I've found that I still have enough vanity left to freshen up. I want it to look natural and effortless, of course.

By the time I went back downstairs and fixed Kit a glass of sweet tea, he was done with cats and coming up the back steps. Perfect timing. As he came through the back door, I did a graceful turn toward him, holding out his glass. *Effortless. Natural,* I told myself. I smiled as I glided across the kitchen floor with his tea, my eyes on his wonderful face.

Only two steps into my effortless, natural glide, I hit a road block. Something hit me right below my knees, and I lurched forward. The glass of tea sailed through the air, and I ended up sprawled on the kitchen floor like a felled tree. The road block yelped, the glass hit the wall and shattered, and I seriously considered just lying there with my face pressed against the floor until The Second Coming.

"Trinket! Are you hurt?" I heard my dream man ask, and I knew I couldn't lie there forever. Too bad. It sure beat having to face humiliation.

"I'm fine," I said and lifted my head to find myself eye level with the little brown road block. Brownie stared at me. He's a beagle-dachshund mix that showed up one cold winter and stole my mother's heart and attention. I narrowed my eyes at him. He licked his butt. I decided I didn't want to be that close to such a disgusting activity and took the hand Kit held out to me.

"I'll get you another glass of tea," I managed to say calmly, once I was standing.

"No, that's okay. Where's the broom? I'll help you clean up this mess."

Who couldn't love a man like that?

Once we swept up all the glass and had the floor mopped clean of sticky tea, I asked how Mama's cats were doing. It was a polite question to bridge the awkwardness I felt.

"They're doing fine. It's a good thing we caught one of the new cats in time. She's going into heat and needs to be spayed. I'll wait until she finishes her round of antibiotics for that though. So—I heard the pilgrimage went well except for Walter Simpson."

His comment wasn't completely unexpected. I nodded and said dryly, "Other than *that*, Mrs. Lincoln, how was the play?"

Kit grinned. "A very close parallel. I'm glad I wasn't there. It had to be horrible."

"I couldn't believe it. One minute he was alive and well, the next minute he's lying dead on the ground."

"How's Sammy taking it?"

"I haven't seen him since the pilgrimage, but I hear he's devastated. He was Walter's closest kin and has been living in his house and taking care of him for the past three years."

Kit shook his head. "That's got to be difficult for him. It's always hard to lose someone close to you."

We both had experience with that, and I'm sure Kit was thinking about those he'd lost as much as I was. After the first shock subsides, the anguish and grief are close behind. Acceptance comes eventually, but it takes a long time. Sometimes a lifetime.

Mama came in the back door, and Brownie greeted her joyfully. They were both wearing blue argyle sweaters. He's never far from her if he can help it. She aids and abets his sneak-thief tendencies. The dog's penchant for devouring inedible objects is how I first met Kit, so I can't complain too loudly. After all, if not for Brownie's afternoon snack of jewelry, I wouldn't have raced the dog to the veterinary clinic to remove the jewelry he devoured while I was busy medicating my mother's cats. I'd had cat spit in my hair next to a partially dissolved pill that had been forcibly ejected from said cat's throat and a wad of straw from the hayloft sticking out like porcupine quills, so I had definitely made a lasting impression at our first meeting.

My curse of being less than graceful hasn't deterred him from seeing me, so I feel pretty good about that. I occasionally have the tendency to react like one of the Three Stooges in a skit, especially when I'm with Bitty. It can be very embarrassing. Kit doesn't seem to mind.

"Does this medicine have to be kept in the refrigerator?" Mama asked him, holding up the bottle. "It doesn't say on the label."

"Yes. Be sure to finish it out. Then bring her in to the office, and I'll spay her for you."

Willow Bend Animal Hospital gives my mama a discount on all the stray and feral cats she manages to bring in to be fixed. I'm sure a large portion of Daddy's pension from the U.S. Postal Service goes toward making life comfortable for the Marshall County cat population.

When Mama brought out a fresh apple pie from the old pie safe and put on a pot of coffee, I knew Kit would linger a while. Very few people can resist my mother's baking, especially her pie crusts. I don't know how she does it. I can cook plain food and make excellent desserts, but I've never been able to master the art of the pie crust.

We sat at the kitchen table over our pie and coffee, and when Daddy came in from his yard duties he joined us. The talk inevitably got back around to Walter Simpson and the puzzle of how he'd happened to be shot.

"Someone just put a live round in their gun, that's all," said Daddy. "A stupid mistake. I don't know how anyone could manage it."

"Especially when it's one of those old guns," Mama agreed. "You'd think they'd know better, using all those old weapons like that. It was just an accident waiting to happen."

After a moment Daddy said, "Maybe it wasn't such an accident."

I was flabbergasted my father even hinted at murder. I recovered enough to ask, "Why on earth would you say that?"

Daddy shrugged. "Walter Simpson wasn't the most well-liked man in town. He had a way of irritating people. I suppose any number of folks wouldn't have minded taking a shot at him."

"Why, Edward Truevine, that's a terrible thing to say," Mama got out after a moment of stark silence. "No one deserves to be killed for being a trifle irritating."

"I didn't say he deserved to be killed, Anna. I just said there are a lot of people who might want to take a shot at him. That's different."

"Well, don't you go letting anyone hear you say that, or you might end up as a suspect."

Daddy sighed. "Since I was here where at least four dozen people saw me during the time of the reenactment, I doubt that's going to be an issue."

"You just never know these days," Mama said with a shake of her head. "The world's gone crazy. Anything can happen."

I had just opened my mouth to say I was sure it was a terrible accident when the kitchen phone rang. I got up to answer it, since I'd already eaten every bite of my apple pie. I might have even licked the plate if Kit wasn't there. One should never horrify their attractive male guest, however.

"Hello," I said into the receiver as cheerfully as I could. For a moment there was no response, then I heard a rather hysterical voice babbling something I couldn't understand. "What did you say?" I asked. "Who is this?"

There was a scuffling sound, a cough, and then: "It's Bitty—oh Trinket, come quickly. I need you."

Alarmed by her obvious panic, I asked, "What's wrong?"

"Oh, Trinket," she said in a sobbing voice, "they're arresting my baby!"

For a moment, the words didn't sink in. I stood frozen to the spot beside the phone base on the wall as I tried to make sense of what she'd said. I couldn't imagine why one of her boys would be arrested or for what.

"But why?" I asked. "Which one and what did he do?"

"Brandon . . . they said he killed Walter Simpson."

Stunned, I couldn't say anything but, "Call Jackson Lee as soon as we hang up. I'll be there in ten minutes."

"Jackson Lee was here. He's on his way to the police station now. Just come be with me. I don't think I can get through this without you."

"I'm on my way."

When I hung up, I started for the stairs. "Brandon was arrested for killing Walter Simpson. I'm going to be with Bitty as soon as I get my purse," I said.

Kit stood up immediately. "I'll drive you there. You look too upset to drive yourself."

He was right. My hands were shaking, and I had a slight tremble in my voice as I thanked him. Mama had gasped and covered her mouth with one hand, and Daddy had uttered an oath I would have gotten smacked for saying once upon a time.

This didn't make sense. I hoped it was all a mistake, but the sense of foreboding inside me warned there was trouble ahead. I wasn't that surprised.

Chapter 4

"HOW CAN THIS BE?" I asked Jackson Lee as we perched on chairs in the police station and waited for Brandon to be released on bail. "That rifle doesn't even fire."

Jackson Lee shook his head. "Apparently, it fired this time. The rifling on the bullet is consistent with the rifling on the gun barrel of the weapon he used. The prosecutor believes there's enough evidence to charge Brandon with involuntary manslaughter. I'm sure I can plead accidental death at most, but of course, I'm going to try to get all charges dismissed."

Bitty looked up at him with horror in her eyes. "He's going to have another trial?"

"That was just an arraignment, sugar. He'll have to surrender his passport and make bail, and you know I'll do everything in my power to get him cleared of all the charges. We just have to figure out what happened."

Bitty seemed dazed. I'd put my arm around her shoulders, and I gave her a squeeze. "It's going to be okay, Bitty. You have to believe that."

She turned toward me, eyes shiny with unshed tears, and I wanted to hug her and make it all go away. I didn't know what else to say. The usual platitudes seemed so inadequate.

Kit cleared his throat. "You have the best lawyer in all of Mississippi on your side, Bitty. If anyone can make all this go away, it's Jackson Lee."

Jackson Lee looked at Kit with a faint smile. "I appreciate your faith in me. I'm going to give it everything I've got."

The two men nodded. They're both tall, dark, and handsome, and both professionals who don't skimp on assisting clients or patients. Kit was right. If anyone could handle this, it was Jackson Lee.

"Are you sure you don't want to wait at the house, hon?" he asked Bitty. "I can bring him home to you as soon as he's released."

Bitty shook her head. "No. He's my son. I'm not leaving until I can leave with him by my side."

Brandon had to be processed: fingerprinted, photos taken, identifying marks like tattoos or scars noted. The bail bondsman had to pay his bail and get the paperwork signed. I expected Rayna's husband, Rob Rainey, to show up at any moment. It wouldn't be the first time he'd come to our rescue with bail bonds.

The old cliché that the wheels of justice turn slowly seemed to hold true for the first part. I wasn't sure about the exceedingly fine part of the cliché, but things definitely moved at a slow pace. No one seemed in a hurry to get anything done.

"Where's Clayton?" I asked Bitty as time stretched and the silence seemed too loud. "Is he okay?"

"He's at home. I wouldn't let him come with us. He's too upset, and I don't know if I can handle that right now."

I nodded understanding. Sometimes keeping a lid on our emotions can be ruined by the smallest of things. A lady doesn't make a public spectacle of her grief, and Truevines remember that at the most trying of times. Often a bit late, but we get there eventually. So Bitty and I sat quietly on the outside, while inside we were both in turmoil. I could feel her trembling next to me and knew she was frightened for her son. Mothers invariably go into protective mode when their child is threatened, and I knew she felt helpless, because I did, too.

Since I didn't want to keep saying, "It's going to be okay," I asked her if she wanted something from the vending machine. A lone drink machine stood next to one of those vending machines that spit out bags of chips or candy bars. They both looked shabby but offered variety.

"A Coke will be fine," she said, and I got up and dug into my purse.

"What kind? Grape, orange, water, or Co-cola?" I asked. In the South, all soft drinks are called Cokes. I don't know why. If someone orders a soda or pop, we immediately know they're not from the South. Some Southerners still refer to Cokes as "Co-cola" instead of Coca-Cola. Of course, I speak for older Southerners, not the newer generations.

"Diet Sprite. Oh, and a bag of chips and some chocolate. I really need a big chocolate bar right now."

Disaster can occasionally be eased by the magic of chocolate. It's an equal opportunity therapy that takes the edge off many catastrophes.

About the time her drink clunked into the metal slot, the door opened, and Rob Rainey stepped into the waiting room. Bitty immediately rose from her chair, and when she saw Rayna behind him, she gave a sigh of relief. Things would move along much more swiftly now, I was sure.

It still took some time to get all the necessary paperwork done, but within a half hour Brandon came out of the back. His blond hair was tangled, and he looked shell-shocked. Bitty didn't make a scene; she just went quietly to him and stood by his side. A fifty-thousand-dollar bond had been set, which meant that ten percent equaled five thousand dollars for the bondsman. Rob refused to take Bitty's money.

"No. I know you and I know Brandon, and I'm not worried he won't show up for his court date."

Bitty's eyes filled with tears, and she nodded her gratitude. Rayna hugged first Bitty, then Brandon, then me. "Call if you need me," she said to us. "I'll be right there."

"I know," said Bitty. "Divas are forever."

We left the police station and went out to our cars. A lopsided moon illuminated the night sky and silvered tree tops behind the lights of the parking lot. It had gotten dark without me even noticing. Time had crawled while waiting, but apparently, it was later than I'd thought.

"Will you stay with me tonight?" Bitty asked me when we stood by her car. "I don't want to sit there driving myself nuts about all this, and I can't tell Brandon how terrified I am about what might happen, but you know I don't have Jackson Lee stay over when the boys are home."

Bitty may be a bit snobbish, even bitchy at times, and she'll do the craziest things I've ever seen or heard of, but she's an excellent mother. She never does anything that might embarrass her sons in that way. There's a huge difference between being crazy and being a bad mom.

"Of course," I said immediately. "Kit can take me home for an overnight bag, and I'll be right back."

On the way back to my house, I asked Kit, "Do you think Brandon is going to be cleared of the charges? I mean, how can they say his gun fired the fatal shot when it hasn't worked in a hundred years?"

Kit shook his head. "I don't know. Jackson Lee is pretty near a miracle worker, but if the ballistics report says Brandon's bullet killed Walter Simpson, there's not a lot that can be done. I hope it will be ruled just an accidental shooting instead of reckless endangerment or involuntary manslaughter, but you never know. A lot depends on the prosecutor, I guess."

"We have a new prosecutor, but I haven't heard much about him. He's supposed to be sharp, I think."

"No matter how sharp he is, I'm sure Jackson Lee can handle him. Brandon will be just fine." He reached over to hold my hand, and it made me feel a lot calmer.

By the time I got to Bitty's house, it was almost ten, and she was already in her pajamas. Bitty wears a lot of pink, especially in her nightwear. She almost always looks like she's been dipped in Pepto-Bismol. That night was no exception. She greeted me at the door, pink silk pajamas covered by a pink silk robe, with her pink kitten slippers festooned with pink feathers.

"I thought you'd never get here. I have wine chilled and ready. Come on into the kitchen."

"And hello to you too," I said as I put my overnight bag down by the stairs and followed her to the kitchen. "Mama and Daddy say they're praying for you and Brandon that everything will be all right."

Bitty smiled. "That's so sweet. I know they worry, too. And I'm sure we can use all the prayers we can get. Here we go: I have Zinfandel for you, a crisp, ebullient Riesling for me."

"You've been going to wine tastings again, haven't you," I observed as I took my glass and followed her to the small parlor that used to be a butler's pantry of some kind. She changed a lot around when she remodeled, and it makes a very cozy place to sit and chat.

"Only a few tastings," she said. "I've learned so much about wine."

"And you have new white slipcovers, I see."

Due to a small accident during the fall season, the white slipcovers on her overstuffed chairs met an awful fate. Bitty changes slipcovers with the seasons, just as she changes storm doors for screen doors in the summer. She also rolls up rugs and has them taken out to be cleaned and some of them stored. It's a spring ritual. Heavy bed curtains give way to filmy mosquito nets; her sunporch that was once a kitchen back when kitchens weren't attached to main houses has the glass windows taken off to leave only the screens. Wicker furniture on the front porch is cleaned and pillows refreshed or replaced. Her lawn service removes winter greenery and pansies and replaces them with summer greenery and a host of flowering plants.

I just put my sweaters in a different drawer and shake my tee shirts free of wrinkles.

We live in completely different worlds. When our worlds collide, there's usually a lot of confusion and turmoil, but we muddle along as best we can. Since neither of us wanted to be the first to acknowledge the elephant in the room, we chatted about inconsequential things.

"We don't have a full accounting yet, but I think the pilgrimage went very well this year, all things considered." Bitty took a sip of wine and stroked Chen Ling's furry little head. The dog is rarely far from her. "At least the weather held. And the concert went very well, and the Sunday brunch was lovely, too. You should have gone."

"I was in a coma," I said after another sip of wine. "It was self-induced and lovely. Since I'm not working for several days I have a lot of free time to catch up on things I haven't done for a while. Cleaning out my closet is on the list. I'm not sure I'll get to it, but you never know."

We chatted about tasks we had yet to do and how nice it was that Deelight was having the next Diva Day at her house. She's lived in Holly Springs all her life, and we went to school with her and her sister. We committed many childhood crimes for which we all got in trouble, and now she has young children who are doing the same. Motherhood isn't always easy. Deelight has change-of-life kids. I would rather have a sharp poke in the eye than deal with children at this stage in my life. I've never been that patient. My sister Emerald has six children and manages just fine. I consider her either insane or numb to reality. Probably a little of both.

"Brandon went straight to bed when we got home. He's just drained. I don't know what's going to happen if he has to . . . go away," Bitty said.

"He won't go away," I said. "Jackson Lee won't let that happen. I mean, there's no way that old gun could have fired the bullet, right? I don't understand how they decided it definitely came from Brandon's rifle."

"Jackson Lee said the ballistics report matches the bullet—or minie ball—to our rifle. I just don't understand it. It's never fired in my lifetime or my mama's lifetime. The only reason we kept it is because it has sentimental value. You know how she was, and I'm the same way. I keep something as trivial as a spoon, if it belonged to one of my ancestors."

Since I came from the same kind of values, I completely understood. We keep pieces of charred wood in our basement that was part of the original structure that burned, just because it belongs to the house. Such things aren't worth anything to anyone but us.

"There's probably a mistake," I said. "I'm sure the rifles got mixed up or the bullet isn't the same. Something like that. I just can't imagine who would load their gun with real bullets for a reenactment. It must have been a mistake, but still . . . is there someone else at the reenactment who has a rifle that's similar to yours?"

"Probably. It was a rather common weapon during the war, I understand. Mama's two times great-grandfather brought it home from the war. I'm not sure if he was wounded or had gotten sick, but his old rifle hasn't been used since right after the turn of the century. It stopped firing right around then and ended up just being a conversation piece over the mantel for a long time. I remember seeing it as a child when we went up to the country to visit relatives."

Bitty's mama had come from Tennessee, not far from Shiloh. Like our ancestors, hers had fought under General Nathan Bedford Forrest, one of the South's best commanders, if not the best. Forrest had lived in the area around what is now Ashland, Mississippi, and was revered by many of his neighbors, as well as the soldiers who fought under his command. He wasn't called "The Wizard of the Saddle" for nothing. His descendants carried on his legacy; Brigadier General Nathan Bedford Forrest III died heroically in World War II. We Southerners take pride in such things. We're a rather morbid lot.

I said, "I'm sure the police have checked out the gun pretty thoroughly. If it won't fire then they'd know they have the wrong weapon."

"If it didn't fire, then they wouldn't charge Brandon with killing Walter," Bitty argued, and I agreed.

"I know. I just keep thinking back to the chaos of the last reenactment. Walter Simpson was flailing around, and I was trying to match up weapon to soldier—it was crazy. I could have mismatched gun to soldier, but those were all supposed to be replicas."

Bitty's eyes got big. "You mean our rifle may have gotten mixed up with someone else's gun? But I don't see how that's possible. Brandon would have noticed if he carried the wrong rifle, since ours doesn't fire."

I nodded. "He would have, but I watched the police tag the rifle he carried right after Walter was shot. Maybe we should ask Brandon if he kept his rifle close to him the entire time before the battle. Just in case someone with a similar rifle picked it up, thinking it was theirs."

"So, you think someone else may have accidentally switched them? But if that was the case, the bullet wouldn't match our rifle. It would match theirs. Brandon was holding our gun."

"True." I sighed. "Well, it was only an idea. I'm sure there's a rational explanation for everything. We just have to wait and see what happens."

"Jackson Lee will do a discovery, or whatever it's called, to find out exactly what the charges are and how they've come to their conclusion. Then we'll know what we're dealing with, as far as evidence. I just don't understand how they think Brandon would load real bullets into the rifle and then shoot at people. Even by accident, he's not that stupid or cruel."

I didn't know what else to add, so I said, "It's unlikely that he'll go to trial. We're worried for nothing. The police did what they had to do after the ballistics report, but I'm sure this will all be sorted out soon."

Bitty nodded, but I noticed she held her wine glass so tightly by the stem that I worried it might break. "I'm sure it will, too," she lied.

It turned out to be almost a week before Jackson Lee was able to get what he called a discovery package. That is simply a statement of all the charges against Brandon and depositions or interrogatories that may have been made. To our complete surprise, three people had given depositions stating they'd overheard Brandon and Walter Simpson in an argument before the reenactment, and one interrogatory stated Brandon had aimed his weapon at Simpson.

I sat with Bitty and Brandon at the kitchen table as we tried to make sense of all that Jackson Lee had just given us. He had copies of the police reports, depositions, and interrogation statements. We spread them out on the table, and Jackson Lee sat with his arm across the back of Bitty's chair. Clayton had gone back to school at Ole Miss, but Brandon stayed behind a few days longer to hopefully clear himself of any charges.

"But I don't even know this guy," Brandon protested. He put his finger on the name Ted Burton. "I've never heard of him. How does he know me?"

Bitty shook her head. "I don't know, honey. He said he saw you and Walter Simpson in an argument right before the reenactment. Did you argue with Mr. Simpson?"

"No. He was pretty upset about having to wear the blue instead of the gray, but he didn't say much to me about it. Just muttered a lot. Why would this guy say I argued with him? I don't get it."

Jackson Lee cleared his throat. "Did you perhaps have an exchange of words with Walter that might be misconstrued as an argument? A loud comment between you? Anything like that?"

After thinking a moment, Brandon shook his head again. "No, I'm pretty sure there wasn't. It was so crazy, trying to get everything organized, and Sammy Simpson was directing us where to go and stand, which direction to advance or retreat . . . we did basically what we'd done at the first reenactment, but he had us approach from a different direction for a better effect, he said."

Jackson Lee pulled out a sheet of paper and a pen. "Here. Show me the basic diagram of your movements the first day, then the second day."

Brandon raked a hand through his thick blond hair, looking so young and bewildered that I just wanted to hug him. He had circles under his eyes and looked thinner in just a week. I was sure this was having a terrible effect on him. It would on anyone.

After several minutes of drawing out the depot, freight office, tracks, and adding in his movements as a series of dashes to reach point X, he turned it around to show Jackson Lee. "We came from the east here the first time, see, across the tracks, while the cavalry came from the other side. The guys didn't want their horses stumbling on the tracks, so Sammy had to move it all around. The Yankees are the X's and Rebels are circles. Clayton and I stayed together that first day."

"And the second day? Were you together?"

"No, sir. Sammy split us up because he needed a Rebel to come up behind the depot so it'd be surrounded."

"So that second day you came from the north?"

"Yessir. Mr. Simpson—Sammy—said we'd do what Van Dorn himself had done and attack from all sides. He had Rebels coming from four different points of the compass, and the Yankees were supposed to just give a brief resistance before surrendering. As far as I know, that is what they did. We only had ten Yankee soldiers to seventeen of us. We would have had more, but Royal Stewart went and got himself put in jail for getting in a fight with Skip Whalen, so they were out. But I guess then Mr. Simpson wouldn't have been wearing his suit, would he . . ."

After studying the crude map for a few moments, Jackson Lee sighed and picked it up. "I think I'll keep this a while. I need to see the police photos and diagrams as comparison."

Brandon nodded. "I don't know how old Mr. Simpson got shot, I swear I don't. He was supposed to have surrendered. That's what happened the day before when Royal wore the blue. He gave up right away. Then he sat down and smoked one of those thin cigars, just for fun and to flirt with one of the girls watching. Royal plays around a lot. That's what got him into trouble with Skip Whalen, his flirting with some girl he shouldn't."

Jackson Lee smiled. "I've heard about Mr. Stewart's escapades."

"So have I," said Bitty. "He's always getting himself in trouble. So who is this Brenda Allen? She gave a deposition stating she overheard Brandon and Walter Simpson arguing about a gun too."

"She's one of the tourists. She happened to be standing at the end of the depot right by the street and across from Phillips and said she saw and heard Brandon and Walter in a tug of war over a gun." Jackson Lee shook his head. "That makes two witnesses to say you were in an altercation with Simpson. Do you know why they'd say that, Brandon?"

"No, I didn't argue with him at all. Wait—I know why they think that. Only it wasn't me, it was Clayton. He told me old Mr. Simpson came up to him and wanted to swap weapons. Clayton was bringing me the rifle, and Mr. Simpson stopped him. He thought it was his rifle and said he'd been looking for it. He grabbed it, and Clayton wouldn't let go. They argued about it for a few minutes. Then Mr. Simpson took a good look at it and said it wasn't his after all. That's all there was to it."

"Did Clayton have your rifle all morning? It wasn't ever out of his hands?" Jackson Lee asked.

"That's what Mama asked us. He carried it the day before, so it was my turn. We swapped out days to carry it, and he forgot and left it locked up in the house, so then he brought it to me."

"Have you had any work done on the rifle lately? Cleaning, repairing, anything like that?"

"No, it stays in Mama's gun safe most of the time now. Wait—I cleaned it before we took it to the reenactment. Is that what you mean?"

"A routine cleaning?"

Brandon nodded. "I broke it down like usual, used tung oil, wiped it real good."

"Explain that process, please."

Lifting his brow, Brandon looked a bit bewildered, but launched into a recital of his care of the rifle. When he got to the part where he mentioned cleaning it for the last reenactment a few months before, Jackson Lee stopped him.

"Where were you when you cleaned it?"

"Oh, that was at Christmas when we did the reenactment with Sammy."

"Sammy Simpson?"

Nodding, he added, "A bunch of us sat around cleaning our weapons, drinking a little, and talking about how it must have been during The War."

Jackson Lee looked thoughtful. "Was the rifle out of your sight at any time?"

Now Brandon seemed perplexed, but shrugged. "It could have been. It was just us, you know, and we were messing around a bit. But it's the same rifle. It has the mark on the plate."

"An identifying mark?"

"Guess you could call it that. It's where it got run over by a wagon, and it left a dent in the plate."

"Tell me again everything you can recall about your actions before Saturday."

"Everything?" Brandon slanted a quick glance at his mother. Jackson Lee smiled.

"Just as pertains to the rifle, where it was placed after Friday's reenactment, and where Clayton brought it to you, and if at any point it was out of your hands. I'll also need to talk to Clayton about it," he added to Bitty, and she nodded.

Brandon launched into a rather lengthy recital of his activities, while I marveled at the energy levels of people in their twenties. Jackson Lee honed in on one point: "When you got your cheeseburger at Phillips Saturday morning, where was your rifle?"

"At my side." He paused. "I leaned it against the front of the counter while they gave me my food and drink."

"No one else touched it?"

"Not to my knowledge." Another pause, then he said slowly, "Except that I left it leaned against the counter while I carried my food to the table at the window. Only had my back turned for a moment, though."

"That's all it takes," said Jackson Lee, but his frown wasn't displeased as much as very thoughtful. "If someone switched rifles, that makes no sense. It leaves too much to chance, such as if Brandon would even aim at Walter. Anyone wanting to kill Walter would want more control than that over the situation. After all, Brandon could very well have aimed it at anyone."

"True," I said, trying to follow his line of thought. "But what about afterward? What if someone switched rifles after Walter was killed?"

"I considered that, but the rifle in custody belongs to Brandon," Jackson Lee said with a sigh. "It'd make no sense to switch if the rifle was unusable, but it works. Brandon knows his own rifle."

"Who loaded it for the Saturday reenactment?" I asked, and Brandon smiled.

"Well, there's not much to loading it since it doesn't fire. I poured a little powder down the barrel, but the mainspring is broken so I was just, you know, acting."

Jackson Lee frowned. "So you're sure it doesn't fire at all?"

"Yessir. It has the rod to ram the bullet and paper cartridge in with the powder, but that's about the only thing that still works. I can't fire a rifle when the hammer won't strike the firing pin."

"What about the other reenactors?" I asked. "Most of them had rifles or pistols, original and reproductions. Did any of them have a rifle like the one Brandon had?"

"Probably," said Jackson Lee. "It's an 1853 Enfield. There were over three hundred thousand of them used by Confederate and Union soldiers. It was one of the most popular rifles of the time since it was one of the first rifle-muskets that could be loaded more quickly. It fired a bullet developed by Claude Minié, and became known as a 'minny' ball. It revolutionized the rifled-musket since it was a conical lead bullet with a hollow base that flattened out when it hit a target. The rifling in the bore spun the bullet out with deadly accuracy. The damage it did to the human body was terrific. Caused more amputations and deaths than any other firearm before it."

"You sound like you've studied it pretty extensively," I said, and he smiled.

"If I'm going to argue that Brandon didn't set out to kill Walter Simpson, I'd better know what I'm talking about. If the mainspring is broken, there's no way he could have fired that bullet."

"What about all the noise and smoke from the guns?" I asked. "I mean, someone was obviously shooting something."

"Powder," said Brandon. "Just pour powder and maybe ram a paperwad down the barrel. It makes a lot of noise and smoke, but no bullets, so it doesn't hurt anyone."

"So if someone shot a real bullet, it couldn't even be noticed in all the noise and smoke," I said, and he nodded.

"Right. This isn't the kind of gun you can forget you left a bullet in. You'd have to know it's there, or it wouldn't fire properly."

"What if it was already loaded and someone poured in more powder and just paper?" asked Bitty. "Would that happen?"

"If it did happen, the rifle would probably explode with that much powder," Brandon said. "It'd at least be noticed."

Bitty pressed her face against the pug in her lap. Chen Ling responded with a wiggle and snort, then turned to lick Bitty's chin. I thought it was rather sweet. Dogs often know when their guardians are stressed or unhappy, and most of them respond in some way. I'd never thought the little gremlin she held would be sentimental. Shows how wrong a person could be.

"So you're hoping that someone else with an Enfield shot Simpson?" Jackson Lee asked Bitty. Before she could reply, he said gently, "Ballistics matched the rifling on the bullet to the rifling in the barrel of your gun."

"Are you sure?" Her voice trembled slightly, and I felt her anguish.

"Yes," he said. "It came from the gun used by Brandon. His fingerprints are all over the Enfield. That gun fired the fatal bullet."

"With a broken mainspring," I said, and he must have heard the skepticism in my tone.

Jackson Lee looked over at me. "It sounds impossible. I've called an expert in firearms of the Civil War period to come and take a look at the rifle. His testimony may be crucial."

"This doesn't make any sense at all," I said. "The rifle hasn't fired in over a hundred years, but now suddenly it fires a bullet that kills a man? I don't buy it."

After a moment Jackson Lee said, "We have a lot of things in our favor. For one, these depositions were given by people who are complete strangers, and only one man knows that Brandon and Clayton are identical twins. That sets up reasonable doubt if we go to trial. The interrogatory statements place Brandon at the scene with the right kind of weapon, but we still don't have a motive. The three things necessary for a prosecutor to prove are motive, means, and opportunity. We just have to prove the witnesses' statements are flawed. I'm fairly confident we can do that."

"Fairly confident?" Brandon echoed, and Jackson Lee grinned.

"I don't like to talk in positives. It tempts fate."

"But you're positive you can prove he didn't do it, right?" Bitty leaned forward to ask him. Her eyes were big and anxious, her lower lip slightly trembling.

Jackson Lee sucked in a deep breath, then nodded and said, "I'm positive that I will do everything in my power to keep him from going to prison, sugar. I can't promise, but I'll do my best."

She nodded. Then she surprised me by asking, "What about the guy who ambushed him outside JB's? Any news on who it was or why it happened?"

Shaking his head, Jackson Lee said, "It's most likely random vandalism, just like he said. The guy might have thought Brandon saw him, so he tried to intimidate him."

I knew she hadn't entirely bought Brandon's explanation, but hadn't wanted to mention it just in case. But random events no longer sounded rational, and I said so. Jackson Lee sighed.

"Irrational things happen a lot. Police are still looking through security camera tapes in the court square to see if they can identify the altercation, but the only one that caught it was on the courthouse, and it's too fuzzy to make out who was involved. Frankly, most of the police are working on the Simpson shooting, so it's not getting as much attention as it should."

"Well," said Bitty with a sigh, "I just want this all to be over with soon. I know you'll figure it all out, Jackson Lee."

"I will, sugar. I promise to do everything I can."

At the moment, it was our only hope.

Chapter 5

"A VIDEO? THERE'S a *video* of the shooting?" Bitty sounded hopeful. "Then that should clear Brandon of any responsibility, right?"

Jackson Lee stepped inside from the front porch. He held a briefcase in one hand, and his smile looked rather strained. Uh oh. He hadn't sounded especially pleased about the video. I hoped my first impression was wrong. I'm often wrong. I wanted to be wrong.

I wasn't wrong.

We sat down at Bitty's kitchen table while Jackson Lee took some papers out of his case. He cleared his throat. "Unfortunately, the angle of the video taken by the tourist seems to show Brandon taking aim at Walter Simpson. There's so much smoke, you can't really tell if the bullet comes from his rifle, so that's a point in our favor. There's no visual evidence of flame from the rifle barrel either. I can always argue the video only shows him in the position to aim at Simpson and doesn't prove he did it deliberately."

After a moment of silence, Brandon said, "May I see the video? Maybe I can tell if there's something else going on that made me aim in that direction. I don't remember doing it, but there was so much smoke, and we were all really into it—I mean, we were shooting Yankees. That's what we were supposed to be doing. I could have pointed the gun right at him, I guess. But it shouldn't have made any difference. That rifle *doesn't fire*. I just don't get it."

Another silence fell, and I saw from the expression on Jackson Lee's face that he had more bad news. My stomach lurched.

"Brandon," he said, "the rifle you used during the reenactment is in good working order, according to an expert. It's capable of shooting the bullet found in Walter Simpson."

Brandon looked dumbfounded. Bitty sat in stone silence. I wanted to cry.

Finally I found my wits enough to ask, "Are you sure it's the same rifle? It's difficult to believe that a rifle that hasn't worked in a hundred years suddenly works just fine."

"I had my expert inspect the rifle, and we matched it up to photographs made of the rifle for Bitty's insurance company. There were no serial numbers required in those days like there are today, but there are distinguishing marks that match."

He spread several eight-by-ten photographs on the table. "These are the photos taken for the insurance company," he said, pointing to four of them. "And these are the photos just taken yesterday for verification. Marks on the lock plates look identical."

Bitty and Brandon inspected the photos, and I could tell from Bitty's face that this wasn't the result she had hoped for. Since I wouldn't recognize the rifle if it was used to stir my coffee, I didn't study the photos. It looked like the same rifle from where I sat anyway.

"So now what do we do?" I asked when it seemed Brandon and Bitty were incapable of functioning. "How do we prove that the rifle wasn't working the last time it was used in one of the other reenactments?"

"When was the last reenactment?" Jackson Lee countered.

"April of last year," said Bitty. She sounded so . . . defeated. I couldn't imagine her pain and anguish at all this.

"No, New Year's," Brandon spoke up. "Remember, Mama? We commemorated the 1862 Battle of Stones River."

"Is that what you did? I only recall that I thought it was silly to go off in the freezing rain. I wasn't sure what battle you were fighting."

"Sammy Simpson's ancestors on his mother's side were at the original battle outside of Murfreesboro, Tennessee," explained Brandon. "We did it just like history reported. After the Rebels sang "Home Sweet Home" with the Yankees the night of December thirtieth, they started fighting the next morning and didn't quit until January third, so we did all that too. Except there were only about two hundred of us but twenty-five thousand casualties in the real battle. Sammy was really into the history of it, said it was proportionately the highest loss of soldiers in a single battle during the entire war. He'd invited Clayton and me to join him and some other guys. We were glad we went, since it turned out to be a really cool battle."

Bitty put a hand to her brow. "I think once we're through with all this nonsense, I'm going to stop commemorating all these foolish moments in history. They weren't good the first time around, and for the life of me, I can't figure out now why I ever thought they were special."

"Because those moments are our history," I said to her. "We can't change it, but we should never forget what happened and why. Those who forget mistakes often end up repeating them."

Bitty looked at me. "Does this mean you're going to reconsider your decision not to wear your dress during the pilgrimage next year?"

I stared back at her. "Of course I'll reconsider," I said. "I'll let you know my decision by next March."

A faint smile curved Bitty's mouth. "I can't wait to hear it."

With some of the tension eased, Jackson Lee gathered up the photographs and put them back into his briefcase. Bitty went to get us all more sweet tea. The ice had melted in most of our glasses. I got up from the table to help.

Brandon leaned back in the kitchen chair and looked up at Jackson Lee. "When can I see the video?"

"I'll talk to the prosecutor and arrange it. Meanwhile, make sure your mama doesn't dwell too much on this. It's really hard on her."

"I'm fine, Jackson Lee," Bitty said over her shoulder. "I've come to the conclusion that someone is trying to frame Brandon, so I'm going to do something about it."

There was a sudden, shocked silence. None of us knew what to say, not even Jackson Lee, the silver-tongued arbitrator of many disputes. We all just kind of looked at Bitty.

She turned around with the pitcher of sweet tea and saw us all staring at her. "Well? What? Did you really think I'm going to sit by and do nothing while some monster tries to make it look like my baby deliberately killed someone? No. That's not going to happen."

I sucked in a deep breath and looked at Jackson Lee. He had more influence over Bitty than any of us, I was sure, so he should be able to convince her that doing anything at all could be disastrous. His eyes were glazed; he looked like he'd been pole-axed. No help there. I sighed.

"Bitty," I said, "you don't want to do anything that will hurt Brandon. If you go off and do something stupid, it's not going to help him."

"Then I won't do anything stupid. Here. Give these glasses to them, will you?" She pushed two glasses of ice and sweet tea toward me, and I took them to Brandon and Jackson Lee.

"Do something," I murmured to Jackson Lee when I pushed the glass into his hand. "She is going to get into trouble if she isn't stopped."

That seemed to snap him out of his momentary shock. He gulped down a few swallows of sweet tea and cleared his throat. "Sugarplum," he said, but when Bitty put her hands on her hips and narrowed her eyes at him, he paused. I could see this wasn't going to be easy for him so I intervened again.

"Bitty Hollandale, don't you dare get involved," I said. "I know it's hard to just sit by and not do anything when your child is in trouble, but you cannot help him by causing chaos."

Bitty eyed me. "If it was Michelle who was suspected of committing murder, would you just sit at home wringing your hands? No. I didn't think so."

She had me there, but I still tried. "Okay, maybe I wouldn't just sit at home and wring my hands if it was my child, but I wouldn't make things worse, either."

"Honestly, Trinket, you act like I'm going to go door to door demanding answers."

"It's not like you've never done it before."

"That was different. I was canvassing the area for witnesses."

"Excuse me for thinking it's the same thing. Going door to door asking questions about a crime cannot possibly be the same thing as going door to door asking questions about a crime." My sarcasm was showing, so I shut up for the moment.

Finally Jackson Lee spoke up. "Bitty, sugar, you're upset right now, and I understand that. It probably looks like Brandon has been framed, but this is all circumstantial evidence. There's no solid foundation for a murder charge. Not even negligent homicide. We're still gathering all the pieces of the puzzle, and when I sit down with everything, I'll know which way to proceed. It's going to be okay. You just have to leave everything to me."

Bitty stared at him. "Jackson Lee, you know I trust you implicitly. I do. And I know you're going to do a good job. But you're not an investigator. You're an attorney. There are times only an attorney is needed. This time I think both are needed."

He set his glass on the kitchen table and walked to Bitty and took both her hands in his. "Sugar, I'm not Perry Mason or Ben Matlock. I don't keep an investigator on my payroll. But I do hire one when needed. You don't have to do anything but trust me."

She squeezed his hands and smiled up at him. "Honey, I know that. I do trust you. But if I don't do something, anything to help, I'll go crazy just sitting around here, waiting on other people to act. Do you understand what I mean?"

Jackson Lee sighed. "I understand. Just let me talk to an investigator first. Then I'll send him to you. Will you do that for me, sugarpie?"

"Oh, honeybun, you know I'll do anything for you," Bitty cooed.

I looked over at Brandon. "Quick, get me some insulin. My sugar level is going through the roof."

Brandon just laughed. I imagine he and Clayton were pretty used to all of their mother's mercurial mood switches.

After getting Bitty's promise to wait for an investigator to help, Jackson Lee gathered his stuff up and left. Brandon went upstairs, talking on his cell phone as he did. I looked over at Bitty. She raised her brow.

"We need to make a list of people to talk to first. Then we need to find some gun experts of our own."

I was flabbergasted. "Bitty, you just promised Jackson Lee that you'd wait for—"

"Oh, don't get your knickers in a twist. I'm waiting. That doesn't mean I shouldn't be prepared, however. Someone, somewhere, is trying to frame my son for a killing he didn't do. If I don't do something, this will be on his record forever."

I was silent for a moment, then said, "It's possible that it was an accident, just like it seems, Bitty. You do know that, right?"

"Yes, I know that it's possible. But I'll believe that if you'll believe Miranda Watson is a natural blonde."

I sighed. "Okay. I get what you're saying. I don't want this on Brandon's record, either. Accidental death is not the worst thing, but it's not something you want to follow him the rest of his life. And I think there's something funny about all this, too. I don't know what it is, but it's hard to believe someone just put real bullets in their gun by mistake. What do we know about Walter Simpson?"

Bitty smiled. "Not nearly as much as we'll know by this time tomorrow."

Uh oh. I don't know why I can't keep my mouth shut.

RAYNA SCROLLED down the screen of her huge monitor, reading off the information bits she found on Walter Simpson. "He was born in 1931 in his parents' home of Rosewood in Marshall County. Two siblings died before adulthood. His grandfather started the Simpson Surety Insurance Company in 1898, and his father continued the business, as did Walter until eight years ago when he sold it to MetLife.

Walter had three children, two sons and a daughter. The oldest son died nine years ago and left his son, Sammy, as his heir. His youngest son lives in Alabama. Walter's daughter Myrtle married Richard Grace, and they had three daughters. Deelight Tillman is one of Walter's grandchildren, you know."

"I didn't think they were that close," said Bitty. "Something to do with Deelight's mother. Weren't they estranged? Walter and Myrtle?"

Rayna nodded. "I think so. When Myrtle died, Walter carried on something awful. He never said, but you could tell he regretted being so mean to his only daughter."

"He was mean to everyone. Always was. He wasn't a bad person, but he could be just hateful."

I looked at Bitty. "Somehow, I would think being mean and hateful would qualify as making him a bad person."

"You'd think so, wouldn't you? But he was very generous, gave to charities, always went to church and tithed . . . I guess that's why people still spoke to him. He wasn't all bad."

"Now there's an epitaph I want etched on my tombstone: 'She wasn't all bad.'"

"Or 'Gone but not particularly missed'?" Bitty suggested.

Rayna said, "Put on my tombstone, 'You're standing on my face' or 'You could lose a few pounds.'"

We giggled like teenage girls, amused at our own jokes. It was a great mood changer. Life doesn't have to be all grim, even in serious moments. Bitty and I have always been able to find the humor in anything, and given the choice, we'll definitely laugh instead of cry. It can be unsettling at funerals, we've discovered. Don't ask. Thank heavens we aren't always blood-related to the deceased. Relatives can be so unforgiving.

"Anyway," said Bitty as we got up to head to Rayna's kitchen, "with his often unpleasant nature, I'm sure Walter had a few enemies who might have wanted to see him dead. We can start by talking to them."

I looked over at her. "I hope you're talking about your familiar," I said, nodding toward Chen Ling. "Because I'm definitely not going to be a part of *we* for talking to anyone."

Bitty ignored me and just stroked the pug's furry little head. The dog looked smug. "Do you have any idea who might be angry enough with Walter to want him dead, Rayna?"

Rayna slid her eyes toward me and pretended she didn't hear the question. Instead, she told us she'd just baked a fresh chocolate cream cake. That sounded much better than talking about unpleasant people, and Bitty and I both temporarily put aside all discussion of Walter Simpson.

The garden outside Delta Inn was rich with blooming flowers and impending summer. A wrought-iron table with a glass top provided a perfect place for us to light with plates and glasses of wine. Rayna's big dogs followed us out, black labs that ambled contentedly around the garden and tactfully ignored the pug when Bitty set her on the grass. Chitling returned the favor. I did my best not to look at the railroad depot across the street. Rayna's place faces the garden area behind the depot, now hidden from sight behind a high wooden fence with a sturdy gate. Next door to Rayna's is Phillips Grocery, and across the street behind the railroad depot sits the remains of an old cotton compress that was knocked down by a storm a few years back.

I glanced toward the front of the railroad depot where Walter had died. No traces of yellow tape remained to mark his demise, but someone had placed a flowery wreath and a candle in glass to commemorate his passing. The beautiful swirls and curves of the Victorian and Edwardian era architecture gave mute testimony to the skills of bygone engineers and builders. New trim had replaced old, rotting boards, and the three-story structure with the cupola on top seemed to me like a grand old dame presiding over the area. The family who owns the depot will soon open it to weddings and for other venues, and renovations in the dining area are just being completed. It's a gorgeous building and a perfect spot for festivities.

"So, have you met Jackson Lee's new private investigator yet?" Rayna asked us after we had done major damage to our brunch of chocolate cake and wine.

Bitty was too busy sucking chocolate frosting off the end of her fork, so I said, "No, he hasn't made an appearance so far. Why?"

Rayna waggled her eyebrows and sipped her wine before saying, "I know who it is."

Bitty gave up the frosting to ask, "Who is it, and is he any good?"

Instead of answering, Rayna picked up her cake plate and mine, obviously about to go back inside. Of course we immediately followed. By now Bitty's curiosity made her abandon the second piece of cake on her plate. She trotted behind us back into the hotel.

"Rayna, who is it? Do you know him? Is it someone I'm going to hate?"

I said, "Jackson Lee wouldn't hire someone you're going to hate."

"Catfish Carter," said Rayna, and we both stared at her. Bitty recovered first.

"What?"

"Catfish Carter. His first name is Claude, I think. Anyway, he goes by Catfish. I'm not sure why."

Nonplussed, I didn't know what to say. Finally Bitty asked, "Isn't that a baseball player?"

Rayna said, "No, that was Catfish Hunter. He was a pitcher in the Major Leagues."

"Oh. Well . . . where is this Catfish from?"

"Yazoo City. He's been in North Mississippi about a year and a half now. Jackson Lee first met him on a case he worked on down around Meridian."

"So he's bringing in some stranger? Why didn't he tell me about this?" Bitty asked. I could tell she was getting upset.

"He probably hasn't had a chance yet," I said. "Give him time."

She didn't look convinced. "I'm not at all sure I want somebody named *Catfish* to be the difference in whether or not my son is convicted of a crime he didn't commit."

"Jackson Lee is the difference in whether or not Brandon is convicted," I argued. "An investigator is only his helper."

"It'll be just fine, honey," Rayna assured Bitty. "You know Jackson Lee isn't going to do anything that'd hurt you or Brandon."

"I know." Bitty sighed. "I just get so . . . worried. You know?"

I hugged her. That's better than words in some situations. After a moment, she cleared her throat and said, "So. What can you tell me about this Catfish person?"

We both looked at Rayna. She rinsed off her plate and put it in the dishwasher before answering. "He was a police officer, worked his way up to detective grade, left the force, and got his license as a private investigator three years ago. He's worked on a few high-profile cases, including the bank robberies down in Jackson a few years back."

"You mean the Loan Ranger robberies?" I asked, and Rayna shook her head.

"No, they haven't caught that guy yet. He's all over the South, anyway. Funny, to spell it L-O-A-N. But that's mostly Texas. I'm talking about the Soap Opera Bandit."

"I never heard of that one."

"Oh, I think I remember hearing about that," said Bitty. "The guy wore the mask of an actor from one of the soaps when he robbed banks, right?"

Rayna nodded. "He robbed three banks around Jackson, the last one in Madison County, and Catfish Carter tracked him down and made the arrest. It was right before he left the force and became a PI. Anyway, he's supposed to be very good. You may like him, Bitty."

When I saw the mulish expression on Bitty's face, I had my doubts. She tends to want to be in control of such things. I understood, even while I hoped she wouldn't kick up too much of a fuss. Carter may decide it wasn't worth the money and walk off if she made it too difficult for him.

I misjudged both of them.

I DON'T KNOW what I expected when I thought of a private investigator, but it wasn't a bit like Catfish Carter. There was no rumpled overcoat and cigar, no exquisite mustache or Belgian accent, no craggy good looks and thick blond hair. The man introduced to us in Jackson Lee's office was a portly man, rather neat in appearance but not excessively so, dressed in a pair of khaki slacks, polo shirt, and tennis shoes. He wore thick glasses. Nothing like the TV detectives I'd seen.

Once he opened his mouth, however, he sounded like a cheap detective novel trying to emulate Mickey Spillane. "Jesus, what a dame," he said in a tough, brittle tone as he eyed Bitty. "He said you were gorgeous, but he didn't say you look like a Madonna in mourning, eyes like wet blue stones, hair like cotton candy—don't worry, dollface. I can find the scum that crawled up outa the gutter to shoot down an old man like he's nothing but a dog, old and past his time. It won't take too long to find the rat, run him out of his hole like the coward he is, drag him in front of a judge, and send him up the river to the Big House."

While I stood there in stunned silence, Bitty lifted a brow and studied him. Jackson Lee's secretary kept her expression polite, but I'm sure I saw her stifle an eye-roll. Since we stood in Jackson Lee's outer office and it was a dignified atmosphere, the whole thing seemed totally absurd to me. Carter's choir boy face belied his apparent belief in his own cynicism. The plush carpeting, dark heavy furniture, and professional setting made it feel surreal.

"Would you like to step into Mr. Brunetti's office to wait?" Sherry asked. She's been Jackson Lee's secretary for a few months since his other secretary left to get married. She's not as well-acquainted with

Bitty by experience as the last one. Although I'm sure my cousin's reputation preceded her, so Sherry was quite likely being cautious.

Bitty looked from Carter to Sherry. "No, I'm not sure that's going to be necessary. Will Mr. Brunetti be here soon?"

I could almost read her mind; she wanted no part of Catfish Carter.

Apparently, Carter was pretty quick on the uptake too because he said, "Getting cold feet already? I figured you for stronger stuff, dollface. You want the best, right? Well, I'm it. If you want your boy cleared of suspicion and to find out who cut down that old man before your kid gets sent to prison, stick with me. Maybe I'm a little rough around the edges, caught up in life's big wheel like a lump of tar stuck to the tire, trying to rid the world of sick souls who don't care for nothing but their own pockets, their own greed and lust and need for power, but I can get the job done. I scrape criminals off the soles of my shoes like they're nothing but dog crap, left in the gutter to—"

"Oh lord, give it a rest, Sam Spade," Bitty snapped.

"Mike Hammer," I disagreed, and Catfish looked offended when he peered at me.

"I carry a piece and I get the job done, Stretch."

Bitty finally looked interested. "What kind of piece? Do you mean a gun?"

"Whaddya think, dollface? Of course, a gun. A nine-millimeter semi-automatic."

When Bitty reached into her purse and pulled out a pistol, I nearly passed out. Sherry flung herself backward about four feet and looked terrified, while I protested, "Bitty, put that up! Does Jackson Lee know you bought another gun?"

"This? I've had it for a year. It's a Kimber Solo Carry with the shortest barrel and least recoil of any nine-millimeter pocket pistol on the market."

The last was directed toward Catfish Carter, and he immediately pulled out his weapon and they began to compare. I stepped toward Sherry where she cowered behind her desk.

"If you have a way to contact Jackson Lee and get him here quickly, I'd do it," I said and she clawed at the desk phone with shaking hands.

"She's not going to shoot that in here, is she?" Sherry asked while waiting for Jackson Lee to respond. I shook my head.

Since I couldn't assure her she wouldn't be accidentally shot, and I didn't know if Bitty's gun was loaded and had no idea if Carter was a responsible gun owner, I decided to check out the ladies' facilities. I bolted the door as soon I got into the restroom and sat down on the nice little chair placed in front of an antique washstand with a marble sink. An oval mirror hung on the wall above it, and a glance at my reflection reassured me that I still had all my hair. Sometimes I'm tempted to pull it out when dealing with Bitty.

I had no idea what to think of Catfish Carter. He seemed like a caricature of a detective, and I wondered if Jackson Lee had erred. It wasn't likely, but it was possible. Usually Jackson Lee was pretty shrewd in his business decisions. But there's always a first time. And Catfish Carter may be a good detective, just strange. Most Southerners understand strange. We're used to strange. We usually embrace strange. But then, there's *really* strange, and that's different.

By the time Jackson Lee arrived and I was coaxed out from where I'd barricaded myself, I'd decided that I shouldn't judge people on first impressions. Maybe this guy was okay. And if it kept Bitty from running around, conducting her own version of investigating, I was good with that, too.

We gathered in the inner sanctum of Jackson Lee's office, and he waved us toward the plush chairs in front of his desk. Catfish went to stand against the built-in bookcases, crossing his arms over his chest. I eyed him a bit warily. I wanted to ask where they'd put their guns, but I refrained. Jackson Lee is usually pretty efficient. I was sure he'd make certain they were safely tucked away.

Jackson Lee is a tall man, his Italian heritage obvious in his dark good looks, and as I've said, he absolutely adores Bitty. But he has little patience with some of her more dangerous activities, which includes carrying a pistol in her purse. She's shot the bottom out of a couple of her expensive purses, not always by accident.

"Bitty sugar," he said as she settled her Jimmy Choo purse in her lap, "why are you carrying another pistol?"

"Well, I just felt the necessity. I talked to that Sergeant Maxwell, and he was very snippy with me when I asked if I could get my forty-five back. I know it's being held as evidence until after that other trial, but it's not like it was a murder weapon or anything. I was hoping you could talk to him for me, honey."

Jackson Lee cleared his throat. "And I will, sugar, I'll do that. But I have to ask if you're sure carrying a pistol is truly helpful. Sherry seems to think you were pulling it out and waving it around a bit."

"Oh for heaven's sake, I wasn't waving it around. I was just showing Catfish my semi-auto nine-millimeter. He has one, too. Now let's talk about this investigation. Since you've hired him to help me investigate—"

Jackson Lee quickly interrupted. "No, sugar. I hired him to conduct the investigations. You don't need to worry about it. Remember?"

"Yes, I do recall you suggesting that, but I believe I can be of assistance. After all, I know the Simpson family and their history. I can ask questions without anyone wondering why I'm being nosy. He's a stranger here, and people won't talk to him freely."

I saw a fine mist of perspiration pop out on Jackson Lee's forehead. He was trying very hard not to be too obvious. I could have told him it wasn't going to help. Bitty had reinvented herself again. If it wasn't for the fact I might get tangled up in her schemes, I would probably have rather enjoyed the show. But as it was, I knew I was much too close to the brink of danger. So I decided to help.

"Bitty, the deal is that Jackson Lee found you an investigator so you can focus on all the other things you have to do. Brandon needs your support and attention."

She nodded. "And when he gets home for the summer, he'll have it. Right now, he's on his way back to school and focusing on his studies. By the time school is out we should have all the evidence we need to clear him."

Okay. It wasn't going to be easy. While I scrambled for a way to say what had to be said, Catfish saved me the trouble.

"I work alone, dollface. I'm a lone wolf, a solitary hunter determined to drag out all the dirty little secrets, digging under rocks in people's lives to uncover all the sordid details that rule their darkest desires and make them act like beasts . . . It's a wicked world out there, baby."

A couple seconds crawled past before Jackson Lee said, "Just keep us updated on what you find out, Catfish. You have all my numbers to call, and I can relay the information to Bitty."

"On a need-to-know basis?" Bitty inquired with a smile that didn't fool me at all. She looked positively feral. Jackson Lee sighed.

"Sugar, you know I'll come to you immediately with anything important. There's no point bothering you with unimportant details."

Bitty stood up and shouldered her purse. "That's fine, Jackson Lee. Just let me decide what's important and what's not, all right, sugar?"

Impasse. I didn't hold much hope for Jackson Lee's chances of breaking it without a total surrender. Once again, Catfish Carter came to the rescue, whether he meant to or not.

"Hey chief, I only give important information. I'm wise to what's trivial and which of the daily sins people commit in this weary old world matter in the grand scheme of things. I walk the wild side. I get results. I don't waste time taking on windmills."

Nice, I thought. Even a Don Quixote reference. Catfish might be weird, but maybe weird is what was needed. It wasn't even that different from our usual way of handling things. It just might work.

Of course, if factoring in the Bitty equation, things might just go horribly wrong, too. It was a toss-up.

Chapter 6

"THE READING OF the will is this coming week," said Deelight Tillman as we sipped wine and dipped into buffet offerings at our monthly Diva meeting. We stood in her living room, an expansive space with comfy couches, chairs, and chattering Divas.

Deelight's older sister—christened Deevine Faithann Grace, and now going by her middle name, shortened to Faith—had come into town for the funeral and family gathering. Since Walter had been laid to rest several days before, all that was left were the loose ends that always accompanied a death. Rosewood, the Simpson ancestral home, would be left to Walter's heirs.

"The furnishings are mostly antiques," Faith said. "Grandmother Myrtle had us tell her what we wanted when we were still kids. I remember her writing everything down in a ledger. A Simpson tradition has always been that each heir be able to choose a sentimental piece. That way even if we don't get equal shares, we all have something of the family to hand down to our own children. That old house is chock full of antiques."

"Don't forget the money from the sale of the company and all the stocks and bonds," her sister reminded her. "He always talked about dividing that up equally among his children, with the grandchildren receiving any deceased parent's share. Since there's only one child left, the rest will go to us grandchildren."

"I imagine the house itself goes to only one heir," said Bitty. "Being antebellum, I doubt it's to be sold away from the family."

Deelight nodded. "True. Sammy's father would have inherited, but since he's gone, it'll go to Uncle George. He's the youngest son. I'm sure he never thought he'd be left the property, but he's the closest surviving direct descendant. Since he lives in Alabama, he may want Sammy to stay and manage the property. I would imagine that's what he'll do."

"So when George is gone, the property will go to his closest heir? What's that going to do to Sammy?" I asked. "It seems a little unfair to him to have him stay on to take care of the house and land, yet not share in it as his inheritance."

"Well, George and his wife are childless but even if not, Sammy will still inherit what the rest of us will also get. Once George is gone, the house goes to the oldest grandchild."

"Sammy is unmarried and childless too," Bitty added. "After George is gone, the house will have to be sold and money divided up; or whoever wants to live there will have to buy out the others. That's what happened in my mama's side of the family. One of my cousins bought the rest of us out after they ran out of direct descendants who wanted to live in a big house in the middle of nowhere."

"Since Rosewood is on the edge of town and not exactly in the middle of nowhere, I'm sure there'll be no problem finding one of us who wants to live there," said Deelight. "But it'll be a few years before we have to worry about that."

"We certainly hope so, anyway," said her sister. They exchanged glances. Then Faith smiled. "It's not as if we were that close to Walter, but it's awful that he died before his time. We can take some comfort in the fact he died doing something he loved doing, I suppose."

Guilt nipped at me. "Except he wasn't wearing the right uniform. I feel bad about that."

"Oh, Trinket, it wasn't your fault," said Deelight. "You know how he was. He'd probably rather get a hole in a Yankee uniform than he would in a Rebel uniform anyway. You'd think The War just ended a few years ago, the way he always carried on. It's not that I'm not proud of my heritage because I am, but I admit, I'm not as focused on the sacrifices and hardships our ancestors suffered as Walter was. He couldn't seem to forget even family feuds."

Bitty drained her wine and stood up. "Does anyone else want a refill? All this talk about wills and history makes me thirsty. Deelight, your chocolate soufflé is excellent. Is that an old family recipe?"

Bitty's diversion tactic worked. We talked about chocolate and old family recipes instead of untimely death and ancient feuds. It restored our good moods and led to our Easter egg hunt, Diva style. While Easter was behind us, Deelight had created a fun way to celebrate the illusion of Easter bunnies handing out chocolate rabbits and decorated eggs: a six-foot rabbit we called Harvey arrived, dressed in black tie and carrying a wicker basket full of treats. The real treat, however, was Harvey, a most handsome young man. Did I mention that except for some tight Spandex running shorts, a black tie was almost all he was wearing? And that he obviously worked out and smelled of some kind of tantalizing body oil that made his muscles shine?

It was later decided that the body oil was coconut flavored. I know this only because it was discovered after a tasting that made Harvey nervous and put all of Bitty's wine tastings to shame. Sometimes it's good to be a Diva.

I shall say no more about Harvey here, save that he survived the afternoon and was last seen fleeing up 78 Highway back to Memphis, sans black tie and treats.

BITTY AND I SAT out on her front porch contemplating the restorative properties of wine and chocolate, especially when consumed in tandem. It was the slow time of year at Carolann's shop, and I felt lazy anyway. The weather was almost perfect. Warm days and cool nights that make using air conditioning optional is as good as it gets.

My white wicker rocker creaked as I listened to crickets chirp, bullfrogs burp, and Chen Ling snort. Bitty provided a monologue of irritating facts to prove that someone was trying to frame Brandon, while I tried to tune her out and focus on the sounds of approaching summer. It wasn't easy. I must be getting better at it, because I didn't notice when she stopped talking.

"Trinket Truevine, you're not even listening to me," she accused, and that did catch my attention. I scrambled to cover up my lack of courtesy.

"I was listening. You said the police are trying to railroad your son just because they want an easy suspect, that Rodney Farrell has camped out in an unmarked car down the street to spy on you, and Catfish Carter hasn't found out a single thing so he must be in league with whoever is trying to frame Brandon."

After a brief silence she muttered, "I don't know how you do that when I know you were *not* listening."

I could have told her it was easy to repeat what she'd said because I'd heard it a half dozen times just since I'd arrived two hours earlier, but I didn't. I have a strong sense of self-preservation. Instead I said, "I hang upon your every word. Your every utterance is like a jewel falling from the sky, shining and beautiful."

As I gestured toward imaginary falling jewels with my almost empty wine glass, Bitty said something quite pithy and made her own rude gesture. I smiled. Life is good when we're insulting one another.

"So," I said when she rolled her eyes at me, "it's only been a week, and Catfish is still on the case. Don't give up yet."

"*Catfish on the case*—that's another thing. That man is a parody. He's annoying. He's silly, and I just have to wonder what on earth Jackson Lee was thinking when he hired him. So far, he's not done a blamed thing that I can tell."

"And I thought you had bonded with him. You know—a similar interest in guns and other tools of death."

"Please. You insult me. Okay, so I did have a moment of *simpatico* in regard to similar pistols, but that's all it was. I've been waiting for him to find out something of use, and all I've heard so far is that he's still investigating."

"Did you think it would happen in an hour? Bitty, he not only has to be discreet, but he's working in unfamiliar territory. Give him some time."

"I can't believe you're defending him."

"Neither can I. Maybe I need more wine."

After we retreated to her kitchen for more wine, my favorite Zinfandel nicely chilled in her wine cooler, we returned to the front porch. Dusk had fallen. The street of familiar houses was cloaked in shadows and pink glowing pools from the streetlights. Bitty's overhead porch fixture is a small outdoor chandelier with crystal pendants that tinkle lightly in breezes. It gives off a soft romantic radiance that makes everything look better. It's the kind of flattering light that I look best in, and if I could ever figure out how to keep it around me instead of the harsher light of daytime and reality that usually illuminates me, I'd do it. Since I can't, I just deal with it.

"Do you really think Brandon is going to be cleared of any suspicion?" Bitty asked when we had once again assumed our positions as guardians of her front porch. Chen Ling squatted in her lap, her little bug eyes regarding me with disinterest as I sipped my wine.

"Of course," I said immediately. I believed it because any hint that it might not end well just wouldn't reside long in my beleaguered brain. "Jackson Lee is a wizard when it comes to the defense of his clients, and even if he wasn't, there's no evidence that Brandon loaded his rifle with the intent of causing harm."

I was actually repeating what I'd heard an attorney on *Law &* *Order* say in defense of his client, who had been guilty as sin but got off anyway. I figured if a guilty man could be acquitted, then Brandon was in no danger.

"The new prosecutor can argue that the loading of a rifle is in itself an intent of causing harm," Bitty replied.

I admit I was rather impressed with her response until I remembered that she's also an avid TV addict. She must have seen the same episode. "Well, Mr. McCoy, explain to the jury the difference between a hobby and a deliberate murder," I misquoted.

"I think Adam told McCoy to explain the difference between murder and negligent homicide," Bitty corrected.

"Whichever, we know there's a big difference between intentional and accidental, and I still think it's absolutely strange that a rifle that hasn't fired in over a hundred years is capable of not only firing a bullet, but hitting and killing someone."

"I know. I keep coming back to that too," said Bitty. "It's unexplainable, but the antique rifle expert said it was more than capable of firing a bullet fairly accurately."

"Has anyone actually tried to fire it in the past hundred years?"

"Mama's uncle on her mother's side. It was to celebrate the new century, New Year's Eve 1899. Just as the clock struck midnight, Uncle Jobert pulled the trigger and it misfired. He looked down the barrel—I think he'd been drinking some good Tennessee whiskey—and decided to add more powder and ball, to his immediate regret. The gun fired, a bullet plowed through his right ear, and took it clean off his head. He dropped the rifle just in time for a panicked horse and wagon to roll over it. It never fired after that."

"Good lord. Was he killed?"

"No, but he never did hear well after that, according to family history. Oh, and he walked the rest of his life with his head cocked to one side."

I thought for a moment. "Is your cousin Jobert any kin to your great-uncle?" I wondered aloud.

Bitty nodded. "His great-grandson."

"Well, you know the apple doesn't often fall far from that tree."

"I imagine Jobert's apple didn't bounce much. He's dumber than dirt."

Our character assassination aside, Bitty's cousin makes periodic calls to her with grand schemes of improbable value but always profitable in his own mind. He can get quite cranky when Bitty refuses to fund his latest venture. As you can imagine, Bitty's childhood dealing with Jobert has made her justifiably leery of anything he proposes. She still hasn't gotten over being left high up in a tree when she was only eight; he took away the ladder. Bitty can hold grudges about some things.

I'm familiar with that feeling, too. I'm still miffed about my sister Emerald hiding my favorite sweater so I couldn't wear it on a date when we were in high school. It wouldn't have been so bad except that she forgot where she hid it, and it took nearly three years to find it. By then bugs had gotten to it, and it looked like it'd been barfed up by a billy goat. Barns are not the best place for sweater storage.

"So," I mused after a moment. "If no one has tried to fire that rifle since 1900, you don't really know if it was operable or not."

Bitty looked startled. "Well—no, I guess I don't. Mama said it doesn't work, her mama said it doesn't work, and so I've always said it doesn't work. I never thought to try it. I mean—why would I?"

"Did anyone ever suggest it be fixed? And maybe got it fixed and either didn't tell you, or you forgot it'd been fixed?"

"No, I'm pretty sure not. Mama would have told me if she'd had it repaired. We all just rather liked it broken, if you know what I mean. It's just the way it was left to us, and Mama never would ruin an heirloom by messing with it."

I nodded. "My mama has a cracked pitcher that won't hold air, but she won't give it up. It belonged to her great-great-grandmother and has her initials etched into the glass."

"Daddy kept an empty tobacco pouch that Granddad Truevine used to carry in his back pocket. I've got it in a rubber tub with other family heirlooms."

"Mama still has her mother's embroidered hankies tucked away in a drawer. She says they're part of my inheritance. I'm sure that along with the two hundred cats and a neurotic dog that are also part of my inheritance, I'll end up spending my final days scooping cat poop and blowing my nose into heirloom hankies."

After a moment Bitty said, "We're rather a strange family, don't you think?"

"Of course. Insanity *is* the family tie that binds, you know."

"And here I thought it was a last will and testament."

I shook my head. "Wills tend to bring out the beast in families, not the best."

"Speaking of wills, at least Rosewood is going to stay in the family. So many times these lovely houses get sold at auctions or are abandoned and just gradually disintegrate. And all the antiques. . . . I heard there are some magnificent pieces at Rosewood. An old pianoforte and a solid mahogany armoire are supposed to be nearly two hundred years old."

Bitty is, among other things, an antiques hound. She gets rapturous over old wood and silver teaspoons the way some people get excited over football and the Indy 500.

"Maybe Deelight will let you admire them once the will has been read. After all, according to her, Rosewood will probably be left in Sammy's capable hands in trust for the entire family. I imagine his uncle will be more than happy to know he has the deed but not all the responsibility."

"But he probably won't be able to sell it without all the heirs agreeing, the way I understand it. It's not like my situation when Mama and Daddy died. After Mama passed, we just sold everything that didn't have sentimental value and split the money fifty-fifty. I mean, the house was only forty years old and not really my style or Steven's. He and Tammy aren't very sentimental, so I packed up all the things I'm sure Mama would have wanted passed down after Steven got his portion. If they ever decide they want their kids to have some of those things, I'll be glad to share."

"Steven doesn't get back here often, does he," I remarked, and she shook her head.

"Not since he married the Wicked Witch of the South," she muttered. "They're much too cosmopolitan to visit such a backwater town as Holly Springs. Tammy's used to a *more gracious way of life*."

I had to laugh at the way she said it, mimicking her sister-in-law's rather haughty tone quite well. Since I couldn't think of anything to say that wouldn't sound equally catty, I just said, "Bless her heart."

"Well, Hinds County *is* the Mecca of western civilization, you know." She drank more wine then added, "Everyone has moved to Madison County now anyway. I loved living in Jackson. Philip and I had a house there for when the senate was in session. The people I met were lovely, and not a single one of them made me feel as if I'm deficient in culture. But that's the old money people. It's the *nouveau riche* who have to put on airs. Tammy is not old Jackson or old money. She tries too hard to be classy."

"As Aunt Sarah used to say, 'You can get away with anything if you do it with class,'" I quoted.

Bitty lifted her wine glass in a silent toast to her mother and her wisdom. "Here's to grommets and ratchets, or whatever it is Steven's firm manufactures. And to Tammy, the leader of all polite society. Long may she reign as Queen of Grommets."

We'd no sooner finished our toast than Jackson Lee pulled up in his silver Jaguar. It's not a new car, but it's very nice. Wicker creaked as Bitty immediately smoothed her hair and patted down the collar of her blouse, just in case it'd gotten rumpled or creased. She likes to look her best for Jackson Lee, especially since he's so often seen both of us at our worst.

Chen Ling growled her usual sweet welcome as he came up onto the porch, and I lifted my wine glass in a salute. "Greetings and salutations, Jackson Lee," I said. "What brings you out on such a lovely evening?"

I expected him to say something flowery about Bitty being the lure. Like any good Southern lawyer, he has a way with words. Instead, he dragged over a chair to sit in front of us and looked at Bitty.

"I have a report from Catfish. He's found out some interesting information. Do you want to read it, or do you want me to give you a summary?"

"Just tell me he's found evidence that Brandon didn't kill Walter Simpson, and I'll be happy," Bitty said, and I saw that her knuckles went white around the wine glass stem.

Jackson Lee shook his head. "Sugar, you know that's not exactly what we're looking for here."

"It's not? Why not?"

"Facts say the gun Brandon held fired the fatal bullet. We can't disprove facts. What we can do is muddy them up a bit. We have to prove that he didn't have motive but other people did. We have to create doubt that he knew the gun would fire. I have some good people working to recreate the scene. Crime scene units already did the line of fire, using the video from a tourist to place Brandon in the right position to fire the bullet. But we can state that there was a lot of confusion and chaos and that someone else could have fired the bullet from that rifle."

Bitty looked confused. "But no one else had that rifle. It's an heirloom."

"I know, sugar. But it's supposedly an antique that hasn't fired in a hundred years. For it to fire this one time is pretty unusual, I'd say. So I intend to create doubt about the accuracy of ballistics that report only one rifle could have fired that bullet. Now here. Catfish has transcripts of his conversations with a few people around town. As we all know, Walter wasn't the most beloved town figure. He made some enemies when he ran the insurance company. And he made more enemies when he sold it."

"But that was what, six or seven years ago?" I asked. "What enemy waits that long for revenge? And even if they did, was it a bad enough offense to deserve murder?"

Jackson Lee smiled. "Not for normal people, no. But for someone without conscience or scruples, murder isn't a problem. There are people who have waited a lot longer than eight years to get satisfaction for some slight they feel was done to them."

"So what did Walter do that made him enemies?" I asked. "How did selling the insurance company upset people?"

"When you cut out your investors and make a private deal to sell it for more than market value, that can cause hard feelings," Jackson Lee said dryly. "The company had been in business for nearly a hundred years. It'd gone through a lot of restructuring, but then a national company made an offer, and Walter quietly bought out his investors for pennies on the dollar, then sold it for a huge profit."

Bitty looked bewildered. "How did Catfish find all that out?"

"By asking questions and researching records. He spent a lot of time in the archives. He's also a computer whiz. He already has enough for reasonable doubt, if it comes to that."

"Okay," I said after we had time to absorb the implications, "this is all news, and it names people with reason to want Walter dead. Brandon had no motive whatsoever."

"Except for the tourist who insists she saw him in an argument with Walter right before the reenactment," Jackson Lee reminded me. "We know it was Clayton and just have to convince a jury of reasonable doubt if this goes to trial."

"Do you really think it's going to trial?" Bitty asked.

"It's always possible, sweetpea."

Bitty looked so distressed I could hardly stand it. There's nothing that gets to me more than a mother upset about her child being in danger. Maybe because as a mother, I relate so well.

"See, Bitty?" I said. "There are people with real motives who might have wanted Walter dead. Brandon had no motive whatsoever. It's so obvious, any jury is bound to see that."

"Thank you, Trinket." Bitty managed a smile. "Now we just have to figure out which of the many who wouldn't mind seeing Walter dead was at the reenactment and had opportunity."

"Richard Grace was one of the investors Walter cheated," Jackson Lee said after a few moments.

"But he's been dead for several years," I argued.

Jackson Lee nodded. "Yes. But he has children who are still alive."

It took a moment to sink in. Then I said, "You're talking about Deelight and Faith."

"Yes. Catfish learned that Faith's oldest son, who works for the MetLife Company that bought out Simpson Insurance, has said his grandfather stole the family fortunes from his heirs. And he did it quite loudly, and to anyone who'll listen, in fact. That's not exactly a good sign."

"But he doesn't even live in Holly Springs. And he wasn't at the reenactment." I shook my head. "Walter is still leaving his direct heirs a nice inheritance."

"Some people can never have enough money," Bitty said, and since I'd always thought of her as someone who revered money far more than most, I was intrigued by her observation.

"Do you mean that as in, some people will do anything for more money, or as in, some people have great respect for what money can buy?" I asked.

She thought for a moment. "As in some people will do anything for more money is what I really meant. You all know I have great respect for what money can buy. Sometimes I forget it's not guaranteed as an endless supply, but I think I keep a fairly frugal perspective."

I stared at her. She wore diamond earrings the size of butter beans and had a ring on her finger that was worth enough to support a small town for a month. Her casual slacks and a light blouse cost more than I made in a month. Heck, her shoes cost more than my car was worth. But I didn't say anything. It'd not only be a waste of my time, but would sound pretty petty when all things were considered.

After all, it hadn't been too long ago when Bitty had undergone a traumatic experience with a shortage of available cash flow. I'd half-expected her to start washing out her clothes in a Number 8 washtub and hang them on a line strung from one end of her kitchen to the other; or cook roadkill like Granny Clampett. I hadn't expected her to shop at Walmart. The latter was her only concession to the reality of a budget most people would consider generous but she viewed as poverty. Walmart shares had shot through the roof on Wall Street after Bitty filled six or seven baskets and had to be talked down by Jackson Lee at check-out. Thank heavens for his tact and patience.

"Sugar," said Jackson Lee, "you do real well with your money. Most of the time. Just don't sign anything without me looking over it first, okay?"

"Oh, I learned my lesson about that the last time," Bitty vowed. "Everything that doesn't already go through your office gets sent there immediately. Which reminds me—do you have my latest bank statement?"

"No, it went to your accountant. Is something wrong?"

"Not really. Well, not yet, anyway. I just want to make sure the check I wrote out to the Daughters of the Confederacy posted. Lorene Campbell called to ask me if I'd sent it yet since they don't have my name crossed off the list."

"List of what?" I couldn't help asking. Bitty is on a lot of committees and fundraisers, and I don't know how she has the time to get it all in between her shopping expeditions, her weekly massages by Rafael or Rio or whatever his name is, target shooting at the gun club, and hair and nail appointments. She also sleeps until at least ten every morning.

"Contributors," Bitty replied. "You know the governor proclaimed April as Confederate Heritage Month. There are memorial services for the Confederate dead and reenactments being held all over the state. Local chapters need funds to help with the reenactments and memorials."

I blinked a couple times. "You're going to have another reenactment? The last one wasn't enough for you?"

"You do realize that it's the one hundred and fiftieth anniversary of many battles during The War?"

"Uh, I guess I do. Now, anyway. So every battle is going to be commemorated with another reenactment?"

Bitty sighed. "No, Trinket, but some of the pivotal battles will be reenacted."

"And the purpose of this would be—what?"

"You have absolutely no sense of history, do you." She said it more as a statement than a question, and I let it go. Bitty's history knowledge is mostly confined to local. Now, caught up in her justification for getting involved in another reenactment, she continued, "The Confederacy may not have been part of the United States for four years, but it's still our country. Our history. Our heritage. Honoring those who fought and died in all our wars should be an annual event. I've realized that I cannot turn my back on our heritage because of Walter's death and the trouble it's caused. I have to honor it. He would have wanted that."

"Uh huh. Just so I know—you do realize we have Veterans Day

every November? Fourth of July every summer? Memorial Day every May? Flag Day? Right?"

"Yes, and now we have Confederate Heritage Month in Miss'sippi."

When Bitty narrows her eyes at me in a certain way, I know it's time to shut up. I glanced over at Jackson Lee, who'd had the good sense to stay out of our discussion. So I smiled and did my best to look enlightened.

"That's good," I said. "Really. So when and where are these reenactments? I don't have to go, do I? Or wear anything hot, bulky, and likely to flip over my head at any moment?"

"Good lord, Trinket. How much wine did you drink?"

"Apparently not enough. I'll be right back. May I freshen anyone else's drink?"

An entire vat of wine would not have been enough to prepare me for my dear cousin's next, and might I add—quite insane—adventure. Sometimes Bitty outdoes even herself.

Chapter 7

"WHEN YOU TOLD me we were going to the museum, I thought you meant Holly Springs. I'm not going, Bitty. I already told you—I've had enough reenactments to last me a lifetime."

"Oh, for heaven's sake, Trinket. You don't have to do anything or wear anything. All you have to do is ride along with me."

"If I don't wear anything, I'll be riding along in the back of Rodney Farrell's patrol car," I observed. "Public nudity is prohibited."

Bitty narrowed her eyes at me. I thought about telling her she was making wrinkles that her $500 an ounce anti-wrinkle cream wouldn't be able to erase, but decided against it. If I hadn't already been trapped in her car with her, I might have risked it. Since I was, I didn't.

She sighed at my silence. "You're being cranky, Trinket. Just sit back and relax. It'll be fun."

"Put on your glasses, Mr. Magoo," was all I said, and she muttered something under her breath. She hates wearing glasses. She snatched them off the dashboard and slapped them on the bridge of her nose. I'd be surprised if she didn't end up with a black eye.

"The reenactment won't even be until June," she said after a moment, and I felt more comfortable since she wore glasses and focused on the road unfurling ahead of us. Rain smacked against the Mercedes' windshield in a steady rhythm. Leafy tree limbs whipped in the wind, and the tires hissed over the pavement with an occasional slurp.

"Are you ever going to replace your sports car?" I asked to keep from discussing this latest trip down Madness Avenue.

"Oh, I ordered another red one. I'm supposed to pick it up next week. I've just been so busy, I haven't been up to Memphis yet. The salesman kept calling, and I finally said I'd come up. I'm sure you wouldn't mind giving me a ride."

"Buying a car that expensive, they should deliver," I said.

"He suggested that, but I'd rather see it on the showroom floor first. Just in case there are any dings or scratches."

"Dings or scratches? This from a woman who stripped out the gears of one car last year, then put another one in the lake two months later?"

"That last wasn't my fault, Trinket, as you very well know."

I did know. That didn't mean I wouldn't tease her about it, however.

"You're averaging a new sports car every six months," I said. "Detroit should love you. Or did you buy a foreign car again?"

"German engineering is excellent," she replied after a brief pause, "but I've been thinking about a Maserati for a long time and—"

"No! A Maserati? Are you kidding me? I thought you were getting another BMW?"

"Well, I thought about it. Then I considered that it might be bad luck. You know. After the last foreign car."

"Your Miata was built in America. It lasted you a lot longer than the BMW. I'm just sayin' . . ."

"Then you'll be pleased to learn I bought a Cadillac CTS-V. Now are you happy?"

"Ecstatic. Same color?"

"Yes, it's called Crystal Red. Panoramic sunroof. Very nice."

"Life can go on now, I suppose." I barely kept from rolling my eyes. "It's nice to know the economic recession didn't affect everyone."

"I'm doing my part to kick it into gear again. That's the only thing that's going to help, you know, is for people to spend money."

"Tell that to people who have been without jobs for a year or two. I'm sure they'll be quite gratified to hear it."

"I know. Isn't it awful?"

"Where is it we're going again?" I asked to get away from the depressing topic of people out of work and fiscal struggles. "The museum at Corinth?"

"Yes. There was a battle there, and they're planning a reenactment. I've been nominated to drop off all the club's necessary forms. They have to get permission to go onto state-owned or federally owned battlegrounds."

"Y'all never heard of the internet? Forms can be filled out and filed online."

"I know. But their computer system is down, and sometimes a little one-on-one can be very helpful."

Knowing Bitty as I do, I realized she had to stay busy to keep from dwelling on things that were stressful. Having her son accused of manslaughter fell under that category, I'd think. And I had to admit that prowling around grassy fields full of ticks, fleas, and historical markers was a lot safer than investigating a possible murder. It occurred to me that Jackson Lee may be behind this latest diversion. He can be quite devious at times.

So I settled in and decided to enjoy the day, soupy weather and all. Chitling was at the groomer's, and I had the front seat all to myself. We reached Corinth in a reasonable time. I was astonished at how much the Mississippi town had grown just since my last visit.

"This was a key point for Confederate and Union troops during The War," said Bitty as she parked the car at the museum. "Since Shiloh is only twenty-two miles away, Corinth was a launching point for the battle at Pittsburg Landing. The reenactment is for the Second Battle of Corinth. It happened right after that awful carnage at Shiloh."

"Uh huh," I said as I followed her into the Interpretive Center. Shiloh National Military Park is in Tennessee. Corinth Interpretive Center grounds in Mississippi is studded with cannons, barricades, and bronze statues and markers. A beautiful water feature stands next to a walkway into the center. I waited inside while Bitty spoke animatedly with the lady in charge of the reenactment. When their conversation ended, I followed Bitty back outside.

"I need to get a sense of the scope of the reenactment," said Bitty. She stopped at the trunk of her car, and the lid popped open. She took out rain boots.

I got a sinking feeling. "Why are you putting on boots?"

Bitty gave me one of those *Duh* looks, and I sighed as she said, "How do you think I'm going to give a report if I don't view the grounds?"

I was a bit stunned. "When did you decide nature walks in the rain and mud are a good thing?"

"Since it was suggested I see the improvements done with my donations to Friends of the Siege and Battle of Corinth. Don't be tacky, Trinket. We won't walk long."

"Do you have a mouse in your pocket, Cochise? 'Cause there's no *we* taking a walk."

"Don't be so unpatriotic. This won't take long, and it'll make me look like I know what I'm doing."

"But I don't have any boots with me," I said. The rain had slackened to a fine mist. My hair felt like wet dog ears against the side of my face. "I'll sink down to my knees in that muck. I'll ruin my shoes and get your car dirty."

"I have plastic bags you can use." Bitty stomped her feet into her boots, then lowered the lid to the trunk. She tied a plastic rain bonnet over her helmet hair.

"The bags will get torn on ruts and weeds," I protested.

"They're for after our walk. That way you won't get mud in my car."

"Well, as long as you aren't inconvenienced any—Bitty, I am *not* walking out there. It's raining, and I don't want to."

"You really do whine too much, you know."

"Yes, I believe you've said that a time or ten."

"All right then, just be that way. I'll go by myself."

"Thank you. I will."

I leaned back against the car and crossed my arms over my chest and watched as Bitty set bravely off on her little jog around the area. There's evidence of the long-ago battle left behind in indentations where once there were trenches and lines of soldiers. Grass covers all traces of death and desperation now, but grim reminders remain in the strategically placed cannons.

While I'm interested in my local history, that interest only goes so far. I'm not as avid a scholar of all the dates and events as are others. Bitty, however, has a variety of interests that contradict her reputation as a bubble-headed blonde with too much money and time. Antiques are only one of her passions; she's also caught up in the genealogy of our family and their participation in key historical events. The War—or Mr. Lincoln's War, or the War of Northern Aggression—is just one major event. When properly motivated, Bitty can rattle off trivia concerning battles, generals, and depredations like my mother can list the ingredients in a Lane cake. So I often find my mind wandering when she's on one of her enthusiastic rambles about the number of troops, who won the battle, and what the weather conditions were at the time. You can see my dilemma, I'm sure.

Bitty wanted to show off all she knew about the Second Battle of Corinth.

I wanted to get out of the rain and have a cup of hot coffee somewhere. Or wine. I wasn't feeling that picky.

So when I looked away for a moment at the sound of a train whistle, then I looked back, it was rather dismaying to realize that my dear cousin had disappeared from sight. No plastic-clad head was visible among the historical markers or trenches, no designer clothes and rain boots.

I resigned myself to waiting longer than I had hoped. It'd be a lot dryer if I waited in the car, so I reached for the door handle. It didn't open. That meant Miss Bubble-head had taken her purse and keys with her. Damn. I looked down at my shoes. Suede flats. Not exactly rainwear. I had two choices: Stay by the car and get wetter, or look for Bitty and get muddy and wetter. It didn't take me long to decide to wait it out.

About five minutes after that decision, it began to rain harder. Drops came down like fat water balloons. I retreated to the museum, but the door was locked and the sign said it was closed for the day. I huddled in the relatively dryer alcove outside the door and scanned the field that was getting blurred by rain. The temperature dropped a few degrees. April can be fickle.

I made an executive decision to abandon my earlier decision, which meant I was going to end up muddy and probably pretty irritated. I stomped down the pavement as far as it went then struck out across the battlefield. Markers designated where Union troops had been entrenched and where Confederate troops had dug in for the duration. Cannons stood sentry, and earthworks snaked the green field. Bronze statues scattered across the fields like metal ghosts of long-gone soldiers. I barely noticed as I squished through wet grass and red mud.

I'm not particularly a fan of mud, for a vast number of reasons. I don't even do facials with mud. Its sticky, the red Mississippi mud leaves stains in clothes that never come out, and it is exceedingly unpleasant to wallow around in. I know this from experience. As a kid, I didn't even like it. As an adult, I avoid it at all costs.

Yet there I was, trekking over a wet battlefield in search of my dear cousin, globs of red mud attaching to my now-ruined shoes, and cussing under my breath about the necessity of being out in the rain and muck. I'm not a good sport at such times.

As I crested a fairly high hill, I looked down into the valley of hummocks and saw Bitty. She was engaged in a rather earnest discussion with a slender boy in a gray hoodie. My brothers as boys were able to put their fingers in their mouths and emit a shrill whistle no doubt heard by ocean liners down in the Gulf of Mexico. All I could get out was a rather wet *pfffft!* It was heard by no one.

So I tromped several yards down the slick hill, half sliding in places, irritation growing with each step. Bitty was oblivious to my approach. The boy with her looked up, however, and saw me coming. I'm not sure if it was my no-doubt scowling expression or he figured he'd be outnumbered, but suddenly he grabbed Bitty's purse from off her shoulder and took off across the grass like he'd been shot from a cannon. Bitty screamed. I started running.

I have no idea what I thought I could do to help. I'm not an athlete, and I don't know any karate. All I know is kick and bite, and those aren't always good options. I've learned that lesson the hard way.

Bitty took off after the little thug, too, but her rain boots must have made it difficult to keep her footing. She ran like a two-year-old, feet flailing out to the sides, little arms pumping up and down, screeching, "Stop, thief!" as she floundered up a slope.

I was too breathless to talk, so when I got close enough to her to touch her I reached out to let her know I was there. My hand slipped on her waterproof jacket, and instead of putting my hand on her shoulder I struck her between the shoulder blades. She let out another screech and tried to turn but slipped on wet grass and mud. My momentum carried me a few feet past her, so I couldn't catch her before she slid back down the hill like it was greased. I stumbled to a halt.

I peered down the hill through the pounding rain and saw her thrashing around in a rather shallow ditch. I looked up and saw the purse snatcher a good fifty yards away. He headed for an area of buildings I could barely see in the distance. I looked back down at Bitty and started my descent. Trees shadowed the area and dripped more rain on the ground; I half-fell down the slope trying to get to the bottom. I skidded the last three or four feet and landed almost on top of her. She made a gargling sound that I interpreted as "As last you're here to save me."

By the time I managed to catch my balance and free myself of her flapping arms, I heard her say through mud and rain, "Ge' oth me, ya biggox!" It was a little garbled, but I got her drift.

"Doing my best," I muttered. "Be still a minute. I think I'm tangled in your jacket."

"Trinket? Is that you?" she said, blinking at me with lashes clogged with mud. If I hadn't known who it was, I wouldn't recognize her. She was just blue eyes looking out from red mud.

"Yes, it's me. Are you all right? I saw what happened."

Sitting up in the thin current of water sliding over the grass, she tried to wipe her face. It didn't work out so well. She succeeded in smearing mud from brow to chin instead. "I'm okay, just mad. That little creep stole my purse."

"I know. Come on. I'm going to put my hands under your arms and lift you. Try to help."

I stood up, put my arms under hers, and heaved. My heels slewed, and we both went down. I jarred my tailbone and bit my tongue. I think I said something very ugly. Then I tried again. This time I did better. I got her halfway to her feet, and she managed the rest. We clung together for a few moments, a little breathless from our exertions. I was cold, clammy, and my bare toes squelched in the mud. Apparently, I'd lost a shoe somewhere. Bitty had lost her plastic hat.

"We've got to get back up that hill," I said finally. "Once we're dry again you can tell me just what the hell you're doing so far out here."

Bitty wobbled a little, grabbed my arm to steady herself, then said, "I got lost. I asked that young man which way back, and he seemed so nice at first. Then he got a little pushy. He asked for some money. I might have given it to him but he got ugly, so I told him he had bad manners. Then he grabbed my purse and ran. The horrible little thug took everything. My purse, my wallet with all my money—my new purse!"

"Jimmy Choo?" I asked sympathetically as we trudged back up the slippery hill.

She clawed at a clump of grass to pull herself up the incline. "No," she said after we stood on top of the rise. "Lana Marks. It cost more than I usually pay for a purse."

"I'm not surprised. I'm sure you can get another one."

"Maybe. But I liked that one. Oh, I broke a nail!"

"Come on. Let's go call the police."

Bitty came to an abrupt halt. "My phone is in my shoulder bag."

"That's okay. My phone is in my purse, locked safely in your car—uh oh—do you have the car keys?"

Bitty slowly shook her head. "They're in my purse, too."

"Great. Just great."

"We can use the phone inside the Interpretive Center. You go inside. I'll hide around the corner by my car so no one sees me."

"Don't worry, Princess Barbie, no one would recognize you. And the center is closed. So there goes that idea."

"So early?"

"It closes at four-thirty. We got a late start, remember?"

"I had things to do . . . anyway, I don't get up late every day."

"If you got up before noon, it wouldn't seem like it gets dark so early. Try going to bed earlier at night. That might help."

"It's all that daylight savings time that gets me confused," said Bitty.

"Poor darling. Try setting your clocks ahead an hour. That'll keep you on time."

"Already? I thought that didn't happen until June."

I rolled my eyes. "That explains a lot."

"You're going the wrong way," Bitty said, and we halted.

"No, I'm sure it's this way," I replied after a moment.

"I think it's this way," said Princess Pea-hen, and so we trudged off in the direction she pointed. By the time we passed the same statue twice, I had enough. I stopped.

"I'm going the other way. You can follow me, go with me, or keep walking till you reach the West Coast."

"You're always so irritable, Trinket."

I just looked at her. The lacquer she uses to keep her hair from moving had gummed together in clumps that stuck straight out on one side, flat on the other. She looked like a badger.

"Really?" I said. "I cannot imagine why I would be irritable. It can't have anything to do with the fact that I'm wet all the way to my femurs, I can't feel my right foot, and when this mud dries it's going to turn to cement, and I'll end up immobilized like one of these statues."

"Try to look on the bright side."

"And that would be—where?"

"Your purse didn't get stolen."

I thought about it a moment, nodded grudgingly, then struck off for where I was pretty sure the car with my purse and phone waited for our return. Bitty trailed behind me.

When we were finally in sight of the parking lot at last, I was glad because it was hard to walk in only one shoe. My other was forever left on the battlefield. I felt a pang of loss. They were my most comfortable in-between shoes, not winter shoes but not spring ones, just right for wearing anywhere casual.

As we drew nearer to the paved lot I realized something was wrong. Different. It didn't look the same. The reason hit me just as Bitty gasped, "My car! He stole my car!"

WRAPPED IN BLANKETS and drinking cups of hot coffee, we waited for Jackson Lee to arrive at the police station. We'd flagged down a motorist—who looked startled and frightened by our appearance—and he'd called the police for us. The officer hadn't really wanted us in his patrol car but reluctantly took us to the station. They were very nice. Bitty gave a report and sketchy description of the purse-snatcher; the police gave us blankets and coffee.

Corinth is around an hour northeast of Holly Springs. Jackson Lee showed up and greeted some of the officers as if he knew them fairly well. I imagine in his line of work, he meets a lot of the police officers in North Mississippi. When they were through slapping backs and exchanging quips, he turned and saw Bitty and I huddled in uncomfortable chairs like muddy gnomes. His eyes got a little big, but other than that, he didn't betray his revulsion by word or expression.

"Are y'all ready to leave?" he asked. I noticed that his eyes kept straying to Bitty's hair. It was difficult to see the blond for all the clotted mud. I was pretty sure we looked like two of those termite hills found in Africa, just mud piled up in layers to form cones.

"Past ready," I replied while Bitty did her best to retain her composure and mask her chagrin that he was seeing her in such a state. Again. I figured he was used to it by now.

"You're always our knight in shining armor, Jackson Lee," she said with a bright smile only slightly marred by drying mud flaking off every time she moved her facial muscles.

He smiled back and gestured to the door. "Your carriage awaits, milady."

"I hope it's mud-proof," I said and saw him flinch. He keeps his Jaguar very clean.

"We won't worry about that," he said gallantly.

However, I'm sure he was thinking of his pristine leather seats.

I was thinking of a shower and clean clothes.

Bitty was thinking about her stolen purse.

"It's not a week old," she complained as he guided us out of the station. "And I had my phone in there, my car keys, and my cash—"

"Sugar, he stole your car. It's worth a lot more than a purse."

"Yes, but it's also a lot easier to find. I told them about the stickers on the bumper."

Jackson Lee opened the passenger side door for Bitty, glanced up and met my eyes, and shook his head. I shrugged. My purse had been in that car too. I hoped for a quick arrest. No self-respecting crook would want to drive a Mercedes with a pink bumper sticker that reads: *Zombie Apocalypse Go-to Girl*. It has an outline of a pink nine-millimeter. On the other side is a bumper sticker with a picture of a pug stretched out on a pink rug. It reads: *I'm Too Pugalicious For You, Babe!* They were Christmas gifts from her sons. I think they understand their mother very well.

By the time we got back to Bitty's house where I'd left my car, I was doing my best to stay awake. It'd been a trying day, and I'd tossed and turned the night before. My car was parked at the curb in front of the house, and Jackson Lee thoughtfully pulled up next to it.

Before I could rouse myself enough to get out of the car, he reminded me, "Since your purse was stolen with Bitty's car, I can call a locksmith for you."

Bitty responded, "Not tonight. It's too late. She can stay here. Besides, I have a plan, and I want to see what she thinks about it."

Jackson Lee asked carefully, "What kind of plan, sugarplum?"

"Oh, it's just something I thought of while we were waiting for you at the police station," she replied with a vague wave of one hand. "I'm too exhausted to talk about it now, honey."

A thrum of foreboding quivered inside me, but I was too tired to panic. I was covered in mud from my head to my feet, my clothes were ruined, and my right foot was cold. My left shoe was glued to my foot with red sludge. I had no phone, no purse, no money, no credit cards, or car keys. At the moment, I didn't really care. Concern would come in the morning.

Since Bitty often forgets to set her alarm or even lock her doors, I was a little bemused to see Jackson Lee had a key to the front door. He let us in, reminded Bitty to set the alarm when we went to bed, kissed the tip of her nose—the cleanest place on her face—and told us goodbye.

Bitty called after him, "Don't forget to pick up my precious girl in the morning," and he called back that he wouldn't dare forget.

She shut the door and turned to look at me. "Chitling is spending the night out, I presume," I said.

"I talked to Luann Carey, and she went and got her from the groomer's. She goes to bed early, so Chen Ling will spend the night with her."

Luann runs a small rescue for pugs. She was responsible for matching Bitty up with her little gargoyle, a match made in puggy heaven, I might add.

After calling my parents, I headed for the stairs. "I'm going up to shower. I hope you still have that flower muumuu that fits me in the guest room."

"I bought some more things, and they're in the chest of drawers. Help yourself. I'll meet you back down here after we're clean. Put your clothes in the washer. Sharita came the other day so there's plenty in the freezer. I'll pop something in the oven, and we can have dinner."

"Wine?"

"Of course."

I smiled. I can always count on Bitty to have the necessities of life close at hand.

Showering was pure luxury. I shampooed my hair with Bitty's expensive shampoo, used her conditioner, then wrapped myself in a thick white terrycloth robe. The chest of drawers held a pair of lounging pajamas in size Trinket. They actually fit, and I was rather proud of her for choosing the right size. She likes to pretend I'm six feet tall and weigh a lot more than I do. I like to pretend she's an empty-headed munchkin. We're both wrong but close enough to the truth to be within calling distance. She'd also chosen a nightgown, a shapeless muumuu, socks, and some nice things from Carolann's shop for me. Bitty can be very generous.

When I went downstairs, Bitty was already in the kitchen, and something was in the oven that smelled good. I'm not really comfortable with Bitty using anything but the microwave since she has a tendency to set food on fire, but at least the oven would contain any flames.

"What do I smell?" I asked as I joined her after putting my clothes in the washer.

"Chicken cordon bleu, broccoli, carrots, and wild rice. I've already poured the wine."

"Riesling?" I asked as I lifted my glass and tasted it. "Nice. Not too tart or too sweet."

I set the small kitchen table with one of Bitty's many sets of dishes, using her everyday flatware and cloth napkins. She doesn't like to use paper napkins. They're "bourgeois," in her opinion. I'm more practical and less elegant. It might seem lazy to prefer throwaway napkins instead of nice cloth ones, but I don't have a maid to do the washing at my house either. It's me or Mama in charge of the laundry. Neither of us is particularly inclined to do extra work unless it's absolutely necessary.

"Use the potholders that match the serviettes," Bitty said as I placed condiments on the small round table.

I looked at her. "If you're going to use British terms, at least use the accent. And since the Queen can't make it tonight, excuse me if I don't match potholders to *serviettes*."

Bitty just laughed. "I think the Queen refers to them as linen. I'm not sure. I guess I'm too tired to think straight. We'll both feel better once we've eaten."

I didn't realize how hungry I was until the food was on my plate and the delicious scent tickled my nose. There was very little conversation as we ate like longshoremen shoveling in the food. Delicately, of course, as befits the flower of Southern womanhood. *Right.* Fortunately, there were no witnesses to our piggy party.

After we loaded the dishwasher and refilled our wine glasses, we went to our favorite spot to relax, her small parlor. I groaned as I put my feet up on the matching ottoman to the plush overstuffed chair. "I can't believe the day is ending on a high note after all the trauma."

Bitty nodded. "It was awful. I should have waited for a better day to take the photos of the park."

"You took pictures?"

"I got some half-decent ones, I think."

"Any pictures of your mugger?"

"Maybe. I won't know until I get the camera back though."

"Ah," I said. "You put it in your purse."

"Afraid so. I just hope the police find my car soon, before that jackass sells all the stuff in my purse and my car. Who robs people in a national park?"

"People get robbed every day in cemeteries, parks, grocery stores—even nice places like Oak Court Mall where you go shop in Memphis. That's what happens when they don't have jobs, food, or a decent place to live. And of course, there are plenty of rich people who steal, but they do it with real estate, manipulating stocks and bonds, or passing punitive laws."

"Well, I don't like it. I don't want people going hungry, but I'd have given him money if he hadn't been so impatient. May he rot in prison."

"I'll drink to that." We toasted the hopefully imminent incarceration of her mugger. Then we toasted to Jackson Lee's future successful defense of Brandon, and then we toasted random people and events until we had gone through two bottles of wine and were so relaxed, I felt quite giddy.

Bitty chose that moment to drop her bombshell. I must say, she picks the path of least resistance at times.

"So I've been thinking . . ." she said. Being under the influence of delightfully fermented grapes, my warning bells failed to respond.

"Do tell," I said merrily, still blissfully ignorant of the foolish scheme about to be unveiled.

"Being at the battlefield today made me think of the reenactment when Walter was shot. I saw all those cannon, all the battery fortifications, and the weapons in the Interpretive Center and how much alike they all are. So I think we need to check the rifle the police have in the evidence room to be sure they have the right one. That's the only rational explanation."

Still in my alcohol haze, I said, "That sounds reasonable. Jackson Lee can get you in there to inspect it, I'm sure."

Bitty shook her head. "No, I mean we have to take it from the evidence room and do our own examination."

For a moment I still didn't understand. "Hire your own ballistics expert. He'll be able to verify if it's the rifle that fired the bullet that killed Walter."

"Trinket, you're not listening. I have to see if it's mine. Brandon said he thinks it is, but he only sees it once or twice a year. I'm the one who's most familiar with it. We need to get it out so I can bring it here and study it for a little while, try to fire it. Then I'll put it back."

"Wait a minute—are you saying what it sounds like you're saying?"

"I don't know. Does it sound like I'm saying I want to repossess my rifle for a while?"

"It sounds like you're saying you want to break into the police station and steal the evidence."

Bitty nodded. "Then yes, I'm saying what it sounds like I'm saying."

Flabbergasted, I could only stare at her in shock. No amount of alcohol could make that scheme sound any better, I was pretty sure.

Chapter 8

"WE'VE GOT TO talk her out of it, Rayna. Gaynelle, can you help?" I pleaded. We sat in Rayna's garden, drinking lemonade in the warm sunlight, all traces of rain gone from the skies.

Both Divas stared at Bitty as if she'd suddenly grown an extra head. It would have been nice if she had. Maybe the new head wouldn't be prone to stupid ideas.

Finally, Gaynelle said, "So Bitty, tell me once more how you came to this decision?"

"Well, we had gone to Corinth to take some papers to one of the members of a UDC group for their next reenactment, and she asked me if I had seen the new markers installed and suggested I might want to photograph them to show to donors. So I did, but after I got mugged and my car was stolen, we ended up at the police station. It was while we were there, waiting on Jackson Lee to come after us, that it occurred to me that if all those cannons and guns in the Interpretive Center look so much alike, the gun from my family could be easily mistaken for another. After all, over three hundred thousand Enfield rifles were used by both sides during The War. The most common was the 1853 model. Just like my rifle. So I need to go get it for a while."

A moment of silence followed her explanation. Gaynelle and Rayna looked stunned. I completely understood their reaction. Rayna recovered from her shock first.

"Bitty, hon," she said gently, "not only is that not possible, it's extremely unwise."

"Unwise?" I echoed. "I think the correct term is stupid. S-T-U-P-I-D. Stupid."

Bitty shot me a disgusted glance, then cleared her throat. "It is possible. I think I know how it can be done with no one the wiser. After all, the police won't check the evidence again until it's time for the trial, and we can put it back before then. I'm sure it's not the right rifle. It can't be. Something about all this isn't right. I just have to see if it fires."

"The police have already made that discovery," Gaynelle said decisively. She's a retired school teacher, so she always sounds authoritative. "It fires. They can't lie about that. It's evidence and can be challenged in court by Brandon's attorney. It could ruin the prosecutor's entire case."

Nodding, Bitty said, "Yes, I understand that. But I've had that rifle in my possession for years, and before it was mine it was my mama's, and her mama's before her, and the last time it fired was 1900. My great-uncle Jobert shot his ear off with it. Then he dropped it, a wagon rolled over it, and the rifle hasn't fired properly since then. So, when should we do it?"

"Not me, not in this lifetime," said Gaynelle promptly. "I rather like life on this side of those metal bars."

When Bitty looked at me and Rayna, we said at the same time, "Not me!"

"Well, I can't do it by myself," said Bitty irritably. "I need a distraction."

I shuddered. "That sounds too dangerous. Breaking out of jail would be stressful enough. But breaking in? No way. I'm not eager to spend a few years of my life languishing in prison."

"What can they charge you with if you break into jail?" Bitty wondered aloud. "It's not burglary. Breaking and entering, do you think?"

"I think you don't even want to go down that road," said Rayna. "Tampering with evidence is an offense all in itself. Stealing from the evidence room is still theft."

Bitty looked dejected. "That's terribly inconvenient."

"Yes," I said, "sometimes being a law-abiding citizen can get annoying."

"You're making fun of me, Trinket."

"Yes. Yes, I am. Of all the insane schemes you've come up with in the past year, this one tops the entire list."

"Wait a minute, Trinket," said Rayna. "There was the trip into town on the John Deere. That has to qualify as pretty crazy."

"And what about the time she had you dress up in men's clothes as the owner of a unit at the storage facility? That was not only crazy but very dangerous," Gaynelle reminded us.

Bitty narrowed her eyes at me. This time I held my ground. "And there was the time," I said, "that she had me help her move a corpse in a laundry cart. That was ghastly and crazy."

"Don't forget the body in the carpet," Rayna chirped. "Hiding it in the cemetery didn't work out so well."

"Okay," Bitty said rather sharply, "that's enough. I get your point."

"Thank God," said Gaynelle with a sigh. "You frighten me at times."

"Don't pout, Bitty," I said when she crossed her arms over her considerable chest and gave us a sullen glare. "We love you. We don't want you to go to prison. Think of all you'd miss by not being here."

"You are all tacky, tacky people, and right now not being here holds a great deal of appeal for me."

"You'll get over it," I assured her.

Bitty lifted her brows. "You all do recall that you have been active, if not exactly willing, participants in some of these events this past year, don't you?"

There was a moment of silence. Rayna, Gaynelle, and I looked at each other. Then I said, "You're right. I guess we're all pretty crazy. A rather disturbing thing to admit, but it's true."

Bitty smiled. "See? As the Cheshire cat said, 'We're all mad here.'"

Apparently, I wasn't the only one who considered insanity an appalling realization.

"I need a drink," said Rayna, pushing back her chair.

"Just bring the Jack," Gaynelle suggested. "It'll give the lemonade a nice flavor."

She was right. A little lemonade and Jack Daniel's make for a pleasant afternoon in the garden.

"Catfish Carter is doing very well, I hear," said Rayna as our self-therapy took effect. "I know he's a little peculiar, but he's very smart."

"A *little* peculiar?" Bitty echoed. "He talks like an actor in a Grade Z movie."

"I know. It's odd, but I think it throws off the people he interviews, and they think he's an idiot."

"They're not alone," Bitty muttered.

"But he's found out some very interesting information," Gaynelle said. "I don't think I ever knew about Walter's insurance sale cheating his investors."

"People aren't always eager to let others know they were fooled." Rayna took a sip of her lemonade, rubbing one of her black labs with her sandaled foot in an absent-minded manner. "Of course, there is Brett Simon's discontent, and he's been very vocal about it."

"Isn't he Deevine—I mean, Faith's son?" I asked, and she nodded.

"Yes. He wasn't shy about telling people they'd been cheated."

Gaynelle shook her head. "Since he lives in Tupelo, I haven't heard much about him."

"It happened several years ago anyway," Rayna said. "It took a while to be found out. I'm not sure how Brett discovered it."

"Didn't they read the will this week?" I asked.

Rayna said, "Tomorrow. Maybe things will settle down after that. You know, even though Walter had enemies in town, I still keep coming back to the hope that it was just a tragic, senseless accident. Someone mistakenly fired a loaded gun."

"If that was true, the police wouldn't have charged Brandon with manslaughter," Bitty said glumly.

"They only did that because the rifle was loaded with powder and fired the fatal bullet," Gaynelle said after a moment. "Someone has to be held accountable for Walter's death."

"Who would they hold accountable if he'd been struck by lightning?" Bitty asked.

Rayna smiled slightly. "That's known as an act of God."

"In Philip's case it would have been an act of mercy." Sometimes Bitty flashes back to the senator, her ex-husband Philip Hollandale, a cheating womanizer now buried in his family plot in Hollandale, Mississippi. It was his murder that initiated our current hobby of investigating unexpected and often violent deaths. That's not exactly a good recommendation.

"Do you ever hear from Parrish or Patrice?" Rayna asked, referring to Philip's mother and sister.

"Not in a long while. Sometimes Patrice will get drunk and call to harass me. But the last time she did that, Jackson Lee took the phone and told her he'd drag her incestuous butt into court if she kept it up."

"Did he really say that?" I asked, surprised.

"Well, not in those words. That's what he meant, though."

Senator Philip Hollandale was not greatly missed in our section of Holly Springs. Not just because Divas are loyal to Bitty, either. However, his mother and sister obviously miss him. I understand that. We tend to love our close relatives even when they're terribly flawed.

Our change of conversational topic got us away from the quicksand of Bitty's newest scheme and on to other important matters—like Trina Madewell's latest depredation against local society and Miranda Watson's new male friend. When Rayna's cell phone rang, she picked it up and stepped away from the table for a few minutes while we discussed Miranda's last column.

"She sanctified Walter Simpson," Gaynelle said with an arch of her brow. "Called the family a cornerstone of Holly Springs' gentry."

"Well, the Simpsons have been here since God was a baby," said Bitty as she studied a chip in her fingernail polish. "Not that that's a good recommendation. We've had scoundrels, Yankees, and carpetbaggers take root here as well."

Amused, I regarded her with fondness. I'm always full of goodwill when imbibing. "It makes life interesting, Bitty, you must admit."

"Interesting? I guess you could call it that. I call it downright messy, cluttering up town with all kinds of riffraff."

Gaynelle and I looked at each other and just smiled.

Rayna returned to the table and plopped down in her chair. She tossed her phone to the tabletop and said, "You're never going to believe this."

Immediately intrigued, we all came alert. Rayna shoved a strand of dark hair behind one ear, and her big hoop earring caught the light and sparkled almost as vividly as her eyes.

"What?" Bitty demanded when Rayna's teasing pause drew out too long. "What aren't we going to believe?"

"Remember the Simpson will we were just discussing? Well, that was Deelight's sister Faith who called. I had the day wrong. It was read this morning. Apparently, Sammy Simpson was left the entire estate—house, furnishings, stocks, bonds, and every single thing right down to the last nail in Walter's coffin."

For a moment none of us said anything. I don't think we even breathed. Then Bitty said, "Walter Simpson must have lost his mind before he died. I've never heard of such a thing. The Simpson family always leaves the house and contents to the oldest surviving direct heir, and the rest of the family gets different bequests. Walter was big on tradition. Did he get dementia before he died? Maybe he killed himself at that reenactment."

Bitty suddenly sat up straight and clutched her throat. "That's it! Suicide! Walter killed himself, and Brandon had nothing to do with it!"

I didn't have the heart to tell her that it was fairly unlikely that Walter managed to shoot himself in the chest with a rifle from twenty feet away. Rayna tactfully intervened.

"I'm sure Jackson Lee will take that under consideration, hon," she said. "Anyway, now the entire Simpson family is in an uproar about it. People are threatening to contest the will. Poor Deevine is crushed, not so much because she didn't get anything as she is because her son is so upset, he smacked Sammy right in the mouth and made him bleed all over the conference table. There's talk of Sammy filing assault charges as well as the family suing Sammy."

"Well, Jackson Lee was Walter's attorney, so I'm sure he can settle everybody down," Bitty said. "Maybe there was a mistake with the will."

Rayna shook her head. "This is where it gets really good. There was a codicil filed up in Desoto County with another attorney."

"What?" Bitty looked surprised. "Walter always used the Brunetti firm. He wouldn't go somewhere else, especially up to Desoto County. Does Jackson Lee know about this?"

"Jackson Lee was the one who had to read it to the family."

"Is that legal?" asked Gaynelle. "Can there be two lawyers? Who brought in the codicil?"

"It was delivered by special courier to Jackson Lee's office yesterday afternoon."

"So why did Deevine—I mean, Faith—call?" I asked after a moment.

"She wants to see if Rob will recommend an investigator. She's speaking on behalf of the rest of the family. Deelight must be just as crushed as the rest of them."

"An investigator? You mean the family is really going to fight the will?" Bitty looked intrigued. "This promises to be quite an event."

"It makes you wonder, doesn't it?" Gaynelle murmured. "Why would Walter do that?"

"Faith said the rest of the family thinks Sammy coerced him. He was with him for three years and had a lot of influence over him." Rayna looked thoughtful. "It's possible he got him to sign a codicil. I'm sure Jackson Lee will check with the other attorney."

"No one had influence over Walter," Bitty said. "He was an ornery old coot who didn't like many people and not many liked him."

"Bitty!" Gaynelle and I said in unison. Then I added, "You can't go around saying things like that when Brandon is a suspect in his death."

"Yes, Trinket, I know that. I'm only saying it to y'all. Everyone in town already knows it anyway."

I rolled my eyes. Rayna took another drink of her lemonade.

Gaynelle said, "This certainly put a new wrinkle in everything. Don't you all think?"

"Well, this is going to get good," said Bitty, and we all looked at each other and shook our heads.

Gaynelle dropped us off at Bitty's house after we left Rayna's. She drove her pale blue 1985 Cadillac Seville instead of her Toyota and leaned across the long bench seat to look out the passenger side of the window at Bitty.

"Now Bitty, don't you go and do anything foolish. Just let Jackson Lee and Catfish handle Brandon's case. You have to trust their judgment."

Bitty nodded. "I understand, Gaynelle. Thank you for worrying."

I intercepted Gaynelle's glance and sigh of resignation. Yes. Bitty understood. What she would end up doing was another thing entirely. I shook my head and followed Bitty up the walk.

My car was still at the curb, sitting idle until I got the extra set of keys from my bedroom at home. I'd already called Daddy to bring them. While I'd canceled my debit card, I would have to go to the DMV to replace my driver's license. I didn't relish that inconvenience.

"Do you need a ride anywhere?" I asked my impulsive cousin as we went into her house. "I know you don't have a car right now, and Daddy is bringing me my extra set of car keys."

Bitty set Chen Ling on the floor and punched in her alarm code. Jackson Lee insisted she use it, especially since her house keys and address were now in the hands of thieves. She might come home, and the house would be entirely cleaned out. He'd made her an extra set of house keys, but the locksmith hadn't yet arrived to change out all her locks.

"Who knew we'd have to go to all this trouble?" she asked. "Just because some idiot robs me, now I have to cancel all my credit cards, put alerts on my bank accounts, and get new keys for everything. I just hope that thug doesn't ruin my car before I get it back."

"I assume there's been no word?"

She sighed. "Not yet. But it hasn't been twenty-four hours, so I haven't lost hope."

"Next time we decide to walk in the rain, we'll need armed guards, I suppose." Suddenly I was struck with a horrible thought: "Bitty—were you carrying your gun in your purse?"

"No, it didn't fit in the smaller purse. I left it at home. A good thing, in light of what happened."

"I'll say. I'd hate to think some idiot is running around Corinth armed with your gun, credit cards, and car."

"As opposed to just running around armed with my credit cards and car?"

I laughed. "I guess. He can't do much good with your credit cards now, so we can hope he stops at a traffic light and a cop pulls up behind him and recognizes your bumper stickers."

"That's wishful thinking, but we can always hope."

It was cool in the house, and our footsteps echoed on her wood floors as we crossed to go in to the kitchen. Bitty has one of those state-of-art refrigerators with French doors on top and the freezer below. It serves ice and water on the door and has another smaller door that opens to reveal most frequently used foods or drinks. Like sweet tea. A glass pitcher of lovely golden-brown tea beckoned my attention. I had just taken it out while Bitty got glasses from the cabinet when her house phone rang.

I finished pouring our tea while Bitty answered the phone. Then I opened the refrigerator door and browsed a bit, finally deciding on chicken salad. I carefully opened the plastic lid. All may not be as it seems in Bitty's fridge at times. I've nearly eaten dog food twice. Of course, the dog food is home-cooked—boiled or roasted chicken, green beans, and sometimes rice—but just the thought of eating dog food makes my stomach churn.

Fortunately, the chicken salad was people food. I could tell by the grapes and pecans, not allowed on Chen Ling's new diet. I plopped a big chunk onto a plate, only half-listening to Bitty as I wondered if she wanted some too. About the time I turned to motion to her, she let out an excited squeal.

"Already? You're wonderful! How is it? What?"

I immediately figured her Franklin Benz had been located. From the expression on her face, I also figured it wasn't in the best shape. She confirmed my suspicion with her next words: "Was it completely stripped?"

Good lord, I thought.

"Thank heavens. Why would they burn the tires? But it's okay other than that—did you find the little punk who stole it? I want that skell in jail."

I rolled my eyes. Our *Law & Order* addiction was carrying over into our other lives. We have always been TV fans, but sometimes the line between real life and fantasy blurred a bit too much. If it didn't, I'm sure neither one of us would ever for a second think we were qualified to investigate murders for any reason. A combination of unrealistic belief in our own abilities coupled with an overdose of optimism has gotten us in too many unpleasant situations.

I recognize this. Bitty doesn't. I'm not sure which one of us is the bigger idiot: me for being aware of our idiocy and doing it anyway, or Bitty for not having a clue. It's a toss-up.

One more reason Jackson Lee craftily maneuvered us into leaving the investigating to an actual licensed investigator, I'm sure. He's really good. I was fine with that. I'd had my fill of getting too close to dangerous people.

"Was my Lana Marks purse in it?" Bitty asked the caller. "Or anything else valuable?"

I wasn't sure she was including my purse and other possessions in the "valuable" part of her description. That was okay. I liked my purse. It held what I needed and didn't cost me more than most cars. I wouldn't really miss my cell phone that much, but it was inconvenient to have to replace it. Whether I had a phone or not, I would be paying a monthly fee to AT&T, so getting another one was sensible.

When she hung up and turned to look at me, I held out a glass of sweet tea. "Have some. You look like you might need it."

"What I need," she said as she took the glass, "is for that punk who stole my purse and car to go to jail. The police found my car, as I'm sure you figured out, but someone had started to strip it. The police believe there's gang involvement. The tires were burned for some god-awful reason, and my purse and other stuff weren't with it."

"I assume that means my purse is gone, too. A pity. I rather liked that purse."

"No, yours is there. I'm sure that thug realized it isn't worth much."

I shook my head. "Who would have thought thieves could be so picky?"

"I know. I still wonder how that thieving boy got back around to the parking lot so quick. And how he knew the car was mine."

"It could be because it was the only one in the lot, and we were the only idiots out on the battlefield in the rain," I observed. "Or he could have been watching us when we pulled into the museum parking lot. Thieves do that. They target a place and wait for likely looking pigeons."

"By pigeons, I assume you mean us," Bitty said with a grimace. "I'm sure that's exactly what we were, too. The one time I don't carry my gun with me, and you see what happens? I get mugged and my car stolen. Are you eating my chicken salad?"

"What do you mean, the *one* time, and yes, I'm eating your chicken salad. Want some?"

She nodded. "Well," said Bitty after we took our chicken salad and tea to her parlor, "that was just a figure of speech. I don't really carry my gun all the time. But I do carry it when I think we're going somewhere dangerous. I just misjudged the danger level."

"I'll say." I focused on my sandwich. "We were pretty lucky, all things considered."

Chitling jumped up on the ottoman and nudged Bitty's hand holding the plate. Bitty held the plate higher. "You know, if I'd had my pistol, he wouldn't have gotten away with my purse and my car."

"If you had a pistol, he could have had a gun or a knife. He could have killed you or taken you hostage. Abducted you for ransom money. Or you might have dropped your gun and shot yourself in the foot. Statistics show that criminals have no scruples about taking away a person's gun and shooting them with it, while most non-felonious people hesitate before pulling the trigger. Having a gun with you is not always the safest thing."

Bitty was quiet for a moment. "I don't like shooting people," she finally said. "It's not a nice feeling. But you have to admit, we might not be here if I hadn't had my gun with me a time or two."

"True," I said. "I guess I'm ambivalent about the entire issue. Maybe because I'm the first person who would shoot themselves in the foot."

"I keep asking you to go target shooting with me. You'd like it."

"I'll keep it in mind."

The doorbell rang and Chen Ling barked shrilly. The dog looked at the chicken salad on Bitty's plate and then toward the front door, obviously undecided which deserved its attention. I set my empty plate on the end table next to the chair and got up.

"I'll get it. It's probably Daddy with my car keys."

Instead of my father's familiar smiling face, a stranger stood on the porch, and I didn't unlock the door as I looked out at him. "May I help you?"

"Is this the residence of Elisabeth Hollandale?" A tall, rangy man, he shifted from one foot to the other and kept his head down as he looked at a piece of paper in his hand.

I eyed him suspiciously. Bitty's stolen ID could have lured any criminal to her door. He may not look particularly dangerous, but I wasn't about to trust my judgment on that call.

"Yes, it is. Whom shall I say is calling?" I asked.

"David Smith. I brought her car."

"Really?" My suspicions increased. Bitty had just talked to the police, and they'd said her car had been partially stripped and set on fire. "How are the tires?" I asked, and the man sounded slightly confused.

"The tires?"

"Yes, the tires. Are they okay?" That was my crafty way of finding out if he knew what had happened to her car. If he did, then he must be somehow involved.

He shifted from one foot to the other and peered at me through the door. "The tires are brand new, so they're okay as far as I know."

Aha! "Who sent you here, or did you come on your own?" I demanded. "Where did you get this address, Mr. *Smith?*"

"What? My boss gave me this address." He flapped a piece of paper at me. "I told you—I brought her car."

"I'm calling the police. They might be interested in learning just how you got this address and why you're here."

He took two quick steps back away from the door. "Look lady, I was told to deliver the car here. If you're not Elisabeth Hollandale, there's no need to call the cops. I must have got the address wrong."

"I'll bet."

"Who is it, Trinket?" Bitty asked from right behind me.

"Call the police," I hissed at her. "I think he's friends with the guy who stole your car."

Bitty's eyes got big as duck eggs. She stared out the closed security door, and I was glad she hadn't switched it out for the screen door she uses in summer. This one was much sturdier. Since Bitty stood stock-still in the entrance hall, I figured it was up to me to get to the phone. I took a step back, then two, keeping my eye on the guy on the front porch, wondering why he hadn't yet taken off. Maybe he knew we were alone, knew we were unprotected. Maybe he intended to force his way inside.

One of those fancy French phones always sits on a small table in the foyer, and I edged toward it. I heard the man say, "Are you Mrs. Hollandale? I brought your car."

Bitty moved closer. "My car? How could you? I mean, isn't it still impounded?"

"Ma'am, I don't know anything about that. All I'm trying to do is deliver this car. Wait. Here's my manager. Just open the door, and I'll let him explain it to you."

Before I could stop her, the security door swung open. No time for the phone. I lunged toward the alarm pad set into the wall just inside the front door. It had a panic button. About the time another man stepped up onto the porch, I hit the panic button, and all hell broke loose. Sirens blared, sounding like air raid warnings, lights flashed on and off, and the guy at the door hit the porch floor with his hands over his ears. His partner, who must have come to help, nearly fell off the steps into the yard.

Bitty waved her hands in the air and turned in a circle like a dog about to lie down on the floor, shouting something at me. I couldn't hear her. I looked for a weapon. An ornate umbrella stand stood right by the door. I grabbed an umbrella out of it. It was a man's heavy-duty one. I held it like a baseball bat, ready to smack either or both of those men if they tried to get inside.

"Hurry, lock the door and get behind me, Bitty," I yelled, brandishing my weapon in a threatening manner.

She tugged on my arm, but I kept my eyes on the pair of thieves. I was tired of being a piñata for criminals. It was their turn to get knocked around. I had righteous indignation on my side.

The sirens kept blaring, the lights kept flashing, and Bitty had stepped away from me to answer the phone. I have no idea how she heard it. All I heard was those damn sirens wailing away. Then Bitty was back beside me, waving her arms in the air, her mouth moving but the sirens drowning out everything. Before I could stop her, she stepped to the alarm system and hit the button to turn it off.

The sudden silence was heavy and smothering. My ears still rang. Bitty turned around just as the front door opened again and our visitor came inside. Galvanized by fear and shock, I swung my umbrella, and it hit the target with a solid *thwack*! The man staggered sideways with a loud yelp and fell against Bitty. I grabbed her arm and pulled her away from him.

"Run, Bitty," I yelled. "Run!"

I swung blindly in the intruder's direction, once more connecting with my target. My heart pounded so fiercely in my chest, it was nearly as loud as the sirens had been. My mouth was dry, and my lungs worked like bellows, dragging in just enough air to keep me from passing out. I was terrified.

Bitty's face bobbed in front of me again. She waved her arms in the air. "Trinket, wait!"

What was she doing? She should be running, not putting herself right back in danger. I reached for her just as the man pushed up from the floor where my blows had knocked him, and I started to swing again. Bitty grabbed for my umbrella. I jerked it away.

The intruder stood up, and I saw his face just as I got the umbrella free from Bitty's attempt to help. *Rodney Farrell.* Oh no. He had a cut over his eyebrow and a welt on his cheek.

He also had a badge on his chest. I'd been whaling the tar out of him while the criminals were getting away. He put up his hand and said, "Miz Truevine, what the hell are you doing?"

I tightened my grip on the umbrella handle and opened my mouth to explain, but my thumb must have hit the umbrella's release button. It popped open with a loud snap, blotting him from my view with a large black blossom of waterproof nylon.

I looked over at Bitty. She just shrugged.

Chapter 9

"WELL, I DIDN'T KNOW Jackson Lee got them to deliver my new car from Memphis early, Trinket. I was just as surprised as you. Anyway, if Rodney Farrell hadn't been spying on me, he wouldn't have gotten here so quickly. I'm thinking of complaining about police harassment."

"I wouldn't," I said. "That's like whacking a wasp nest with a stick. You'd get them all stirred up and be sorry for it right after."

"Maybe. Although it might be a good excuse to get inside the police station without them suspecting anything."

"If you're still considering your brainless scheme, forget it. It won't work, you'll get arrested, and it's not even necessary. Jackson Lee is taking care of everything."

I sucked down another half-inch of my sweet tea. Daddy had brought my keys right in the middle of all the chaos earlier. Fortunately, he'd explained to Deputy Farrell about all the trouble at the Corinth museum and smoothed over everything by adding how nervous we were about the criminals showing up. My daddy has a lot of credibility. Me and Bitty—not so much.

"I'm going home," I said. "I want a long bath with bubbles up to the ceiling and a good night's sleep. Things will be better tomorrow."

"I'll come get you in the morning. We can take a ride in my new car."

"I'm working in the morning."

"Even better. I'll pick you up afterward. I think we need to go see Deelight and give her our condolences."

"We already did that at Walter's funeral. And Diva Day."

"I meant condolences about being left out of his will."

I sighed. "You're going on a fact-fishing trip, aren't you?"

"Maybe. Well honestly, Trinket, now there are more suspects than ever about who may have wanted Walter dead. Why shouldn't I see what I can find out?"

"Because Jackson Lee hired Catfish Carter to do that. We—and by that I mean *you*—aren't supposed to ask anyone anything that has to do with Walter's death."

"That's just ridiculous. How else am I supposed to talk to the recently bereaved?"

"Sounds to me like most of them are about as bereaved as you are. Take my advice—and I know you won't—let Catfish handle it."

"Honestly, I get hungry for hush puppies every time you say his name," Bitty muttered. "But all right. That doesn't mean we shouldn't see how Deelight is doing, though."

"Only if you promise not to go around asking a lot of silly questions about who hates Walter Simpson the most."

"I wouldn't do that. Not in those words, anyway. Give me some credit, Trinket. I'm not a child."

"I forget that. Sometimes it feels like we're both in junior high again. I'll see you about one tomorrow afternoon, then."

Bitty walked me out to my car. Evening shadows lay low in the sidewalks, but the street lamps hadn't come on yet. Her shiny red Cadillac sat in her driveway. I could almost detect the new car smell from the front sidewalk. My trusty five-year-old Ford Taurus is paid for and still drives great. I have no desire for a car note. It may not have a new car smell, but my insurance isn't so high I can't pay it, either. That was a great comfort as I opened my car door and slid into the driver's seat. It was hot and stuffy, so I switched on the engine and lowered my window.

"Thanks for trying to save me today, Trinket," Bitty said. "That was very sweet and brave of you."

"Right. I assaulted a police officer with an umbrella. I must have looked like a deranged Mary Poppins."

"You did well, Trinket. Honest."

I looked out my window at her. She held Chitling in her arms and waved one of her paws at me. "T'ank oo, Auntie Trinket, for saving my mommy," she cooed in a voice she obviously thought was how the dog would talk. My guess ran more toward a gravelly voice with the faint whiff of brimstone.

I rolled my eyes. "Good lord, it's Zuul, The Gatekeeper, demigod of destruction."

"Looking for The Keymaster to Gozer," Bitty said right back. We know our movies.

"Goodbye, Zuul. Keep away from the Stay Puft Marshmallow Man."

With our homage to *Ghostbusters* over, I pulled away from the curb and smiled halfway home. Bitty is just as crazy as I am, and I don't necessarily mean that in a bad way. We aren't dangerous. Just annoying. And quite often, we're lucky enough to be right about our suspicions when in the general vicinity of a murderer. Or is that unlucky?

After arriving home and giving a lengthy explanation to my parents about all that we had become involved in just in the past twenty-four hours, I went upstairs for my bubble bath. It was pure luxury, lying in the old clawfoot tub with my feet up on the curved edge, listening to music from my CD player I set atop the wicker hamper, letting my mind drift lazily along. I avoided any thoughts of the current situations, instead thinking of my daughter over in Georgia and the recent news that she'd gotten a promotion at her job. I was thrilled for her, especially since she's also taking college classes at night. Michelle has always been a hard worker.

I must have dozed off thinking about her. Suddenly she was there, smiling at me, telling me how excited she was to have a great new job and studying for her master's in business ed. And best, she said, was the fact she was going to have a baby. I was going to be a grandmother! I was half-terrified, half-euphoric. I danced around, then stopped to smile down at my grandson in my arms. I already loved him as much as I did my daughter. He was beautiful, with blond hair like my mother had in her youth, big blue eyes, and a smile that promised a lifetime of joy.

It was one of the best dreams I've ever had.

While I'm not exactly ready to be a grandmother yet, I know that when Michelle does have a baby, I'll be thrilled. Grandparents get the best in their grandchildren, no responsibility and all the fun. It's one of the perks for having survived your children's adolescence with some sanity and money left. If you're very, very lucky.

I was sitting at the kitchen table telling my mother about the dream when the phone rang. It was Kit, calling on the house phone to ask me out to dinner. Not being completely stupid, I said I could be ready in fifteen minutes. He laughed and said he'd pick me up in an hour. There are times when I have the best of both worlds.

It was a beautiful spring night. The sky was clear and full of glittering stars, and the wind was cool and just brisk enough to keep away hungry mosquitoes. We sat at a table outside the restaurant in Red Banks, having fried catfish, hush puppies, and coleslaw. Candlelight flickered, and tiny bulbs lit up the patio. Kit smiled at me, and my heart did a rapid little *thunk-thunk-thunk*. There went my sixteen-year-old reaction to him again.

"I hear you've been keeping busy," he said.

"Already?" I sighed. "You heard correctly. I've been with Bitty. She always has an activity planned whether it's sensible or not."

"Her extracurricular activities give me heartburn. Jackson Lee must have ulcers."

"He's made of sturdier stuff than that. After all, he's used to the company of murderers and arsonists. I hardly think Bitty would affect his health. It's me she's killing."

Kit grinned, and I thought again how handsome he is. "You're made of sturdier stuff than that, too," he said. "You amaze me at times."

"Because I live through Bitty's manic schemes? I'm like a cock-roach. I have the ability to survive nuclear disasters."

"Let's hope that ability isn't needed again in the future."

I tilted my head to the side. "We're talking about Bitty, right? She's a walking disaster. I don't know how she comes up with the things she does, but sometimes, she even makes some off-the-wall scheme seem plausible. That's usually right before everything turns to mud."

Kit lifted his beer in a salute, and I clinked my glass against his. "To less mud and more blue skies," he said, and I nodded.

"I'll drink to that."

"Too bad about Walter," he said once we'd finished our dinner and walked out to his car. "I heard the reading of the will was excit-ing."

"Brett Simon hit Sammy Simpson smack in the mouth and made him bleed. Then he said Sammy had somehow swindled the rest of them, and he'd see him in hell before he got a penny. I think that's when Jackson Lee stepped in to separate them."

"And Brett Simon is an heir, I take it?"

"He's Deevine Faithann Grace Simon's son, Walter's great-grandson. Deevine goes by her middle name now, Faith. For obvious reasons."

"Hunh. She's Deelight Tillman's sister, right?"

I nodded. "She moved away years ago but comes back for family occasions."

"Sounds like her son is a hothead."

"I've never met him. I know Faith is worried about his reactions and wants to get all the mess about the will straightened out before she has to leave town again. She called Rayna to see if she knew an investigator who could help."

Kit opened my car door for me, and when we pulled out of the parking lot, he said, "An investigator into breaking a will might have a difficult time going up against Jackson Lee. I imagine he dotted every *I* and crossed every *T*."

"It's not Jackson Lee's handling that's in question. Apparently, there was an attorney up in Desoto County who wrote a codicil for Walter, giving Sammy everything."

Kit was quiet for a moment; then he said, "You know, I ran into Sammy and Walter up in Southaven not too long ago—about four or five months, I think. It surprised me, since Walter didn't leave Holly Springs that often. Sammy said he'd been seeing a new doctor up there by the Baptist Hospital. Walter was his usual cantankerous self, bullying Sammy like he always did. I wouldn't have thought much of it if Walter hadn't asked me what I thought about a grandson who'd drag him off to a new doctor when he liked the one he had. He went on about it for a few minutes and seemed—well, out of it. He kept ranting about unrelated things—I just thought his new meds weren't agreeing with him so when they left, I didn't think any more about it."

"And now you suspect there might be more?"

"I don't know what to think. Walter wasn't himself, but that happens a lot with older people. New doctors are a part of aging. Their medications have adverse effects or don't work at all. The elderly often tend to blame those closest to them for their problems. They can even have hallucinations. Brain cells misfire. So it could be that Walter was just having a bad day."

I thought about it a moment. "What unrelated things did he rant about?"

"For one thing, lawyers. He called them 'bloodsuckers' and worse. It just seemed at the time to be a random comment along with many others. He rambled on about people stealing from him, how his things were disappearing from the house and so forth."

Surprised, I asked, "Is any of that true, do you think? What kind of things disappeared?"

"Sammy said he'd been insistent that someone stole the kitchen stove and replaced it with an inferior one. Walter agreed with that, saying it looked the same, but he knew it wasn't since his eggs had burned."

"So he was just reflecting medicine or age-related issues. I remember that my grandfather had the same type of problems. He had trouble getting enough oxygen to the brain, I think."

"It's likely that the family members who know about these kinds of issues will use them to challenge the will," Kit said, and I agreed.

Night air filtered in through the open car windows as we drove down 78 Highway, bringing the scents of meadows and cows inside the car. I thought about Walter's behavior right before he died. He'd certainly done a few odd things, but I'd seen nothing like what Kit described. He'd been more upset about wearing a Yankee uniform than anything else.

"I'm sure any investigator the family hires will find out a lot of this," I said. "I'll tell Faith or Deelight to be sure to have him talk to you, if you don't mind."

Kit reached across the seat and took my hand, squeezing it slightly. "That's why I told you about it. It may mean nothing, but if it does, then they'll have the info at hand."

AS IT TURNED out, Kit's information was of great interest to not only Deelight and her sister Faith, but to Jackson Lee as well.

"Knowing the state of mind of an individual who amends his will is an important aspect for those who want to challenge it," he said.

"Are you going to represent the family?" asked Bitty, and Jackson Lee shook his head.

"No. It's a conflict of interest. I represented Walter with his original will, and now I'm Brandon's attorney in the matter of Walter's death. Our firm cannot represent their challenge."

We sat in Bitty's kitchen at her table, drinking sweet tea and going over the information Catfish Carter had relayed in a written report. He was thorough, I had to admit, and even Bitty grudgingly agreed he'd found out a great deal in a relatively short time.

"He's done better than I thought he would," she said. "Maybe people tell him things just so he'll go away."

"Whatever works," Jackson Lee said blandly, and I hid my smile.

"So what we now know is that there were several people at the reenactment who wouldn't have minded seeing Walter Simpson shot, right?" I asked. I pointed to three names on a sheet of paper. "Riley Powers surprises me. The other two, Mitchell King and Royal Stewart aren't that big a shock, I guess. But Royal Stewart was supposed to be in jail. That's why Walter had to wear the blue instead of the gray."

"Royal was released at ten that morning. While he wasn't in uniform, he did attend the reenactment. Mitchell King wore a gray uniform, and Riley Powers was General Van Dorn."

"I wouldn't think Riley would be able to get away with shooting him," I said. "He was on horseback, and everyone was watching him. He'd have to know he'd be seen. What reasons do the three of these people have to dislike Walter enough to shoot him?"

"Over the years, a lot of people have had run-ins with Walter. He wasn't the most popular man in town. He and Riley had a business deal involving a piece of land out by Highway 4. Walter sold it to him as ten acres, but when a surveyor came in, it turned out to be only eight-point-two acres. Walter refused to refund him any money or do anything to make good on it. He said Riley should have checked it out before he bought it, and buyer's remorse didn't get refunds."

"Did Riley take him to court?"

"Yes, but the contract was ambiguous in the size of the parcel and listed it as between eight and ten acres, which it was. Riley didn't read it carefully before he signed it and he lost."

I shook my head. "What about the bank that loaned Riley the money? Surely, they would make sure it was what it was represented to be before issuing payment?"

"Certainly they would have, but Riley paid cash."

Bitty sniffed. "Walter knew what he was doing, the old reprobate."

I agreed. "No wonder Riley was mad at Walter. And Royal? What was his problem with Walter?"

"Royal and Walter had it out after a fender bender. Royal was driving down Memphis Street when Walter came up behind him too fast and hit him in the rear. It dented the fender of his car, and Walter said he'd take care of it if Royal didn't call the police to file a report. It'd make his insurance rates go up, particularly because of his age."

"And then Walter wouldn't pay," I said, and Jackson Lee nodded.

"Right. When Royal showed up with the estimate from the body shop, Walter chased him off his property with a loaded shotgun."

"Were the police called?" Bitty asked.

"Yes, but it was a he-said, he-said situation and nothing was done. Walter had put away the shotgun by the time they got there, and Royal didn't have any witnesses." Jackson Lee shook his head. "Mitchell King sold Walter a lawnmower, and Walter took it back after the summer was over and said that it didn't work and he wanted his money back. Mitchell refused, of course, so Walter stood out in front of his small engine repair shop and told everyone that he did shoddy work and cheated his customers. When police told him he couldn't be on Mitchell's property, Walter just stood across the street with a sign. It infuriated Mitchell."

"You know," I said, "I don't feel nearly as bad about not giving Walter the gray uniform after all."

Jackson Lee laughed. "He was something else, even before he got old and senile."

"I'll say." I shook my head. "I'm glad I didn't know him better. Then I'd be on the short list of people with reasons to shoot him."

Bitty scooted her chair back from the table. "Well, all those people have reasons to kill Walter, and Brandon doesn't, so I don't see why the police won't drop the charges against him."

"We have to show cause, sweetings," said Jackson Lee. "I'll file motions. It's not as simple as just saying he didn't have motive so he shouldn't be charged. His fingerprints are on the murder weapon, and he was there."

"Isn't all that circumstantial evidence or something like that?" Bitty asked.

Jackson Lee nodded. "Yes, but it's an inference that can add up to corroborating evidence when presented. There's a video showing him aiming the rifle almost straight at Walter. That's direct evidence. We have to show that Brandon didn't know the rifle was loaded, that he didn't deliberately aim the weapon at Walter, and that the rifle was long-held to be inoperable. We have to muddy the waters, in other words."

It sounded nearly impossible, and I saw from Bitty's face that she thought so too. It's hard to prove a negative, and that essentially is what Jackson Lee had to do.

After Jackson Lee left, I thought Bitty might cry. Instead, she drew herself up, sucked in a deep breath, and said, "Let's go comfort Deelight."

Even though I knew it wasn't just a mission of mercy, I nodded. "I'm ready when you are, Jessica."

"Jessica?"

"Jessica Fletcher. *Murder, She Wrote*. You know. Angela Lansbury."

"Good lord, Trinket. I'm much younger than the character she played. Although I do admit, I'm not bad as an amateur sleuth. Maybe better than her, since she had a script, and I'm dealing with real-life killers."

It was my turn to say, "Good lord."

When we arrived at Deelight's house, her sister was still there, and so was Brett Simon. One look at his face was enough to tell me he was furious. A rangy young man with blond hair already thinning on top, Brett paced back and forth in Deelight's living room. Faith perched on the flowered sofa, hands clasped around her knees, a worried expression on her face.

Bitty sat on the couch between the two and turned to Deelight. "Oh honey, I'm sorry that things haven't worked out. I just can't imagine what Walter was thinking."

"Neither can I," said Deelight with a sigh. "I thought I was going to fall out on the floor when Jackson Lee read the codicil. My mama would be shocked by all this. I mean, it just flies in the face of family tradition. The Simpsons have always held together at family tragedies. I just cannot imagine why he'd do this."

"You know," Faith said, "it's not the loss of any part of the inheritance that bothers me, as much as it is the way it was done. Sammy should have told us about the codicil. For that matter, our grandfather should have told us."

"How long ago was the codicil written?" I asked.

"In January. The twentieth, I think," Deelight answered.

"Four months ago. Kit saw Walter and Sammy in Southaven about that time. He said Walter was complaining about lawyers, among other things. There may be a connection if you want to check it out," I said. "Perhaps there's been a mistake."

Brett wheeled around to look at me. Rage twisted his features. "Sammy forced Walter to name him as sole heir. I'm sure of that. He's been living with him for three years and had plenty of time to talk him into cutting out the rest of us. My mother should have her fair share! It's not right, and I'm not going to stand for it."

Faith reached out a hand to snag his shirt sleeve. "Brett, honey— it's not as if I expected to get much of anything. The house and land always goes to the oldest direct descendant, and that would be Mama's brother, Uncle George. Not even he is supposed to inherit it all. I knew all that, and it's never been about the money or house. Not for me, anyway. I wanted just a few things, the painting in the dining room and one of the Limoges vases that Grandmother collected over the years. That's what was agreed upon, nothing else."

"Yes, we all chose something," Deelight agreed. "I asked for one of the Fabergé eggs our great-grandmother collected. Grandmother used to take them out of the display cabinet and let me touch them when I was little."

"Only children and grandchildren inherit," Faith explained to me and Bitty. "Unless there are no living children or grandchildren, and then the house and land would go to the eldest niece or nephew. In this case, that's not an issue."

"So you're only going to inherit the things like the eggs and vases?" I asked.

Faith shook her head. "We get nothing. Not so much as a pencil, according to the codicil. I don't understand it."

"That seems extreme. Walter surely left you the things you were already promised."

Deelight shook her head. "No, everything was left to Sammy. If he wants to keep to the promises already made, that will be up to him."

"Everything?" Bitty echoed in astonishment. "That's awful!"

"It's complicated," Deelight said.

"It's not tradition," said Faith.

"It's outright theft," Brett said loudly. He was fuming. I thought steam would come out of his ears at any moment, he was that mad.

Bitty and I shut up. It seemed the wisest thing at the moment.

Deelight managed a smile and asked, "More tea or cake?"

I still had half a glass of sweet tea and a few bites left of Hummingbird cake. Bitty took more tea and "a small piece of cake," so that left us alone in the living room with Faith and Brett.

Bitty immediately leaned forward and asked in a hushed tone, "Who do you think killed Walter?"

Faith started to shake her head, but her son had no qualms about replying: "Sammy. He's the only one who stood to gain. Of course he killed him!"

I could tell Faith was caught between wondering if Brandon had really killed him or if it was someone else, so I said, "The police will no doubt find the real killer eventually. It's unlikely that someone deliberately loaded live ammunition in a rifle being used in a crowd of people."

Brett turned to look at me. "I wouldn't put it past Sammy. He directed the reenactment, didn't he? He'd have known who was supposed to be where."

"That's true, but it's rather obvious. Would he be foolish enough to commit murder in front of half the town and busloads of tourists? I don't think so."

"Walter is dead, isn't he? Someone killed him. I don't for a minute think it was just an accident."

I hesitated, then said, "It seems extremely risky to shoot someone in full view of all those people. I just keep thinking it has to be an accident of some kind."

"Are you kidding?" Brett stared at me. "It's the perfect alibi. Sammy wanted Walter dead, so what better way to do it than have it look like an unexpected tragedy?"

"But what you're forgetting is that my nephew was arrested for something he didn't do, even accidentally. The heirloom rifle he carried is incapable of firing. I don't know how it might have happened, but I do know that Brandon didn't deliberately shoot him. And since he had the rifle that did kill him, it couldn't have been Sammy. It's dangerous to go around accusing a man unless you're positive he did it, you know."

Brett snorted. "I'll risk it."

Faith stood up. "I wish you wouldn't talk like that. It's bad enough that all this has happened. Must you make it worse, Brett?"

"I'm sorry. Maybe I should go on back home. I'm only upsetting you, and that's not why I came."

Faith patted his arm and said softly, "We're all upset. First the shock of his death, then the funeral, now all this about the will. . . . It's just too much. None of us are ourselves lately."

I had the thought that some of us hadn't changed too much as Deelight returned, and Bitty took her second piece of cake with a smile. "Thank you, Deelight. Faith, Brett may be right, you know. It's true that my son had nothing to do with loading the gun that killed Walter, but Sammy has to be the most obvious suspect. Who benefits the most from Walter's death? He does. And since Walter didn't drive anymore, you know Sammy had to be the one to take him to a new lawyer to write up that codicil. I wonder whose idea *that* was. Somehow, I doubt it was Walter's."

As Bitty took a bite of cake, I hurried to fill the appalled silence. "Of course, all that is just conjecture. None of us know what might have happened. The police are still investigating."

"Not to mention Catfish," said Bitty after the bite of cake disappeared. "He's running around town asking a lot of questions and poking his nose where it shouldn't be, so maybe the truth will come out soon."

Faith blinked in bewilderment, and I explained, "Catfish is the name of an investigator who's trying to find out what happened."

"Oh," she said. "I think I heard that Jackson Lee had hired someone to help. He's been doing some work at the insurance offices."

"I thought y'all didn't have anything to do with the insurance office anymore," said Bitty. "Not since Walter sold it, anyway."

"Brett works at a branch of MetLife, the parent company. They do the underwriting."

"And Catfish Carter has been doing some work there?" Bitty asked.

I could almost see the wheels turning in her hamster-brain. When she turned to look at me, I said, "No. Leave him alone. He knows what he's doing."

"For heaven's sake, Trinket. I wasn't going to suggest we bother him."

"Good. He's doing just fine without us."

"Of course he is." Bitty ate the last bite of cake and stood up. "Where shall I put this, Deelight?"

There was the usual polite exchange of Bitty offering to clean up and our hostess saying she would do it later, and after a few more minutes of light conversation we left. As we went out to Bitty's car, I said, "Well, that was slick, Ace Ventura."

"What are you talking about? A pet detective movie? Did you put whiskey in your tea?"

"No, but it sounds like a good idea. Honestly, Bitty, you were about as subtle as a tank. Why were you accusing Sammy of murder?"

"Doesn't it seem odd to you that he's the only one who benefits?"

"It seems sad and disappointing. But we can't go around accusing him of murder, Bitty. Not to his relatives, anyway."

"Maybe the police need a nudge in the right direction."

I opened the car door and turned to look at her. "Don't even think about it. If you do, I'll tell Jackson Lee that you're not keeping your word."

"Did I say I'm going to do anything?" She slid behind the wheel of her car, and I bent to get into the passenger seat. The Cadillac still had that wonderful new car smell, and I breathed it in for a moment. Bitty started the car, and the engine purred. I closed my car door before trying to talk sense to her again.

"You don't have to say you're going to do anything. You just do it, and then it's too late. I know you're worried about Brandon, but getting things tangled up won't help him."

"I think Sammy did it, Trinket. He's the only one who benefits. He has motive, he had opportunity, and he had the murder weapon. He switched it with our rifle. I'm sure of it. I don't know how he did it, but I know he did."

I hated to admit it to her, but it sounded plausible. The more I heard, the more plausible it became that Sammy Simpson had been responsible for his grandfather's death. He got the most benefit, and he had been there. Then again, even though I'd been not fifty feet away, I *hadn't* seen him shoot Walter. I hadn't seen anyone shoot Walter. No one had really seen Walter shot.

The reenactment had been the perfect screen for murder.

Chapter 10

"YOU KNOW HE DID it, Trinket."

"Maybe," I said, still unwilling to let Bitty know I agreed with her. That could lead to acts of idiocy on her part. She'd have us staking out his house or breaking and entering to get evidence. I wasn't up for that.

We had renewed the subject of Sammy's guilt as we sat out on her front porch waiting for Jackson Lee to come by. He had another report from Catfish Carter, and I was interested in hearing what the investigator had to say next. He'd been pretty good so far. About every four days, he handed in a report, and Jackson Lee faithfully brought it straight to Bitty. As far as I knew, he didn't leave anything out. It'd been four days since the last report, and I wondered if this one would incriminate Sammy.

"Deelight said Faith left this morning. Brett left yesterday," Bitty commented, and I looked over at her, waiting for her to elaborate. She didn't disappoint. "Apparently Brett made a big scene at Rosewood, and Sammy called the police, and they told him he couldn't go back there without the owner's permission. Soooo . . ."

"The owner being Sammy Simpson," I said, when it became obvious she wanted me to respond. "And he said none of the family can show up at Rosewood."

"Yep. None of Walter's grandkids or even his son George can step foot on that property unless Sammy invites them. Or at least, gives them permission to visit."

"That's one way to avoid trouble, I suppose."

"Or a way to keep everything for himself. He's greedy, Trinket. I think he's planned this for a long time. We have to stop him."

"*We* don't have to do anything. There are people a lot more qualified who can do a much better job. Trust me."

Bitty eyed me over the rim of her wine glass. I tried to ignore that. I knew how badly she wanted to find someone to blame besides Brandon for Walter's death; I did too. But getting in the way of the truth wouldn't help any of us. If the two of us got involved in any kind of awkward situation, it could blow up in our faces.

Bitty responds to catastrophe with action. I respond to catastrophe with retreat. I like to know what I'm getting into. Bitty is more, *Full speed ahead and damn the torpedoes.*

There are drawbacks to both responses.

Fortunately, Jackson Lee arrived before Bitty could try to persuade me that we should stop Sammy Simpson from getting everything. I lifted my wine glass in a salute.

"You're just in time, Mr. Brunetti. What news have you brought your fair maiden today, or should I ask?"

Jackson Lee smiled at my obvious attempt at levity. He probably figured that Bitty was getting restless. Keeping her well-informed was his way of putting off her eventual involvement in the situation. It was inevitable, but if he could keep her in line for as long as possible, perhaps there was a chance things might be resolved before she did too much damage.

"For one thing, an antique gun expert disputes the original findings that the rifle Brandon held is the only one that could have fired the fatal bullet. How does that sound?"

Bitty sucked in a sharp breath. "*Really?* You mean he says the gun doesn't work? That it couldn't have fired the bullet that killed Walter?"

Jackson Lee dragged a wicker chair over to sit by us, looking much too big for the fragile chair. "No, I didn't say that, sweetpea. He disputes that the bullet could be fired by only that one weapon. It may have fired the bullet—but there are other old rifles that could have fired it too. Apparently, the bullet was mangled enough to make it doubtful."

"Oh. Well . . . that's good, right?"

"That's definitely good. I'm sure now that we can make this go away. No charges can stick if there's doubt that the gun Brandon held fired the fatal shot. Along with the other people Catfish found with actual motives for wanting Walter dead, I can make a pretty strong case for a dismissal."

Bitty sat rock still for a moment, then she heaved a big sigh of relief. "Then he's safe."

"He will be safe. Just hang in there, sugar-pie."

I relaxed and realized I'd been holding my breath. Relief swamped me. I looked over at Bitty and saw her smiling from ear to ear. Maybe this was all over. Brandon would be cleared of any charges, and our personal lives would go back to normal. Whatever normal is. At least, none of us would be charged with murder.

"So who do you think killed Walter?" Bitty asked. "Someone did. And it wasn't an accident. I'm pretty sure of that."

Jackson Lee riffled through some papers in a folder he pulled out of his briefcase. "That will be the police's problem, sweetie. All we have to do is get Brandon cleared of charges. Here. I have Catfish Carter's latest report. It sums up his findings. There are enough ambiguities for the police to follow up. There's no shortage of other people with motive, as you'll see when you read through it."

"Catfish isn't so bad after all," Bitty said after a moment. She flipped over another page of the report. "Although he doesn't say who he thinks is responsible for Walter's death."

"That's not his job. He just lists facts. I do the conjecturing." Jackson Lee smiled. "And I provide facts so the prosecutor can decide if he wants to risk losing in court."

"That's good. What do you think of him? The new prosecutor, I mean?"

"Hard to say. I haven't gone up against him yet, but he seems pretty sharp. He's an Ole Miss law school graduate moving closer to home." Jackson Lee looked over at me. "So now that the worst is over, you ladies can get back to life as usual. I'm filing for dismissal and don't expect any unpleasant surprises."

I read between the lines: *Keep Bitty from doing anything outrageous.*

That was a lot easier to ask than to accomplish, but I didn't anticipate any problems. Her determination to keep him from going to jail had succeeded. Brandon would be safe. I smiled as I left them alone for a few minutes to exchange nauseatingly sweet endearments.

After Jackson Lee left, Bitty turned to me and said, "I need more wine. So do you. We need to free our minds to figure out what to do about this."

I followed her into the kitchen. "Do about what? And there's not enough wine in all of Mississippi to free our minds from jail, if you're still talking about snooping around."

"Sometimes your views are so limited, Trinket. Expand your mind. Dream the impossible dream. Reach for the horizons."

"Good lord, when did you start channeling Timothy Leary? If you start chanting 'tune in, turn on, drop out,' I'm going home."

"How about 'question authority' as a quote? That's one of your old favorites."

"I was such a rebel. I drew the line at LSD, however, so don't even go there. I was never into illicit drugs. Or even legal drugs. My preference for mind-altering substances is limited to liquid enhancement like wine or other delicious products of distilling processes."

"I'm in complete agreement with that viewpoint. More Zinfandel?"

Bitty poured us both another glass of wine, and we went back out onto her front porch to enjoy the balmy weather. April is usually almost perfect. Except for rain and the occasional tornado, it's the kind of weather that makes Mississippians want to linger outdoors. May is good up until the last week or so, and June turns so hot, crawfish can boil in muddy ditches. July is like a blast from an iron-smelting furnace, and August has temperatures that rival our solar system's hottest planet, Venus. September usually limps in with sultry days for the first couple weeks, then drifts into more bearable temperatures in October. Once upon a time in the olden days when I was a child, the end of September was coat and gloves weather. Now it's shorts and tee shirt weather most of the time. I won't argue the cause, just the effect: our planet is heating up.

"So what do you think we should do first?" my reckless cousin asked, jerking me from my pleasant reverie of heat-scorched planets. "Talk to Sammy or interview Royal, Mitchell, and Riley?"

"Do you really want me to answer that? You won't like my reply." I sucked down an inch or two of wine in anticipation of her response.

"There's always the insurance company, I suppose. We can find out who the investors were and if they were mad enough at Walter to try to kill him."

"Brandon is going to be exonerated. There's no need for us to do anything. Let the police handle it. They have excellent methods and manpower."

"Yes, that would be lovely, Trinket, but we both know they're hampered by all the rights criminals have these days. We don't have to Mirandize or provide search warrants."

"We don't have to do anything. We're no longer involved. It's none of our business who killed Walter."

"I think Brett was right. It has to be Sammy who killed him. We just have to figure out how he did it. He must have switched the rifles. I really need to get in the evidence room and inspect my rifle."

"Wait a while, and it'll be returned to you. As soon as Jackson Lee gets the charges against Brandon dismissed, you should be able to get it back."

"If you, Gaynelle, and Rayna provide the distraction, I can get in there and sneak it out. I mean, it's my property, so it's not like I'm really stealing anything."

I stared at her. "Have you heard a word I've said? There's no reason for us to get any more involved than we've already been—it's over."

Bitty cuddled her bug-eyed little gargoyle closer to her chest, stroking the fur between Chitling's ears. "Of course, I could do it myself, but it'd be so much easier with your help."

"Are you insane? It can't be the heat because it's not hot enough yet, so I doubt you've had a heat stroke. How much wine have you had today?"

At last she looked at me. "Not enough, or your disinterest wouldn't bother me."

"Bitty—Brandon's charges will be dismissed. You know that, right?"

"Yes, Trinket, I know that. But surely you realize that until the real killer is found, he'll still be considered guilty by some people?"

"Do you really care what some people think?"

"Not usually. But I've no intention of letting anyone say that Brandon is like his father. Frank was guilty and should have gone to prison, but for the first few years after all the scandal, I could barely hold my head up in this town. He cheated people we knew, friends, even family, and I thought it'd never die down. It wasn't just me who had to deal with stares, whispers, the speculation that I was somehow aware of what he was doing or even involved. I don't want my sons to go through anything like that again."

For a moment I was silent. I hadn't lived in Holly Springs when all that happened ten years ago, but I knew how it must have hurt Bitty to go through the humiliation of having her husband accused, then arrested, tried, and convicted of investment fraud, perjury, and false statements. He's serving time in a Federal prison and probably has a hot tub in his cell while those he cheated try to scrape together enough money to pay their rent.

"I understand," I said at last, and Bitty nodded.

"I knew you would."

"That doesn't mean I want to risk a prison term doing something crazy and reckless. I'm not sure I'd do well in jail."

"I have a foolproof idea—"

"NO," I said as loudly as I could. "Not just no, but hell no!"

Bitty lifted her waxed, perfect eyebrows. "My, my, that's rather emphatic."

"Yes, it is. Pay attention. One of these days your schemes are going to get us maimed, killed, or locked up for ten to twenty. I empathize with your need to exonerate Brandon. I do. But there are times when it's much wiser to sit back and wait, than it is to rush out and do something stupid."

"We've already been maimed a few times," Bitty reminded after a brief silence.

"Yes, but not permanently. I'm in no hurry to change that."

"Fine, we'll talk about it another time."

I rolled my eyes. "Heaven forbid."

Bitty leaned over her familiar and whispered in the pug's ear. Chitling fixed me with a baleful stare. Sometimes I think she understands whatever nonsense Bitty imparts in her floppy little ears. It's a bit scary.

"They're returning my Mercedes tomorrow," Bitty said after a moment, and I gratefully seized the change of conversational topic.

"With or without the tires?"

"Jackson Lee had them put on new tires, check it for other damage, and clean it. So the Franklin Benz rolls again."

"Did the police find the thieves?"

"Not yet."

"Will my purse be in it?" I asked.

Bitty blinked. "Why . . . I don't know. I didn't ask. There's always that possibility."

"I still haven't replaced my driver's license. The thought of waiting in line at the DMV is pretty horrifying."

"What about your bank card?"

"Oh, I did that first thing. What little I have, I like to keep. That's why I don't play the stock market."

"If you ever want to invest, I can put you in touch with my broker," Bitty offered, and I shook my head.

"No, thanks. I'd rather just set fire to my money than put it in the hands of someone who has very little personal stake in using it."

"But they get money if they make you money, Trinket."

"I follow the Edward Truevine school of thought on that issue. They don't mind taking risks with other people's money, not their own, so I choose not to participate in that dangerous game."

"Very safe of you. Not particularly beneficial, but safe."

"If you're making fun of me, I don't care. I'm fine just the way I am. I'm not in debt, and I like it that way. What I don't have, I don't need."

"'But you ain't got no legs, Lieutenant Dan,'" Bitty quoted *Forrest Gump.*

"'Yes . . . yes, I know that, you idiot,'" I paraphrased right back at her.

Bitty smiled. "Well, if you're happy without money, that's fine, I suppose. Money may not make you happy, but the lack of enough can make you miserable."

"That's very philosophical, Bitty," I said. "Sometimes you surprise me."

"Sometimes I surprise myself. I've been rereading a few classics lately, trying to get my mind off all the troubles. At first it was okay, you know, Austen and Brontë. Then I read a few other authors, and I've decided that far too many classics are depressing."

"Let me guess—Thomas Hardy?"

"*Jude the Obscure.* What a downer. I realize it's a classic and has to do with social mores of the times, religion and all that, but really? All that death, disappointment, and tragedy? Give me the *Daily News* anytime. It has death, disappointment, and tragedy but in a much more optimistic way."

I barely kept from rolling my eyes. "Hardy's work reflected a feminism ahead of its time and socialist views. It's a devastating portrayal of a man conflicted with repressed sexuality, who makes bad choices and inevitably suffers the consequences."

Bitty lifted her nicely waxed eyebrows. "Other than that, it's a laugh a minute. I'd rather read obituaries."

"In a way, you did. But never mind. Read Dickens or Lewis Carroll. They're much more entertaining."

"I love *Alice in Wonderland* and *Through the Looking Glass,*" said Bitty. "'The time has come, the walrus said, to talk of many things. Of shoes—and ships—and sealing wax—of cabbages and kings.'"

"'And why the sea is boiling hot and whether pigs have wings,'" I finished. We may quote a lot of TV and movies, but on occasion, we can quote more cerebral characters, if you want to think of Lewis Carroll as highbrow. "You know there are people who analyze the Alice books and compare the characters to religious and political views, don't you?" I added.

"That thought gives me a headache. Why can't people just enjoy the book?"

"Some people have to give every act a deeper meaning," I said. "Not everyone has an ulterior motive behind their words, thoughts, or actions."

"If you're talking about me, I don't know whether to be insulted or pleased."

"See what I mean? You're thinking I had an ulterior motive in my comment."

"Yes, sorry. Maybe that's just experience talking."

I smiled. "Maybe it is."

"Then again, it could be the wine."

"That's possible, too."

Afternoon shadows deepened to dusk as we sat on the porch listening to a symphony of crickets serenade us as night fell. It was peaceful, the quiet broken only by the occasional bark of a dog or slow passing of a car down the tree-lined street. Small town America at its best. A Mayberry of sorts, I fancied, although more sophisticated people might view it as a town too large to be as simple as Mayberry, and too small to be as urbane as Memphis. Holly Springs sits on the cusp of both worlds.

I can walk the downtown area in less than fifteen minutes unless I run into people I know from church or my childhood. Then my walk may run to an hour or so, depending on if I've been greeted by a dear old thing or a former school friend. Dear old things are little old ladies who have little else in life to do other than reminisce, usually about the past crimes of people they've known since childhood. Sometimes the past and present intermingle to produce conversations that are often fraught with consternation and confusion.

Mrs. Tyree, who lives next door to Bitty and has occupied her home for over twenty years, is an excellent example of a sharp-witted dear old thing. She's a tiny little woman who started a cleaning dynasty back during the aftermath of civil rights and Rosa Parks. Bitty's maid Maria was employed through her former company. Mrs. Tyree can be a force of nature.

Therefore, as she appeared on the sidewalk in front of Bitty's house, pushed open the iron picket-gate, and came up the bricked path with a determined set of her narrow shoulders and a grim expression on her face, Bitty said, "Uh oh. I hope Chen Ling hasn't been pooping in her flower beds again."

Ida Tyree's wooden cane tapped against brick as she approached. She wore an elegant dress with a slim skirt that probably cost more than I made in a month, sensible shoes that were stylish, and a gorgeous gold chain around her neck. A Pandora bracelet jangled on her slender wrist as she put one hand atop the other on the crook of her cane, positioning herself on the bottom step.

"Good afternoon, Mrs. Tyree," Bitty said. "Care to join us? We're drinking wine."

"Don't mind if I do," said Mrs. Tyree. "Although I prefer sweet tea. I'm not that fond of strong spirits."

"No problem," Bitty assured her, and got up and pulled a chair closer to us, then went inside to fetch a glass of tea.

That left me alone with Mrs. Tyree. She scares me a little, in the same way a teacher used to scare me, with that knowing glint in her eye and lifted brow, as if she knows exactly what I've been up to and disapproves.

"It's good to see you weren't too terribly affected by being witness to a murder," she said as she sat down in the cushioned wicker chair next to me. "Or should I say, another murder?"

Mrs. Tyree is tactful. We'd become notorious for finding bodies in the last year, not the kind of fame I prefer. I blame Bitty's last husband, since he went and got himself murdered, and we had to be the ones to find him. It was very unpleasant. Unfortunately, it seemed to encourage other murders in our vicinity. Or maybe it was just our luck to know people who got murdered. Bad luck must be contagious.

I managed a smile and tried for a light tone. "Our reputation has spread, I see."

"Indeed. You and Bitty have become famous."

"Some say infamous."

A twinkle lit her dark brown eyes, and a smile curved her mouth. "Yes, that, too."

"It's very inconvenient," I confided. "My parents sometimes look at me as if I have two heads. If I knew how to control this newfound talent, I would be more than happy to live the rest of my life without falling over another body."

"I can well imagine. Do the police still think Brandon did it?"

"He's not yet been cleared as a suspect, but Jackson Lee is working on that."

She nodded. "If anyone can get him cleared, it's Jackson Lee."

A lot of Holly Springs' residents have that view of Jackson Lee. It may be part education, part sharp wits, and part magic, but he has an excellent track record defending his clients.

By the time Bitty returned with Mrs. Tyree's glass of sweet tea, we had moved on in our discussion to the issue of property taxes and politicians. We'd decided we weren't in favor of either.

"Politicians lie," I said to bring Bitty up to date on our conversation.

"Tell me about it," said Bitty as she gave Mrs. Tyree her glass. "My marriage to the senator was a lesson in restraint. Not his—mine. I couldn't believe that he felt it perfectly fine to lie about everything. But of course, the man didn't have the morals of a billy goat, a requirement to win and hold any public office. I think it's even written in the bylaws: No Morals Allowed. Do you need more wine, Trinket?"

"No, I'm good. Two glasses are my limit when I might have to drive."

"Do you ever hear from the Hollandale family?" Mrs. Tyree asked, adding, "I was told Miss Parrish asked my cousin Nettie about you not long ago."

I nearly choked on a sip of tea. Old ghosts kept popping up. It made me wonder if the universe was trying to tell us something.

Bitty echoed my concern. "Good God, that's the second time in recent memory I've been asked about them. I hope this isn't a cosmic warning they're going to show up soon."

"There's no reason why they should," I said. "All litigation is over with now. The senator's estate has been settled and all claims satisfied. Including yours."

"Yes, one would think they would appreciate all I did for Philip during our marriage, but instead, they tried to cheat his poor widow."

I remembered it a bit differently: "You weren't married to him when he was killed, Bitty, so you were never technically his widow."

She peered at me over the rim of her wine glass, eyes narrowing a bit. "Yes, Trinket. I know. But I was married to him long enough to earn the divorce settlement they tried to cheat me out of after he was murdered, and I deserved that money."

"Yes," I agreed. "You certainly did. Philip treated you horribly. Thank heavens you have Jackson Lee now."

That smoothed her ruffled feathers. She smiled. "Yes, I do, don't I?"

Mrs. Tyree sipped her tea, then leaned forward, her voice soft as she said to Bitty, "It will be just fine with Brandon. You'll see. Mr. Brunetti is wonderful at these things."

We all nodded, then Mrs. Tyree added, "Besides, I know who

killed Walter Simpson."

I stared at her while Bitty nearly dropped her wine glass, sloshing some of it over her lap and pug.

"Excuse me?" I asked politely, a tad worried that Mrs. Tyree may have suffered some kind of mental aberration.

I needn't have worried. She sounded quite sane when she repeated, "I know who killed Walter Simpson. I overheard him talking about it at Budgie's the day before yesterday."

I looked over at Bitty, who was busily wiping wine from her damp pug, and she looked back at me. Then we both looked at Mrs. Tyree.

"Do tell," we chorused, and she smiled.

Chapter 11

"WELL," SAID THE elderly center of our attention after she took a delicate sip of tea, "I sat at the table in the corner, where I've sat once every week for the past twenty years, and I suppose I was out of sight, or he wouldn't have talked so loud. It's been my experience that most people think the elderly have lost their hearing anyway, so they don't credit us with the sense God gave a goose, but as you see, it's not true of everyone."

Bitty and I nodded our earnest agreement, and I urged, "You are so right. Do go on."

"Budgie has chicken fried steak and milk gravy as the special every Tuesday; you can't make it yourself as cheap as she sells it in the special. It's always pretty crowded in there on Tuesdays. Budgie had just brought my plate to me when the oldest Grace sister came in and sat down with a young man at the table right behind mine. You know who I mean?"

"Yes. Faithann Grace, now Faith Simon," Bitty said. Her hand stilled atop Chen Ling's head, her huge diamond ring glinting in the fading daylight. "Who was with her?"

Nodding, Mrs. Tyree said, "Yes, that's her. It must have been her son who was with her. He called her Mama. Thirty-ish, hair thinning on top, angry."

"Brett Simon." I glanced at Bitty then back at our elderly visitor. "He's rather disturbed by the reading of the Simpson will."

"I gathered as much by the direction of their conversation," she said wryly. "Normally, I don't eavesdrop. It's rude. My mama would have boxed my ears for it. But he spoke so loudly, I couldn't help but overhear before his mama shushed him." She paused to take another sip of tea.

Bitty and I waited, probably looking like two hound dogs leaning forward with our ears perked, heads cocked to the side to catch every word. Mrs. Tyree held her tea glass between her palms and smiled, recognizing an attentive audience.

"They weren't sitting there two seconds before he came out and said, 'I loaded that gun myself, Mama. I aimed it right at him.' I nearly fell out when I heard that, but I kept on eating. His mama hushed him pretty quickly and said that they were just going to have to put it all behind them as best they could. Now that Walter was buried and the will read, there wasn't any reason for them to stay in town any longer."

Flabbergasted, I didn't know what to say. Bitty did.

"We need to call the police immediately. Call Jackson Lee. Call Catfish Carter." Bitty stood up, excitement in her voice. Clutching Chen Ling tightly to her ample bosom, she added, "I think we should notify the prosecuting attorney, too, and get the ball rolling."

I hated to burst her bubble, I really did. "Bitty," I said gently, "just where do you think you can roll that ball? What Mrs. Tyree just told us is important and definitely something to get Catfish to look into, but it's not firm evidence. It's what Jackson Lee would call hearsay."

Bitty looked disappointed, then quickly rallied. "Well, we have what I call a witness. Would you be willing to tell this to the police and Jackson Lee, Mrs. Tyree?"

"Of course. That's why I came over here. Oh, except for one more thing. My gardener stepped in a pile of pug-size poo and tracked it all over my back deck."

"I'm so sorry. Lately she's been getting away from me so fast. There must be a hole in our fence. Shall I send someone over to clean it up?"

"No, it's already been cleaned. I just thought you should know she's been getting loose. She may get lost if she wanders too far."

Mrs. Tyree is too polite and well-bred to say what she really thinks, but it was evident in her tactful comment that she didn't appreciate pug poo on her porch. Bitty apologized again and scolded Chitling, even though the dog looked more bored than ashamed.

I looked at Mrs. Tyree and smiled. "I'm sure whoever found her would bring her right back. Just like in an O'Henry story. Once they found out what they had, they'd be eager to get rid of her."

Mrs. Tyree laughed. "Yes, she is a rather spoiled little thing. If she wasn't so cute, she couldn't get away with it."

"Are we talking about Bitty or the dog?" I asked, and Bitty said something tart and Mrs. Tyree laughed again.

Still shaking her head, she said, "You two remind me of my sister Ruth and how we used to carry on. She's been gone nearly ten years now, and I still miss her every day."

"You should join us at our next meeting," Bitty said after a moment of contemplative silence. "I think you'd enjoy it."

"Lord no, child! I remember the last one I attended. I don't have the stamina or stomach for some of the stuff you ladies get up to, and that's the truth. I'm fine watching y'all from a distance." She set her empty tea glass on the little wicker table and stood up. "Thank you for the tea and hospitality. Let me know how it works out with the police. I'll be glad to go in and make a statement anytime they want me."

Bitty could hardly wait to call Jackson Lee. He expressed cautious enthusiasm that I could hear from my spot huddled in the parlor chair close by. I contemplated the impact of Mrs. Tyree's revelations. On one hand, it added to the suspect pool and lent validation to our suspicion of Faith's son; on the other, it only muddied the waters.

I wondered what Jackson Lee thought about it all, and in only a few minutes, I had my question answered as Bitty hung up her cell phone and gave me a triumphant smile.

"He's contacting Catfish immediately. Just to confirm, of course. I know it has to be Brett Simon now."

"Fifteen minutes ago, you were positive it was Sammy," I argued and was dismissed with a wave of her hand.

"Roll with the flow, Trinket, roll with the flow."

I rolled my eyes instead. "Honestly, Bitty, sometimes you worry me."

"I don't know why. This is all coming together at last. Brandon won't be suspected of something he didn't do."

"That was already decided when the gun expert gave his deposition," I said. "I don't think it's wise to run around saying that Brett is the killer until he's been arrested and convicted."

"So you think he's guilty too," she said with a wide smile.

"I didn't say that. Although it's a definite possibility."

We were still discussing—arguing—about the social rules in accusing a friend's son of murder when Bitty's doorbell rang. Chen Ling is a reliable backup just in case we don't hear it, and for several moments, neither of us could hear anything but indignant pug. While I tried to shush her, Bitty opened the door. Our visitor did not assuage the dog's indignation. Strangers tend to have that effect on Chitling.

Panting from my efforts at catching an old pug with bowed legs and more determination packed into fifteen pounds than most fifty-pound pit bulls, once I had her firmly in my grasp I looked up to see Catfish Carter stepping into the entrance hall. I nearly dropped a pug.

"Mr. Carter," I managed to say, wheezing a little from hefting a heavy, wiggling dog while trying to remain upright, "what a surprise."

"Life is full of surprises, dollface. Nasty ones, nice ones; the big wheel just keeps on turning."

Ignoring the CCR chorus of "Proud Mary" that immediately popped into my head, I stepped aside as Bitty showed him into her living room. My cousin, however, showed no such restraint.

She sang about big wheels turnin' as she seated him on the uncomfortable horsehair settee infamous for rearranging spinal alignments in guests.

At first Catfish looked confused, then he said, "Rollin' on the river, right? Yeah. I get it. John Fogerty."

"CCR and Tina Turner," I added, contributing my limited musical knowledge to the strange conversation. "CCR is my favorite version."

"She's talking about Creedence Clearwater Revival," Bitty said when Catfish gave me a baffled stare. "Now that we have that out of the way—I assume you've heard the good news?"

"Do you mean that your son may be cleared of suspicion? Yes, I heard that."

"So I assume you have been taken off the case now?"

Catfish shook his head. "I'm working a related case now, dollface. What can you tell me about Sammy Simpson?" He shot me a glance as well, lifting a bushy eyebrow. He reminded me of a portly Groucho Marx. All he needed was a cigar and a sneer.

I kept my mouth shut and let Bitty wade in with both feet.

"He's an unprincipled scoundrel," she said promptly. "Why?"

"I need facts, not opinions, sweetface. You saw him and Walter in Southaven?"

"No," I said, intervening before Bitty could dig a conversational hole. "That was Doctor Coltrane, the vet at Willow Bend."

"Well, somebody got that wrong." He took out a small notebook and ruffled the pages as he searched for whatever he'd written.

"Would that somebody be Brett Simon?" I asked, and he glanced up at me. I shrugged. "We told him about it, so that must be where you got your information."

"Think you're a sharp cookie? Well, I've got eyes and ears all over this little burg. It doesn't take me long to find out what people know."

Before he could launch into another bad imitation Philip Marlowe recitation, I asked, "Does this have to do with the recent will reading of Walter Simpson? Are you Faith Simon's investigator too?"

"Oh, he can't be, Trinket," said Bitty. "It'd be a conflict of interest. Wouldn't it?"

Catfish shook his head. "No. I'd be a free agent if no longer employed by Mr. Brunetti. If I was helping Mrs. Simon, which I haven't said I am, there's no conflict."

That pretty much answered my question. Faith had hired him, too, I was fairly sure. Then Catfish Carter confirmed it by adding, "I heard you two dames reported Brett Simon made a café confession about killing Mr. Simpson. Now why would that be?"

If this was an example of his interrogation style, it left a lot to be desired, in my opinion, and I opened my mouth to tell him just that when Bitty intervened.

"Now who told you that? It was Mrs. Tyree who heard it, not us. I just now found out and told Jackson Lee, so he'll report it to the police."

"Way to go, Greyhound," I said and lifted my brows when she gave me a baffled look. "Under the bus?"

She blinked. Then whatever passes for reality in Bitty-World must have hit because her eyes got wide. "Oh. Oh yes, but of course, that's all hearsay, isn't it? And Mrs. Tyree has made an appointment to talk to the police, I'm sure."

The conversation didn't go much better from that point. Catfish tried to wheedle more information out of us, we resisted, and finally Chen Ling took offense at his presence and bit his ankle. It was really more like a nibble, and that's how we discovered he wears pink socks. I was intrigued. As Catfish likes to project an aura of ultra-macho man, it seemed incongruous. Not that alpha males can't wear pink socks, I suppose, but it does lead to titillating questions. I refrained.

After closing the door behind him when he left, Bitty leaned back against it. "I locked it, but should I set the alarm?"

"It couldn't hurt." I thought a moment. "Chain lock, too?"

Bitty slid the chain lock, and we both smiled. Then Bitty refilled her wine glass, and we assumed prone positions in her parlor. Chen Ling joined us, coming to a stop by Bitty's chair to stare up at her fixedly until her wine-drinking servant bent and lifted her up to sit in her lap.

"How are you going to stop her from pooping on Mrs. Tyree's deck?" I asked as if we had nothing else to concern us but pug poo. "Install concrete block fencing? Razor wire on top? Turret towers with armed guards?"

"How many glasses of wine have you had, anyway?" Bitty readjusted the portly pug atop her lap.

"Not enough, or I'd be blissfully napping. Instead, I can't help thinking about Brett Simon and why he'd say he shot Walter if he didn't. Unless he was talking about something else, and that's still saying he shot someone. Faith just doesn't strike me as the kind of person to condone murder."

"It's her son," said Bitty after a moment and lifted her hand to stop me as I opened my mouth to protest. "I know. I wouldn't allow my son to get away with murder either, even though I'd get him the best attorney possible after he turned himself in to the police."

That's true. Bitty will go to any length to protect her children, like most mothers; but she doesn't condone criminal activity, I consoled myself.

Then she suggested we commit a criminal act, and I figuratively slapped my forehead with my palm.

"Bitty, may I ask why you think it necessary to steal your rifle from the police evidence room? Brandon will be cleared, and not because of some iffy information about Brett Simon but because there's not enough evidence to convict him. Isn't that what Jackson Lee told you?"

"More or less." She sipped from her glass, gazing at me over the rim. Chitling gazed at me because she's plotting ways to remove me and have all Bitty's attention for herself. Never underestimate a pug.

Despite the scrutiny, I said, "No. I will not willingly be part of a criminal enterprise."

"Honestly, Trinket, it's not criminal to reclaim your own property."

"It is when you break and enter to reclaim it from police who are holding it as evidence," I argued. "Didn't we recently discuss this? And wasn't it decided that would be foolish?"

Bitty sniffed disdainfully. "If you don't want to go with me, Trinket, just say so."

"I don't want to go with you."

"No, really."

"Really."

"Well, if *that's* the way you feel . . ."

I almost felt bad. Not bad enough to encounter the police while breaking into their evidence room, however.

"It is. Sorry to disappoint you. I have an aversion to prison, you see, and some of your plans go terribly awry."

Bitty sucked down the rest of her wine. "Not always. But I see I am alone in this."

I sighed. "Why must you reclaim your rifle now instead of wait for the police to bring it to you? Don't they always return confiscated items?"

I referenced the previous times her pistols had been confiscated and had been duly returned, although with serious reservations, I'm certain. Lieutenant Maxwell had been quite specific in his requests—demands—that Bitty refrain from firing them at people.

"Because, Trinket," she said slowly as if explaining to a small child, "they are holding my rifle until they locate a suspect, arrest a suspect, charge a suspect, indict a suspect, and then convict a suspect. I could be ninety by then. What if they never settle on a suspect? My heirloom will be lost forever."

"And you don't think they might suspect you are the one to steal the rifle? If so, you aren't giving the police very much credit."

"Well, of course they'll suspect me. But I can put it away where they'll never think to look, and then once they've settled on a suspect—what are you doing?"

"I'm going home." I had stood up and tried to remember where I left my purse. It held my car keys. Then I recalled that I had a new purse now and readjusted my expectations. I found it quickly.

"You're being so contrary, Trinket."

"Yes. Yes, I am. I'm usually contrary when someone suggests I break into a jail to steal weapons."

Bitty smiled. "We don't have to break into the jail, silly girl."

I stopped fishing around in my purse for car keys and stared at her. "We don't?"

"No. We just walk in, you distract the desk person, and I—what are you doing now?"

I'd dumped my purse upside down on the ottoman in a desperate search for keys. As I spotted a metallic glint reflecting lamplight, I said, "Getting out of here as quickly as I can. I'm not involved in this. Do what you will. I'm going home, where I intend to soak in a tub, then talk to sane people." I paused before clarifying, "Reasonably sane people. Maybe a crazy dog. Any of whom will be an improvement."

Keys rattled in my hand as I scooped up loose change, used tissues, lipstick, an empty wallet, a hairbrush, and a tattered grocery list that was probably a month old but my mother insisted was current. Then I straightened and looked at Bitty.

She sat glowering at me like a modern Medusa, and it was a miracle I didn't turn to stone. Her gargoyle glared at me, too. I sighed.

"Sorry. I just can't do it, Bitty. Jackson Lee will do his best to get your rifle returned to you intact and quickly as possible. You know that."

She surprised me by taking a deep breath, then saying, "You're right, Trinket. Jackson Lee will handle everything, and it will all be fine. At least Brandon is safe, and we can go on with our lives now."

"Uh, yeah," I managed to reply. "Are you all right? Your eyes are kind of glassy."

"Allergies. Pollen in the air, you know." She waved a hand at me. "I'm fine, really I am. Don't worry about me, Trinket. You go on home to Aunt Anna and Uncle Eddie."

"Uh huh. Bitty, what are you planning?"

Her eyes opened wide and she blinked. "Honestly, Trinket you say the strangest things at times. Now go on. They'll be calling here looking for you if you don't get home soon."

She followed me to the front door, carrying her gargoyle, and I turned to look at her as she punched in the code to unlock the security alarm and then slid the chain free. She wouldn't meet my eyes. Prickles of suspicion danced along my spine.

"If you do what I'm sure you're planning to do, don't call me. I don't want to know about it. Call Rob Rainey for bail money. Or Jackson Lee. Bitty, are you listening?"

"Of course, Trinket. I always listen to you. Have a nice drive home."

I would have lingered to press her, but her gargoyle snapped at me when I got too close, so I just waved one hand in the air in a gesture of surrender and left. Oh, I knew she was going to draft some unsuspecting person into helping her go after her damn rifle, despite all common sense and police with badges and guns. I just knew it.

Sometimes I would rather be wrong.

DADDY WOKE ME by yelling up the stairs to come to the phone. I opened my eyes, blinking and wondering why I couldn't see. Then I realized it was in the middle of the night as my eyes adjusted to total darkness except for my bedside clock. The big hand was on the three, the little hand was on the two. I tried to make sense of that.

"Eureka May Truevine, pick up the phone," my daddy bellowed up the stairs, and I promptly got tangled in my covers trying to get up.

"Coming," I yelled back, then fell out of bed onto the floor. Fortunately, there was a nice soft rug to break my fall, but I still said some ugly words.

It occurred to me, of course, that it was Bitty, and she'd either been arrested or was in trouble and despite my warning, calling me to come help. I intended to be strong. I intended to be firm. I intended to remind her she was crazy.

The road to hell, it is said, is paved with good intentions. I figured I was pretty much at my destination on that road.

At first I didn't recognize the person on the phone and pressed it closer to my ear as I asked her to repeat what she'd said, following that request with, "Who is this?"

"Miranda Watson, and I need help. She's stuck, and I can't get her out and I'm afraid she's going to be arrested—are you listening?"

Actually, I was stuck myself, wondering how Bitty had come to enlist Miranda Watson as her accomplice. I rallied and shifted from one foot to the other, curling my toes up from the cool kitchen floor. "Uh huh," I answered brightly. "Stuck in what?"

There was a moment of silence, a sigh, and then, "A garbage can."

I tried to picture that and failed. "Okay, so what—"

"Oh, for pity's sake, Trinket, just haul your ass down here and help me get her out of this damn garbage can."

That sounded direct. "Okay. Where are you?"

"The police station."

Visions flashed before my eyes: me in an orange jumpsuit or black and white horizontal stripes; me stretched out on dirty pavement while police handcuffed me; Bitty, arms flapping and butt in a garbage can while police cuffed her. I sighed.

"I'm on my way," I said, and Miranda muttered something that sounded like, "You bet your ass you are," but I could have been mistaken.

The Holly Springs Police Department is now in a nice, one-story new building close to 78 Highway, on JM Ash Drive just off Highway 7 before it turns into Craft Street. It's a red brick and fairly new structure, much too modern to allow break-outs or break-ins, even if suspects were incarcerated there. They're usually taken to the building where we'd gone to pick up Brandon. The larger jail for longer-term convicts is also on the outskirts of town, with razor wire and all the accoutrements necessary for prisoners. Apparently, the newer building is where the evidence room is located, with Bitty's heirloom rifle tucked away in a cubby somewhere. I had no idea where the garbage can was located.

It was dark, of course, but low lights were on inside. I saw no blue lights, nor did I see Bitty's car or any sign of police officers dragging off a bubble-headed blonde. Nor did I see any sign of a gossip columnist, even though I drove to the back of the parking lot. As I turned my car to head back to the front, the lights happened to catch a dark shadow that moved. Uh oh. I stopped and peered into the night. Several cars were in the lot, most seeming to belong to government employees. I waited, and in a moment, the shadow moved closer.

Beckoning furiously, Miranda Watson said as soon as I got close enough to roll down the window to ask about Bitty, "You should have better sense than to drive in here like this. Go park the car at the gas station, then walk back."

It made sense, although I didn't much appreciate being scolded by a gossip columnist. I reflected it was a good thing I'd worn comfortable shoes. Unfortunately, they were my bunny slippers because I'd been too rattled to remember to put on sensible shoes like Nikes. By the time I parked at the corner and walked back to the parking lot, Miranda was pacing. She wore a dark hoodie and jeans, with a black turtlenecked sweater that she had pulled up over her chin almost to her eyes.

"Cameras," she said in a muffled voice when I reached her, and alarmed, I glanced up and around.

"Here? Never mind. Where's Bitty? If they have cameras, we're all in trouble, so let's get this over with before they happen to see us out here."

I followed Miranda around the back to a small area behind the building. Trees, bushes, and dirt lined the rear parking area. Oddly, no light illuminated the space.

"I think they're burned out or something," Miranda muttered and pointed.

I looked where she pointed, but all I saw was a dumpster. Then it dawned on me. Oh no. Bitty must be horrified. And how could I get her out of there, if she couldn't climb out?

I stood on my toes and peered into the abyss. My eyes slowly adjusted to the lack of light. It was empty, except for a Bitty cowering in the bottom like a rat in a leather jumpsuit. "Are you still wearing that thing? I thought you had it made into cushions 'cause it didn't fit any more," I said as I tried not to touch any part of the huge metal dumpster.

"Shut up and get me out of here," she snapped and stood up. There was nothing for her to stand on, and I wasn't tall enough to reach over and drag her out. I turned to ask Miranda if she had any ideas, but she'd disappeared. I didn't blame her, but it did irritate me. "Trinket!"

I turned my attention back to my dirty Diva. The dumpster may be empty, but it had a vivid reminder of previous occupancy in a ripe odor that wafted toward me. I held my breath, stood on my toes, and offered my hands to Bitty. If not for her blond bubble hair, it wouldn't have been easy to see, it was so dark back there. The pale helmet wobbled toward me, and I felt her grab at me. She missed, I tried again, found her skinny little arms, and clasped her tightly.

"You're going to have to jump while I pull," I muttered.

"I can't jump. My cheerleading days are behind me."

"Do tell. Look, you'll have to help, or I'll go get my car, tie a rope around you and the bumper, and put it in reverse. These are your choices."

"All right! You're terribly cranky tonight."

"Yes, I get that way when I get hauled out of bed at two in the morning to come on some rescue mission for something I told you not to do in the first place. You can explain later just how you got in the dumpster and what you hoped to accomplish here."

"Where's Miranda?"

"No idea. That's something else you can explain later. Now, ready? On the count of three I'll pull, you jump."

The first attempt did not go well. I pulled, she forgot to jump, and her slick leather arms slid out of my grasp. She landed with a thud on the bottom of the dumpster. I swear, the scent of pizza with sausage and peppers gusted up into my face like a Domino's tornado. Bitty cussed a little, then stood up and waved her arms at me until we connected again. I was rather glad that I couldn't see her that well.

The second attempt failed, too. I wasn't strong enough, and Bitty couldn't seem to leap high enough, since the dumpster was probably five feet deep, and that's her height.

"I'll get my car," I said, and Bitty made a sound like a distressed frog. "What else can I do? Go inside and ask a policeman for help?"

"That may be difficult to explain," came the woeful response from the garbage well. It kind of echoed. She really sounded pitiful.

I thought about it a moment, then said, "Cats."

"Honestly, Trinket, this is no time to talk about a Broadway play."

Now she sounded cranky, so I said, "No, Princess Pew, I mean, we can say we're out here trying to rescue a stray cat. You know. Everyone knows my parents are the local homeless shelter for stray cats."

"Oh! Yes, that's good. Okay. Go inside and get someone with a ladder to get me out of here. I'm going to have to soak in a tub, do a sauna, and shampoo something sticky out of my hair. Don't ask."

"Don't worry, I didn't intend to." I rubbed at my shoulder where it felt like I'd strained it trying to heft Bitty out of her unsanitary nesting spot, then turned to go into the police station to ask for help.

I immediately bumped into a solid wall that said something like, "Oof!"

My heart leaped, my stomach dropped, and my knees got wobbly. "Miranda?"

"No," said a familiar male voice. I felt better.

"Jackson Lee?"

"Who else? I got a call from the station saying I needed to come get my significant other out of the dumpster before they have to arrest her."

"A cat," I said, squinting into the darkness to try and see his face. He was a big dark shape and that was it. I tried again. "We were rescuing a cat."

"Of course you were. Is she still in there?"

"I'm afraid so. We may need a ladder."

We didn't need a ladder. Jackson Lee reached in, took Bitty by the arms, and hauled her out like a sack of flour. Then he immediately released her and took a step back. "You smell like pizza."

"Thank you," she said with an obvious attempt at dignity.

Jackson Lee blew out a breath he'd obviously been holding and said, "Bitty, we can talk when it's daylight, and you can tell me all about this adventure then. I'd like to get some sleep in what's left of the night. I'm not up to sorting out your no doubt tangled reasoning."

In a small voice, Bitty said, "You're mad at me."

There was a brief silence, then another sigh, and he said, "I won't be when I wake up again. Please go home, sugar. Straight home. Shall I follow you?"

"No, that's fine. I'm sure Trinket won't mind. If it's any consolation to you, she told me not to do this."

"It's not, but good to know. Good night, ladies."

And with that, our tall, dark, handsome hero walked off into the night. I smiled, then I realized I was stuck with Bitty. That put a damper on the situation.

"Can you take me home, Trinket?" Bitty asked, adding, "We came in Miranda's car. I assume she has abandoned our mission and me."

"Probably the smartest thing she's done all night. I have cloth seats. You smell like pizza and garlic. I'm not sure I want that lingering in my car."

"I'll buy plastic bags at the gas station."

"A deal," I said, and we walked toward Cousin's gas on the corner where I'd left my car. Fortunately, it was still there. Not much traffic on Highway 4 to witness our curious arrival, me in sweat pants, sweatshirt, and bunny slippers, and Bitty disguised as a giant pizza slice. All in all, it wasn't the worst situation I've been in with Bitty.

"I wonder how the police knew we were out there," Bitty said as I drove down Craft, and I shook my head.

"It's a police station. They have cameras everywhere. Just because the lights were out, that doesn't mean they can't see you. I'm amazed they didn't arrest you. What did you think you could do, even if you hadn't fallen into the dumpster? And how did you manage that?"

"It's a long story." She shifted to look at me, and plastic made a snicking sound under her leather-clad thighs. "I was told the evidence room was at the rear, so I figured I could go and see if I could at least look inside and spot my rifle. But the only window was high up, so I needed something to stand on. Miranda suggested I look in the dumpster for a box. Other than that, she was no use at all. She was the one who told me the lights were out because they were changing to new lighting, so I decided it was the perfect night to try, you see. And she graciously agreed to help me."

"I'm astounded you're talking casually to Miranda. You usually have unkind things to say about her."

"Well, perhaps I misjudged her. Then again, she left me, so perhaps I didn't. But at the moment, I had no one willing to do the tiniest little favor for me, so—"

"Hold it right there, Miss Martyr. Breaking into a police station isn't a 'tiny little favor.' It's usually suicide. Or at the least, incarceration-icide."

"That's not a word," she protested, making the plastic squeak as she crossed her arms over her ample chest.

"It should be. Do us all a favor and just buy prison denims or an orange jumpsuit. Stop trying to earn Jailhouse Fashion."

"I've often thought about starting my own clothing line, you know. I studied design in college, so perhaps I could share my visions with the world."

I turned onto Van Dorn and sped up to beat the light at Memphis Street, and headed for Randolph Street. College Street would be the next turn off Randolph, and I could leave my deranged cousin at home. Only a couple more blocks to go . . .

But as we passed the courthouse, a police car pulled out to follow us. I kept an eye on my rearview mirror, only half-listening as Bitty rambled on about designing prison clothes for the un-incarcerated as well as more fashionable garments for those inhabiting prison dorms on the government dime. I expected lights to flash at any moment so I paid scrupulous attention to turn signals, speed, and no rolling stops. That had been an issue in the past that I did not care to repeat. If Rodney Farrell was in that patrol car, I may well be called to account for a misdeed I hadn't taken into consideration. It's happened. My intentions to read the *Mississippi Driver's Manual* from cover to cover had yet to be realized. The road to hell narrowed.

The light changed at S. Market Street, and I braked to a halt while Bitty rambled on about measuring the stride, whatever that means. The patrol car pulled up next to me. I tried not to look out my window, but a quick "burp" of the siren drew my attention. The officer motioned for me to pull over. I stared at him. It wasn't Rodney Farrell. I made a right turn and nosed in my car across from Tyson Drugs, closed for the night as most sensible people were safe in bed.

Bitty didn't even seem to notice; she kept talking about denim and duck cloth and horizontal stripes. I turned off my engine. That got her attention. She glanced around.

"Tyson's is closed, you know," she said. "So is JB's."

"I don't think that officer cares about laxatives or whiskey sours, Bitty. Do you know him?"

"What? Oh. The police. What did you do?"

"I have no idea." I hit the button to roll down my window before the delayed action safety feature ended. The officer appeared in the opening. He had his cap pulled low over his forehead, but it was the little ticket book in his hand that caught my attention.

"Officer, was I speeding?"

"License and proof of insurance, please."

Uh oh. That was going to be a problem.

"My purse was stolen. It had my license and insurance card—wait.

I have a card in my glove compartment. Move, Bitty, so I can get it—"

"Put your hands on the wheel," the officer said sharply, and I froze in reaching over Bitty for the glove compartment. "Back where I can see them."

I slowly complied. My heart beat so fast it sounded like thunder in my ears. The street was empty, even late-night people having deserted this part of town. Bitty, oblivious to the nuances of an armed man at my window with the law on his side, leaned forward.

"Who are you? I don't know you. Are you new?"

The officer had stepped back to speak into some kind of radio he wore like a pin on his lapel, and I hissed at Bitty to shut up. She ignored me. She squinted out the window to try and see his face or maybe his badge number, I didn't know. I just didn't want any complications when I still hadn't replaced my driver's license. I was pretty sure I had an insurance card in the glove compartment, but I certainly wasn't about to reach for it now.

Then the officer stepped close, bent down to look into the car at my passenger, and asked, "Are you Miz Hollandale?"

Before I could reply, Bitty said, "I'm Mrs. Hollandale, yes. Who are you?"

"Officer Barron Stewart. I just moved back to Holly Springs."

"Barron—are you Royal Stewart's brother?"

"Yes, ma'am. What are you ladies doing out so late at night?"

Bitty bridled. "Is that a crime now?"

Officer Stewart shook his head. "No, ma'am, but the car's right taillight is out. This was a courtesy stop."

I didn't like the sound of *was*, so I said, "Thank you so much, Officer. I'll have my daddy take a look at it first thing in the morning."

"Can your daddy explain why you don't have a driver's license?"

I sighed. "Yes, but it won't help. My purse was in Bitty's car when it was stolen a few days ago, and I haven't yet replaced my license. I did cancel credit cards and things like that but hoped when the car was found, it'd still have my identification in it."

Officer Stewart was busily writing in his little book. He glanced up at me. "You said you have your insurance card in the glove box?"

"I do." I motioned to Bitty, and she opened the glove compartment and found the little slip of paper with insurance information, handed it to me, and I handed it to the officer. He read it, wrote more in his ticket book, then gave it back to me.

"Miz Truevine, you should go get your license replaced first thing tomorrow too. I'd normally give my own brother a ticket for something like this, but I'm giving you a warning instead. This is a written warning, so if you don't get a new license and get stopped again, it will be a definite ticket and fine."

Filled with the warmth of having escaped paying a ticket, I gushed, "Oh, thank you, sir! It's been so awful, getting the car stolen, then police finding it stripped, and after the murder and all, it's been a terrible time lately."

Officer Stewart tore the warning from his pad and held it out. "Yeah, the murder at the pilgrimage was bad. My brother can't stop saying that it could have been him, since Walter was wearing the uniform he'd been wearing the day before. If not for that bar fight and going to jail, Royal might have been the one killed."

That struck me. All this time I'd been thinking Walter Simpson was the target. What if he wasn't? What if it truly was an accident, or at least, the wrong victim? Even Bitty caught that and leaned forward to look past me as I took the warning from Stewart.

"Why would you say that? Was it an accident after all?"

Officer Stewart didn't answer. He just touched a finger to the brim of his hat and turned and walked away. I looked over at Bitty and did an imitation of *The Twilight Zone* theme. She rolled her eyes.

"Royal Stewart is a terrible flirt, you know," she said as I backed my car out of the diagonal slot and had to go around the block to come up at the light on Randolph Street. "He hit on Skip Whalen's girlfriend right in front of him while at JB's. She apparently liked it, and that really set Skip off, the way I heard it from the boys."

"Tell me about Skip Whalen," I said, and Bitty, who loves to gossip, even though she says otherwise, launched into a lengthy history of the Whalens and their son Skip—whose name really was Skip on his birth certificate, and didn't that sound like a dog's name rather than a baby's—saying they'd only been back in town for a few years. . . . I shall spare you the finer points.

After sorting out the non-essential details when she finished, I parked in front of her house. "So what you're saying is that Skip is rowdy, but don't get him mad? I wonder how mad he got at Royal Stewart."

"Maybe we should ask him. I'll pick you up in the morning."

"No, I have to drive up to Olive Branch to get my driver's license before I do anything else."

"I'll go with you."

As she opened the car door, plastic bag rustling a farewell to leather, I said, "Isn't the Benz being delivered?"

"Yes, but Jackson Lee wants to take it for a test drive before bringing it to me. Just in case. You can take me by his office when we get back from Olive Branch. Or Nesbit, if it's too busy at the Olive Branch DMV."

I groaned at the thought of driving an extra fifteen miles each way, an hour extra in the car. "I'll hope for short lines."

Bitty bent to smile at me. I got a good whiff of sausage and peppers as she said, "You do that, honey. Optimism is a fun exercise."

I hate it when Bitty is right.

Chapter 12

"MAY I SMILE?" I asked the lady manning the DMV camera, and she looked amused.

"Will you be smiling when an officer stops you?"

"Probably not, but since I have to use my license as ID to write a check at grocery stores, I'd prefer looking pleas—"

The click of the camera warned me that I would definitely not be looking pleasant on my laminated license. The lady—and I now use that term loosely—manning the camera gave me a nice smile, however. "All done. Wait over there, please."

I sat down next to Bitty, who had a driver's manual in her hand and flipped through the pages. "Listen to this, Trinket. It says that mud flaps are required on all trucks. Did you know that?"

"No."

"Well, it's on the test, I bet. 'All motor vehicles, trailers, and semi-trailers must have fenders, wheel covers, or flaps to prevent mud, water, or other material from being thrown from the wheels up onto other vehicles.' Can you believe that? I wonder if the Benz should have mud flaps."

"The Benz should be plastered with signs warning other drivers that it's subject to sudden stops, swerves, and general insanity instead of pink bumper stickers with pugs and pistols."

"You're just jealous. I'll get a bumper sticker for your car. You'll like it, I'm sure."

"Not if it has a pug or pistol on it. And I'm not taking a test. Just replacing a lost license."

"Oh, that's too bad. You'd have the right answer to at least one of the questions."

I didn't bother pointing out that she had only gotten out of driver's ed because she wore a low-cut blouse to class and a form-fitting sweater on test day. And she wouldn't have had to take driver's ed if she hadn't run a car through the front of the McDonald's while still driving on a learner's permit. I'd been the licensed driver foolish enough to let her take the wheel, so I remembered it quite clearly. My daddy did too, I was pretty sure. Age might have robbed him of the memories of my first school play, my winning a spelling bee, and other minor childhood triumphs, but he definitely still recalled the disasters.

"So riddle me this," I said instead. "Would Skip Whalen be angry enough at Royal Stewart to try to kill him?"

Bitty closed the driver's manual. "He's been known to carry grudges, so he might. But his eyesight is still good, so I can't imagine him mistaking an old man like Walter Simpson for Royal. After all, Royal is young and good-looking."

"And Walter looked like a peach pit," I mused aloud. "Both were tall and thin, though. And with the smoke and chaos—he might have still thought Walter was Royal."

"But didn't Royal go to jail? Skip might have thought he was still there. And anyway, Royal looks nothing like Walter. Gray hair and wrinkles aside, he even walked like an old man."

"All very true. It just seemed that perhaps I'd found a rationale for his murder."

"There's nothing rational about murder, Trinket."

"No, but rationale is defined differently from rational. It's a justification for doing something insane, while rational means balanced thinking."

Bitty flapped a hand at me. "There are a lot of murderers who think killing someone is rational and balanced thinking."

Still thinking aloud, I said, "But of course, profit is a common rationale for murder too, and there were people who profited from Walter's death." I pondered the possibilities. While I hated to think Walter's death was a mistake—random murder seems so unnecessary, capricious, and impossible to prevent—I hated even more thinking someone hated him enough to kill him. Just because people are cranky, that doesn't mean they deserve the death penalty. If so, the world would have maybe a hundred people left.

A sharp elbow in my side earned an "Ouch!" and some stares my way as Bitty got my attention.

"They're calling your name, Trinket."

I got up and went to the desk to get my license. As I suspected, the photo caught me with my lips pinched in the act of saying a word beginning with *P*, but it was the name that got my immediate attention. *European Treevine*. I had been reduced to a botanical phrase. It took a moment to get the clerk's attention, as she was busily chatting up a handsome man and had no time for a woman with pinched lips, but finally she sauntered over.

"Everything accurate?" she asked in a bored tone. She looked to be about fourteen going on thirty, but since she worked at the DMV, I assumed she was at least eighteen.

I smiled. Her eyes got big and she took a step back, so maybe it wasn't as pleasant a smile as I intended. Still, I proceeded to show her my license.

"This information is incorrect. My name is Eureka May Truevine."

She peered at the license. "Yes, ma'am. That's what it says here. European Treevine."

I inhaled deeply. "It can't just be my accent, as I filled out the card and gave two forms of identification. Here they are. See? The names do not match."

I spoke clearly and concisely. The girl looked puzzled. I understood that my forms of ID were a bit unusual, but it'd been all I could find that I didn't already have in my purse—the purse that was stolen: My birth certificate and a former work ID when I lived in Nevada and worked at a casino-hotel named Hot Pants and Hot Slots. I was there less than a week, but it was the only ID with my photo and signature that I still owned. The other IDs I had presented were judged unreliable. And no, I did not wear hot pants while working there. My job was in Human Resources and writing workmen's comp claims, so I stayed out of sight in the back. It still hadn't been enough to calm my anxiety over working at a hotel-lounge-casino named Hot Pants and Hot Slots. The parent company had a normal name, something like Casinos Ltd, or I'd never have taken the job in the first place. A warning to those who apply online for jobs.

At any rate, as I was laboriously explaining to the girl behind the counter that while my name may be unusual, it is authentic, Bitty tugged on my sleeve quite firmly. I jerked to one side and turned to glare at her. "What?"

"We have to go, Trinket. There's an emergency. Come on, Trinket, let's *go!*"

By now the girl behind the counter was looking at me suspiciously. Trinket is not quite the same as Eureka or even European, so I decided to forego the possibilities I saw looming in my immediate future and left with Bitty, clutching my new license in my hand. I could come back, and perhaps to another DMV where people knew how to recognize computer entry errors.

"We should have stayed at the DMV in Olive Branch," Bitty fumed. "Now here we are on the other side of the state when we need to be in Holly Springs."

"The lines were halfway to Marshall County, Bitty," I said, but didn't bother trying to correct her location miscalculation. Nesbit is fifteen miles west of Olive Branch, and Olive Branch is twenty-five miles from Holly Springs, give or take a mile or two. Mississippi is a lot wider and longer.

"So what is this emergency?" I asked as we got to my car. I clicked the remote, the horn beeped, and the doors unlocked. Daddy had put in a new lightbulb, so I didn't anticipate being stopped by the police for a taillight, and all was well in Taurus-world.

Bitty-world was another matter.

"Chen Ling is missing."

I absorbed that as I slid into the driver's seat and started the car. Bitty slammed her door. Normally, I would think of something insulting to say, but still rattled at my unrequested name change and all its implications, I said, "From where?"

"My house. Sharita was there, and Chen Ling just loves her, so I let her stay while we were out. Sharita already called Jackson Lee, and he's coming to look for her. I'll just die if she's gone—or been abducted."

I could tell Bitty was about to ratchet up the already dire situation, so I said, "No one will abduct her. She bites."

"She does bite. Maybe she got away. She could be hiding and terrified somewhere and wondering why I'm not there to rescue her . . ." Her voice ended in a little catch.

"It's more probable that she's on Mrs. Tyree's back deck planting pug piles."

Bitty brightened. "Of course! I'll call Sharita and tell her to go next door."

"I'm sure she's doing that now. After all, how far can Chitling get so quickly?"

"You'd be surprised," Bitty said as she dialed on her cell phone. "Sharita? Have you checked next door with Mrs. Tyree? Oh? And she wasn't there. All right. Oh, Jackson Lee just got there? Yes, he'll find her. Thank you."

By this time we'd gotten to Pleasant Hill Road, and I could see the I-55 on-ramp ahead; I sped up a little. Even if I drove as fast as possible, it'd still take an hour to get back to Holly Springs. A lifetime for Bitty. I had faith in Jackson Lee that he'd leave no stone unturned in a search for Chitling.

While I dodged traffic and tried to keep to the speed limit, Bitty dialed everyone in a three-mile radius of her house to enlist their help in scouring the neighborhood. Rayna said she'd go right over, bless her heart.

"She's taking Jinx," Bitty said as she scrolled through her contact list to find the next victim—I mean searcher. "He's good at rescuing people from disasters. Remember how he found that child after the tornado?"

I did and tried to envision the poor dog's confusion at searching for a wandering pug. But it may work out better having the dog look for her. A dog should know where another dog might go.

While Bitty called Gaynelle and alerted her to the missing pug, I focused on the traffic and wondered when so many people had moved to North Mississippi. Most of the roads we traveled had been dirt roads not so long ago. Now they were six-lane highways. Progress wasn't always good.

Bitty clicked off her phone and blew out a breath. "Gaynelle is going to take a walk and see if she can spot her."

"That covers a good portion of Holly Springs," I said. "I was just thinking, doesn't Royal Stewart live close to you?"

My effort to distract her didn't work for long.

"Off Randolph. There's a rooming house there. Oh! Do you think he stole Chen Ling? Maybe he wants to hold her for ransom, or—"

"No, no, I didn't mean that. For one thing, Royal has no reason to abduct your dog, and for another, he'd be more likely to abduct Sharita's biscuits than any dog. I just thought that once we have Chen Ling safely home, we can pretend she's missing and go knock on his door and ask a few other questions, too."

"Oh. Well, as long as my precious girl is safely home, we can ask all the questions you want. Like what kind of questions?"

"I wonder if he'd discuss the bar fight and Skip Whalen, or even the girl they fought over. It might give us an idea if there's enough there to warrant someone trying to kill him. If nothing else, we can at least cross him off our suspect list."

"Royal? Is he a suspect?"

"No, Bitty, he's a potential victim, remember?"

Her cell phone rang, and she quickly punched it to answer. Her immediate squeal let me know she was no longer pug-less. "All the way to the depot? That's crazy. How did she get in their back yard? She did? Tell Gwen I'll send my landscaper over to fill in the hole and replace the plants. Yes, thank you!"

Being on the Bitty side of the conversation did not leave me out at all. I already had the picture of the Great Escape firmly in my mind. It's walking distance from Bitty's house to the railroad depot, unless you're a fat old pug with bowed legs and smushed face. Then it's a bit of a stretch. Still, Chitling had acquitted herself well, I thought, walking that far and having enough energy left to dig a hole and destroy plants.

"I take it Gozer the Traveler is fine," I said in between Bitty's calls to alert the posse that the dog was found and in protective custody. I don't think she appreciated my *Ghostbusters* reference. She stuck out her tongue at me. I smiled. Then she sat back with a sigh of relief.

"Thank heavens. Gwen found her in the back yard of the depot making friends with her pit bull. And a cat."

I correctly interpreted that as Chitling terrorizing Gwen's pit bull and a cat. But all I said was, "Then we have time to go by to talk to Royal Stewart before going home."

"I prefer going to get my precious girl first. Then we can go talk to Royal Stewart."

I thought about it. Faced with me, Bitty, and the gremlin, Royal might find it easier to answer questions just to get us to leave. I'm flexible. I just hoped he was home.

First we met with Rayna and Gwen, who had a grumpy gremlin on a leash. Gwen's family has owned the railroad depot for decades, and it's on the Historical Register and has the former dining room renovated to cater weddings, hold meetings, and we hope—to entertain Divas one day soon. It was also the scene of the reenactment, and I couldn't help glancing toward the front where Walter had died. It was so lovely and peaceful, with pots of flowers, hanging baskets, nice old bricks laid out in front, basking quietly in the noonday sun.

Bitty scooped up her pouting pug and hugged her tightly. "My poor, precious girl! Are you all right? Why did you run away? Mommy's back now, and I won't leave you again."

That precluded a visit to Budgie's for lunch, I reflected, but perhaps that wasn't as bad as it could be. Too much of a good thing always went straight to my thighs. As I said, I'm flexible.

All I said to Bitty, however, was, "Your precious is pooping on your white pants."

Bitty reacted appropriately, holding Precious out so she could finish her deposit on the grass. Rayna said, "Oh my," and Gwen went for paper towels to wipe pug poo off Bitty's white linen pants.

I said, "Don't squeeze her so hard next time," and Bitty flashed me a peace sign. She forgot one of the fingers, but due to the unsanitary circumstances, I let it pass. I'm sure it was an oversight.

Once Bitty and pug were poo-less if not fragrance-free, we got into my car and drove to her house. Jackson Lee was there, as well as the Franklin Benz. It sat in gleaming splendor in the double driveway that led to the garage. It still had pink bumper stickers on the rear bumper.

Obviously having forgiven Bitty for her midnight madness, Jackson Lee gave her a big hug, then got a puzzled expression on his face. "Sugar, is that a new perfume?"

"Chitling Number Five," I said in between snorts of laughter.

Bitty ignored me. "Chen Ling had a little accident, so I need to bathe her. Is Sharita still here?"

Jackson Lee shook his head. "She said to tell you she had to run, but she labeled all the food and put it away for you. I'll just wait out here on the porch while you get Chen Ling all cleaned up."

I figured that was his tactful way of requesting that Bitty do the same. Since I had no intention of being roped into assisting, I said, "I'll get us something to drink and sit out here with you, Jackson Lee. Tea?"

After I filled two glasses with sweet tea, I joined Jackson Lee on the porch. I'd left my purse on one of the chairs and moved it to sit down. My wallet fell out, and I picked it up and put it in my lap as I sat in the wicker rocker.

"Is it legal for a DMV employee to change your name without permission?" I asked as a way of forestalling any questions about what Bitty and I might have planned. Sometimes it's better to avoid dire warnings and disapproval.

"Not yet," he replied, laughing a little. "I take it not all went well at the DMV?"

I opened my wallet, took out my new license, and handed it to him. He scanned it, then grinned. Really, he's a very handsome man, and I completely understood Bitty's infatuation with him. I wasn't quite as sure of his reasons for returning that emotion, but then again, Bitty does grow on people.

"European Treevine sounds very botanical," he said, and I nodded.

"That was my first thought. But is it legal?"

"I'd be interested in seeing the forms of identification they used to come up with this, but I'd say, no, it's not legal. Oh, that reminds me—I got a call from the Corinth police. They found your purse, and it has your wallet in it. They're sending it to me."

"Thank heavens. I hope my identification is still there. I'd hate to have to use this license if I'm stopped by the police again."

"Again? That sounds ominous."

"Oh, I had a taillight out," I said and took a cool swig of tea. It was sweet and delicious. And it kept me from verbal diarrhea. Jackson Lee can flush out information like Chitling can root out the last corn chip in the sofa.

As he handed me back my license, he said, "What on earth was Bitty thinking to try and retrieve that rifle last night?"

"Oh, she has this idea that it all hinges on the rifle, that people will continue to suspect Brandon even though he's innocent and charges have been dropped—that goes back to her first husband, you know— and since no one has been arrested or charged yet for the murder, the town will still think Brandon is guilty."

"I see," he said in the tone of a man who obviously doesn't see, and I sympathized.

"It was very hard on Bitty when Frank was arrested, and then, of course, when she was suspected of killing her last husband. And you must admit, people talk about us now that we have been involved in recent investigations."

He sighed. "That's why I hired Carter, to keep Bitty from getting involved."

"Well," I said, "he was very helpful. But Bitty has been insistent on getting that rifle from the beginning. She gets obsessed. Perhaps you noticed."

"I noticed. And she may have a point."

My ears perked up. I probably looked like an Irish setter. I blame that on the box of hair dye from Walmart. Apparently Fire Red means just that. At any rate, I leaned forward. "What do you mean by that?"

"It's possible that the rifle she identified as hers has either been switched or possibly tampered with at some point so it fires. The experts disagree."

I thought that over. "So Brandon could still be accused of having fired the fatal shot?"

"It's possible."

"Until it's a certainty, I think Bitty would prefer not knowing about it," I said after a moment.

"I agree. No point in making things worse."

"Making what worse, sugar?" Bitty chirped as she stepped out onto the porch, and I hoped she hadn't heard what he'd said about the rifle.

I said the first thing that popped into my head: "Putting up an invisible fence to keep Chitling from wandering. After all, you already have a fence around the yard. If she figured out how to squeeze her plump butt through the bars of the fence, she'll figure out how to turn off the electricity."

Bitty looked thoughtful. Perhaps I had achieved my goal. Unfortunately, that brought up an entirely new set of issues.

"That isn't a bad idea at all, Trinket. But then, do I want my precious girl subjected to electric shocks? I don't think so, but I don't want her lost or hit by a car, either. Maybe I should hire a dog sitter for when I have to leave her home. Sharita must have been frantic, and I don't want her to feel responsible if it should ever happen again."

I envisioned a series of thieves and irresponsible transients drifting through Bitty's house as dog sitters. Apparently, so did Jackson Lee. He cleared his throat.

"Let me help you figure out which is best, sugar-pie," he said with a smile, and Bitty smiled back, adjusting Chitling to fit under her other arm as she leaned forward to kiss him on his forehead.

Chitling snapped at empty air, Jackson Lee recoiled, and I finished off my tea and got up to let them sort it out. He'd know what to say or do to alleviate if not prevent Bitty going off on another tangent.

It was cool and quiet in the house as I replenished my tea. Overhead ceiling fans shed a cool breeze, the air smelled faintly of garlic and lemon due to Sharita's recent culinary expertise, and the old house nestled comfortably around me as I wandered into the front parlor where Bitty kept a sofa and plush chair, desk, chair on wheels, ferns, and business papers. It looked out over the front porch, and I saw Bitty sit down next to Jackson Lee and settle Chen Ling in her lap. This could take a while. I considered a nap. I regretted leaving my book at home, a marvelous romance about a medieval knight and his damsel in distress. Then I wondered if I should go and interview Royal Stewart myself. It might be best. Bitty and Chitling could be intimidating.

I retreated to the hall and the fancy French phone on a mosaic table to call Rayna. She could give me his exact address. I briefly explained my mission when she answered, and she offered to go with me. Perfect.

It took only a moment to negotiate the Bitty gauntlet with vague references to seeing how Rayna was doing and I'd be right back, and thankfully, Jackson Lee aided my cause by asking Bitty if Sharita had baked any of her famous muffins or made Aunt Sarah's pimento cheese. Saved.

Rayna came out of the house before I could even turn off my car engine and got into the front seat and buckled up, smiling at me. "I've missed engaging in skullduggery. Thank you for thinking of me, Trinket."

"You must not have heard of my recent name change," I said as I maneuvered my car out into the street to turn around and head back toward Randolph Street. As with most things in my life since my return to Holly Springs, it was a lot funnier in the retelling than it had been in the experience, so that Rayna giggled all the way to Randolph Street and the boarding house. We parked on the street, and I looked at the steep staircase leading up to the second floor. It had been an obvious add-on once the old home was turned into a boarding house, and I didn't quite trust the rickety-looking stairs.

"Are you sure those are safe?" I muttered as I followed Rayna across the yard. It had been neatly mowed and trimmed, flowers grew in tidy beds, but the stairs were a nightmare waiting to happen.

"Probably not," Rayna replied cheerfully. Of course, she's the kind of person to whom bad things are considered learning experiences. Which doesn't explain why she's still hanging out with me and Bitty and is a founding member of the Divas. You'd think she'd have learned by now that lightning can and does strike in the same place more than once.

Still, I followed her up the narrow, steep steps to the tiny landing at the top. I clung to the side-rails while she knocked on the door. Royal came to the door, his dark hair tousled, and looking sleepy-eyed.

"Oh, did we wake you?" Rayna asked pleasantly, and he shrugged.

"I worked late last night but need to be up anyway. Aren't you Rob Rainey's wife?"

Rayna smiled. She's one of those beautiful women who can enchant men and probably random frogs with just a smile, and he stepped back to invite us into his efficiency apartment that was little more than a room and kitchenette. It was surprisingly neat and tidy. My gaze was immediately drawn to an antique rifle hung on the wall. It looked very similar to Bitty's.

While I walked over to look at it, Rayna said, "We hope you can clear up confusion for us on the reason you went to jail the night before Walter Simpson was killed."

I glanced over my shoulder and caught the puzzled expression on Royal's face. "I'm not in trouble for something else, am I?" he asked.

"Heavens, I hope not," Rayna replied with her most beguiling smile. "We just can't help thinking that somehow that fight is connected to the mess surrounding Brandon Caldwell."

"Yeah, I heard all charges against him were dismissed. Glad to hear that. It wouldn't have been Brandon involved in that fight with Skip, anyway. Clayton was the one who Skip tried to beat down over Jenna a while back. Skip can't ever tell the twins apart."

That got my immediate attention. "Were Brandon and Clayton at the bar that Friday night too?" I asked.

"Yes, ma'am. Just for a little while, though. Clayton saw that Skip was drunk and mean and figured it was a good time to leave."

"But you stayed," Rayna said, and he grinned.

"Yes, ma'am. I don't mind a little scrap every now and then, and Skip asks for it when he's been drinking. Besides, after Clayton and Skip got into it at the last reenactment, I figured he might have it coming."

A dozen different ideas rattled in my brain. None of them concrete, just crumbs that had little connection to facts. But I still asked, "What reenactment was that?"

"Stones River reenactment. It was right after Christmas. Why?"

"That's up around Murfreesboro?"

He looked surprised. "Yes, ma'am. Not many people are familiar with the more obscure battles, just the famous ones."

"I know lots of useless trivia." I abandoned the rifle on the wall and moved closer to him where he stood by a small sofa set in front of a sixty-inch television hooked up to gaming systems. As in multiple. He wore a tee shirt, Spiderman pajama pants, was barefoot, and looked very young. "Is that your rifle?" I pointed to the one on the wall.

He nodded. "Yes, ma'am. Well, it's not an heirloom or anything. I bought it at one of the reenactments."

"Does it fire?"

He looked puzzled, then wary. "It did last time I used it. Why?"

"And the last time you used it was at the pilgrimage the day before Walter was killed?"

"I told all that to the police already. They gave it back to me last week. It's not the gun that killed Walter Simpson."

"I'm sure it's not." I walked back over to the rifle and studied it.

"When you clean it, do you break it down completely? Take the barrel off and everything?"

"That's the best way to clean a weapon."

"Did you clean it at the last reenactment at Stones River?"

I turned to look at him when he hesitated, and he still looked mystified. "Yes, ma'am, as a matter of fact several of us cleaned our weapons. There wasn't much else to do except drink, and you can only do that so long."

"Do you recall who else was there?" Rayna asked, and I saw that she'd caught the drift of my interrogation.

He nodded. "Brandon and Clayton, of course, and Sammy Simpson . . . let me think, oh yeah, Arlie Newton and Tommy Gibbons were with us too, as well as Skip."

Rayna glanced at me, and I lifted my eyebrows. Then I looked at Royal. "Do you know what kind of rifle Skip Whalen owns?"

"Enfield, like the rest of us. It was the second most common weapon used, although the 1861 Springfield was the most popular the last few years of the War."

"So tell me about Jenna. That's who Clayton and Skip got in an argument over, right?"

Royal shrugged. "She's a pretty girl. I think she's screwed up messing around with Skip since he has a reputation for getting, ah, rough with his girlfriends, but some people just don't get wise until it's too late."

"So how did you get involved that Friday night?"

Royal shifted, crossed his arms over his chest, obviously getting tired of our questions. "Look, I don't want to be any more involved in this than I am. Skip got rough with Jenna, I got mad, he took a swing at me, and I tried to break his nose. We both went to jail."

"And how was Clayton involved in that?" Rayna asked.

Royal shrugged. "He wasn't. Not that night. They'd got into it over Jenna a while back. Clay cleaned his clock. Skip said he'd get even with him for that, but they must have patched it up because he didn't have much to say to him that Friday night."

"I appreciate your information," Rayna said. "I think it will help a lot."

"Just keep my name out of it, please." Royal shoved a hand through his hair, a rueful smile on his face. "My brother says if I get in trouble again he's going to make sure I spend some quality jail time."

I understood that. We walked the few steps to the door, when I thought of something and turned. "Can you tell me when Skip got out of jail?"

"Oh, he got out before I did. His daddy came and paid bail before he even got to a cell. He was bleeding everywhere. My brother let me sweat until early morning."

I smiled. "You've really helped Brandon and Clayton, I think. Thank you."

I made it almost all the way down the steep stairs without tripping but did have to take the last two steps in a giant leap to keep my balance. Rayna had glided down as if greased. There are times I find her quite annoying.

"So what do you think?" she asked once we were back in my car.

"I think we have some intriguing possibilities: a fight over a girl, an angry boyfriend, an opportunity to sabotage his rifle, and someone attacked Brandon after the fight at JB's. Are you still grounded from doing any kind of investigating?"

Rayna made a rude sound. "Rob can advise, he can request, but I draw the line at orders. I take it we visit Mr. Whalen next?"

I smiled. Rayna is very quick. I like that about her.

Chapter 13

WE WENT BY HER house so she could look up information on Skip Whalen on the programs installed in their computer, while I let her dogs out into the garden to do their business. She has an old dog named Belle, a lovely black lab with a friendly temperament that regards everyone she meets as a friend. Jinx is much younger but seems to realize Belle is slower and has her limitations. They ambled slowly around the garden while I breathed in the scents of spring and essence of Mississippi. Lovely fragrances that recalled my childhood.

As I reflected on childhood memories, one of the depot owners emerged with a dog on a leash. Both black labs ran to the fence and barked welcomes, and she waved. I waved back. Next door, the lunch crowd at Phillips had picked up, and I was glad I had a parking spot. Rayna said they intend to eventually pave the narrow driveway that leads to the back of the property and the alleyway where their garage/former carriage house is located. Old properties require constant maintenance—a reminder to me whenever I thought of buying my own house once I won the lottery. Of course, I'd win enough to pay someone else to do all the maintenance, but as long as I was dreaming, I included a magic house that cleaned itself.

Rayna whistled from the door, and I took that as my cue to follow the dogs.

"Sorry to take so long," she said when I joined her inside the huge former hotel lobby. "I did some sleuthing while I was at it. Oh, and I made us some lunch. Hope you're hungry."

She'd put a small buffet atop the former registration desk, and I realized I was pretty hungry. "I'm starved. Reminiscing and fantasies always make me hungry."

Rayna pulled up a stool next to me. "Reminiscing about . . .?"

"Childhood. Spring and summer when everything was green, and the world had no sharp edges. Hopscotch. Swinging on vines over the creek, falling into cool water and pretending I had slipped, chasing fireflies at dusk, roasting marshmallows on a green stick Daddy cut for me, sleepovers where we giggled and made up stories."

Rayna smiled and pushed a dish of strawberries toward me. "Picking strawberries in June, blackberries in midsummer, blueberries in late summer, apples in the fall—we used to have such fun. What are your fantasies? G-rated, please."

I laughed. "Old houses that magically clean themselves."

"I keep looking for that bottle with a genie inside. I understand perfectly."

"So what did you sleuth?" I asked as I chose a fat red strawberry.

"Just some background on Skip. We did his bond and Royal's that Friday night. Rob took care of Royal, and I wrote Skip's bond. He's got a record of arrests, mostly for fighting and malicious mischief. Nothing major, mostly vandalism."

"I so look forward to meeting him," I said with a sigh, and Rayna laughed.

After we finished ham sandwiches with tomato and lettuce, ate fresh fruit and cheese, and drank sweet tea, we tidied up and headed for my car.

"I have another fantasy," I said as we got inside and I rolled down the windows to let in fresh air.

"G-rated?"

"My fantasies usually are, unfortunately. Which way do I go?"

Rayna consulted her printout. "Oh, not far at all. Close to Cady Lee. What's your other fantasy?"

"That we find out who killed Walter and why before Bitty does something else stupid. Did I tell you what she did last night?"

"Oh Lordy, she called me to ask for my help, but I was bonding out someone and couldn't get away. She didn't tell me what she had planned, though. Do I want to know?"

"She tried to break into the police station in the mistaken belief that her rifle was kept in an evidence room there. And she incorporated Miranda Watson as her accomplice."

Rayna laughed, and I entertained her with Bitty's latest escapade all the way to the Whalen house.

It turned out to be close to Cady Lee's house, not far from the cemetery in a lovely old area. Several of the houses are always on the pilgrimage. It was quiet and serene, basking in the spring weather, sunlight and soft breezes that could be deceptively balmy. April is a fickle month in the South. A gorgeous day can turn into a night of tornadoes and hail that destroy crops and shred fruit blossoms. Not to mention turn lives upside down.

So I just enjoyed the weather while possible as we turned into the driveway of the house where Whalen lived with his parents. It was a charming little house, brick with arched doors and wooden shutters and window boxes, gently sloping lawn, and a garage out back that held a monster truck behind the open doorway. It had huge wheels. I assumed it belonged to Skip and not his middle-aged parents.

"Rob would love that truck," said Rayna as we got out of the car. "He has a fantasy where he's in a monster truck rally."

"That's frightening to know. And I always thought Rob had good sense."

"He has his moments," she said, and I nodded.

Rob did indeed have his moments. He'd saved our lives not an awful long time ago, and I still talked nicely to him and brought him slices of cake when my daddy didn't eat it all. He's a big fan of Hummingbird cake.

Mrs. Whalen answered the door. She was about my age, with tidy brown hair and a nice smile. Until Rayna asked if her son was home, then her smile turned into a grimace, and she looked at us as if we were bugs in her salad.

"Who are you? Wait—I've seen you before. You're that crazy woman who runs around getting mixed up in murders."

Since that could have applied to both of us, I let Rayna take the lead. Besides, the woman was intimidating. She was slender but wiry, and confrontational. Then her husband popped up behind her, and he was definitely intimidating. He had brawny shoulders, a bald head, arms like a wrestler, and tattoos on his neck and face.

Rayna stood her ground. "Is your son in? We handled his bail bond, if you recall, and I have a few questions for him."

Mr. Whalen pushed his wife aside and filled the open door with his bulk. He did not look at all friendly. "What kind of questions?"

"As your son is not a minor and capable of response, I must address those questions to him."

Rayna remained cool and calm, and I goggled with admiration.

Mr. Whalen leaned against the door frame. "He ain't in. I'll tell him you came by."

"Do you know my name?"

"Don't need to. You're the bail bond lady. He'll know it."

He had a point. I took a step back. Rayna stood firm. "Rainey Bail Bonds. He must ask for Rayna."

Whalen guffawed. "Rayna Rainey? Sounds like a boy band."

Rayna didn't move. "My name is Rayna Blue. If he does not contact me soon, I shall consider him non-compliant. There are consequences."

She sounded very professional and confident. I believed her. Apparently, so did Skip Whalen's father.

"Fine. He's in the garage. Talk to him."

Then he stepped back and shut the door in our faces. I was relieved.

"I didn't know you could do that," I said as we walked down the short brick path to the driveway. "What consequences would there be if he didn't contact you?"

"I'd be bummed."

When she didn't add anything, I said, "That's it?"

"That's it. Did you believe me?"

"I did. You're good. Ask Skip if he killed Walter. Tell him there are non-compliant consequences for lying to a bail bondsman."

Rayna just laughed.

Skip was under the monster truck when we found him. He was on some kind of rolling board, and when Rayna called his name, he rolled out to peer up at us. He squinted slightly. "Whaddya want?"

"Do you remember me?" Rayna asked, and he blinked.

"Naw. Who are ya?"

Grease smeared his forehead, and his nose looked a bit off-center, but other than that, he could have been handsome, if I fancied female abusers. Since I do not, I found him rather repulsive.

Rayna remained calm and in charge of the situation. "I bonded you out of jail the night you got in a bar fight with Royal Stewart."

He grunted. "Which time?"

"The night before Walter Simpson was killed."

"Huh. Yeah, I remember that."

"That's a good start. What else do you remember of that night?"

Scowling, he pulled himself the rest of the way out from under the truck by grabbing the frame and rolling backward. Then he got to his feet. He was built a lot like his father, brawny but with hair. He had peculiarly light eyes, and I couldn't decide if they were blue or gray. He wiped his hands on a rag he pulled from his back pocket. He wore mechanic's overalls; they might have been gray. It was hard to tell.

"What's this about?" he demanded, and Rayna didn't flinch when he towered over her. I thought she looked splendid and uncowed.

"It's about the fight that night with Royal Stewart. What is your version of the event?"

"What does this have to do with my bond?"

"You haven't been to court yet. I want to be sure you'll make an appearance, and it's more likely you'll show up if the consequences are likely to be light."

"The charges are creating a public disturbance and property damage. I'll pay a fine and go home."

"Perhaps. Don't you have a previous record?"

Skip looked uneasy. "Yeah."

"Now, please give me your version of the events of that night."

Skip tried once more: "I already gave my statement to the police that night."

"Yes, and now I want the truth. After hitting Jenna, what happened next?"

"Did she tell you that? Don't believe anything that lying little bitch has to say." He added a few more comments it's best not to repeat, ending with, "Fine. She got all uppity, and I gave her a reminder of what happens when females act stupid. I didn't hit her. Hard, anyway. Then Clay had to put his nose in it, but his brother had the good sense to make him leave. After that, Royal decided to stick his nose in my business, and it ended up in a fight."

"I heard you got whipped," Rayna said, and Skip's face turned bright red.

"The hell I did! He might have broke my nose, but he ended up spending the night in jail for it. My daddy got me out and took me to the ER. They put a splint on it, but it still ain't right. Now I have to go to court and pay fines—he shoulda minded his own business."

"So you're pretty mad at Royal, I imagine."

"I don't get mad. I get even. My daddy taught me not to take nothin' off nobody, or I'd be kicked around in this world, and he's right. So I don't. Now, get out of here if you're through asking stupid questions."

Oddly, he reminded me of Catfish Carter. Maybe it was his way of speaking, tough and covering up a multitude of deficiencies, I was quite sure. Except Catfish was efficient in his job, and Skip seemed to lack even basic decency.

"Lovely family," I remarked as we returned to my car.

"Yes, I found them obnoxious too." Rayna buckled her seatbelt and leaned back. "Skip has motive, opportunity, and means. And I didn't even get around to asking him about his rifle. I wonder why he wasn't in the pilgrimage reenactment since he goes to the other ones."

I was struck by that. I looked at her as I started the engine. "That's a good point. Did he try to join and was turned down? Did he elect not to join in because he had other plans? So maybe he was at the depot but not dressed as a soldier. Wouldn't carrying a weapon be noticed then?"

"It's possible. Or it's also possible he dressed as a soldier and slipped into the crowd and joined the fight without anyone noticing."

"But the police should have caught that if he did," I mused aloud. "After all, they were questioning everyone and even made the spectators stay for questions."

"Once they got there," Rayna said.

A lightbulb went on in my head. "True! There was a span of time after the murder was even noticed. Plenty of time for the killer to escape. But that doesn't explain how Brandon's rifle was the one that fired the fatal shot."

"And there's no evidence that Walter wasn't the intended target all along." Rayna got quiet, and we both pondered all the new information.

Then I said as we reached Van Dorn Avenue, "Jackson Lee says there's a discrepancy in the rifle identification. The experts don't agree. Did I already tell you that?"

"No, but I deduced something like that from the questions you were asking Royal. What kind of discrepancies, did he say?"

"No. We were being secretive on the front porch while Bitty cleaned up her pug. We'd rather Bitty not know anything about that. She worries, and when she's worried she does crazy things."

"Like try to break into police stations. Lord, sometimes I wonder what goes on in her brain."

"Don't go there. It's frightening." I braked at the light on S. Market, glanced in my rear-view mirror, and saw a patrol car behind me. Secure in my new taillight, I smugly waggled my fingers at the officer. He responded with a friendly flash of light and siren burp. The light changed, I moved forward, and the siren and light repeated. Maybe it hadn't been friendly.

"What'd you do?" Rayna asked, and I shrugged.

"No idea." I pulled over at the gas station next to the Methodist church and parked. I recognized the officer as he emerged from the patrol car and walked toward me. Officer Stewart. Maybe he was just checking on the taillight. Maybe Royal had complained we'd questioned him.

He bent down and said, "Did you get your new license yet, Miz Truevine?"

I gulped. "Yes, I did that first thing this morning."

"Good. May I see it, please?"

I glanced at Rayna, who gave me a smile somewhere between concerned and tickled. I knew what was about to happen, but what choice did I have? I took my license out of my red wallet and handed it to him. He frowned at it, then squinted up at me.

"European Treevine?"

"There was a miscommunication." I tried a smile. "The young lady who entered the data misread my birth certificate. And apparently my work ID."

"Uh huh. Do you have those with you?"

I sighed. "Yes, I do."

When I handed the birth certificate and ID to him, he scanned the former and then lifted his brows at the latter. "Hot Pants and Hot Slots? Is this your stripper ID?"

Rayna tried to muffle a snort of laughter, but I heard her.

With as much dignity as I could muster, I replied, "No, it's a casino in Nevada, and I was in Human Resources. It was the only photo ID I still have, so I used it. My others were stolen, but I've just been told that my purse was located by the Corinth Police Department, so I hope to have my original license and ID returned soon."

After a moment, Stewart blew out a heavy breath. "You know, you're either the worst con-woman I've ever met, or you're telling the truth. Since I recognize Miz Blue, I'll go with the last. If I'm wrong, I'll find you."

That sounded ominous. He handed me my license and photo ID, and I slipped them into my purse. "If you contact the Corinth Police, they'll verify what I told you."

He nodded. "I might do that. Good day, Miz Blue, Miz Truevine."

As he walked back to his patrol car, Rayna managed to ask with a straight face, "Why didn't you tell him Sergeant Maxwell can verify your identity? Or Deputy Farrell?"

I started the car. "Are you serious? Either of those two would be very happy to see me do a nickel in the pen."

Rayna snorted laughter through her nose. It was very unladylike. "Where did you hear that phrase?"

"I think it was *Law & Order* reruns. Or it could be *The Big Bang Theory*. Who knows."

"Trinket, hanging out with you and Bitty can be traumatic, but you never disappoint," Rayna said, and I feared she was right.

Just to be polite, I stopped by Bitty's house before I went home. I had to work the next day and wanted to be home early to recover from my trauma. Jackson Lee had gone, and Bitty came to the door to let me in, wearing a pug in a sling. It was a familiar style for her. I avoided the front fangs of a grumpy pug and sidled in the door.

"I'm on my way home but thought I'd stop by for a minute. Really, doesn't that hurt your neck? That sling looks uncomfortable, and Chitling isn't that light."

"Fifteen pounds, and sometimes it does ache. Where have you been? I wish you'd replace your cell phone."

"They're mailing me a new one. Then I'll have to figure out how to use it again."

"It should be easy enough, since it's just like your last one, Trinket," Bitty said over her shoulder as she headed to the kitchen with me behind her.

"No, of course they've discontinued the last model I had, and now I'll have a new one with new features, and—just keep me away from hammers for the first week, and I'll be okay after that."

"Are you hungry?" Bitty asked, opening her refrigerator, and I shook my head.

"I had a sandwich at Rayna's. She had fresh strawberries. I think they were from Mexico or California, though. It'll be nice when they ripen here. Wait—what is that?"

"Carpenter's is open. They have ripe strawberries."

I put my purse on the counter as she pulled out a tub of strawberries. Greed gleamed in my eyes, I was sure. "Do you have whipped cream?"

"Of course. Sharita sliced strawberries earlier, so you can have whole ones or sliced ones. Take your pick."

We ended up with both. Bitty ladled strawberries atop shortcake, added whipped cream, another shortcake, more berries, then more whipped cream, and we cautiously carried our towering structures of deliciousness to the kitchen table. We might have tried the parlor, but we both knew we'd never make it that far.

Halfway through, I said as I dipped a whole strawberry into the container of whipped cream Sharita had left, "Rayna and I talked to Royal Stewart."

"Without me?" Bitty paused with a strawberry poised in front of her mouth, and the pug she wore decided it must be meant for her. Chen Ling grabbed for it, Bitty tried to pull back, but the pug won. She chomped delightedly on whipped cream and strawberry. Bitty shrugged and reached for another one. "I can't believe you went without me."

"You were busy with Jackson Lee. You don't feed her grapes, I hope. They're deadly for dogs."

"I'm happy you care about Chen Ling's health, but you know I don't feed her grapes. So what did y'all find out? Anything good?"

Rayna and I had decided to limit the information so Bitty wouldn't get her hopes up too high, and I relayed the bare details about our conversation with Royal.

"Maybe we should go see Skip Whalen tomorrow," Bitty said as we reached the last bit of strawberries and shortcake. She fed Chitling a strawberry without whipped cream. The pug grunted happily, sounding similar to how we'd sounded moments before, I'm sure.

"I have to work tomorrow, but Rayna and I talked to Skip after we talked to Royal. He's pretty obnoxious. But so are his parents, so I can understand where he gets it."

"I see," Bitty said, eying me over the depleted plates of strawberries. "You did all that without me."

"Did you really want me to come drag you away from Jackson Lee? He didn't look in the mood to let you out of his sight."

"Well, he could have, and I'd be fine with it. All he did was fuss at me for trying to get my rifle. It wasn't like I was going to steal it, not really. How can you steal what you own? And besides, I just know there's something not right about those rifles. I want to see it and hold it, not just look at pictures."

"You know since it's the murder weapon, they have to keep it until they arrest someone and they go to trial."

"Which means I'll never get my rifle back," Bitty said glumly. "Jackson Lee said he'd see about arranging a visit tomorrow so I can see the rifle, but the prosecutor is protesting."

That told me Jackson Lee truly did think the rifle may not be the murder weapon. Unless he was stalling Bitty until he was certain. That was possible. I felt duplicitous for not saying anything to her about it but reasoned it was for her own protection. One more midnight raid at the police station may see her learning to make license plates at Parchman.

"You'd think the prosecutor would want the truth instead of

putting obstacles in the way," I said as I put dirty dishes in the sink and started rinse water.

"You would, wouldn't you?" Bitty agreed. "You don't have to rinse those, you know. The dishwasher does it all."

"Habit. And unless your dishwasher has a disposal grinding up food left on plates—not that we left much—it's more sanitary. Did Jackson Lee say what he thinks about the prosecutor? I know lawyers like to get together even when they're on opposite sides, but just wondered if he had an opinion on him yet."

"He's reliably vague. Wine or tea?"

I thought a moment. "I really need to go home. So, tea. I don't want to get stopped again today and have to French kiss a breathalyzer."

"Again today? You're making a bad habit of that."

"I know. Meeting law enforcement in strained circumstances is getting old."

We took our tea out to the front porch. Her lawn service had tidied everything up and trimmed bushes, raked leaves, planted spring flowers, and removed any pug piles.

"Did you know there's a dog poop service?" I asked, dredging up trivia from a brain sated with strawberries and whipped cream.

Bitty looked at me. "To make deposits or clean it up?"

"The last. They come on scheduled visits, clean up poop, dispose of it properly, and charge a fee. I read about it somewhere."

"Is there one in Holly Springs?"

"No idea. There's always something for entrepreneurs to do. Just look at Mrs. Tyree. She started out cleaning houses, built a reputation, added more houses, hired help, and when she sold the business years ago, it was worth a fortune. Put her kids and grandkids through college. All it takes is ingenuity and hard work."

Bitty was silent for a moment, then said, "I married rich men."

I lifted my tea glass in a salute. "And prospered. I'd rather clean houses, myself, but I know you didn't marry them for money."

"I've thought about that. I think perhaps I married Franklin for his money, although at the time I thought it was love. It just didn't work out."

"Probably because you were still trying to get over Frank. You even married a man with a similar name. You were broke and frantic and had young sons. You did the best you could."

"Marrying for love is really the only reason to get married, I've come to realize."

"You married Philip Hollandale for love, and look how that turned out. Never mind, Bitty. You're smarter now. Experience has taught you a few things. When you marry again, it will be for all the right reasons."

She looked at me. "Jackson Lee brought up marriage."

I stared at her. When she didn't elaborate, I said, "And? Did he propose? Give you a ring? Buy you a car?"

"Don't be silly. He just suggested that when we marry, I retire from the Divas."

I didn't like the sound of that. It was one thing for him to get exasperated at the dumb things we do, but quite another to try to control her choice of friends, including crazy ones.

"And what did you say?" I asked cautiously.

"I said that any man who expects me to give up friends isn't the right man for me."

She sounded rather sad. So I said, "I'm sure he didn't mean it the way it sounded."

"That's what he said. He said he meant Diva activity like trying to solve murders. I understand that. But now I'm wondering if we did get that serious, would he change down the road? Would he expect me to give up friends? And if I did, what next? Give up family for him? My dog? I can't do that, Trinket. I won't do that."

"Bitty, I think you've had a traumatic day and may be overly sensitive. Jackson Lee has never struck me as the kind of man who demands control. He already has enough control in his daily work, and he's not at all insecure. You're especially careful about that because of Philip. But he was a completely different kind of man. Wait and see. Y'all have been together for about a year, and this is the first time he's said anything like this, so just take it slow and easy and see what happens."

Bitty sighed. "You're right. And it has been traumatic. I almost lost my precious girl, and that scared me."

Precious Girl looked at me smugly as Bitty hugged her. I decided it was time to leave the two alone to snuggle. Bitty walked me to my car.

"Come by tomorrow after work. If I get in to see my rifle, I'll give you an update on our case."

I nodded wisely, thinking all the time that the only case we really had was our shared mental instability. I asked my mother about it when I got home.

"Mama, were Bitty and I always crazy, or is this some kind of midlife crisis we're going through?"

Mama looked over at me, a faint smile on her face as she chopped vegetables at the sink. "Well, hon, Sarah and I used to ask each other if it was healthy for you two to be together so often. You just seemed to gravitate toward trouble. We tried to keep you apart at times, but it never really helped. I blame the Truevine genes."

"So it's genetic?"

"Oh no, honey. I think it's just you two are so much alike."

That stunned me. "Alike as in how?" I finally got up the courage to ask. "I don't think we're anything alike."

"Really?" Mama looked thoughtful. Then she went back to chopping carrots. I got the point: We've always been crazy. That thought lingered with me the rest of the day.

Kit called me that night, sounding weary. "A long day, a bowel resection, and two dogs hit by cars. Almost lost one of them, but I think he's got a good chance. I brought him home with me for the night because Mrs. Taylor worried about him dying alone."

One of the things I appreciate most about Kit is his compassion for not only the pets he treats but their owners. He knows that most of them think of their dog or cat or bunny as a member of the family.

"You probably won't get much sleep tonight," I said, and he chuckled.

"Probably not. I'm monitoring Rebel pretty close, but his vitals are good. So what have you ladies been doing the past few days?"

We hadn't seen each other much lately. Sometimes it's like that. But we always picked up right where we left off when we got together, and I really appreciated that, too.

I gave him a brief rundown of the past few days and what Rayna and I had learned from Royal and Skip, and added, "And Jackson Lee thinks the rifle may not be Bitty's."

"He said that?"

"No. He's a lawyer. He said there are discrepancies. I read between the lines."

Kit laughed. "Jackson Lee is a cautious man. I'd be careful with the Whalen family, though."

My ears perked up. I hadn't mentioned my suspicions that Skip might be involved in the death of Walter, whether by design or accident. It could be he was trying to kill Royal, or he could have been trying to frame Brandon or Clayton, although the last was pretty weak.

It'd take too much planning and machinations, and he didn't seem bright enough for that. Skip was more a reactive kind of guy, in my opinion.

At any rate, I asked, "Why do you say that?" about the Whalen family.

After a pause, Kit said, "I base my opinions of people on how they treat their pets a lot of the time. It's usually a pretty close indicator of their characters."

It was what he didn't say that really grabbed my attention. "Are the Whalens your clients at the clinic?"

"They were. I wasn't impressed with their compassion."

If Kit said something negative about someone, I listened. He usually tried to stay in a middle-of-the-road mode. I didn't ask for details, and I don't think he would have shared them anyway.

"I see," I finally said. "They're no longer clients?"

"No. Their pet died despite all I could do. They're a sporting family. Used to have dogs."

That said a lot. "Sporting. Like hunting?"

"Yep. The entire family."

"Oh." That meant either Skip or his father could be marksman enough to shoot straight. Which meant if they were going to shoot someone, it wouldn't be an accident. "I'll keep my distance during deer season," I said lightly, and we went on to talk about going up to Memphis for the barbecue contest in May. Memphis in May is always crowded, usually turns out to be Memphis in Mud, but it's great fun, and the barbecue is delicious if you know someone who's cooking. Even if not, you can get delirious on the tempting fumes. We made plans to go.

There are times when I miss something important that's right under my nose.

Chapter 14

"DO YOU THINK Bitty and I are alike?" I asked Carolann at work the next day.

She looked over at me, brows lifted, a faint smile on her face. "I didn't used to think that. You always seemed more cautious."

"But now you do?"

Carolann hesitated. It was obvious she didn't want to distress me. I sighed. She put a hand on my arm, her voice earnest.

"Oh Trinket, it's a good thing, most of the time. Really. If not for you, Bitty would be dead or in prison by now. But then again, I don't recall her ever finding a body before you got back to town, so it's possible that the universe has put you together again for a reason."

Entertainment? Vengeance? What on earth could the universe have to do with me and Bitty and our newfound predilection for finding bodies and creating chaos? I was stymied.

But I only said, "Yes, I suppose that's possible."

Carolann smiled and nodded. "Synchronicity is a strange thing, but Carl Jung made very good points that coincidences can be connected for a purpose. Perhaps the purpose is to learn why you and Bitty have recently been involved in helping to solve murders."

That sounded as reasonable as anything else I'd heard. I nodded. "You know, that makes me feel better. I think. Thank you, Carolann."

She laughed. "You're not convinced."

"Well, no. But it still sounds better than just being crazy."

Bitty showed up just as I got off work and was walking out to my car. I'd parked behind the store in a small area for employees. She angled her huge Mercedes into the lot, rolled down her window, and said, "Get in, Trinket."

I hesitated. Did the universe expect me to go off with Bitty on an obvious mission? It could create combustion like splitting the atom. Was the universe ready for that? I didn't know how to request or receive answers, and Carolann was busy, so I got into Bitty's car.

"What's up, buttercup?" I asked as she backed out onto the street without looking behind her, inviting an annoyed driver to honk. She ignored it.

"It's not my rifle."

Oh boy. "What did Jackson Lee say?"

"Technically, it was in Brandon's possession, so the ownership of the rifle doesn't matter as much as who pulled the trigger."

"That doesn't sound good, but I suppose it makes sense. You can always shoot someone with someone else's gun, I guess. Can they recharge him?"

"They can. That doesn't mean they will. It's up to the prosecutor once he has all the information he needs. There's been enough doubt raised that it can be regarded as circumstantial evidence, but there may be extenuating circumstances."

Bitty sounded calm. That made me nervous. I peered at her. She concentrated on aiming the car down Memphis Street. When she turned onto Van Dorn, I had a sneaking suspicion I knew our destination.

"Are we returning to the scene of the crime?"

"Yes. I want to look around and see if something comes to me. It wasn't Brandon. Not even by accident. I know that. Don't ask me how. I'm a mother."

I was quiet for a moment, then said, "I bet Faith Simon thinks that about Brett, too."

"Oh, he's been cleared. I didn't tell you?"

"I haven't talked to you today, Bitty. So no, you didn't tell me."

"Police questioned him, and he ended up confessing he'd made it up because he thought his mother might have done it. That was after a polygraph."

Alarmed, I said, "I hope that doesn't mean the police are going to arrest Faith."

"No. Actually, they both have alibis for the time of Walter's death that are pretty solid, so I think they'll be fine. Brett was just telling his mother he'd aimed at him so she wouldn't confess, and neither of them realized they'd been overheard."

"Well, that's good, but it takes us back to square one."

Bitty stopped at the light on S. Market. "I hate square one. I want square end. I don't think I can stand it if police start looking at Brandon again."

"I know." I thought about telling her what I knew but wondered if that would only make it worse. I wasn't sure of anything yet. A frantic Bitty can be a dangerous Bitty. I'd decide after we looked at the railroad station again. Maybe an idea would come to me, or maybe I'd see that there was no possible way it could have happened as I suspected. I kinda hoped for the first.

Bitty parked in front of Phillips, and we walked over to the depot. I stayed out front while she went in the side door to ask for Gwen.

Gwen wasn't home, but her niece was, and she gave us permission to prowl around all we wanted. She'd been away at school, and I don't think she realized our reputation for getting into trouble did not come close to the reality.

Workmen had been redoing the baggage claim area, the former waiting rooms, and had finished the dining area. Only a few remained, painting newly repaired walls and making sure no nails or broken floorboards remained to injure tourists. There's usually a craft fair in May where people come to sell paintings, crafts, jellies and jams and jewelry, reenactors roam around in blue and gray uniforms, tours are given, and the depot is open for the curious and those who appreciate history. It can be entertaining as well as enlightening. It had been postponed this year.

Sunlight flirted with clouds, and the wind bent smaller trees and tulips. The lunch crowd had long left Phillips, but the teasing scent of fried food wafted through the open door as a patron exited. My stomach growled.

"Can we eat before we prowl?" I asked Bitty.

She gave me an exasperated look. "Can't you wait?"

"I haven't had lunch, and it's nearly four in the afternoon. Phillips closes soon."

"I take it that's a no," Bitty said and shook her head. "Fine. That gives the workmen time to finish up anyway."

We went into Phillips, and I ordered a fried bologna sandwich, fried peach pie, and onion rings. I got an Orange Crush out of the cooler and added it. Bitty got the cheeseburger. We'd both end up regretting all the grease, but at the moment, it smelled too delicious to care.

Once we sat at a table in the window, the cloth-covered tables and iron chairs comfortable and familiar, I reacquainted myself with huge metal tubs holding bottles of Coke, memorabilia hanging on the walls and lining old shelves; the history of the building was recalled in old photographs. Phillips Grocery had been established in 1948, but in the nineteenth century, the building had housed a saloon, and local legend claimed it had been a house of ill-repute as well. I hoped it was true. I rather liked the whispers of a scandalous past.

I sipped my orange soda while waiting for my food, gazing out at the tracks and trying to see the depot reenactment with fresh eyes. It had been earlier in the day, but it had been crowded, the sun shining, with caution tape strung up to keep spectators from getting caught up in the fray. From the perspective of Phillips across the street, they'd only be able to see some of it. The main action had been directly in front of the depot. Down by the freight office, the supplies to be "burned" had been stacked, and just past the baggage claim room of the depot was where Walter had been killed. No one at Phillips could have seen it. But what about someone at the freight office? Could they have witnessed something?

"Did the police question any workers at the freight office?" I asked Bitty after we picked up our food at the counter and returned to the table.

"Jackson Lee said they questioned everybody but the horses." Bitty took a bite of her burger, closed her eyes in brief ecstasy, and we both paid attention to our meal for a few minutes.

"Well," I said when I'd polished off my sandwich and onion rings and unwrapped my peach pie, "no one would have seen it from here, even if the crowd hadn't been there. Wrong angle."

"And Phillips is usually busy on Saturday," Bitty said. "They stay open until six."

I tried to reimagine the scene. It was odd, as I'd been there, yet trying to see it from a different perspective required imagination. I squinted and concentrated.

"Gas?" Bitty said, and I opened my eyes wide and looked at her.

"What?"

"You look gassy. Are you all right?"

I rolled my eyes. "I was thinking, Bitty."

"Oh. It looked painful."

"It wasn't. What are you hoping to find at the depot?"

Bitty shrugged. "I don't know. A clue as to how someone else could have shot Walter Simpson, I suppose. I just don't believe Brandon could have done it, even if the rifle he had is capable of firing. Can you imagine this following him the rest of his life? He's so young, and all he did was take part in a silly reenactment. I tell you, Trinket, I'm really rethinking all this reenactment business. I mean, yes, I want to remember our history because we sure don't want to repeat it, and it was part of our heritage, but what lesson should we take from it? That war is evil? We've known that. Are we supposed to avoid conflict with other Americans? I mean, we do disagree, and politics is a mess, but why should we ever get to the point of hate enough to fight each other over our differences?"

"I've never heard you so contemplative before, Bitty. You're scaring me."

She sighed. "I know. I'm just so worried that somehow this will all end up with my child being charged with a murder he never planned, never wanted, and didn't know happened."

I thought about the video we'd seen, the eye witnesses, most seeing the same thing but interpreting it differently, and wondered if we were looking at it from the right perspective.

After a moment I said, "Did you say the depot is open so we can go inside?"

"Gwen's niece gave us permission, so yes."

"I was standing under the overhang, and if I remember correctly—and I may not—one of the baggage room windows was open. What if someone inside fired the fatal shot?"

Bitty stared at me. "Who? Why?"

"I don't know that for certain. Let's go look."

I ate the last of my peach pie as we walked across the street. Pots of flowers lined the front walk, mulch had been replaced, and bushes that had been trimmed were bursting with new shoots. Most of the action had taken place at the north end of the depot due to space, and the freight or express office resided in a small square building across a graveled open space. That was where the "supplies" had been stacked. I stopped by the baggage room. One of the long windows had been left open by workers and the door was open. I stepped inside. The old floor creaked slightly, but was quite sturdy, and I went to the open window to see if there was anything to my theory.

I calculated for the crowd of tourists, the angle, and realized that it would not have been possible for a shooter to make the shot. He'd have had to lean out the window with his rifle; surely someone would have noticed. All the reenactors were outside the depot, not inside. Disappointed, I walked back outside.

Bitty stood under the freshly painted gray corbels holding up the overhang at the far end of the depot. I walked down to stand by her.

"Searching for a new theory here," I said, and she looked up at me and smiled.

"So am I. But look, Trinket, someone could have stood right here around the corner and fired the shot, and none of the tourists or anyone not acting would have seen them. The main side window of the freight office has an AC unit in, so it's unlikely anyone in there would have seen them."

I stepped around the corner. She was right. It was a wide-open area, but on the day of the reenactment, it had been filled with blue and gray soldiers and a lot of action. Gravel and grass led to the back of the depot and personal living quarters of the family; no doubt cars had parked out of the way. But right here, unless someone was looking, it would have been easy enough for someone to fire a rifle and not be noticed, or be thought to be part of the show. All it took was a uniform and Enfield rifle.

"Tell me about the rifle you saw today, Bitty. How do you know it's not yours?"

"It has the mark on it like the wagon wheel that ran over it a hundred years ago, but it's on the wrong side. It's that simple. And it didn't feel right. Jackson Lee is having the experts look at it again and compare it to the insurance photographs just to be sure."

"So, why and when would that happen? I mean, the rifle has been in your safe since the last time the boys used it, so it'd have to have been switched with another recently."

"I don't know. I called the boys earlier, but they're in class and haven't called back yet. They're usually so careful, but they must have let someone borrow it."

That made sense. It also shot my theory out of the water. Pardon the pun. Several different scenarios ran through my head. I mused aloud, "Did someone plan to kill Walter and switch them, or were they intending to kill someone else and blame Brandon?"

"Who else would they want to kill, though?" Bitty asked.

I leaned back against the red brick wall. "The only person I can think of is Royal Stewart. Walter was wearing his uniform. He wore a hat. Someone had to think he was Royal."

"But that's preposterous. They look nothing alike."

"Think about it, Bitty. Smoke haze, men running around shouting and waving guns, the guy you want to shoot is right there, wearing a hat and uniform you recognize. So you hide around the corner here, probably in a uniform as well, holding an old gun, and you wait for the right moment to take your shot. You're focused on the uniform and hat, not the face, and then your victim is right in front of you. You shoot, then blend into the other reenactors. After it ends and Walter doesn't get up, you join the others who run to him, and take the first chance you can to switch rifles with whoever lays his down."

"Brandon must have laid his rifle down when he tried to help Walter," Bitty said after a moment. "That's when it happened."

"Who would notice something like that? I mean, his rifle is right there, and he picks it up and doesn't think any more about it."

"But the dent in it—how do you explain a dent almost identical to mine?"

"I can't imagine all the rifles got through the war without some kind of damage. It could be a coincidence."

"I'm not sure I believe in coincidences."

I smiled. "Let me tell you a short story about Carl Jung and his theory of synchronicity, and you might change your mind."

Bitty stared at me. I nodded my head encouragingly.

It all seemed to fit.

JACKSON LEE HEARD us out patiently and nodded appropriately but reserved comment until we were through telling him of our theory.

Then he said, "Impressive. It does stretch the bounds of credulity as both rifles had such similar damage, but it's always possible."

"That's it?" Bitty made a rude sound. "It's more than possible. Trinket has told me some very interesting things. You need to look at Skip Whalen."

Jackson Lee glanced at me. I shrugged. Yes, I had told her. He'd have to deal with it.

"Someone should see if Skip Whalen has my rifle," Bitty added indignantly.

Jackson Lee began to explain about things like probable cause, evidence, and so on, but somewhere in there he completely lost Bitty and even me. He ended with a plea.

"I beg of you, don't go snooping. You may get shot, and if you're on their property, there's nothing I could do about it. Please tell me you won't do that."

Bitty crossed her arms over her chest, a rather amazing feat in light of her small arms and big chest. "Do what?"

After briefly closing his eyes in what was probably a prayer, he opened them again and sighed. "If you trespass on private property, you will go to jail at the least, as I doubt the Whalen family will hesitate to call police, or you'll be shot at worst. There are laws. My job is not to skirt the laws, but to uphold them while I defend my clients.

Interpretation of law only goes so far."

"Jackson Lee, honey, I do not intend to be arrested or shot. Neither sound especially fun. So don't you worry your pretty little head."

Uh oh. That was the killer phrase. "Pretty little head" had been a chauvinistic motto far too often in women's lives, but I'd never thought Jackson Lee the kind of man to use it. He blinked in confusion.

"Bitty, I have never said—"

"You don't have to say it to think it or mean it," she said, and I saw her point, but still didn't think it belonged to Jackson Lee. Besides, he was right. Bitty unfettered could be a danger to herself and others.

I held my tongue. It's usually unwise to interfere in other people's arguments unless directly involved, and while Bitty would certainly directly involve me in any manic scheme, it was best to wait for proof.

That came rather quickly.

After Jackson Lee left—on uncertain terms—Bitty shut the door behind him and bit her lower lip. That sign of distress moved me to ask, "Honey, are you all right?"

"No, but there was no other way to manage it. I had an idea. Do you want wine or tea while I tell you about it?"

"Straight whiskey couldn't ease my angst if you plan on prowling around the Whalen house looking for your rifle."

"Well, I have that, too. Maybe a valium somewhere. It's probably expired, though. I never take them."

"It's for me, not you," I said unkindly, and she just smiled and waved me to follow.

I followed her into the kitchen while she poured wine. I knew it was futile, but I had to try. "Bitty, whatever you have planned—don't do it. Please."

"I'll need your help. And maybe someone like Gaynelle or Cady Lee. Who do we know that the Whalens might not know we know?"

"Three hundred and fifty million Americans, for a start."

She gave me a disapproving look. "I said that we know, Trinket. Do try to keep up, or this may take a while."

"Whatever you have planned, I'm not helping. Neither will Gaynelle or Rayna or even Miranda Watson."

Bitty perked up. "Yes, I could ask Miranda to do it. She might. She owes me after leaving me in a dumpster."

"I'll call her and suggest she go on vacation."

"I'll offer her a diamond tiara for her pig to wear."

I took the glass of wine she held out, sucked it down, and gave it back to her. "More. And I can't fight bribery."

"I know. Let's just take the bottles into the parlor with us."

We carried the wine into the parlor, where I sat across from her on my cushioned chair with matching ottoman and put my feet up. I briefly considered leaving, but that wouldn't stop Bitty. If nothing else, I could find out her plan and work to prevent it.

It rarely turns out that way.

"Once I realized Jackson Lee wasn't going to arrest Skip Whalen," Bitty said as I thought about just sticking a straw into my bottle of wine, "I realized I'd have to manage it all myself. So I had to make him leave, you see. And now that he's probably irritated with me, he won't be hanging around so won't find out our plans."

"Your plans. I wonder if there are bags of wine I could just fit with an IV and mainline."

Bitty stared at me. "You say the oddest things, Trinket."

"I've been told that. Do go on. How are you going to arrest Skip? And you do know Jackson Lee is an attorney, not a police officer, right?"

"Really, Trinket, you talk to me sometimes as if I'm stupid."

I sucked down two inches of wine and tried not to choke.

"Anyway," she continued, "I wondered if I could lure Skip away from his house with an offer to buy his rifle. Then I realized he wouldn't sell it to me, even if he admits he has it. But he can't keep it, you see, for that is evidence, and he has to know if he's caught with it, it can get him in trouble. Right now he has no idea that the rifle in custody has been proven not to be mine. When he finds out, he'll have to dispose of my rifle. Right?"

It made a convoluted sort of logic. I nodded. "Go on."

"So, I'll get Miranda to write in her column that the rifle in police custody is not my rifle, so police are still searching for the killer, then get her to offer to buy it from Skip."

I waited. She stared at me with a smile, pug in lap, wine glass in hand, hope in her eyes. I almost hated to point out the obvious flaw. Almost.

"You don't think Skip might find it odd that Miranda would offer to buy the rifle after printing that police may be looking for it?"

"Well, she won't say that, of course. She'll just say she wants to buy an antique rifle so her boyfriend can join the next reenactment."

"Bitty, what's to keep Skip from just dumping the rifle in the nearest lake?"

She blanched. "It's an antique! He wouldn't do that!"

"It's easy, and he obviously doesn't care about antiques. He may have already gotten rid of it anyway, and this is all a moot point."

"Okay, so I got bogged down in wishful thinking. What would you suggest?"

I actually thought about it. I blame the wine for that. It didn't seem preposterous to make suggestions for what might work when I had no intention of doing any of it. When will I ever learn?

But I blithely mused aloud, "First, if Skip still has the rifle, which I doubt, I'd think he has it stashed at his house, or garage, or maybe even a rented space. Once he switched it, the sensible thing to do would be get rid of it before police investigated closely enough to realize the murder weapon doesn't belong to you. That wouldn't prevent Brandon from having used it, of course, if one follows police logic, but they'd certainly want to know who the owner of it is. So they'll investigate that. Once the news is known, if Skip hasn't done the practical thing and disposed of the rifle he took in the switch, he has to get rid of it quickly. So perhaps he breaks it down and disposes of it in several different places, barrel here, stock there, and so on. Or he might panic and bury it. He strikes me as the kind who'd panic and not be smart enough to act in his own best interests. Most murderers are just people too lazy or stupid to think of legal means to get rid of enemies, anyway."

I paused, sipped my wine, and realized Bitty hadn't interrupted me. She gave me an encouraging nod. "All that makes sense, Trinket. So what would he do?"

"Well, if he buries it on his property, it would definitely be found once police trace the murder weapon to him. I'm not sure these antique rifles bought and sold at reenactments are that traceable, but police are amazing at tracking down leads and eventually reaching conclusions. So it may happen soon, or it may take them a little bit. Maybe he takes a load of trash to the dump and gets rid of it that way, but police can often trace that, too. So if he's done any research at all on getting rid of a murder weapon—also doubtful—he goes fishing or hunting and manages to leave it in the lake or woods. Not so easy to find then."

Bitty said, "If they're a sports family like Kit said, they have a cabin somewhere."

That struck me as very possible. Bitty leaned forward. Her eyes glistened.

"We could maybe go hiking, don't you think? See if we notice anything unusual?"

"Like what, ripples in the water? Disturbed leaves in the forest?"

"Oh, Trinket, you know what I mean."

"Yes, I do, and I don't want any part of it. You want us to see if they have a camp or cabin somewhere and break into it."

"Well, not *break* into it, exactly. I have a key."

I didn't know what she meant, and my confusion must have shown. She smiled.

"Do you remember the cabin I bought with Philip? It was supposed to be our little getaway in the woods?" When I nodded, as if I could forget the cabin that had been the scene of a murder, she added, "I sold it, if you recall. Guess who bought it?"

Lightning flashed, thunder rolled, the air smelled like sulfur in her parlor as I waited for the devil to appear in a puff of smoke and brimstone. All imaginary, of course, but there are times Jung really is appropriate.

"Synchronicity," we chorused.

Chapter 15

"WHY DID YOU keep a key, if you don't mind me asking?" I inquired as we drove up the narrow, rutted road to Bitty's former cabin.

"I didn't mean to. I happened to find it not long ago when I cleaned out a drawer in my front parlor desk."

"I'm shocked. You cleaned out a drawer?"

"Very funny," Bitty said and focused on getting the Jeep she had borrowed up the incline. It was as steep and narrow as I remembered it. "I don't know how Cindy drives this thing around. It's like aiming a dump truck," she muttered.

"Grinding gears doesn't help," I offered, but she didn't appreciate my critique.

"Do you want to drive this bucket of bolts? 'Cause I'm fine with it if you do."

"I'm good. You're doing a great job. Grinding gears is musical in its own way."

"Can you even drive a straight stick, Trinket?"

"Of course. Maybe. It's been a while." I didn't add that I'd never stripped the gears like she had, as that might have ended with me either driving or walking. So I refrained.

We bucked on up the hill and finally ended in the peaceful front yard of the cabin Bitty had once owned. Crows still nested overhead, noisy and protesting the disturbance. There was no other vehicle in sight. I still shuddered as I recalled our last visit.

"I wonder if the Ashland police ever recovered from our visit to their station?" I mused aloud, and Bitty laughed.

"Probably. They seemed more annoyed than shocked. Very nice people, as it turned out. I think they liked us."

I recalled our visit a bit differently, but then, I'd been rather shell-shocked at the time. And Cady Lee Kincaid had been tipsy. It had been a memorable moment. I didn't want another one like it out in the wilderness too far away from civilization to walk. I'm sure the Ashland police felt the same way.

Bitty seemed to have no such reservations. She unfastened her seatbelt and got out of the Jeep—Cindy Nelson's husband's hunting vehicle that had absolutely no comforts—and went straight up to the front porch and locked door. I hesitated. I stood on the bottom step while Bitty unlocked the door and went inside. No alarms went off, no one came screaming out at us, and as far as I know, no bodies lay inside. I put a tentative foot on the next step up.

"Trinket!" Bitty shouted, and I froze.

"Is it a body?" My voice quavered a little.

"What? No, you idiot. It's a mess. I can't believe they're so untidy. And I had it all decorated so nicely, too. Looks like all they do is drink cheap beer and microwave pizza."

"Do you see your rifle?"

"No, but it could be lying under the pizza boxes for all I know. Come on in here."

I knew it was illegal. The property no longer belonged to Bitty. She shouldn't even have a key to it. But we didn't intend to steal anything, after all, so if her rifle was here, we were going to call Jackson Lee or the police immediately. Probably the former. He was much better at explaining our intrusions to the police. Anyway, Bitty had promised me we wouldn't touch anything if we found it, but take photos and then call authorities. That was the only way I'd agreed to come along on this ride to insanity. Plus, I felt a bit responsible for it since I'd been the one to talk about the possibilities of the rifle being in the woods.

I got to the front door and peered inside. Bitty was right. It was a mess. I'd seen worse in my time, however, so stepped over discarded camouflage overalls lying on the floor to join her.

"Is that it?" I indicated the rifle rack over the fireplace; it held several rifles, and one looked old.

"No. You've seen my rifle, Trinket. Does that look like an antique?"

"Uh, it looks old."

"It's not that old. Here. I brought a photo of it." She took out her cell phone, scrolled through, then held it out to me until I took the phone.

I immediately hit the wrong thing, and it went to a photo of Chitling drooling on her little pink bib. Bitty snatched it away from me and held it under my nose so I had to draw back a bit to see it without crossing my eyes.

"Oh. Yeah, now I remember," I said. "Okay. I'll look for one like that."

After a half hour of cautious searching—although I doubt Skip or his father would have noticed if we did anything other than clean up—we had to admit defeat.

"Maybe it's buried outside," Bitty said, and we exited the cabin and looked around in the yard for a while. I had foolishly worn capris although I did wear tennis shoes and ankle socks; apparently ticks and fleas were awake from winter naps. My white socks held black polka dots that bite.

I got in the Jeep, dangled my legs over the side, and stripped away shoes and socks and gave them a good shake. My ankles looked like I had been attacked by flesh-eating bacteria. I glanced up in time to see a truck on the road below the cabin. The drive up cut back and forth a few times, but it was the only way to the cabin. My stomach dropped.

"Bitty! Someone is coming!"

My shriek startled the nesting crows, and they flapped wings and shrieked louder than I had. Bitty ran over, climbed into the Jeep, and started it. "Seatbelt!" she ordered as she wheeled the vehicle around in a wide circle, backing it up into the mounds of pine straw beneath the towering pines. I buckled in. Bitty gave me a quick look. "I meant buckle me in, Trinket."

"Oh. Sorry." I unbuckled and did my best to pull the seatbelt around Bitty's ample chest but had issues. For one thing, the Jeep was bouncing around, and when the Jeep bounced, so did Bitty's huge boobs. When Bitty's boobs bounced, the seatbelt jerked, and a few times my nose came perilously close to her bouncing boobies. I think she bruised my chin. I persisted; however, as women are wont to do in extreme circumstances, and despite my precarious position between being tossed out of the Jeep or smothered by Bitty's boobs, I managed to buckle it at last.

By then we had reached the bottom of the first curve, and in a moment we would be met by the oncoming truck. The road was too narrow to pass. One of us would have to move over. I put my money on Bitty to force the issue.

I was struggling to buckle my own seatbelt but managed to get out, "What a-are you g-going to d-do?" as we jolted and bobbed like fishing corks.

"Ab-bout what?"

Bitty had a death grip on the steering wheel. I couldn't find one of my socks, but maybe it was on the floorboard.

"When we m-meet up w-with them?"

We hit a deep rut, and I bit my tongue. It hurt and I yelped. Bitty didn't even glance at me. She kept that Jeep on the road, riding the middle of the gravel like a demon, barreling on to our fate. A Valkyrie. Boudicca. The warrior queen wrestled that Jeep like her own personal dragon and bore down on the larger truck with spitting gravel and dust billowing behind us like smoke. It was almost thrilling, if I ignored the danger and discomfort.

As luck would have it, we met in a narrow spot that had a small verge on one side, and Bitty didn't even slow down. The truck quickly pulled over when the driver obviously chose life instead of an igno-minious death. We went past too fast, and the dust boiling up around us was so thick, that I barely got a glimpse of the driver.

"Did you see who it is?" Bitty asked as she kept going, taking a curve at a speed that scared the liver out of me. I glanced behind us. The truck sat still on the verge, not having moved. They might not follow. Probably cleaning out their pants.

"I think there were two of them. The driver was bald."

"Sylvester Whalen."

I laughed. "He didn't strike me as a Sylvester. Unless Stallone is the last name."

"Sly is his nickname, of course—pothole!"

We hit it full on, my side dipping down so sharp and hard that it jarred my teeth. Fortunately I didn't bite my tongue again. I expected to hear a tire blow, but the Jeep just kept going.

"Nice dragon," I said in relief as we surged on, and when we finally reached the paved road again, I wanted to get out and kiss the asphalt.

"You're a strange one," Bitty said as we rolled up Highway 5 to-ward Ashland. When we passed Highway 4 back to Snow Lake and toward Holly Springs, I looked at her. She just said, "Gas and car wash."

Ah. Yes, it'd be best to take Cindy back a clean Jeep full of gas. I was amazed we'd actually made it this far without undue damage. I had no intention of saying that aloud, or we'd end up in the kudzu. The universe has an often perverse sense of humor.

We bought cold drinks at the Citgo, and even though the fried chicken smelled good, I was still too queasy from our roller coaster ride to eat. Since I had lost a sock, I volunteered to take off my shoes and man the water wand in the car wash. I figured Bitty would end up washing the inside of it if I didn't anyway. It didn't take me long.

"There," I said as I got back in the Jeep and buckled up. "All done. We can return it in good shape and get your car back."

"Yes, so she shouldn't mind loaning it to us again later."

A cold chill ran down my spine despite the heat. "Later, as in when?"

"Maybe tonight. You don't think Sly and Skip went up there to hunt, do you? It's too late for turkey, too early for squirrels."

I looked at her. "You frighten me."

"Why, because I know when hunting seasons are? You forget, Philip liked to pretend he was a hunter. I was expected to keep up so he could do photo ops for the papers. It got him the votes he needed."

"Politics is a strange business."

"Indeed."

"But that's not what I meant," I said. "You intend to come back to the cabin later?"

"Trinket, they may be hiding the rifle as we speak."

"If they recognized us and still have it, they're dismantling it and dumping it in the Tippah River by now."

"Don't say that."

"Sorry, Bitty, but the likelihood of you getting it back is getting smaller by the hour. I hope for the best, but expect the worst."

"It does save time, doesn't it," she said with a sigh. "But I can't give up until I've done everything I know to clear my son's name and, if possible, get the rifle back. My mama was so proud we'd saved it all these years. Things so often get sold, or lost, or just fall apart."

I understood. Having heirlooms, even small things, keep that person's memory alive. "This was my great-grandmother's," people will say with obvious pride, holding up a quilt or hat or book. Most people want that continuity in their lives. It's a kind of immortality. It's not just a Southern thing, either. People all over the world hold onto family possessions as if they're a great treasure. And to that family, they are.

I thought of Faith and Deelight, both crushed at the loss of promised heirlooms. It's not the value. It's the connection.

"I'll help you, Bitty," I heard myself say and immediately wanted to slap my own mouth shut.

Bitty gave me a surprised look, as if she had never thought I might refuse. It figured.

We swapped vehicles at Cindy's and went back to Holly Springs in Bitty's car. I had begun to regret my rash promise to join her insanity, but it wouldn't have mattered if I had said *no* anyway.

"We need to wear dark clothes," Bitty said as we pulled into her driveway and parked. "Just in case they're still there."

"If they're still there, we need to be wearing police uniforms. Better yet, we should tell Jackson Lee and let him send police out there."

We went in the back, through her covered porch that used to be the kitchen when the detached kitchen was outside; it's attached to the house now, accessible through the porch with storm windows in winter, screens in summer. It has lots of green plants and comfortable chairs that beckoned me to linger. Bitty ignored their summons and went up the steps into the new old kitchen, where Chitling greeted us with her customary disdain.

"Police only muddy the water, Trinket, even if they'd go. You know Jackson Lee can't know what we're doing. He'd be cranky."

"More like furious. But whatever." I followed her into the kitchen and pulled a stool up to the granite counter. Or maybe it's quartz. Whichever it is, it's pretty. I watched while Bitty got her little gremlin's food out and heated it in the microwave, tested it for temperature, then put it in a good china bowl on the floor.

The gremlin gobbled it without tasting. It could have been sawdust for all the notice she took. But it did smell good. It should. Sharita boils chicken, rice, vegetables, and adds vitamins suitable for fifteen-pound gremlins and puts it in freezer containers that Bitty thaws out. Dog kibble is fed twice a day, as Kit told Bitty it has nutrients essential for dogs. I hope when I die I'm reincarnated as Bitty's dog.

"Tea?" I requested hopefully as she reached back into the refrigerator.

"Of course. You know where the glasses are."

I did. I put two on the counter, and Bitty added ice, then the tea. Then we trotted from the kitchen through the entrance hall and into the small parlor, our favorite war room, with Chen Ling following right behind us.

"Tell me what you have planned," I said when I had imbibed about eight ounces of my sixteen-ounce glass of tea. "I need to know when my last stand will be made."

"You sound like Custer."

"I feel like Custer. Why dark clothes?" Bitty gave me a *Duh* look, and I shrugged. "Yes, so we blend in better, I assume, but do you intend to walk there? If not, the Jeep will let them know we're there, and dark clothes will be superfluous."

"We can park down the road. There's a lay-by that's clear. As long as it stays dry, we can leave the Jeep there."

"I see a lot of surprises that can pop up. One, they're armed and waiting and shoot us; two, they're drunk and armed and shoot us; three, they're not there and have already ditched the rifle somewhere."

"Four," Bitty said, "we find the rifle and prove Skip killed Walter."

I sighed. I realized her desperation but had hoped Bitty would see the madness in her scheme and change course. Perhaps that had been in vain.

Sometimes Bitty surprises me.

"But you're right, Trinket. In retrospect, it does sound insane to go up there alone in the dark. But I know Skip is the killer. Did I tell you what Brandon said?"

Almost overcome with relief, I could barely speak so shook my head. Bitty smiled.

"Brandon said he and Clayton hadn't wanted to worry me so had never told me about the confrontations with Skip a while back. They know I don't like it when they get in fights. I reared my boys to be gentlemen, not thugs. It seems that Skip stole my rifle last year when they were at the reenactment in Stones River. Sammy Simpson made him give it back, but it was after Skip and Clayton had a big argument. Then Skip went out and bought his own antique rifle, so it blew over and they didn't think any more about it."

"I thought their argument was over a girl," I said.

"Oh, that's what started it. Skip is abusive, and Clayton told him Jenna was too nice to be with him. They'd been drinking, you see. Apparently, a lot goes on at these reenactments that I didn't know, but we won't worry about that now. At any rate, that's what started their feud. It seems to have escalated."

"An understatement. So, do you think Skip was aiming at Clayton?"

"I don't know. He's mean as a snake and could have just wanted to kill someone, or he could have thought Walter was Royal, or he could have been aiming at Clayton, or he could have not realized his gun was loaded, then panicked and switched with the first person he saw—or deliberately switched with Brandon."

"You've got some solid reasoning there," I said in admiration.

Bitty preened, smiling and nodding and stroking Chen Ling between her cute little ears. The world was looking better. We weren't going to go off on some madness, Bitty made sense, and I wouldn't have to ride in that Jeep again.

One out of three isn't what I'd call good odds.

"We just have to trick Skip into admitting it, and I have a plan," she said, and I looked down at my empty tea glass and thought about switching to wine. Or Jack.

"How do you change course so quickly?" I asked as she joined me in the kitchen. "You go from planning a midnight raid against armed men to luring them to some godforsaken spot and getting a confession, all in sixty seconds."

"Oh no, I've been thinking about this a lot. Ever since Brandon called me back last night and told me about their Stones River confrontation. It just would have been easier to find my rifle in Skip's possession. If that isn't possible, I had to have plan *B*. Or *C*."

"Does Jackson Lee know about the confrontation?"

"He doesn't have to know everything."

"Of course he does." I found my favorite wine in the cooler tucked next to her gigantic refrigerator. In proper doses, Zinfandel helps soothe jangled nerves. It's rather like Xanax; too little doesn't work, too much can put you into a coma.

"Don't tell me you're taking Jackson Lee's side against mine," Bitty said, and I added a little extra wine to my glass.

"Okay. I won't tell you. Cheers." I took a healthy sip of the cool, delicious beverage that could alter even Bitty's drama into acceptable behavior.

Bitty poured red wine into her glass, narrowing her eyes at me as she sipped. Her long fingernails drummed against the counter with an annoying click like dog nails on a wood floor. We had a stalemate. Mexican standoff. Staring contest.

Then Bitty caved. I was temporarily elated.

"Very well, Trinket. Tell Jackson Lee anything you like. I just won't give you any details so you can rat me out."

You can see why I said it was temporary elation.

"Just so you know," I said after a moment, "my primary concern in this is you. I prefer you being out of jail and alive, not shot by a man who has already murdered in full daylight in front of a hundred people or more. He's either reckless, stupid, or a sociopath. Neither of those things are good."

"I take your point," Bitty said. "And thank you. I know I get carried away sometimes, so I appreciate your looking out for me. And yes, I know Jackson Lee feels the same. But if no one is taking this seriously, how will the police know to look at Skip?"

"Are you sure the police aren't already looking at him?"

Shrugging, she said with a sigh, "Not according to Jackson Lee. He's not a suspect because there's nothing to tie him to the case. They're focusing on other evidence."

I thought for a few minutes and more wine. Then I said, "Do you still have that DVD of the reenactment? Maybe we need to look at it again."

We went back to the war room. Bitty pushed a button, and the painting over the mantel slid up to reveal a big-screen TV. A cabinet under the window held things like cable boxes and DVR players. She turned on the DVD player, found the case holding the right disc, and slid it in. Then we literally sat on the edge of our seats to watch.

"My God, you look like a porpoise in a bonnet," Bitty said when the camera scanned across me, and I said, "I told you so."

"I'll get you another gown made for next year."

"That will be a waste of your mon—oh look, who is that?"

We stood up and peered closely at the screen, Bitty rewound, then paused. It was a fuzzy picture because of the transfer from phone to YouTube to DVD, but I recognized Brandon—no, it was Clayton. He held the sword. Brandon had the rifle. Smoke poured thickly into the air, and the man who came up behind him had caught our attention.

"It's Skip!" Bitty exclaimed, and I shook my head.

"Put on your glasses, Bitty. It's not Skip. It looks like . . . *whoa*!"

Our jaws dropped.

Chapter 16

"WHAT WAS HE DOING in the reenactment, and did anyone mention it?" Bitty asked Jackson Lee, who shook his head.

"I don't know. Since the police have this as well, I'm sure they've investigated and have cleared him. If not, we'd have heard about it."

"If not, he'd be off the force," I said. "I'm just wondering why it wasn't mentioned at any time. Royal didn't even mention it."

"Maybe Royal doesn't know," Bitty said darkly. "This certainly shoots my theory out of the water, if Skip didn't do it."

"Mine, too."

Jackson Lee leaned back in the chair. Chen Ling sat in his lap. He didn't seem to mind. "I can't see how Barron Stewart taking part in the reenactment would impact the case, as long as he didn't shoot Walter."

"But that's just it," Bitty said. "How do we know he didn't? He could be mad at Walter because of that fender bender his brother had, or maybe Walter did something to him. The old man sure seems to have ticked off the rest of the town. And it's odd he never mentioned being in it, you know."

"Is Barron Stewart bald?" I asked, and Jackson Lee and Bitty both stared at me. I put my hands out in a Scooby-Doo shrug. "I just got a glimpse of the driver of the truck. It wasn't a monster truck, so it has to belong to someone."

"What truck is that?" Jackson Lee inquired, and Bitty looked daggers at me. Uh oh.

"Oops," I said.

Jackson Lee turned to Bitty. She sucked in a breath and explained it.

When she finished, Jackson Lee said slowly, "So you're telling me that you and Trinket trespassed on someone else's property, then tried to run them down?"

"Why do you always have to look at things so negatively," Bitty complained. "It wasn't like that."

"Did you have an invitation or the Whalen's permission to be there? No? Then it's trespassing. As for nearly pushing them off the road . . ."

He went on for a few minutes scolding us like children, and I thought it well-deserved. Bitty sulked a little but nodded meekly enough in all the right places. That in itself told me she knew we'd gone too far. Again.

Finally, Jackson Lee said, "I know you both just want to help. I'll look into the Whalen family. I'll also see what I can find out about Barron Stewart. Just give me a chance to do that before you commit any more crimes against humanity, please."

"That's a little strong," Bitty objected, but she agreed to let him look into it before going on to plan *B* or *C*. For all I knew, she had a plan *Z*, too. It was daunting.

"Why don't you stay for supper, sugar?" Bitty asked him, and I decided it was time for me to make my way home. The day had been exciting enough. When I gathered my purse, Bitty said, "Oh, do stay, Trinket. There's plenty of food in the freezer. It won't take long to heat."

"I should go. These shoes are rubbing blisters on my heels without socks. And I have things I need to do that I've let go for a while."

I did have blisters, and I didn't have a thing to do but get away before she thought of some godawful plan that would be worse than the others. She may have promised Jackson Lee she wouldn't do anything until he'd done his own investigations, but that wouldn't keep her from plotting. Sometimes her plotting takes a more active turn. More active turns can be scary.

By the time I made my escape, it was the middle of the afternoon, and I felt lucky to have the rest of the day to myself. I would go home, take a long, luxurious bath, probably wash my hair, then perhaps relax and finish reading my novel. It had all the requirements for an exciting book: knights and damsels and love and danger. I liked danger when someone else was dealing with it. Not so much when it was me.

Of course, when I got home, I found guests there, and Mama and Daddy were out at the barn with them. No problem. I could just sneak in and go upstairs and have the entire floor to myself. I parked out front and walked around the back.

Brownie greeted me with vociferous barking, as if he'd never before seen me, and I was there to burgle the house. I tried to shush him, but Mama saw me and waved me over. I wanted to just wave back and go inside, but I knew better. I joined them at the barn, Brownie sniffing me as if I'd rolled in cow patties.

The two ladies visiting were from a cat rescue. My heart leaped.

"Are you here to take all the cats?" I asked, hope no doubt gleaming in my eyes.

"Oh no, not all of them. Your mother was just telling us about the tame ones we think we can place in good homes."

Well, that would do. Next time my parents went out of town, there would be less cats demanding my attention and hissing when I was five minutes late with their dinner.

"The kittens in particular should be adoptable," Mama said, and the ladies nodded. "People drop them off here in boxes, or even bags, just left on my porch or doorstep. It's awful, what people do," Mama said with a sigh.

I agreed. People have some notion that dropping an animal off in the country is better than taking it to a shelter or even euthanizing it. It's not. Most die of starvation, dehydration, or are struck by cars, killed by other animals, or die in the elements. Winters are cold, summers are hot, spring brings flash floods and storms—it's much kinder to take the poor thing to a shelter than abandon it. I've seen dogs sit by the side of the road waiting for their people to come back, resisting rescue for weeks. It makes me feel murderous toward the heartless owners who left them there. Most rescues are overwhelmed with the sheer number of homeless pets.

So as Mama chose lucky kittens to go with the ladies, who had brought about ten pet carriers with them, I tried to ease away. Daddy caught my arm. "You'll help load them, won't you, Trinket?"

What could I say? "Of course, I will."

Nearly an hour later, the last of the lucky kittens were loaded up into the van, off to new lives and hopefully, wonderful new homes. Mama looked tired and pleased but had tears in her eyes as the van pulled out of our driveway. She saw me looking at her.

"I do my best, but it's hard to say goodbye, sometimes. I get attached. Those are the ones that were left last month, tiny little things. Dr. Coltrane took them to his office for the techs to help bottle feed them, then brought them back to me. They're doing great."

I didn't know quite what to say. My mother has such a big heart, but I worry that as she gets older, this will all be too much for her. It's too much for me, now.

"You've saved their lives," I finally said. "If not for you, they'd never have made it this far."

Mama nodded. "I know. I'm just a silly old woman."

I hugged her. "No, you're a wonderful person who cares. That's too rare these days. It will be—*agh!*"

A sharp pain in my ankle made me shriek in her ear. Mama jumped back, accidentally stepping on a cat. The cat screamed, Mama screamed, Daddy came running with a rake in his hand, and the little horror attached to my ankle gnawed voraciously on my unprotected skin. I shook my leg. Brownie remained firmly attached. Mama immediately came to the rescue.

"Oh, be careful, you'll hurt him . . . let go and come here, Brownie. It's all right. She was just giving me a hug."

Just before I was ready for the Jaws of Life to pry the dog off my ankle, Mama got him detached. I sank to the grass to inspect what I expected to be gaping wounds. It was rather deflating to see only red scratches. He hadn't even broken the skin. That seemed impossible. It felt like puncture wounds.

Daddy inspected my ankle while Mama cuddled Brownie against her, looking worried. I didn't flatter myself it was about me. She nodded encouragingly. "You're scratched up a bit but not bleeding. It must be because his teeth are worn down. The poor thing ate rocks before we got him, you know."

"Did he. I'm not surprised."

Daddy helped me stand. "I'll fix you up, princess. Come on."

It was the "princess" that made me smile. He hadn't called me that in a long time. I think I'm really a Daddy's girl at heart.

While Daddy fussed over me with hydrogen peroxide, warm water, then antibiotic cream, Mama peeked into the downstairs bathroom to check on us. "No deep cuts, I hope?"

"No, she's just bruised. Wonder why he did that?" Daddy mused, and I answered.

"Well, you'd think the car wash would have cleaned my feet off good enough, but it may be that he smelled other animals on me. Bitty and I went for a short hike in the woods."

Mama and Daddy both stared at me in disbelief. They know Bitty and I don't hike. Or wash cars. Not willingly, anyway. I sighed and gave them the Disney version of our morning, leaving out all the parts about Skip Whalen being suspected of Walter's murder.

"Bitty does carry on about heirlooms," Mama said when I finished.

Daddy stood up, shaking his head. "Bitty beats all I've ever heard. Remember the time in the fifth grade when she insisted Darlene

Landers had stolen her favorite sweater?"

Mama laughed. "And then Darlene's stepmother showed up at church wearing it the next Sunday. Bitty made a big scene right there, claimed it'd been her grandmother's, and then proved it with a little label sewn inside. Her mother verified it. The pastor gave a sermon about coveting a neighbor's possessions not long afterward, but poor Sarah was mortified that Bitty had been involved. And of course, it turned out that Shirley Landers had just coveted the sweater and had Darlene steal it in Sunday School, so Bitty didn't get in trouble. But that was a scandal for a while."

"Good lord," I said, "I don't remember that at all."

"You should. You asked me why some mamas can be bad and not get in trouble for it. I asked if there was something I'd done. You said, 'Not yet.'"

I laughed. "I don't recall you ever being bad enough to warrant that question, so I'm sure it had nothing to do with you."

"That's a relief. I've often wondered." Mama cuddled little Brownie closer to her and whispered something in his ear, and the dog smiled blissfully.

"I can understand why you've replaced us with animals," I said as I put my foot on the floor and gingerly tested my mobility. "Please explain to him that I know my place, so he doesn't have to bite me again."

"Oh, he says he's sorry. He just got confused." She held up the dog's paw and waggled it at me. I swear, I thought of Bitty.

"Why is it *I'm* the one who's considered the weird one in our family?" I asked no one in particular, and Daddy laughed. He stopped when Mama gave him the evil eye.

"You can't top Bitty," Daddy said, and I nodded.

"Yes, but she's extended family."

I thought about that when I went upstairs. Bitty and I were closer than my twin sister and me, and we always had been. I love my sister, but she and I are from different planets. We're no closer than other sisters, despite simultaneously sharing a womb and a room. She looks like Mama; I take after the Truevine side of the family. No one ever believes we're twins.

Whereas Bitty and I look nothing alike, we're both regarded as family outliers. It has become apparent since my return to Holly Springs that we have always generated mischief, although of a much less dangerous kind than we do now. It's not as if we seek it out. We just seem to attract it, like magnets. Perhaps we should learn to channel this talent in more positive directions. I wasn't sure how that could be managed.

I opted for a quick shower and shampoo instead of long bath and tied a plastic bag around my ankle and foot before getting in the tub. It's one of those old-fashioned clawfoot tubs, and the shower apparatus is rigged to the faucet, and the curtain is hung on metal rods dangling by hooks and chains from the ceiling. It wobbles a bit unless you know just how to manage it. Old houses refitted with bathrooms that were once bedrooms have to make concessions.

After wrapping my wet hair in a towel, I put on a cotton robe over light pajamas and went downstairs for a glass of sweet tea. It was still daylight outside, and as I reached the foot of the stairs, I heard Mama in the kitchen talking to Daddy. I decided to join the conversation.

"Hello, gorgeous," said the man of my dreams, grinning at me from across the kitchen table as I came to an abrupt halt in the doorway. "New slippers?"

I blinked, then remembered the plastic bag I still wore on one foot. "Yes. It's all the rage in flood zones, I hear. I'm surprised to see you."

A glance at my mother was filled with reproach for her not warning me Kit was there, but she ignored me. "Dr. Coltrane came out to bring me the litter of kittens someone left here a few days ago. They got a clean bill of health and should be adoptable soon," she said.

Brownie stood staring into a cat carrier, nose pushed against the wire door. One of the kittens popped him on the nose, and he yelped and jumped back. I smiled. Mama picked him up immediately, of course, and I took the opportunity to walk around the table to the refrigerator. I noticed Kit already had a glass of tea and slice of pie.

It rattled me anytime I saw Kit, but especially when I wasn't at my best, like wearing pajamas and a plastic bag on my foot.

I took my tea and pie to the table and sat down across from Kit. "I hope Brownie's shots are up to date," I said. He grinned.

"Always up to date. Your mother tells me he bit you earlier."

"Gnawed on me like I was a pig's ear. He didn't break the skin, but he did leave marks. I'm scarred for life."

My mother rolled her eyes at me. I smiled and cut into my chess pie. Kit laughed, and Daddy chuckled.

"You're fine, princess. Why are you wearing a plastic bag?"

"I wanted to keep my scratches dry and not wash off the antibiotic in the shower. I can probably take it off now."

I bent to remove the bag, and when I straightened, my pie was gone from my plate. It was clean as a whistle, although I shudder to think about how dirty whistles can get. At any rate, I inspected the three innocent faces gazing solemnly at me. Then Daddy visibly swallowed, and I said, "Aha! Thief!"

We all laughed, and good humor ignited family stories that had Kit laughing at some of the antics Bitty and I used to commit on a regular basis. After I went upstairs and made myself more presentable, I joined my parents and Kit out on the back deck. Daddy had gotten the lawn furniture from the barn and cleaned it the week before, and Mama put out the good cushions. A nice breeze kept the bugs at bay as we drank sweet tea and watched the sun go down behind the trees. I could almost feel the family unit draw close around me, a secure, lovely feeling. As dusk fell, Mama lit citronella candles; the fragrance mixed with the scent of privet hedge and roses. It was a nice, peaceful evening.

I walked Kit to his truck when he left, and we stood chatting in the glow of the outdoor light on what used to be the stable and is now the garage where my parents keep their car. My car was still parked out front. We chatted for a few minutes more, then I kissed him goodnight and watched as he pulled out of the driveway and onto the road. I thought about moving my car, but I'd have to go upstairs and get my keys, so just left it. It'd be safe until tomorrow.

After such a nice afternoon and evening, I ate leftovers from the light supper Mama had fixed, then went to bed and slept quite soundly, not even stirring until morning. Maybe I would have slept even later, but about nine thirty Daddy called up the stairs that I needed to come down and see about my car. Confused, I opened my eyes in the shadowy confines of my room, loathe to leave the comfort of my bed. My car? When he called the second time, I gave up any thoughts of more sleep and got up. I grabbed my car keys and robe, then stuffed my feet into slippers.

Yawning, I met Daddy in the kitchen. "Is my car blocking you?" I asked, and he shook his head.

"Just go look."

That was a strange reply, but I dutifully stumbled outside and around the house to look at my car. It would have been easier to go out the front door, but for some reason, I never think of that. I always use the back door. I'm a creature of habit.

My bunny slippers made crunching noises on gravel as I rounded the corner of the house, then came to a dead stop. All four of my tires were flat. Someone had spray-painted figures and words on my car. Nasty words.

"At least they could have bothered to spell them right," I said as I tilted my head to read, and Daddy muttered something under his breath.

"What have you and Bitty really been up to?" he asked after a moment.

"Nothing. Much. Just trying to find her rifle."

"Uh huh. You seem to have upset someone. What's a—" He cocked his head to one side. "Snope?"

"I think they mean *snoop*. Obviously, didn't graduate at the top of their class. I may have to get a new paint job. This one looks permanent."

My lovely beige Taurus had red paint all over it: on the windows, the hood, the trunk, doors—the paint had dripped in places so the words looked bloody.

"I'll call the insurance company," I said after a moment. "They'll send someone out to fix the flats. I hope I don't have to get new tires."

"I'll try my air compressor first. If that doesn't work, you'll have to get new tires," Daddy said, and I sighed.

Mama met me on the back deck before I went in to dress and call the insurance company. "Who would do such a thing?"

I had my ideas, but there was no way I intended to confess participating in Bitty's scheme until I absolutely had to. "There are a lot of crazy people out there," was all I said and went inside and upstairs to escape.

When I came back downstairs, a package with familiar lettering lay on the kitchen table. It was my phone from AT&T. Mama sat at the table. She had a look of determination on her face that warned me she intended to ask questions.

"I need to call my insurance agent," I said, but she motioned for me to sit down.

"Daddy saw your car when he went out to get the mail," she said. "This was done while we slept. Who have you upset?"

I sighed. Confession was about to be committed. If I were Catholic, I'd have crossed myself and asked for mercy. Since we're Methodist, I winged it. "Remember how I told you that Bitty and I were looking for her rifle and drove out to a cabin to see if the people had it?"

"Yes, Trinket. Since that was just yesterday, my feeble mind can recall it."

When Mama is sarcastic, I know she's annoyed. I nodded.

"No reflection on your abilities, just a reminder that I told you most of it. I didn't add that we suspect the person who might have it of also killing Walter Simpson."

Mama's eyes got big. She was quiet for a moment. Then she asked, "Why would he keep the murder weapon if he's a suspect?"

"He's our suspect. As far as I know, the police aren't investigating him. And the rifle that belonged to Bitty's mother isn't the murder weapon. It hasn't been publicly announced yet."

"Oh. It's that rifle. I don't know why I thought you meant the other antique rifle."

I looked at her, blinking. "What other antique rifle?"

"It belonged to the Truevine family. Your father can tell you more about it than I can. I thought perhaps Tommy had given it to Bitty instead of Steven. Of course, it's supposed to go to the eldest son, but since Eddie got the house and land, Tommy got the rifle."

Thomas Truevine was Bitty's father. He'd died years earlier of complications from a stroke. This was the first I ever recalled about him having a rifle, but it also explained why Bitty was so determined to retrieve her heirloom, besides just being Bitty. If her brother had the other rifle, she'd be even more determined to hold onto the Jordan rifle that had belonged to her mother's family.

"Steven doesn't care anything about antiques or heirlooms," I said after a moment. "His wife considers anything more than two years old to be obsolete and worthless."

Mama shook her head. "She sold some of the lovely things Sarah left Steven, and it caused quite a rift at the time. You were living in New York then, I think. Or maybe it was out in Oregon. One of those states with mountains."

"There's a little difference between the Cascades and the Catskills," I said, but let it go. I wondered if Bitty knew what Steven had done with the rifle. Was it like the other one? Did it even matter? It could be one of those weird coincidences despite what Jung said.

After I called my insurance agent, I called Bitty. I used the cordless kitchen phone and let my new cell phone stay in the box. It was safer there.

Bitty answered on the second ring. She sounded breathless.

"Is this a bad time to talk?" I asked.

"Oh, Trinket! I'm glad you called. Do you know what someone did? And I can just bet it was that Skip Whalen, for only he would do something so nasty."

"Spray painted your car?" I hazarded, and there was shocked silence on the other end.

"How did you know?" she recovered enough to ask.

"Mine, too. Red paint all over my Taurus."

"White paint all over the Benz. I'm beginning to think the car is cursed."

"Insurance will cover it," I said, then asked, "What do you know about the Truevine rifle that your daddy had?"

"Oh, he left that to Steven. I don't know why. He never gave a hoot about heirlooms. It's probably still in a trunk somewhere. That's why Mama left me all the Jordan stuff. She knew Steven wouldn't appreciate the sentimental value, just the cash value."

"Does it look like your mama's rifle?"

"It's an Enfield, so probably. It's been a while since I've seen it. I remember Daddy getting mad at Steven when we were kids, after he—oh, Trinket! Steven took a hammer to the lock plate when he was about nine so it'd look like Mama's rifle. They were hung on the wall, and he said they didn't match. I never even thought of that!"

"I wonder if Steven still has that rifle," I said, and Bitty made a rude noise.

"Probably not. That may be why both those rifles look so alike. I'm going to call him and ask if his peasant bride got rid of it. I'll bet she did."

Bitty doesn't like her sister-in-law that much. She puts on airs, Bitty always says. I left that in Bitty's capable hands and went outside to find my father. He had a noisy compressor hooked up and was putting air in my tires. Two were fat and full again.

I studied my car for a moment. It looked awful.

"I wonder if I could scrape the worst words off with a paint scraper," I said, and Daddy looked up at me.

"Better wait on the insurance company to look at it first. I think your tires are okay. Good thing I had some extra valve caps in my shop. They took the other ones with them."

I asked Daddy about the Truevine rifle, and he confirmed all that Mama and Bitty had said. "I sure hope Steven didn't sell it. It belonged in my family, too, and that'd be an insult," he added.

"Well, if he did, I think I know who may have bought it," I said and reflected on the probability of the Whalen family owning two former Truevine possessions: Bitty's cabin and now the Truevine rifle. It just seemed too fantastic.

In my opinion, Carl Jung has a lot to answer for.

I STUDIED BITTY'S car, noting the misspelled words. "They left out the *T*," I said, and Bitty nodded.

"*Bich* just doesn't sound as awful, so I don't mind. And they used a *K* instead of a *C* on that four-letter word. My adjuster is due shortly, but I just need it repainted. Oh, and the tires aired up again."

When we went inside, I said, "Okay, tell me what Steven said."

Bitty smiled. "Wine or tea?"

"You tell me."

She poured wine, and I thought I must be wrong. Then we settled in the parlor, and I prepared to hear that Steven still had the rifle, and my theory was shot.

"Tammy the Twit sold it," Bitty said, and I paused with the wine barely touching my lips.

"She sold it?"

"Yep. Steven doesn't even care. He told her she could. I'll have words with him later. I told Tammy to find the receipt, because she can't recall the name. After all, it was four months since she sold it because it doesn't really go with her décor, and it's just taking up room—she has no soul."

My hand trembled in my eagerness as I asked, "She got a receipt? That's amazing! If she has the receipt and it's Skip Whalen . . ."

"She said it was a woman who bought it. I'm wondering if Jenna or his mother got it for him. Or if he sent them after it. After all, it's all the way down in Jackson."

"His mother, maybe. She seemed very protective of him."

"I can understand that. I'm protective of my sons, and if they wanted a rifle, I'd get them one, too."

I nodded in satisfaction. Whether there was a receipt or not, surely Tammy would be able to describe the woman who bought it. That might be enough to get the police to investigate Skip. It struck me that perhaps Jackson Lee should be made aware of all this.

"Have you told Jackson Lee what you learned?"

"Not yet. He's not in, and his secretary said he's either in court or in a meeting, and she'd have him call me."

"He'll be the one to get the police involved. Then we can step back and let them handle everything," I said.

Bitty readjusted Chitling in her lap and sipped her wine. When she didn't answer, I said, "Right?"

"Right what?"

"We'll let the police take it from here?"

"That would probably be the easiest thing to do," Bitty agreed, and I got a funny feeling she wasn't going to be cooperative.

"Tell me it's what you plan on doing," I demanded.

Bitty lifted her brow. "Why, Trinket, you know I will do what is best. Don't I always?"

I wanted to groan. Instead, I said, "My my, it's so vairy vairy wahm in heah," and we both laughed. Although I signaled an end to the conversational quagmire, there was no way I would let Bitty do something stupid and dangerous. Not this time. We'd had enough close calls.

I just wouldn't tell her that. I had a terrible feeling that Skip Whalen was too dangerous to cross. And yet there was something that didn't quite fit. I didn't know what it was, but it had all come together too smoothly to feel entirely comfortable. Some niggling piece of information kept rattling around in my brain. I didn't know what it meant, but it couldn't be good.

Really, I should trust my instincts more.

Chapter 17

RAYNA AND GAYNELLE showed up before I left to see my insurance adjustor, and we all sat out on the front porch chatting. Of course, we shared what we knew with Rayna, who already knew a lot anyway, but poor Gaynelle was astounded by it all. Her eyes got big.

"Any more wine, Bitty?" she asked, and our hostess graciously complied. I refrained from refills. One glass of wine was more than enough when about to meet my insurance adjustor.

After Gaynelle was amply fortified, she listened to my theory and then Bitty's and let it all soak in for a few minutes. Being a retired school teacher, Gaynelle is able to quickly get to the heart of a matter and cut through the clutter. She summarized concisely: "So Skip Whalen is the likely culprit, he has the gun originally thought to be the murder weapon, purchased the actual murder weapon, yet the police do not regard him as a suspect, is that it?"

Bitty blinked. "That's about it."

"Well then, the answer is to direct attention to him so the police investigate."

Rayna and I exchanged glances. I figured this could go one of two ways: Bitty would allow Jackson Lee or even Catfish to take our suspicions to the police in any form they chose, or she would do something insane herself to move things along. My money was on the latter.

"And your suggestion on how to do that?" Bitty asked before I could interject a warning to Gaynelle.

"Let Jackson Lee do it," Gaynelle replied promptly.

Relieved, I looked at Rayna and smiled. Perhaps the emergency was over.

Since it was almost time to meet the adjustor, I said goodbye, bent close to Rayna, and said in her ear, "Keep an eye on her."

Rayna nodded. She knew who I meant and why. Once Bitty decided something should be done, it was difficult to dissuade her. Only a harsh dose of reality worked.

I drove up to the shopping center close to 78 Highway and met the adjustor. He seemed rather startled by the extent of paint covering my car, but at least the tires weren't ruined. He took photos, wrote in his book, inspected it inside and out, then got on his computer. Within fifteen minutes, he handed me a check. I was stunned.

"That's it?"

"Yes, ma'am. Unless there's something else, damage done to any contents?"

"No, I didn't have anything left inside." I looked at the check. It was more than enough to repaint it, I was pretty sure. "What do I do what what's left over? Send it back to you?"

He looked startled. Then he grinned. "You're the first person to ever ask that. That's the average rate for repainting a car at a reputable dealer. You're entitled to the entire amount."

I felt rich. I smiled. "I'll get a good job done on it. Thank you."

And that was it. It had been so easy. Not all modern conveniences are convenient. This certainly was very convenient. I considered going on home. After all, driving around in a car that has blood-red curse words painted on it wasn't my idea of fun. But rescuing Bitty from some manic scheme was even less fun, and that was likely if she hadn't gracefully accepted the verdict that she should allow Jackson Lee to handle it.

So I drove back to Bitty's to be sure all was well. Someone had put a tarp over the Benz in her driveway, and no one came to the door. Rayna's car was gone. Inside, Chen Ling barked a protest at my knocking. Bitty must have gone somewhere with Rayna and Gaynelle.

I remembered my cell phone. It had only a partial charge but should have enough life for a phone call if I kept it short. I called Bitty's cell. No answer. I called Rayna. No answer. I couldn't remember Gaynelle's phone number and hadn't taken time to update my contacts, so I got back in my car and drove over to Rayna's. Her car was there. I parked and started up the path when I saw Rayna and Gaynelle in the garden, so switched course. I went through the garden gate, stopped to pet the dogs first, and then joined them at the table.

"That didn't take long," Gaynelle said as I sat down in a wrought iron chair. Rayna pushed a glass of lemonade toward me, and I took it. Fragrant mint added a nice flavor.

"I was shocked. Things are so much simpler these days. I rather like the convenience, even when I moan about the good ole days. Pay no attention when I do that, by the way."

"We never do," Rayna said with a smile. "Where's Bitty?"

I paused with the lemonade at my mouth. "I thought she'd be with you."

"No, we left her with the insurance adjustor. The woman said it'd take a while, so we told Bitty to come over after they were through."

"Really. Huh. Well, her car is there, covered up with a tarp, and her dog is there, making loud noises, but Bitty didn't come to the door or answer her phone."

"Maybe she's in the shower." Gaynelle frowned a little. "Or maybe she had to go off with the adjustor for some reason. To sign papers or get the check."

"They do all that on a laptop and print out the check right then," I said. "Unless this was an old-fashioned adjustor who doesn't know anything about that kind of technology."

"I doubt it," Rayna said. "She looked awfully young. I thought she was a little old to be selling Girl Scout cookies when she first came up, but she said she was from the insurance company."

"Huh," I said again. "Did she have a business card or identifycation?"

Gaynelle nodded. "She did. She showed it to Bitty. Quite poised, although she seemed a bit nervous. She said this was her first time out on her own."

For some reason, it sounded off to me. Apparently, it did to them, too.

"I don't like it," said Rayna, and we both nodded. Without discussing it further, we got up and I started toward my car. Rayna detoured to tell Rob she was leaving. Gaynelle stopped before we got to the curb.

"Let's wait for Rayna. I'd rather ride in a car without misspelled vulgar language, if you don't mind."

"I don't mind at all."

Rayna quickly joined us after grabbing her purse and letting the dogs in. Gaynelle got in the back seat, leaving me to get up front with Rayna. It was less than three minutes to Bitty's house, but it seemed like a half hour. I worried that she'd been duped by unscrupulous adjustors into signing a release for much less money than was needed to repaint her car; abducted by con artists and would be held for ransom; beamed up by aliens to be dissected. Yes, sometimes I get carried away with my creative problem solving.

Nothing had changed when we got to Bitty's house. The Benz was still covered, and no one came to the door. I went around back. It was unlocked. I knew I risked setting off alarms, but that didn't deter me. I went in through the back, into the kitchen, and no alarms sounded, if you didn't count the pug. She yodeled at me from the middle of the kitchen floor, looking indignant. I couldn't get her to hush so risked losing a finger by picking her up. She quieted immediately.

I went to the front door and let Rayna and Gaynelle in. "I'm going upstairs to see if she's napping, but I doubt she'd leave Chitling down here alone."

Everything was tidy and serene upstairs, but no Bitty. I checked every room. Chen Ling started squirming, so I set her down. She immediately headed back downstairs and went to the front door, barking. I followed.

"What is it, Lassie?" I asked as she pawed at the closed door. "Timmy's in the well?"

My attempt at gallows humor made Gaynelle giggle but didn't make me feel any better. I checked the first floor, then went down to the basement, through the boys' redecorated den with giant TV, game consoles, and a refrigerator stocked with snacks and soft drinks. I even looked in the wine cellar. It was unlocked. No Bitty. Then I thought about the upstairs coat closet. I'd once found a body in it and was rather squeamish about looking there again. But I went back up the stairs and sucked in a deep breath, then opened the door. No Bitty, no body. I was relieved, actually.

Meanwhile, Rayna went next door to ask Mrs. Tyree if she'd seen her, and Gaynelle went out back to check the garage. Chen Ling still fussed at the front door. She seemed quite upset.

"She just went off and forgot to set the alarm again," I said to the dog, then stopped. It was stupid to try to explain to a dog, even if she'd listen. Instead, she scratched at the front door with her pink-painted claws, her little pink bib with *Mommy Loves Me* on the front bobbling with every frantic movement. Maybe Bitty had fallen in the yard. I took a chance and opened the door.

Chen Ling shot out like a missile and went straight to the Benz. She tugged at the tarp, growling and shaking her head in efforts to dislodge it. About that time Gaynelle came from the garage.

"She's not out there but her new car is still here. What is that dog doing?"

Dread began to form in my chest. "I think she's trying to tell us where Bitty is."

Gaynelle and I immediately began yanking at the tarp. It was one of those heavy ones that had cords to keep it tight, so it took us agonizing moments to get it untied. Chitling kept underfoot, but I didn't fuss at her. She was as frantic as we were.

I finally got the tarp off and saw a huddled shape on the back seat; blond hair spilled across leather. The doors were locked. I turned to Gaynelle.

"I need a hammer. Since her garage is unlocked, get a hammer or something."

"It's locked too. I looked in the windows."

I turned around, looking for something to break the glass while Gaynelle cupped her hand to shade her eyes and peered inside. I saw a metal garden stake and ran to yank it out of the dirt. It came up easier than I thought it would, and I staggered backward, regained my balance, and returned to the car.

"Stand back," I ordered Gaynelle and took up a batter's stance, judging where to hit for the most effect.

Gaynelle grabbed the dog, Rayna came running across the yard, and I swung the metal yard stake as hard as I could. It bounced off the window and nearly decapitated Rayna on the backswing as she came up behind me.

"Yikes! Trinket, wait! I have her keys."

She caught me just before I started to swing again, thank heavens. I'm not sure my arm could have endured another shock.

"It's not Bitty," said Gaynelle as she held Chitling against her. The dog gave her no trouble at all but rested quietly in her arms.

I looked at her. "What?"

"That's not Bitty. The hair is too long, and the clothes are wrong. No spike heels."

"What?" I said again as Rayna hit the remote, and Bitty's doors unlocked.

Gaynelle nodded. "It looks like what the insurance adjustor was wearing."

As I absorbed that, Rayna opened the back door and pulled the woman out by her legs. She was unconscious. It wasn't Bitty. I just sat down on the driveway, deflated. Chen Ling howled mournfully, and I felt like doing the same. Where was Bitty? What had happened here?

Panting slightly, Rayna checked the woman's pulse once she got her halfway out of the car's backseat. "She's alive. I'm calling the police and an ambulance."

Gaynelle said, "It's the insurance adjustor. This is so odd."

I put my palm on my forehead and closed my eyes. "Where's Bitty?"

No one answered. I understood. They didn't know either.

AS THE AMBULANCE carried away the adjustor, whom I was willing to bet was not an adjustor at all, the police questioned us. Just my luck, Rodney Farrell drew the short straw.

"Now tell me again, Miz Truevine, what happened here?"

"Has anyone called Jackson Lee?" I asked instead of answering. "He needs to be here. He'll know what to do."

"You're asking for your lawyer?"

I wasn't sure if he was shocked or excited. "No, I'm asking for Jackson Lee. He's *a* lawyer, not *my* lawyer."

Farrell sighed. "I think Miz Blue called him. Now, tell me again what happened."

"Deputy, that's why you're here. I have no idea what happened. Bitty's gone, that woman was unconscious and locked in her car—after which, someone pulled a tarp over it—and we can't find my cousin."

"That's very strange." He wrote in his little book, squinting in the sunlight that felt hotter by the minute. Then he looked up at me again. "Could she have gone off with someone else?"

"She could have sprouted wings and flown to the moon for all I know," I snapped, and Farrell took a step back. I sighed. "Deputy, I'm very worried. I'm hot, and I haven't had a good day, and I want to know she's safe. That doesn't seem to be too much to ask."

"Yes, ma'am, I understand. I'll be back in a minute."

He walked off, leaving me standing in the hot sun in Bitty's front yard. Two police cars were at the curb. The ambulance was long gone. Another officer talked to Rayna, and the third talked to Gaynelle. He glanced my way, and I recognized Barron Stewart. That wasn't very reassuring.

I turned and went up on the porch and sat down in one of the wicker chairs. It was a lot cooler, and I felt light-headed. If they wanted me, I was in plain sight.

It wasn't five minutes before Officer Stewart came up on the porch. He stood looking at me for a moment before saying, "You've scared Farrell, I hear."

"Really? If only I'd known it was so easy."

He pushed his hat to the back of his head. He had hair, I noticed. My mind raced. So not the bald guy driving the truck. Had to be

Sylvester Whalen, just as Bitty said.

"Miz Truevine, I seem to be running into you a lot lately."

I eyed him. "It's a small town. Who's the woman we found in the back of Bitty's car, and what are you doing about finding her?"

"It's not that small a town. Her name is Jenna Jones, and we've put out a BOLO for your cousin. She's probably just gone off to lunch somewhere."

"And left an unconscious woman in her car?" I had sat up, the name triggering memory. "Did you say, Jenna?"

"That's what was on the business cards we found with her. She only had four of them. Miz Truevine, from what I hear you and your cousin are always getting into situations that you shouldn't and think you're detectives. Don't try that with me. How do you know Jenna Jones?"

"I've never met her," I said honestly.

"Lying to the police is never a smart move, you know."

"That's why I'm not lying to you." Behind him, I saw Jackson Lee's Jaguar roll to a stop at the curb. He got out almost before the engine died and approached the police talking to Rayna and Gaynelle. "Excuse me," I said when Stewart started asking me why Jenna Jones was at the house and who would spray paint Bitty's car. I pointed to Jackson Lee. "Address all your questions to Mr. Brunetti, please."

He half-turned, muttered something under his breath, and then said, "Did you get your license corrected yet?"

I should have expected it. I hadn't, of course. But then I remembered, and said, "You can ask Mr. Brunetti about that, too. The Corinth police are sending him my stolen items."

All in all, I felt I acquitted myself fairly well, even though I had obviously irritated the police. Again. Stewart left me alone, and I waited for Jackson Lee to join me. No point in bothering him when he was obviously asking the police questions. He'd find out all he could.

In just a few minutes, the police finished dusting Bitty's car for fingerprints, packed up their kits, and left, along with the officers who had questioned us. I saw Mrs. Tyree coming up the walk. She rarely used her walker, but had it this time, and clumped up to the porch with the look of a woman who neither expected nor wanted help.

"It's Bitty again," she said without preamble. "I wondered why she gave me her car keys this morning. I thought she must have something in mind to give me her extra set."

"We don't know where she is. Have you seen her this afternoon?"

"No, but I did see that blond woman helping her put a tarp on her car. I was rather glad of that. Some people get offended at those words."

"Not since then?" I couldn't help asking even though I knew she'd tell me if she'd seen anything.

"No, dear. I know you're worried. I told the police already, so I'll tell you. I didn't see Bitty, but I did see a truck driving past a few times when I came out to sit on the porch. It seemed odd to me, because it slowed down, then sped up, then turned around and came back." She paused, but before I could ask, she said, "It was black, with wide tires, and a rifle rack in the rear window. If it had come by again, I might have tried to read the license plate, but I didn't see it before I went back inside. Just thought you should know. The police like to keep things private, but sometimes you ladies actually manage to figure things out before they do."

Jackson Lee and Rayna stepped up on the porch, and they chatted a few minutes with Mrs. Tyree while Gaynelle came to see how I was doing.

"You all right?"

"Not yet. I will be when Bitty turns up. If she's gone off somewhere on a wild chase or to get her nails done, I may yank her hair out, so stop me if it comes to that."

"No, I'll just let you yank out her hair. We're all worried."

"I assume Jackson Lee hasn't heard from her," I said.

"He's about frantic, I think. He tries not to show it. We all know Bitty always has to have a partner in crime on her excursions into insanity."

I laughed. "Usually. But we all warned her we wouldn't help, so maybe she didn't ask."

Rayna came to sit with us while Jackson Lee walked Mrs. Tyree back to her house, being a gentleman and opening the front gate for her, then making sure she got safely home. Chen Ling sat in Rayna's lap; her little bug eyes looked moist, and I could swear she had tears.

"Something's happened to Bitty," I said. Rayna and Gaynelle looked at me, and I pointed to Chen Ling. "She knows. Whatever it was, she saw it."

As if to prove my point, the dog whimpered, then lay down on Rayna's lap and put her smushed little face between her paws. She fit from Rayna's stomach to her knees.

"I don't know. She thought Bitty was in the car," said Gaynelle doubtfully.

"Maybe that was the last place she saw her." Rayna stroked the pug's head, earning another whimper. Biting her lip, she looked up at me. "I think you're right, Trinket. But how could she see anything? The door was closed, and she was in the house."

"I don't know. Maybe Bitty threatened to bring her along with whoever talked her into leaving—or abducted her."

That last seemed the most likely. Bitty wouldn't normally go off and leave Chen Ling in the house and the house unlocked, and I didn't really see her attacking Jenna Jones and locking her in the car, either. I told Rayna and Gaynelle about the truck Mrs. Tyree had seen.

"Do you know anyone with a truck like that?" Gaynelle asked.

"Just the truck Bitty and I saw going up to the cabin. It had to be the Whalens. Either Skip and his father, or Skip and an accomplice. I thought it must be his father, because of the bald head."

"That's more likely," Rayna agreed.

When Jackson Lee returned, we went inside and discussed our options. He had no more news than we did, as the police were being tight-lipped. Or he was.

"So what do we do?" I asked him, and he shook his head.

"I don't know. I'm going to stay here, make some calls, find Catfish, and see if he has any information. He may know more than we do. I don't want to leave in case Bitty comes back."

In the end, because there wasn't anything we could think to do, we left him there with Chen Ling. Rayna took me back to her house, where we went inside and talked to Rob. He always had information, and I gave him a description of the truck Mrs. Tyree saw and added what I recalled of it from that brief glimpse as we passed it. Rob started running details through a computer program, and Rayna beckoned Gaynelle and me to come with her.

"He works better without distractions," she said, and we nodded understanding. "Let's go out in the garden for a while. I'll let the dogs out, and we can see what we can figure out."

"Skip Whalen has her," I said. "I just know it. Somehow he got close enough to her to grab her. Jenna Jones has to be his girlfriend. It'd be too big a coincidence for an insurance adjustor to be named Jenna, too, Carl Jung or not."

"Ah," said Gaynelle. "Synchronicity. It seems likely that it's Skip

Whalen. I don't see who else it could be. Maybe now the police will investigate."

"Jackson Lee said he's calling Catfish, so maybe that will help," I said, but I didn't really think it would. "There has to be probable cause, evidence, some reason other than suspicion to arrest him. He has to know Bitty has proof he bought her father's rifle, and it's the murder weapon. Or we'll have proof if Tammy can find the receipt."

We sat at the same table we'd sat at earlier. The pitcher of lemonade was still there and our unfinished glasses. I peered into mine. A fly did the backstroke, so I didn't drink any.

"I'll go get ice and more glasses," Rayna said and got up and went inside.

I looked over at Gaynelle. "Do you really think he kidnapped her?"

"I can't imagine what he thinks he'll do with her. He'll have to either kill her or get her to agree not to tell the police what she knows, neither of which is a guarantee he'll get away with it. The police may be hindered by rules, but they're certainly not stupid. They may already know more than we do and just be gathering evidence."

I put my face in my palms and pressed fingers into my eyes. My head hurt. I didn't know where Bitty could be or if she was even still alive. After all, Whalen had killed once. After that, it might be easy for him to kill again.

When I lifted my head, my vision was blurred. For an instant, I thought I saw a familiar dog trotting down the sidewalk outside the railroad depot. I blinked, then looked more closely.

"Chen Ling," I said, and Gaynelle nodded.

"She's so upset, poor little thing."

"No," I said and pointed. "There she is."

Gaynelle turned; Rayna came out with a tray of ice and glasses and set it down as she saw her, too.

"I'll get her," said Rayna, and I went with her while Gaynelle called Jackson Lee to tell him the dog had come visiting again.

I called over my shoulder, "Tell him I'll bring her home shortly," as I followed Rayna out the garden gate and across the street.

It had gotten late, and the light was waning as we reached the depot. It was quiet. Phillips closes at four in the afternoon, and no one comes down to the depot unless there's a function. Apparently, there were no weddings or celebrations planned, for the depot was dark on this side except for a few outside lights. Chen Ling trotted right past the dining room and white screen door leading to a small office and went around the front of the depot as if she had a destination in mind.

"Is she looking for Gwen's dog again?" I wondered aloud as we picked up speed. "She sure seems to know where she's going."

"Well, I know Bitty's brought her down here during the Tracks of the Generals tours and crafts fairs, so maybe she's looking for her here."

"They postponed it because of the murder this year," I said, and Rayna nodded.

"Apparently, Chen Ling has a long memory."

I thought about that while I tried to keep up with Rayna. It seemed unusual for even Chitling to do something as inexplicable as follow a memory.

"She's fast for a bow-legged old dog," I muttered as we got to the front of the depot. Long shadows stretched across the old bricks and pavers, and the planters of flowers and tall bushes screened the tracks from the depot. I didn't see any sign of the little dog. "Where did she go?"

Rayna stopped. "I don't know. She couldn't have gotten all the way to the end this fast. Wait—is that door open?"

We moved closer and saw that the door to the old baggage room was ajar. No lights were on, and it seemed unoccupied, but we moved closer to check as it was unusual for the depot to be left open. The long windows were uncovered and let in faint light from the street lamps that lined the tracks.

As soon as I stepped inside, I felt as if we'd walked into trouble. I stood still for a moment, and Rayna paused next to an old table set up across the small room. To the left is the old waiting room, and a bathroom has been added recently. The old floors have been repaired but were left much as they were a hundred years ago, creaking slightly with every step. I heard the familiar clickety-click of dog toenails on the boards, and Rayna whispered, "I hear her."

It sounded as if Chen Ling had gone into the waiting room. I looked for a light switch, but couldn't find it in the murky shadows and hazy light that didn't penetrate very far through the windows and open door. Rayna whistled for the dog, but she didn't respond.

"Can you see anything?" I asked as we made our way into the waiting room. It was pitch black, no windows or open door to allow in light. I felt my way along, fingers tracing wood panels and brick walls. My voice seemed to echo in the high-ceilinged room. Rayna made her way to the bathroom and found a light switch.

Light spread across the floor, and I saw the folding chairs stacked against the wall along with long utility tables used in presentations. Chitling was nowhere to be found. I looked at Rayna and said, "I don't think Gwen will appreciate us rambling around in her depot without permission. Maybe I should go tell her we're looking for the dog again."

"Drat. I left my cell phone. I'll do that, if you want to stay here and try to catch Chen Ling. Don't let her get back out again, or we may never catch her."

"Be careful," I said and pulled one of the folding chairs away from the wall and unfolded it to sit down. I placed it right in front of the door so Chen Ling couldn't get past without me seeing her. I was grateful for the light. It was really kind of spooky being in there alone.

It might take a Rayna a few minutes to alert Gwen to our intrusion. She'd have to walk out and around to the back of the depot that was a personal residence now. Three big new garage doors had been installed, and I was sure Gwen kept the gate to the garden locked. I would.

So I settled in and waited for Chen Ling to finish her prowling, although I couldn't imagine what the dog wanted here. The back garden, I could understand. Gwen had dogs. What on earth would she want inside the empty train depot? Honestly, I was rather grateful for this distraction. Worrying about Bitty but being unable to do anything to find her was frustrating. At least now I had a purpose.

A clicking sound on the other side of the room caught my attention. Aha! I stood up. The door on the far side creaked, and I realized that somehow the dog had gotten it open or found it open. I thought I recalled a small office on the other side and a staircase that led to what used to be rooms for rent. I don't think they'd been used since the late 1920s when the depot closed and still looked as if they were ready to receive guests; beds were made up with antique linens, and old wash stands with towels.

If Chen Ling got up those stairs, I may never find her. So I crossed the room and pushed open the door. I caught a glimpse of a curly tail in the hazy light that came through a small window, and I moved toward her. I had to get her before she went up those stairs.

"Come here, you little varmint," I said, and Chen Ling looked at me and growled. That did not deter me. It wasn't the first time she'd expressed displeasure with me. Fur bristled along her back, and I could tell she was really angry when she let out a shrill bark.

I lunged for her, and she evaded me, skittering to the side into deeper shadows. I wasn't sure what lay beyond, except the dining room, but it was closed. The staircase would be her only escape. I tried to put myself between her and the stairs, but that left the way clear to the waiting room and the open door beyond. So I tried coaxing her. She kept growling.

"What is wrong with you," I muttered and moved forward to back her into an alcove between the wall and some file cabinets. Then I heard Rayna behind me and said, "Here, help me catch this dog. She's not at all cooperative."

When Rayna didn't answer, I half-turned, and then lights exploded in my brain and I hit the ground, dazed but still conscious. Had I hit my head? Had Rayna hit me?

Chen Ling barked fiercely, and I tried to sit up, groggy and saying words that weren't even spray painted on my car. Then a shadow detached, and I knew it wasn't Rayna and tried to duck, but couldn't get out of the way in time. Starbursts of light exploded again.

Everything went black.

Chapter 18

THIS WASN'T THE first time I'd been hit in the head. You'd think I'd have had some sense knocked into me, but apparently I'm too thickheaded. *Don't go into dark places*, I told myself as I lay there blinking. It hadn't yet occurred to me that such advice would have been more useful *before* I'd gone into dark places. But I lay there, trying to get my bearings, realizing that I'd been immobilized somehow. I wasn't yet sure how. Or why. Or who. Or even where, because I didn't seem to be in the same place.

I tentatively tested my limits. Arms behind me, wrists bound together, ankles tied. I felt like the goat in a goat roping competition. I rather gingerly moved my head and found that if I tilted it back, I could see gray light. It seeped in from somewhere. I blinked again to focus my eyes. It was mostly black shadows and thin gray blurs. I didn't know if I'd gone blind or was locked in a closet. It could go either way.

"Dammit," I muttered and then heard a soft, "Trinket? Are you awake?"

"Bitty?"

A sob answered me. I knew it was Bitty.

"Where are you?" I asked, all of a sudden so glad to know she was alive and okay that I momentarily forgot we weren't okay.

"Propped up against a post at the moment. How did you find me?"

"I didn't." I squirmed around a little, trying to find her in the dark. "Chitling found you. Is she with you?"

"Oh, my poor precious. She took off somewhere, and that monster chased her—I hope she gets away."

Oddly, so did I. Chen Ling may not be the most lovable dog in the world, but her loyalty and love for Bitty can't be matched.

"Rayna is with me. She'll be looking for us soon. What does he intend to do with us?" I asked to distract her, as she'd started sobbing again. She sniffled.

"He who?"

"Skip Whalen. That's who has us, isn't it?"

"No. I'm not sure who it is. She looks vaguely familiar, though. I'm sure I've seen her. If I could just remember. I should never have thought she was nice, but then she zapped that poor girl with a stun gun and made me leave with her. She must have nerves of steel, because it all happened in broad daylight. Not that anyone was out to see it."

"It's not Skip Whalen?" I repeated stupidly, and Bitty sounded irritated.

"Just how hard did she hit you in the head? No, it's not Skip Whalen. You were wrong about him."

"I'd say you were wrong about him too, but you've named almost everyone in town as a suspect except Jackson Lee, so I'll just say you're wrong, period." I wasn't in a great mood either.

Bitty sounded indignant when she said, "I have not named everyone, just those who fit the profile."

"How CSI of you. Never mind. We need to think about how to get out of here instead of argue over who's right. Are you tied up?"

"If I wasn't, would I still be sitting here?"

"Good point. Can you scoot toward me?"

"I can, but I'll have to bring the entire bed with me. I'm tied to it."

"Bed?" I echoed. "Are we upstairs in the depot?"

"From what I can tell, we are. She zapped me too once we got here. Whoever she is, she works out. She's got arms like Jerry Lawler."

"Maybe she's a female wrestler. She apparently got me upstairs on her own."

"Did she zap you too?" Bitty asked, but I didn't know.

"I don't think so. It felt more like she hit me in the head with something. Okay. Let me see what I can figure out here . . . yeah, she has me tied to something, too. I wonder if there's a way to wiggle loose."

I wasted a few minutes and the top layer of my skin trying to twist out of the ties that held me to something pretty solid. It wasn't going to happen. I leaned my head back, but it was empty space. Maybe I was tied to something short. I pulled my feet up under me, which wasn't easy when they were tied at the ankles, and the ties were scraping against my already bruised skin, so I was pretty sure I'd end up bleeding into my sandals before long. Still, I persisted. It took a few tries before I finally managed to wiggle one foot free of the ties and got my body in a crouch, but whatever held me, it was too heavy to go with me. I ended up flopping back down.

"And to think I polished my toenails for this," I said into the dark, a completely irrelevant comment that earned an interested response.

"What color?"

I briefly closed my eyes. "Murder by Mango."

Silence greeted that, and I understood. It did seem appropriate for the moment. If I survived, I decided I would throw that bottle away the instant I got home.

"I think I got one hand free—wait. I hear someone coming," Bitty said. "Play dead!"

We both went into possum mode, and the footsteps got close. Then a circle of light bobbed, and I squinted before the flashlight could catch me.

"Still here," said a female voice. Blue light illuminated a cheek and ear. A cell phone?

A male voice said loud enough for me to hear, "Did you kill them?"

"Not yet."

I tried not to shudder. Whoever the "she" was, she sounded determined. I wondered if Chen Ling had gotten away and if Rayna had noticed yet that I was missing.

"I'm almost there," said the male. "I've been looking for Jenna."

"Stop it. I need you now before someone starts looking for these two."

"Two? I thought it was just the rich bitch."

Sounding irritated, the female replied, "Sasquatch showed up with the dog. I can't find the dog, but I've got them both tied. And I found the rifle up in the attic. We need to get out of here *now*."

"I'm at the curb. I'll be right up."

The blue light clicked off, and the flashlight flipped up. I closed my eyes real quick again just in case. I heard her moving around, then the unmistakable sound of a cell phone vibrating.

"Yeah?" she answered. A pause, then a different male voice asked if she was through yet. "No, Skip just got here. Did you take care of the other guy?"

My mind went momentarily blank before I thought, *What other guy?* The male voice rumbled indistinctly.

"Good. He knew too much. We might have to go down to Jackson, too. No, the woman. This has turned into a nightmare. It should have been easy, but these two idiots and that Fish guy have made it complicated. Yes, we'll need to leave town. Not too soon, though. I talked Darlene into inviting us up to her place. No, me either, but just until they convict the Caldwell kid."

Darlene? The fish guy had to be Catfish. I got queasy thinking he might be kidnapped too. Or worse.

"Gotta go," she said. "He just got here. It's about time."

"I don't like this," said the male, breathing noisily, and I recognized Skip Whalen. It sounded like him, petulant and whiny.

"Shut up. I did it for you. The least you can do is help me get rid of them."

"This ain't like the other. Someone's gonna look for these two. That bail bonds lady was with the tall one earlier. She'll be back."

"We got what we came for. Now we just have to get these two out of here so it takes a while to find them. Come on. I'll take the crazy one, you get the mouthy one."

I had no idea which one was supposed to be me. I wavered between playing possum and biting. Those were the only options I had available at the moment.

"What about the dog?" Skip asked.

"It can't talk. That rich bitch can and will, though. Her sister-in-law said she's looking for the receipt on that rifle I bought you. She called and told me to mail her a copy."

Skip laughed. "Pretty stupid."

"Aren't they. Think money will get them everything they want. We've got to get rid of all the evidence. Police can suspect all they want, but without evidence, they can't touch us."

"Well, I still say you shouldn't have done it, Ma. I could have handled Royal on my own. You didn't need to try and shoot him."

His mother made a rude noise. "He broke your nose. Even that wimpy kid beat you up, and you're twice his size."

"Clay caught me off-guard." He sounded defensive. "I had a plan to get him back."

"Get her up, and let's get going before that bonds lady and the depot woman figure out what's going on. I've got the rifle downstairs already. We just have to get these two and get out of here."

If they took us off, we were dead. I knew that. Screaming in this part of the depot would be a waste and probably get me zapped or hit in the head again, or at the least, gagged. So I waited, hoping Bitty wouldn't scream or make noise until we got outside where someone was likely to hear us. Gwen and her family live in the opposite side of the depot so would never hear us here. It was too risky to hope that Rayna was back, although I wondered what was taking her so long. I did my part, pretending to be unconscious, and therefore a dead weight.

Skip got me unfastened from my post and hefted me up to sling me over his shoulder like I was a side of beef. He may not be the sharpest crayon in the box, but he was definitely strong. I imagined Sally Whalen was strong, too. Well, Kit had said they were a sporting family. He must have meant Sally as well. I'd never dreamed a woman had shot Walter. I can be so sexist.

The hard curve of Skip's shoulder dug into my belly as he jostled me about, and I got a quick look at the hallway leading to the stairs as he carried me. The flashlight his mother held wobbled around a bit; I imagine she wasn't having as easy a time with Bitty. I tried to calculate the best time to pitch a hissy fit that might alert anyone nearby, but at night, this side of the depot was deserted. Few cars come by. Phillips was closed, Gwen and family on the other side of the depot, and even the express or freight office empty at night. Rayna's hotel/house faced the road and depot, but since she was somewhere with Gwen, probably looking for Chen Ling, she may be too far away to hear me or know what she was hearing when I did scream.

The odds weren't good.

Blood rushed to my head as I hung over Skip's shoulder, dangling down his back, but I peeped and caught a glimpse of Bitty carried in much the same way over Sally Whalen's shoulder. Appearances can be so deceptive. Who knew she was that stout a woman? Not stout as in fat, but stout as in sturdy. She certainly hadn't seemed like it in our brief meeting at her house. It wasn't that we'd underestimated her; we hadn't even considered it. We'd focused on Skip, not his mother.

I thought about kicking him, as my free foot dangled right about at the best place to kick a man. I flexed my feet and realized I'd lost a shoe. Maybe I could leave a trail of clues behind. Eventually they'd be looking for us. It was a good bet they'd start at the depot for me, at least, since this was the last place Rayna had seen me. With luck, Bitty had left something of hers for them to find, too. In case neither of us survived to tell them she'd been here, too . . .

All these things ran through my mind on my uncomfortable journey down the stairs and through the waiting and baggage rooms. Night air struck, smelling of privet hedge and roses and tar. Trains aren't the best smelling things. Boxcars sat on one of the track spurs; lights atop tall poles spread fuzzy pools. Down the hill, car headlights sped past on Boundary Street. In front of the depot, it was shadowy and deserted. As I bounced against Skip's shoulder, I caught a glimpse of a truck; it idled at the curb. It had a double cab and a huge bed and was black. It looked very much like the truck Bitty and I had passed on the road to her former cabin. I tried to turn my head to see Bitty without making it obvious, in case Sally had her eye on me. Sally seemed to be struggling to breathe. Maybe she wasn't as strong as I'd thought.

A few steps behind, Bitty's spike heels swung in front of Sally Whalen as if she had no use of her feet. If they got us to that truck, we were as good as dead. I waited, gathering my courage and trying not to wet my pants, and when we were about twenty feet away, I drew back my foot with the shoe on it and kicked as hard as I could, catching Skip Whalen right between his legs. It was awkward, and I wasn't sure I'd connected.

He dropped to his knees, dropping me in the process, groaning out breathless grunts for air as I landed hard on the pavers. Apparently, I'd connected. I rolled, screamed at the top of my lungs, "Bitty!" but Sally had a tight hold on her. She kept trying to hit her with something in her hand, and I saw to my horror that it was a stun gun. It sizzled, but it sounded more like sparklers fizzling than a stun gun.

Bitty reared back, grabbed a huge wad of Sally's hair in each of her hands, and yanked hard, as Sally tried to fight her off. Much cursing went on, most of it coming from Bitty. Sally finally dropped her but kept a tight hold on her arm as she kept trying to jab her with the stun gun. It had lost its charge, and I stumbled to my feet and toward them. Just as I reached them, Bitty lifted one dainty foot and slammed her high heel right in Sally's instep, putting as much weight on it as she could. Sally cursed and jerked, knocking Bitty off-balance. I managed to reach Bitty as she fell backward. Sally lunged at us with the stun gun.

Using me as her counterweight, Bitty reared up with both feet and caught Sally right in the chest with those spikes she calls high heels. I fell back as Sally hit the pavers, screaming blue murder. She rolled, got to her knees, and probably would have come after us if it hadn't been for one really pissed-off pug. Chen Ling came out of nowhere, grabbed Sally by one ankle, and held on for dear life as she tried to kick free. When Sally lifted her fist to bring it down on the dog, Bitty was on her like Batman. I've never seen anything like it. Weird sounds rose into the air, the pug growling and snarling, Bitty growling and snarling, and Sally cussing and crying.

That was how Rayna found us, with Officer Stewart and Gwen in tow. Gwen's eyes were big as saucers, and she kept saying something like, "Oh sunny beaches," over and over again, but fortunately, Stewart got right to work and clapped some handcuffs on Sally. I glanced toward Skip, but he had disappeared.

It had seemed like a half hour, but it had all happened in only a matter of a minute or two, I think. I stood there, and my knees wobbled, my bare foot suddenly spasmed, and I sat down abruptly. The truck at the curb screeched away but didn't get far. Two police cars screamed down the hill, and another one came up Van Dorn from the curve below, cutting off escape. Lights flashed, and I put my face against my drawn-up knees and thought about moving to a mountaintop somewhere.

The babble ebbed and flowed around me as Bitty demanded Officer Stewart arrest Sally for animal abuse, while Rayna kept saying murder charges were more likely; I sat there, vaguely aware that we had once more narrowly escaped death. Christian Louboutin would be so proud his shoes helped catch a killer. I was so proud Chitling had helped catch a killer.

Then Jackson Lee arrived, and Bitty went into instant Belle-mode, feeling faint and declaring that she had never been so frightened. "I just kept praying you would get here," she said to Jackson Lee, and he put his arms around her, squashing the pug between them.

I lifted my head at that. "Is that what you were doing?" I asked, and Bitty gave me the evil eye. I shook my head. "It sounded like no praying I've ever heard."

She flashed me the unmistakable sign of friendship, once more forgetting the second finger, and I smiled.

Rayna came over to kneel down next to me, untying my hands. "Are you all right?"

I thought about it. Then I shook my head. "I'm unhurt, but I'm not at all sure I'm all right. I'm so glad you showed up when you did. It could have gotten much worse."

"Yes, Bitty might have killed her."

I actually giggled. "She might have. Of course, to look at her now that Jackson Lee is here, she acts like she might wilt at any moment."

"Jackson Lee saw her in action. He's just letting her have her moment."

"Where the heck were you?" I asked. "I thought you'd never get here."

"Well, I went to tell Gwen we were here looking for Chen Ling, and she thought she might have gone into the back garden again, so we looked there. Of course, she wasn't out there, so we chatted a few minutes, standing out in the driveway. Then the next thing I know, here comes the dog, barking at us like she'd gone mad. I tried to catch her, but she kept running back toward the front of the depot. I got to the corner there between the freight office and the end of the depot and started to go out front, when I saw Skip Whalen get out of the truck and go toward the baggage room. I knew there was trouble, so I got Gwen to call the police while I used her niece's phone to call Rob and Jackson Lee."

"Y'all got here just in time. If they'd gotten us into the truck, we wouldn't have lived much longer. Sally Whalen is lethal. All this time I thought it was Skip, and it was his mother. She's nuts. She's the one who killed Walter, although she thought he was Royal. I don't know how she made that mistake."

"It might have been the uniform and hat. Royal fancied it up with that red armband and the Stewart coat of arms. It stood out from the others. And he always stuck a red feather in the blue captain's hat."

"That explains it. I wondered. Murder is so cruel. Oh God—I forgot. Catfish!"

Rayna looked quizzical. "You're hungry?"

"No, Catfish Carter. I think Skip's father has done something to him."

Rayna went at once to tell Officer Stewart, who had three other officers with him by then. One of them went immediately to his patrol car and used the radio. Rayna returned and said, "They're going to look for him."

I nodded. "Can you help me up? I don't think I can manage it by myself."

Rayna helped me up. It had gotten cool, and I shivered now, as much from the breeze as the aftershocks of danger and drama. I watched as police led Sally Whalen past us toward a waiting car; she limped and blood dripped from her foot, but the look she flashed toward me was pure malevolence. Yes, a frightening woman.

"Here comes Rob," said Rayna. "Why don't you stay at my house tonight? I have that extra guest room, and it'll save you having to drive all the way to Cherryhill."

"It sounds tempting," I said, and it did. I didn't want to think about pulling myself together to drive the cursing car home. With my luck, Officer Stewart would give me a ticket for driving a public nuisance.

"Trinket?" a familiar voice said, and I turned to see my daddy hurrying toward me across the gravel between the depot and the freight office. He'd come in the back way to avoid the police cars, it seemed, and all of a sudden, I was a little girl again and just wanted my daddy to keep me safe.

He came straight to me and took me in his arms as if I were twelve, hugging me. "I came as soon as Jackson Lee called, although I thought it was Bitty in danger, not you."

I pressed my face against his chest. He smelled of Old Spice. I've always loved that scent because it always makes me think of my father. I loved it even more right then. He held me and said over the top of my head to Rayna, "Is it okay if I take her home?"

"You'll have to talk to the police, since I know they'll want a statement from her, but I'm sure it won't take long."

Daddy looked down at me, tilting his head back. "Do you want to go home, or do you want to talk to the police first?"

"Home," was all I could get out, and he nodded.

I don't know what he and Jackson Lee told the police, but within five minutes I was in my mother's car, and Daddy was telling me to buckle up. I did.

Maybe it's silly for a grown woman to regress like that, but there's something very safe and comforting about knowing someone who loves you has your back. I liked it.

OFFICER STEWART came out the next morning to take my statement. He was very nice and respectful, surprising me, and just took down all I said and nodded, and asked questions at the right times, and then finally it was over.

"How's Catfish?" I asked when he closed his notebook. "Did you find him?"

"He's alive and in the hospital. Condition is serious but not critical. Apparently he shot back when Sylvester Whalen ambushed him. That may have saved his life, but he's lucky all the same. If Whalen hadn't been in a hurry, he'd have finished him off."

I nodded. "I'm glad he'll be okay. And Jenna Jones?"

"She'll be fine. It seems that stun gun malfunctioned and gave her such a high dose of electricity, she was out for a while. It messed with her blood pressure, too."

"I take it she was not a willing accomplice," I said.

"Officer, would you like a piece of Lane cake and something to drink?" Mama asked him as he stood up, and he looked surprised.

"Why, yes ma'am, I sure would. Thank you."

He sat back down, and I silently blessed my mother. Or maybe she was curious, too. Whichever it was, we had him talking until he finished his cake, anyway.

"I know the investigation is ongoing, and y'all still don't know everything yet," I said, "but I don't understand why Sally turned on Skip's girlfriend like that."

Mama put a generous slice of cake in front of him, and he picked up his fork. "If I had to guess, I'd say it was because Jenna balked at going along with murder. Maybe she thought she was just there to play a prank or get some petty vengeance. Once she figured out Sally had a lot more than that on her mind, she chickened out. This is delicious, Mrs. Truevine."

"Thank you. That was my mother's recipe. I have half a cake left, so you just eat all you want, Officer. There's plenty of coffee, too. Aren't you Royal's brother?"

He grinned. "Most of the time. I don't always claim him. He can get pretty rowdy on occasion."

"He's got a good heart," I said, "and he's very polite. Mama would say he's been reared right."

Stewart nodded. "Our parents tried. We lost Mama when Royal was just fourteen, so I tried to help out. He resented it, I think."

"He's turned out fine," I said. "You know, when you see someone like Skip, who has been such a bully, you'd think he's just mean on purpose. Then you meet his parents, and it explains it. I wonder if his father was involved in Walter's murder."

"We're still investigating that," he said evasively.

"Is Sally saying anything?" When he didn't answer, I added, "I heard her telling Skip that she had to handle it all because he wouldn't, you know. So maybe Skip didn't know what she had planned."

Stewart shrugged. "Royal said Skip can't hit the side of a barn with a shotgun, so it's likely that's why Sally decided to take care of it, since she used to hunt all the time."

I asked a few more questions but didn't get much more information. I realized I'd have to wait until Jackson Lee got all the details. I wasn't quite ready to leave the house yet, so the answers would have to wait a while longer. I enjoyed just being home and safe.

Later that afternoon, my day got even more perfect. Kit showed up with a picnic basket and a bottle of wine, and we went out to the cherry orchard and spread blankets on the grass and ate fried chicken and biscuits and slaw.

I sighed happily. "The Colonel does amazing things with chicken, and Mama has almost a half a Lane cake in the kitchen, you know."

Kit laughed. "I'll save dessert for later. More wine?"

I held out my glass, and he poured my favorite Zinfandel. "How did you know I didn't want to leave the house?" I asked as he leaned back against the trunk of a cherry tree. Old bark held interesting patterns. And ants. He quickly realized his error and stretched out on the blanket.

"I just figured you'd rather be where it's safe and quiet today."

"In other words, not at Bitty's house."

"That, too." He looked at the marks still on my wrists, his expression serious. "It scares me to think of how easily you could have been hurt."

I held out my foot. Daddy had the doctor come out, so it had bandages on it where I'd cut it somehow, and still bore the marks of Brownie's teeth, too. I tried to lighten the moment. "But I *was* wounded. Even worse, I lost a sandal."

"Trinket—"

"I know," I said quickly. "It scares me, too. But this time we really tried not to do anything crazy. Too crazy, anyway. Trouble seems to find us, even when we don't look for it."

"I suppose that's something I'll have to get used to then," he said after a minute. "I asked Jackson Lee how he handles it, you know. He said he has to think of it in the context of whether he'd rather have Bitty with all of the craziness, or sanity without Bitty."

"I'm not sure I like being compared to Bitty or called crazy, but it makes sense in an odd sort of way."

"Come here," he said, smiling, and patted the blanket in front of him. "Let's lie down and watch the clouds for a while. We can deal with crazy when it shows up again. Let's just deal with us now."

Blushing like a sixteen-year-old, I stretched out on a quilt my grandmother had made and stared up at the cherry tree as Kit started talking about a place he'd once visited that had clear mountain streams and waterfalls that tumbled over rocks into small pools below, and how he'd like to show it all to me. Smiling, nodding, I drifted into his world and lingered peacefully.

There's just something so soothing about a man sharing his dreams.

Then crazy showed up in the form of Bitty and Jackson Lee. They were in his car, and he parked it next to Kit's Chevy. Bitty bounced out, looking none the worse for our adventure, wearing spike heels and capris. It actually looked nice, to my surprise; although I'd have never thought spike heels went with cropped pants. But then again, fashion is not the biggest concern to a woman wearing a pug in a baby sling across her chest, I'm sure. Chitling's dark brown little face wore a bored expression as she peered over the edge of the sling.

"Where's your cape, Batgirl?" I asked as Bitty tottered over grassy ruts to reach the cherry orchard. "You and your trusty sidekick should get a commendation for taking down a killer."

"We should, shouldn't we? Help me, sweetheart, so I don't drop my precious girl."

Jackson Lee helped Bitty sit down on the quilt, and precious girl formed an immediate attachment to the fried chicken. I had to snatch an extra crispy leg from the plate before she got it, and her jaws closed on empty air. I felt rather bad at treating a heroine shabbily, so I said, "Don't watch," to Kit, and tore off a piece of chicken and gave it to Chitling.

"Honestly, Trinket," said Bitty as she tried to stuff her dog back into the sling. "You're only encouraging her."

"As if you wouldn't buy Chitling her own bucket if Kit wasn't sitting here," I scoffed. "So tell me what you know. Did Sally Whalen really kill one and try to kill four other people just because her son got a bloody nose?"

"Four? Oh yes, Jenna Jones. And to be specific, it was Sly who tried to kill Catfish. But I'll let Jackson Lee tell you all about it."

I looked at Jackson Lee. He seemed bemused, but he perked right up when Bitty gave him a look, and said, "Yes, but first, I have to point out that Bitty was right all along. It was the wrong rifle. As you know by now, Sally Whalen shot Walter, thinking he was Royal Stewart. From what I've pieced together—and she's made no confession yet, but Skip keeps talking—it was the rifle she found online that gave her the idea. Most of this is conjecture, mind, but she went down to Jackson to buy an 1853 Enfield, and after meeting the seller—Tammy Truevine—she thought she knew a way to get back at Clayton for his fight with Skip. I think at first she only meant to steal Bitty's rifle at the next reenactment Skip attended, or do something underhanded and mean, but then Skip got into a fight with Royal Stewart, and Royal broke his nose. She was furious. She wanted vengeance, and her plan altered. Skip is a terrible marksman, but Sally used to be on the rifle team and is expert. They got Skip out of jail, and because they knew Royal's brother is an officer on the Holly Springs police force, she was certain he got out early, too. It never occurred to Sally that Barron would make him stay all night to teach him a lesson.

"So, she put on her son's uniform, brought the rifle she'd bought from Bitty's sister-in-law, and waited around the corner of the depot near the freight office. No one would think anything about one more soldier. It was smoky, and there was confusion and shouting and shots being fired, and she simply took aim when she saw Royal's uniform and shot him in the heart."

He paused, and I felt suddenly terrible. I'd inadvertently been the cause of Walter being killed. As if he knew what I was thinking, Jackson Lee looked at me.

"Don't for a minute think any of this is your fault, Trinket. Sally meant to kill Royal and would have found a way. It was Walter's bad fortune to have taken his place, but Royal's good fortune to be a spectator instead of participant. If she'd seen him, she may well have shot him anyway, causing two deaths."

I nodded. "Thank you, Jackson Lee." Kit reached over and squeezed my hand, and I smiled at him before a thought struck me.

"Is Sally responsible for the attack on Catfish?"

Jackson Lee grimaced. "No, that was all Sylvester Whalen. Catfish had figured it out, and he thought he could find the rifle and prove it. He made the mistake of showing up at the depot before Whalen left the work site, and started poking around. So Whalen told him he'd seen someone hide an old rifle, and if Catfish wanted to meet him after he got off work, he'd show him where. Catfish showed up prepared, but he didn't expect two of them. Good thing Skip can't hit the side of a barn. Sylvester got him, thought he'd killed him, and dumped him in the weeds down JM Ash Road in the industrial park. Catfish had shot Whalen in the shoulder, though, so he didn't stay to make sure he was dead."

Then Kit asked, "So how did Sally Whalen get away without being seen after shooting Walter?"

Jackson Lee took Chen Ling as Bitty handed the dog to him and settled her in his lap as he said, "She knew the police would confiscate all the weapons, so when people ran over to help Walter, she went with them. Anyone would have done, but she saw Brandon kneeling next to Walter, his gun next to him, and simply switched them. That way when Brandon picked it up, thinking it was his, his fingerprints were all over it. She wore gloves, so no other prints were on the rifle. Skip said she thought Brandon was Clayton and was very annoyed when she learned later he wasn't."

He paused, then added, "She thought Brandon had seen her shoot Walter, and according to Skip, tried to ambush him at JB's after sabotaging his car. But when he was arraigned and no one accused her, she knew he hadn't. Brandon going to prison was a better revenge anyway. Maybe it wasn't Royal, but I believe she intended to kill him later."

He glanced at Bitty. "The two rifles look so much alike, it was difficult for even the experts to agree. If we'd known the history of the Truevine rifle, we might have figured it out a lot sooner."

Bitty looked smug. "I just knew it wasn't my mama's rifle. That thing hasn't fired in a hundred years. I thought maybe someone had switched the barrel, or somehow repaired it, but I never thought of Daddy's rifle. After all, it's supposed to be safely in Jackson, Mississippi, not in the hands of someone like Sally Whalen." She looked over at me. "Do you know who her sister is?"

I had to admit I had no idea. Bitty smiled. "Darlene Landers. Sally is her half-sister, ten years younger. I remembered that when she told Sly that Darlene said they could come for a visit. Darlene detests Sally. Calls her a half-wit half-sister, so no telling what Sally said to get her to agree. I know Darlene is glad she doesn't have to let her visit now."

"I'm sure," I agreed. "So Sally hid your rifle in the depot, knowing the police might come looking for it, and planned to get rid of it later. Why didn't she do so before last night?"

"Her husband Sly works construction," Bitty replied. "He was part of those renovating the depot, so he got a key to the baggage room where she hid it. But then other workers went in there and moved stuff around. He didn't know where it'd gone. So he gave Sally the key, and she had to wait until it was clear to look for it. She'd already been there twice without finding it. Last night she found it up in the attic where someone must have thought it belonged. I doubt they would have known there was a disagreement between the weapons' experts, so never thought anything of it but that it was just an old rifle that belonged to the depot."

"And how did Jenna get roped into this? Did she know Sally killed Walter?"

Bitty pointed to my wine glass, and I handed it to her. She sipped, and then handed it back. "Not bad wine. It turns out that Jenna really does work at an insurance company, and Sally convinced Jenna to 'mess with' me, as she put it in her statement, and deny my claim. She didn't know Sally had other plans. If I hadn't given Mrs. Tyree an extra set of my keys after locking myself out twice in one day, poor Jenna might have died in there. It got pretty hot with that tarp on the car. Who knows when we would have found her? And don't look at me like that, Trinket. I didn't mean to lock my keys in my car. It just happened. I'm glad you thought to look in the Benz."

"I didn't. Chitling did."

"She did? My precious girl," Bitty crooned, leaning over the pug. She misjudged her audience. Chitling still had her mind on the Colonel. As Bitty leaned toward her, the dog leaped from Jackson Lee's lap into the middle of the quilt, snagging a chicken thigh off a plate, and then taking off across the yard.

Maybe it would have been better if Mama hadn't chosen that moment to let Brownie out into the yard, but apparently he spied Chitling with chicken and took off after her. I'm sure he just meant to help her find her way back, but the result was that both dogs raced across the empty field next to the house and into the woods. While the men went to retrieve them, looking less than pleased, Bitty and I shared a glass of wine.

We chatted for a few minutes before Bitty said with a sigh, "Sometimes things work out better than hoped, don't they?"

"I guess that depends on whether you're Darlene or Sally," I replied and took a deep sip of my wine. Bitty held her left hand out to me. I raised my brows. "You still have five fingers. Or is that four fingers and a thumb?"

"Ring finger, Trinket."

I looked. A slender gold band circled it. I nodded. "Nice."

She glanced down, muttered something under her breath, then used her thumb to twist the band. A diamond as big as a robin's egg came into view. It had two small rubies on each side. I gasped.

"You're engaged?"

"A pre-engagement. I want to take my time and so does he."

"If this is a pre-engagement ring, I don't even want to think what an actual engagement ring will look like." I took her hand and inspected it. "It's perfect, Bitty."

"I know."

"So I take it the two of you worked out your little difference of opinion?"

"Oh, that." She waved her hand, the diamond catching sunlight and flashing messages to an OnStar satellite. "I misunderstood him. He'd never be so mean as to ask me to stop seeing any of my friends, but he does want to help me channel my energies in a different direction. You know, like art, or cooking, or a book club with my friends, something like that."

"Uh huh. I would ask what you have in mind, but I'm not sure I want to know."

"Oh, you'll see. I think I have a perfect idea for our next Diva Day."

I reached for the wine bottle. I would have asked for details, but our stalwart hunters of pugs and pups returned, bearing their prey home. It wasn't pretty. Obviously, the prey had won round one. Jackson Lee and Kit looked bedraggled and worse for wear.

The dogs, however, rode securely in each embrace, eyes closed in satisfaction, smiling as they probably planned their next coup. Really, I want to come back as Bitty's dog in my next life. It may be a short life, but it would be wonderful.

Chapter 19

"WHAT ON EARTH," I exclaimed, pausing just inside the railroad depot dining room. It's a large room with a high ceiling, white-painted walls and woodwork, and huge blow-ups of novel covers everywhere: on easels, hanging from the ceiling, perched in the tall alcove windows; smaller ones decorated each cloth-covered table. Some were tasteful, some were lurid, some exotic, and some plain trashy. I gravitated toward the last.

A nearly nude man with rippling muscles looked down at the woman kneeling in front of him, his hands in her hair. It was very suggestive. I was very intrigued. Nice theme.

We had all been sent invitations that requested we come dressed as one of our favorite romantic fiction characters. I had chosen Holly Golightly from *Breakfast at Tiffany's* fame. I felt rather silly with my hair in a twist, pearls around my neck, and a tiara borrowed from Bitty, but I loved the long cigarette holder, elbow gloves, and slinky black dress.

"Trinket, where have you been?"

I turned to answer my cousin's siren call and came nose to navel with a muscular man wearing a breechclout; to my sorrow, it was a life-size cardboard replica of one of the romance novel heroes I'd been admiring. The real thing eluded me. The cardboard cutout waggled.

"Don't just stand there, Trinket, help me with this thing," Bitty complained.

So I licked it.

Glaring at me around the ribcage, Bitty said, "Stop that! You'll lick the ink off. Take this and set it somewhere strategic. I have more to bring inside."

"Who are you supposed to be?" I asked, eying her. She wore a skintight white dress and jeweled cap on her head and, of course, high heels. I couldn't imagine who she was supposed to represent.

She smiled. "Mata Hari."

"That's not fiction. Or romantic."

"It's not?"

I rolled my eyes. "She was executed by firing squad for being a German spy."

"But the book made her so glamorous—oh well, I'll make her romantic."

"If anyone can pull it off, I suppose it's you," I said, and she blew me a kiss.

I carried my trophy across the dining room. Several fantasies flitted through my head as I placed him against a wall across from the entrance. He should be admired. It's my understanding that real models pose for romance novel covers, and the artist provides the costume, or lack of one, according to the book requirements or artistic preference. They may not all be like Fabio, but they are all muscled and gorgeous. I approve.

Perhaps Bitty's book club idea would prove to be successful, after all. I'd had hints of what she planned in the past few weeks, but she'd refused to divulge details, just saying, "You'll like it."

She was right.

By the time she brought in all the cutouts, with a little help from Brandon and Clayton, who refused to carry the male models but had no problems with carrying in the females, she had about fifteen situated around the dining room. There were some from Faulkner novels, just to honor the man who had once sat in this very dining room watching train passengers board and disembark, and Hemingway and Tennessee Williams, but most were romance novels. Naturally, she had included the *Fifty Shades* novels as well. That should provide conversational starters for the uninitiated. If there are any women left in America who haven't heard of *Fifty Shades*, that is, which I doubt.

Rhett Butler and Scarlett O'Hara cutouts were stationed just inside the front doors, so there would be no mistaking the theme for the day: romance. Trust Bitty to think of that. Since she had gotten "pre-engaged," she'd been like a teenager with her first love; it was all about the wedding that would happen sometime in the next five years, and where it would be, and what she would wear, and did I think summer or winter better, and off-white might work—until I had taken to avoiding her. I finally suggested a ladder and elopement. She took the hint.

So now it was mostly all things romance, and I was very happy for her that she had settled on Jackson Lee. They were wonderful together. I was happy with Kit, and it promised to be a lovely summer.

There are times I'm an optimistic fool, but all indications were that it would at least be a lovely Diva Day. The afternoon weather was perfect, sunshine and warm, but not too hot.

Divas began arriving: Marcy Porter as Jessica Rabbit again, Cindy Nelson as Maleficent or Bellatrix Lestrange, we couldn't quite decide, Cady Lee Kincaid as Pocahontas or Princess Tiger Lily, and Gaynelle as Cinderella; all arrived at the same time. Marcy and Cindy were immediately captivated by the cardboard cutout hunks, while Gaynelle admired Rhett and Scarlett, then moved on to Boon Hogganbeck and Corrie from Faulkner's *The Reivers.* I have no idea where Bitty found cardboard cutouts of Steve McQueen as Boon and Sharon Farrell as Corrie from the movie, but they were perfect. Cady Lee discovered the hero in the breechclout and snagged a passing Clayton to take a selfie of her. I had the impression a selfie was a photo one took by one's "self," but then again, what do I know.

Behind me, Rayna said, "So where are the characters from the *Fifty Shades* books?"

"Ask Bitty," I replied. "This is her show."

"That's frightening. Remember the Chippendales?"

I certainly did. We looked at each other and smiled. Then we found a table near the front where any action was likely to take place. A crystal water pitcher sat in the middle of the table, and crystal glasses glistened in the light through the long windows. Flowers in crystal vases had been placed on each table, along with canapés on small plates, and delicious fragrances emanated from the back area where food was prepared. A buffet table stretched halfway across the front of the huge room.

"Who are you?" I asked Rayna, trying to guess her assumed identity.

She smiled. "I started out as Elizabeth Bennet but then decided that Emma is more my style."

I nodded, appreciating her practical choice; the long skirt, modest blouse, and wide-brimmed hat fit Rayna. We watched as more Divas arrived, guessing who they were supposed to be, drinking chilled water and snagging canapés off silver trays. Carolann and Rose arrived together, both wearing Zeigfield girl costumes, reminiscent of F. Scott Fitzgerald novels, and joined our table. Gaynelle found us, looking very pretty in a ball gown and glass slippers. She even wore a tiara atop her hair and had colored it with blond streaks. Talk drifted to Bitty's engagement, then turned to the recent murder at the depot.

"Poor Deelight was so upset," said Gaynelle as she held a shrimp canapé, looking at it critically. "After all, Walter was her grandfather. And then the trouble with the will—I hope I convinced her to join us."

"So do I. But it's turned out all right now, hasn't it?" I asked.

"Well, Sammy relented and allowed everyone to have the items they were promised after Faith and Deelight apologized for all the trouble, but I think it was Jackson Lee's involvement that really turned it around. He pointed out that Walter's doctor said he was suffering from dementia, so the codicil could be called into legal question, and it was best for all if they came to some kind of amicable agreement." Gaynelle smiled. "So they did."

"That's a relief," Rayna said. "I'm just glad it's all over with now. Life can go back to normal. Whatever that is."

Leaning forward, Carolann said in what passes for a whisper with her, "I heard that the entire Whalen family is going to jail. Sally's sister wants to take possession of the house, since it was in the Landers family for a long time, and she says it should stay that way. Mr. Landers just died a few years ago. Darlene's mother remarried when she was very young and they raised her."

"I thought Darlene lived up north with her husband," said Gaynelle and held up her canapé to look at it in the light.

"Oh, she does, but grew up in Oxford after her parents divorced. She always came back here for the summers to spend time with her father, so I suspect she thought the house should be hers, since her father divorced Sally's mother, too. They left town when Sally was in junior high. Sally came back after he died to live in it, but of course, there was a squabble about that. It ended up that the court let her stay since he was Sally's father, too, and he hadn't said which daughter could have it. Gaynelle, what are you doing?"

"Is there something the matter with that canapé?" I couldn't help asking, and Gaynelle held it out.

"Does this remind you of—of anything?"

Rose Allgood took one off the tray, then laughed. "Naughty Bitty. I wonder who she had create these canapés."

I looked more closely and started fanning my face with one hand. "Oh my—is that what I think it is?"

Carolann hooted with laughter. "Butterfly shrimp with that dollop of pink cream cheese looks like something out of an erotic movie. I haven't seen that since my last boyfriend."

"It looks obscene," I said frankly, and we all laughed.

That was only the beginning. Waiters that looked like romance heroes—no shirt and tight pants—came in carrying silver trays. Pink drinks filled martini glasses; Rayna and I exchanged glances, but Rose knew what they were immediately. Of course.

"Pink Panty Dropper. Delicious. Waiter . . ." Rose beckoned one of them over, and I sat with my tongue hanging out while he smiled, flashing teeth that were so sparkling white, I was momentarily blinded. He flexed his pecs as he lowered the tray, and naturally no one refused a drink. I didn't care what was in it. I just wanted him to come to my side of the table.

I took the drink, smiled coyly up at him, ogled his abs, and he winked, grinned, and moved on to the next person, Gaynelle. She looked frozen, still holding up her canapé, her mouth slightly open, and he bent especially low, brushing her arm with his six-pack as he leaned forward to put her glass on the table. I saw her swallow. Her eyes were glazed.

Then he was gone, leaving us with pink martini glasses with rims crusted in pink sugar, and a vague restlessness. We all drank. It was delicious.

"What's in this?" Gaynelle inquired of no one in particular.

Rose promptly replied, "Vodka, pink lemonade concentrate, and beer."

"*Beer?*" Rayna and I said at the same time.

"But I don't taste beer," Rayna said. "Are you certain?"

"Yes. It's served at a lot of bachelorette parties."

I looked around at the others. "Maybe we need to inspect the buffet table. I have a feeling Bitty has a lot of interesting items for us."

I was not wrong. Jell-O shots in condoms, cheese balls shaped like erect males, gummy-bear phalluses soaked in alcohol, pecker straws—you name it, it was there. I won't even mention what the meat trays looked like. Just think of sausages and strategically placed olives and you'll get the right idea. My face felt on fire, and a strange flush enveloped my entire body after just cruising the buffet table. So of course, I had another Pink Panty Dropper to cool off. It came to my attention that the ice cubes were also suspiciously shaped, and I found that quite funny.

Deelight showed up at our table on our third round of drinks. She had opted for the Jell-O shots in colored condoms, which I thought a bit incongruous with her Tess Durbeyfield costume. Gaynelle stood up to greet her but apparently was feeling the vodka because she swayed a little.

"I'm sho glad to shee you," she gushed.

Laughing, Deelight said, "I couldn't miss a Diva Day. Miranda is here, too. Have you seen her? She looks fabulous as Eliza Doolittle."

"It's the hat," said Carolann. "And parasol."

Gaynelle slurred, "Miranda lovesh working for zhee Memphish paper."

Rather alarmed at the reminder, I said, "She's not going to write about this, is she? Or take photos? I'm not real fond of having my picture in the paper when I'm not at my best. I'm never at my best."

"God, I hope she's not taking photos," said Rayna. "Where is she, Deelight?"

"She's over there, drinking Pink Passions. I might try one. I love raspberries."

"Ooh," said Carolann. "So do I. What's in it besides raspberries?"

Again, it was Rose who knew: "Raspberry juice and liqueur, Grey Goose, lime, simple syrup, and frozen raspberries. Pink sugar crystals on the rim. Also delicious."

"Who's the bartender?" I asked. Not that it mattered. It wouldn't surprise me if Bitty had hired Fabio to mix drinks.

"Bitty's boys are in the back. They refuse to come out here, so they're playing gin with Gwen and her family in between making drinks. None of them want to join us," said Rayna. "I cannot imagine why."

"Because they're smarter than we are," I said, and we all nodded agreement.

Bitty, the Queen Bee of the festivities, floated past, her gilded chains and cap gleaming like real gold beneath the lights. "She's Mata Hari," I said to Rayna's questioning glance, and she rolled her eyes.

"Wasn't Mata Hari executed by the French?" Gaynelle inquired with a slight hiccup, and I nodded.

"Daring choice, in light of all that's happened," said Rose.

"That describes Bitty rather well." I drained my Pink Panty Dropper, considered why it was named that, and opted for water. In my younger days, I had learned the wisdom of lots of water in between drinks. It saved hangovers and making a complete fool of myself but allowed me an enjoyable buzz.

I do not always do what is best, however, and when the soft music that had been playing changed to a pulsing beat and the overhead lights dimmed, I knew something was coming that required liquid fortification.

The Pink Passion was as delicious as the Panty Dropper and equally potent. I sucked down two of them as undulating waiters went into a dance routine right in front of our table. A glance at Rayna showed her to be just as mesmerized, and I studied the taut, tanned bodies with what I pretended was a clinical eye. After all, I had my own hot body in the form of Kit Coltrane and he was imminently more mature. Sensible. I wondered if he could—or would—rotate his hips like that in time to "Pony." My eyes must have glazed over. The next thing I knew, the music changed to "Earned It" from *Fifty Shades* movie fame, and the four men turned their backs to us as they moved in time to the music. Sensuous melody wafted from the boom box speakers, curling around us as we sat riveted.

We held our collective breaths, knowing that more was to come, and it did. Light through the long windows illuminated every ripple of muscle as the tight pants were suddenly jerked off, revealing four young men in thong underwear and black leather boots to their knees. Someone squeaked, then a voice that sounded a lot like Cady Lee called, "Shake it, baby!" and they did.

Black thong underwear did a remarkable job of molding to bodies as they shook their derrieres, brandished short riding crops, and undulated across the floor. Leather strips curved under taut cheeks as they moved in perfect unison, turning and sliding the riding crops across their chests, then lower, drawing all eyes to their, ah, attributes. Someone in the back whistled, a piercing sound, and the dancers grinned, enjoying an appreciative audience.

Next to me, Gaynelle sucked down another Pink Panty Dropper. My mouth was too dry, and I did the same. As the song ended, it went right into a lively beat that had us all tapping our feet, blood racing, and the dancers roamed through the tables, pulling women to their feet to dance.

Someone should have warned them that might not be the thing to do. We can be rather rowdy in our enthusiasm. Especially with barely-dressed young men. One young man chose Rayna, and she gave him a pitying smile before grabbing his riding crop and showing him how to use it. I think he made some kind of sound, but she obviously interpreted it as encouragement as she teased him with the flexible strips on the end, brushing them over his chest and down his ribs, lightly flicking him here and there. His companions laughed as he bravely attempted to reclaim his property, but for all her fragile appearance, Rayna is not a woman to be trifled with in these situations.

Divas clapped and hooted, and Carolann jumped up from our table, and she and Rayna made a dancer sandwich. The poor boy never had a chance. He got a look on his face like a deer in headlights, and then Divas surrounded the other three dancers.

If they survived, they would all go home with lots of money stuffed in their thongs, as well as whatever Bitty paid them. All in all, it could have been worse.

I wish I could say that I sat at the table, maintaining my dignity and enjoying the show. I did, for a short time, anyway. Then something came over me. It could have been the music, or it could have been the Pink Passions, but suddenly I found myself in the midst of the dancers and Divas.

As usual, what happens with the Divas, stays with the Divas.

But I regret to report that the next issue of the *Commercial Appeal* printed photos barely suitable for a family newspaper, along with a short description of festivities that left out a lot of details. For that, we were somewhat grateful.

However, I was dismayed that one photo showed a rather inebriated Holly Golightly holding a long cigarette holder in one hand and a whip in the other, posed quite suggestively with an obviously alarmed young man.

All I can say is, *Well, sunny beaches . . .*

The End

Acknowledgements

Thank you to Gwen, Jo, and Alexa for allowing me to use the Holly Springs Railroad Depot for murder, and to Larry Dixon for informing me about Civil War weapons, and to the great town of Holly Springs, Mississippi, for being so welcoming and patient. You are all kind and wonderful!

For those who want to know more about Holly Springs and upcoming events, or just visit some of the places you've read about, visit these links:

http://hollyspringsms.org/

And for a tour of the elegant and historical railroad depot:

http://thehollyspringsdepot.blogspot.com/

About the Author

Since her first romance novel came out in 1984, VIRGINIA BROWN HAS WRITTEN over 50 novels. Many of her books have been nominated for *Romantic Times*'s Reviewer's Choice, Career Achievement Award for Love and Laughter, Career Achievement Award for Adventure, and 2 EPIC eBook nominations for Historical Romance. In addition she received the *RT* Career Achievement Award for Historical Adventure, as well as the EPIC eBook Award for Mainstream Fiction. Her works have regularly appeared on national bestseller lists.

A native of Memphis, Tennessee, Virginia spent much of her childhood traveling with her parents as a "military brat," living all over the US and in Japan. This influenced her love of travel and adventure, which she indulges with research trips to England and Scotland as often as possible. While Ms. Brown spent her formative years in Jackson, Mississippi, she now lives near her children in North Mississippi, surrounded by a menagerie of beloved dogs and cats while she writes.

facebook.com/virginiabrownbooks

Made in the USA
Middletown, DE
12 April 2023

28732374R00151